MW01504456

DEATH IN
WHITECHAPEL

A Supernatural Mystery
with a Dash of Romance…

Miss Adventure goes international when the Order sends Adina and Chief Inquisitor Breitling to London, where the local affiliate is contending with a series of murders that mirror the infamous Jack the Ripper killings. But things work differently on the other side of the pond, and when Adina discovers that this "Ripper" may not be the callous monster everyone believes him to be, the blustery lead constable refuses to listen, and even Breitling questions her objectivity. Stuck in a foreign land and stymied at every turn, Adina must find a way to make her case before the mounting frustrations break her—and Breitling—for good.

DEATH IN
WHITECHAPEL

S.G. Tasz

The Uglycat Press
Las Vegas, NV

You know it's up to you

Anything you can do

And if you find a new way

You can do it today

You can make it all true

And you can make it undo

You see

It's easy

You only need to know.

-Cat Stevens-

For as much emphasis as the Order places on research and awareness in the name of protecting its members, there's a lot they still don't know. In this way, if in no other, the field of magic looks a lot like the field of science: at every level, from the Chief Inquisitor down to the lowliest Page, everyone in the Order shares a deep desire for answers. This, of course, inevitably leads to more questions, which they then must answer anew. It's an endless cycle, and one that requires unquenchable curiosity and tenacity.

And yet…something is missing. Not an unknown, and not a theory to be confirmed. It's a void, hovering at the edge of thought and consciousness, its tattered edges the only indication that it had once been anything else. But what was it? A question that they didn't want the answer to? Or an answer that scared them so badly they had to rip it from the fabric of reality itself?

That doesn't make any does it? See, this is exactly why reference books should be written by people who know what they're doing.

I'm sorry. Let's move on.

-Don't Call It Magic: An Insider's Guide to the Order of the Presidium

THANK YOU FOR VISITING
The **TOWER** of ~~L**ONDON**~~
THE ORDER

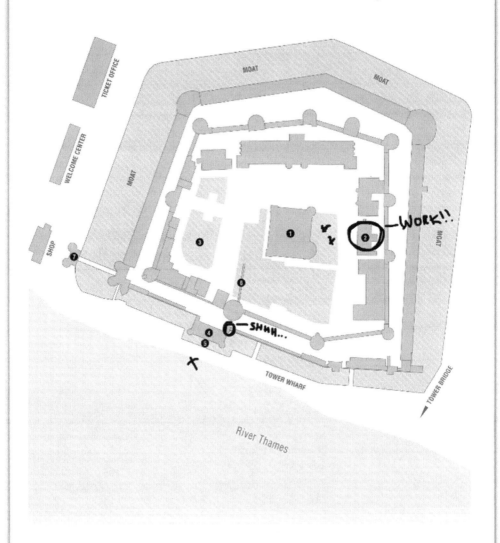

Prologue: June

I've never cared for the sunrise; in my experience, it means the end of a good time. Today, it's the start of a bad one.

My limbs buzz with caffeine and adrenaline as I stumble down the hall toward Breitling's office. I spent the entire night trying to figure out what to do with all the shit Mama dumped on me, and I'm nowhere. It was either come here now or continue to stare at the ceiling and listen to Shiva's whistling snores. I think she may have a deviated beak–or whatever crows have.

The biometric security on Breitling's office door is disengaged, and I go in without knocking. He looks up from his desk as I enter. His appearance leaves me stunned. Instead of his black three-piece suit, he's wearing a white, loose-fitting thermal shirt that looks insanely comfortable. His bed-tousled blond hair falls in front of his glasses as he glares at the fool who's dared to interrupt his work. When he sees it's me, his irritation melts into surprise, and then alarm.

"Adina." He springs to his feet, and the hits keep coming, this time in the form of charcoal gray sweatpants. "I wasn't expecting you until much later. Not that you're not welcome, of course." He runs his fingers through his hair to tame it, then crosses his arms over his chest as if that will hide his casual attire. His discomfort would be funny if I wasn't so freaked out.

Ah, who am I kidding? It's still a little funny.

"Sorry," he says on an exhale. His eyes travel up and down my figure, and a smile rises to his lips as he comes around the desk. His hands fall to mine, and he presses them to his mouth, first one and then the other. "I'm glad you're here, my darling. Very glad."

He leans forward, his head tilted down.

"Umbralists," I whisper.

He freezes. I study him for signs of shock, fear, or guilt, but all I see is confusion. "I beg your pardon?"

"Um-bra-lists," I repeat. "What do you know about them?"

His brows lower. "I have no idea what you're talking about. Is everything alright?"

Dammit, I'm already blowing this. I free my hands from his and rub my eyes. If I tell him the whole story, what will he say? He's told me his Pledge trumps everything else, and I'm not dying to test that. What can I reasonably expect from him here? And will it be enough?

"Adina?" He grips me by the shoulders. "Tell me what's wrong, and I'll do whatever I can to help."

"I hope so." Gritting my teeth, I jump in headfirst. "I talked to Mama last night. About my dad."

His eyes widen. "Good. And?"

"She told me he would have been a Master Umbralist if the Order hadn't rounded them all up and disappeared them from the face of the Earth."

He tightens his hold. "So, that would make you…one of these people?"

My heart sinks. That's not the takeaway I was hoping for. "Maybe. At least, Mama thinks so."

"I see," he says. "Can I assume your mother has made efforts to discuss this accusation with Order personnel?"

"Yes, on the day it happened, or soon after," I confirm. "*No one* knew what she was talking about back then either."

"I see," he says again. His drawn features and hard stare suggest discontent. At what, exactly, I don't know.

"Say something, Levi," I prod after a full minute of silence.

He swallows, his eyelids fluttering like they always do when I say his name. My relief at that is short-lived, however; when he opens his eyes again, they're as cold as granite. "Adina, I swear, I know nothing about this. I don't recall hearing the term 'Umbralist' until now. And as far as the Order's alleged behavior, I will be honest with you: I'm finding it difficult to believe."

Shit. Now what? Will he try to detain me for spreading malicious rumors about the Order? Or will he tell me to leave and never come back? I'm not sure which idea terrifies me more, and both make me want to burst into tears.

"Difficult," he continues, "but not impossible."

I let out a breath. It sounds enough like a sob that his expression softens, and I narrowly resist the urge to throw myself into his arms. If I do that, it'll be hours before we get back to the matter at hand, and this can't wait. "What do you think may have happened?"

He leans back against his desk. "As far as what became of these Operators, I couldn't surmise. Did your mother have any ideas?"

"No, but…" I perch on the arm of the chair across from him. Should I tell him my suspicions? I don't want to risk straining his credulity when he's already said this is hard for him to believe. But then again, if there's something wicked slithering around the same building he spends his entire life in, doesn't he deserve to know?

"Adina." He reaches out with one large hand to cover both of mine. "I understand this is difficult. But if there is a potential threat to Operators out there, no matter the discipline, I am duty-bound to act in their defense. That's my job."

Even if the threat is the people you work for? God, I wish I was brave enough to say that. But I'm also smart enough to know you shouldn't ask questions you don't want the answer to.

His fingers tighten over mine. "Like I said, this is difficult. But keeping secrets doesn't help. Tell me what you're thinking. Please."

I heave a sigh and lift my gaze to his. "I don't know what happened to the Umbralists or where they are now. But…I'm pretty sure that they were detained in the Theatre, at least for a while."

His jaw clenches as his eyes slide to my left arm. The skin is still covered in gray blotches and striations from when I put my hand through a wall full of Deathwalker repellent. "That…could be."

Okay. One more hurdle surmounted.

With a final squeeze, he relinquishes his hold on me. "Whatever may have occurred, it seems they did a thorough job of erasing the event, as well as the entire history of this discipline, from the global consciousness."

"Is that even possible?" I ask.

"Of course. It's a rare Operation, thank God, but there are about half a dozen Memorists with mass effect capabilities scattered around the world. Any one of them could have done it."

I suppress a shiver. "Not sure I wanted to know that."

"I understand." He flashes me a rueful smile. "If I may ask—how are *you* coping with the…personal aspects of all this?"

I laugh, but it comes out as a broken whimper. I hadn't expected him to ask that. "Honestly, I'm terrified. My dad is a traitor who abandoned his community when shit went down, and then he goes and registers his daughter with the same people who kidnapped all his friends. Why would he do that? Was he hoping they would…disappear me too?"

Breitling's stony eyes ignite. "*That* is not going to happen."

"How can you be sure?" I try to inhale, but it's a struggle. My chest feels like it's banded with iron. "They think they wiped away all memory of Umbralists, but my mother remembers. What if there are others? Ones who still *hate* Umbralists? What if the memory Operation fades? Or malfunctions? Or—"

Or what if they order you to destroy me, is what I'm about to ask. But the words catch in my throat, and I choke.

The next thing I know, Breitling has me in his arms, my head tucked beneath his chin. "It's alright, darling. I've got you."

His words pierce my heart. I believe he believes that. But how far does that promise go? Maybe I should push harder for an answer, but I can't make myself do it. There will be a time for tests later. Right now, all I can do is bury my face in his downy white shirt, inhale the sandalwood scent of his skin, and get my shit together.

"It doesn't make sense," he muses, stroking my hair with his palm. "The Order puts almost no restrictions on what Operators do as long as it doesn't undermine or betray our philosophy. To eradicate a whole discipline…that's not the Order I know."

I look up at him with a smile. "I told Mama the same thing. She didn't believe me, of course. But I suppose it would be hard to sell anyone on a group that made your husband abandon you and your three-year-old daughter."

He returns my smile with a wistful one of his own. "Yes, I suppose it would be."

"I'm not talking about me. *I* barely even remember him. But…thank you anyway." Freeing my arm from his embrace, I press my hand to his cheek.

His shoulders sag with a contented sigh as he tilts his head into my touch. "What do you need from me, darling?" he asks, his lips grazing the inside of my wrist.

Well. That is the question, isn't it? Between what I need and what he's Pledged, finding the right words is like trying to thread sixteen sewing needles in a row. "I…I need you to…keep your eyes open, I guess. And if you see or hear anything strange, or if they ask you to…well, just give me a head's up, okay? At least then I can get a decent head start."

He stares at me for a long time, his mouth a single line and his eyes unreadable. I'm starting to get itchy when he breaks his silence. "I promise, Adina, I will do everything in my power to keep you from harm."

Again, I believe *he* believes that. But that question, that one big problem, still lies between us. And this time, no matter how much it may hurt, I can't let it go unasked.

"The Order has a claim on your power, too," I say. "More…more than I do. What will you do if—"

"It won't come to that." He takes my face in his hands and lifts my chin. "If there is a threat to you inside the

Order, I will find it and eliminate it before it gets anywhere near you. I swear it."

His intensity makes every inch of me surge with heat. "How can you say that? You don't even know what kind of monster we're dealing with."

"True." He pulls off his glasses and tosses them on the desk behind him. "But I know what kind of monster *I* can become."

The corners of my mouth lift. "I can relate."

"Oh, I *know* you can." He lowers his head, his smiling lips searching for mine.

I don't stop him this time.

One

I hit the button on my Killer Kash slot machine, take a sip of my Diet Coke, and try to ignore the five-man security detail struggling to break up the brawl at the blackjack table behind me. If, of course, you consider two women in their seventies smacking each other with their oversized purses a brawl.

"You screwed me, Eunice!" one of them screeches. "You stole my ace!"

"Like you stole my boyfriend?" the other, presumably Eunice, screams back. "Arnold had been about to ask me to the Bellini Beach Bash, and you know it! But you go flouncing by in your low-cut blouse, and suddenly I'm chopped liver."

"Is it *my* fault that he prefers steak?"

A feral yowl pierces the air, followed by a series of male grunts as the guards drag the two away amid scattered applause from everyone except me. Under different circumstances, I'd find an old lady catfight as entertaining as the next bored person, but not now. Not when their fight is my fault.

Though, in my defense, three is the designated must-bust threshold, aka the number of consecutive wins a person can have before a Chaotic backlash becomes inevitable and someone (usually me) needs to intervene. But that number has been dropping for weeks. Back in June, it was seven. And now...well, it seems like we're down to one.

I glance up at the ceiling. A cluster of shiny black half-orbs stare back at me like the eyes of a spider. I swear, I can feel Russ's anxiety radiating from those cameras. As the head of the Chaos Intervention Initiative, he's warned me that the rules can change on a dime. Until now, I hadn't realized how irritating that would be. Or how scary.

This septuagenarian slap fight is the latest of many embarrassments for CI-2. We've spent over a month integrating and testing the Mach 3 Invocation Early Detection software into Seychelle Casino's eye-in-the-sky security suite, and the results have been nothing short of disastrous. We've failed to break no less than six incidental invocation cycles before they closed. Those failures resulted in multiple broken bones, a three-car fender bender on the third floor of the parking garage, and (our greatest sin of all) financial losses to the casino in the tens of thousands. It's gotten so bad that the Order's head honcho, Prime Castillo, has been on site for the past week to run interference between Russ and Seychelle's board. But even the Prime's clout only goes so far. At our last meeting (or rather, our last ass-chewing), the casino suits made it clear that six financial hits are all they're willing to suffer.

This little love triangle loop makes lucky number seven.

I smack the Bet button. At least Eunice got something out of all this. She chalked up a multi-hundred-dollar win before her friend purse-whipped her in the back of the head. The CI-2, on the other hand, is about to lose everything.

"Stupid incidentals," I grumble. The NOs don't even know they're inciting them. They can pop up anywhere, and the loops can close any time after the fact. All that randomness makes them almost impossible for the system to track.

An *intentional* invocation, on the other hand…that would be much easier.

My stomach churns at the prospect. Intentional invocations require conscious contact with Chaos, and for a longer period of time. Long enough to make the request and come to terms, at least. In theory, that would give the Mach a better chance of detecting its presence. Great plan, except for one thing: The Order only has a couple of hard and fast rules, and intentionally invoking the power of Chaos breaks the mother of them all.

And yet…

I look up again at the cluster of cameras. Chaos tracking is Russ's life. If the Initiative goes down, so does he. Am I really going to sit here and let that happen if there's something I can do to prevent it?

It's not even a question.

Dropping my head to either shoulder, I open my mind to the surrounding space. After months with the CI-2, I've learned that Chaos tends to linger covertly near a recently closed loop, basking in the residual insecurity and discontent. Plus, not to brag, but I *am* one of its favorites. It shouldn't take long to—

"Yes, Miss Adventure?"

The words surface in my head like a soap bubble, leaving an oily trail from the center of my brain to the inside of my ear.

Hello.

"Lovely to hear from you again. It's been too long. How may I be of service?"

I fight the urge to roll my eyes. Service. That's one way to put it. But if you ignore its metaphysical abilities and the wriggling realm it occupies, Chaos is no better than a low-level drug pusher selling mediocre product for too high a price.

"A winning spin, perhaps?" it prompts. *"Everyone likes a good pile of cash, after all. You will have every digital coin in the coffers as soon as you acknowledge the terms."*

I tap my finger against the Bet button and stall for time. If they spot something on the cameras, they will notify security, trip the fire alarm, do whatever it takes to break the invocation.

But so far…nothing.

"Miss Adventure? Are you still with me?"

Its impatience yanks at each individual hair on my scalp. Chaos is not an omnipresent force, and I've kept it waiting long enough. After all, it's got places to be. Dumpsters to ignite. Lives to ruin.

I can shoulder the backlash, right? If not entirely, at least better than someone who doesn't know it's coming. Besides, it's not like I haven't done it before.

I close my eyes and take a deep breath. This one's for you, Russ.

I—

"I beg your pardon, miss?"

My brain freezes along with the rest of me. That voice. Deep. Soft. British. There's no mistaking it.

I spin in my chair and look up at Chief Inquisitor Breitling. He's wearing his typical black suit, but he's swapped his black shirt for a simple white one. The top button is undone, and I don't see his collar. He must have it on underneath his clothes. Picturing the glossy red chains lying in the blond curls of his chest hair, against his bare skin…

The middle three fingers of my right hand tremble as my sigil squashes the lustful meanderings before they burn through me. "What are you doing here?" I ask.

His face remains stern and cold, a perfect facsimile of a security guard. "My apologies, but I'm afraid you need to come with me."

A slow smile spreads across my face. "Is there a problem…sir?"

To anyone else, his expression would seem unaffected. But to me, the twinkle behind his otherwise dull gray irises and the tiny twitch at the corner of his mouth are as blinding as a spotlight.

He liked that.

"Just do as I ask," he says, "There's no need to make a scene."

I arch a brow at him, then leap to my feet and proceed to do just that. "This is an outrage! I win *one* junior jackpot and you're going to kick me out? I am an American citizen, and I have rights!"

He clears his throat and glances around. The earlier fight still has everyone on high alert, and a sea of intrigued, hungry stares greet him.

"I assure you, you're not in trouble," he announces for their benefit. "Come along and everything will be explained."

"Fine." I whip out my phone and aim it at him. "But I'm going to be filming this. For future use."

With a wink, I hit Record. He rolls his eyes at the camera before stalking away. As I follow, phone pointed at the back of his head, I telegraph one last message to Chaos.

Maybe later.

"Anytime, Miss Adventure," it burbles in my head. *"Anytime at all."*

Breitling escorts me to the elevator and presses the button to the top floor. I wait until the doors close before dropping my phone. "Okay, what's going on? Why didn't you tell me you were coming here today?"

"*I* didn't know I was coming until an hour ago," he says. "Castillo summoned me. I tried your cell, but you didn't answer."

"That's because I don't answer calls from numbers I don't recognize, and yours still shows up as Unknown."

He shoots me a puzzled look. "But you *know* it's me."

I roll my eyes at the ceiling. "Anyway, you don't expect me to believe he made you drive all the way up here to play security guard, do you?"

"That was an accident. Russ called me the moment I walked through the door, told me to intervene on a Chaotic invocation, and that I should pretend I was an employee so as not to draw attention. He failed to mention on *whom* I'd be intervening, however."

I shrug and pretend to be fascinated with the numbers above the door. Technically, I didn't do anything wrong. Chaos and I had been talking, that's all. He'd interrupted me before I'd been able to–

"Oh shit!" My shout echoes extra loud in the small space. "Does that mean the Mach worked? Russ saw Chaos manifesting near me on the video feeds?"

He smiles at me. "It would appear so."

Chills rush up my arms as my eyes sting with tears of relief. "I can't believe it."

"Indeed. The first successful test of Chaotic detection integrated with a Non-Operational security suite. It's a historic achievement. Castillo will be proud." He leans over until his mouth brushes the top of my hair. "So am I."

My cheeks warm, and I'm about to thank him when I make the critical mistake of looking up. His eyes burn into mine, and he leans closer.

"Cameras." I jerk my head at the small box mounted near the ceiling over my left shoulder.

He blinks as if waking up from a dream. "Right."

As he steps back, I face the door and press my lips together until the throbbing stops. God, I wish I could kiss him. Now, and later, and all the time. But we both know there are people who need to be kept in the dark about the exact nature of our relationship. People who, at this moment, may be watching.

The elevator opens onto a dark maroon vestibule with frosted sconces shaped like seashells. The thick carpet swallows our footfalls as we head for the double doors at the end of the hallway.

"So," I ask, "if you're not here because of the Mach 3 rollout, then why did Castillo summon you?"

"I don't know," he says as he opens the door for me. "He said he'd explain when he saw us in person."

"Us?"

He nods. "Whatever he's got in mind, you're a part of it too."

Two

As a downtown resort, Seychelle is several decades older than the cutting-edge properties on the Strip. It wasn't built with a high-tech surveillance suite, so they retrofitted one of the smaller penthouses to serve the purpose instead. The large picture windows have been plastered over and affixed with high-def screens that show every inch of the gaming floor. Three long tables filled with computer workstations run the length of the room. There are twenty people in here, but it's almost silent as the security techs sit fully absorbed by their work.

"Miss Venture!"

Everyone's shoulders hike up to their ears as the sudden ebullience ruffles the quiet. From the antiquated kitchenette on my right, Prime Castillo approaches me with wide arms. Not a hugging gesture, but a presentational one, like I'm a visiting royal arriving at his court.

"Excellent work, my dear." He grabs one of my hands in both of his and shakes it like a Magic Eight ball. "I was quite certain the board would invite us to leave after the fracas at the blackjack table, but my, what a turnabout! I don't know how you did it, but well done."

Bullshit, he doesn't know. My special connection to Chaos is the reason I ended up with the CI-2 in the first place, and Castillo isn't stupid. But if he's not going to throw up barriers—or retributions—I'm sure as hell not going to say anything.

"This is a red-letter day for the Order," Castillo continues. "And for the security industry all around. Wouldn't you agree, Chief Beale?" He turns back to the kitchenette, where Russ stands next to the head of security, Oswald Beale. He is almost as tall as Breitling, but at least fifteen years older and dozens of pounds heavier. With his thick beard and wire-rimmed glasses, I'd say he looks a little like Santa Claus if he wasn't sneering all the time.

"Haze in the feed," Beale grumbles into his collar. "Black haze. That's all it was."

"Indeed!" Castillo beams as if this were a full-throated endorsement. He extends his hand to Russ, who dashes forward, away from Beale. "Now then, Mr. Landry. Since we know the system *can* work, how do we get it the rest of the way?"

Russ rubs his bearded chin. "Well, I've got some backend work to do. Evaluate the threshold matrix and reinstall the visual manifestation driver for starters. If that doesn't solve the issue, things could get complicated."

My eyes glaze over. From the regretful wince on Castillo's face, I suspect I'm not the only one who hears technobabble and instantly feels twelve shades dumber.

"How long will it take?" Breitling asks. Leave it to him to cut to the cold, dead heart of things.

Russ shrugs. "A couple of weeks, I'd guess. In the meantime, we'll keep using the proximity system on the Operationally-configured cell phones. I've got a small team trained on that now. They should be able to handle things while I work the bugs out of the integration."

"Excellent." Castillo says. "In that case, you won't mind if I borrow Miss Venture for a few days."

Russ's brows knit. "Uh, no, Prime Castillo. Not at all."

"Thank you, Mr. Landry. Your flexibility is much appreciated."

Castillo's supercilious tone makes my teeth snap together. I mean, it's a request from the *Prime*. What is Russ gonna do? Say no? Of course not, and for the same reason I'm not about to get all sassy and ask whether *I* get a say in all this. I already know the answer. So does Russ— and so, for that matter, does Castillo.

"In that case, if you will excuse us." Castillo inclines his head to me and Breitling as he exits. We follow him across the hall into a vacant, windowless office, where he takes the only chair behind the bare desk. As Breitling closes the door, Castillo withdraws a key fob from his pocket and presses a button. The rattling of the ancient air conditioner deadens, and the atmosphere grows as thick as a wool sweater.

"Cone of Silence?" I ask.

"Marvelous, isn't it?" Castillo rolls the fob between his fingers. "The Order will make a small fortune when we take it to market. Minus Mr. Landry's generous licensing fee, of course."

He puts the item back in his pocket and spreads his hand over the maple veneer of the desk. "Now then, Miss Venture, Chief Breitling. Tell me—how much do either of you know about Jack the Ripper?"

I blink. Did I hear him right? "You mean, Jack the Ripper, the 19th century prostitute disemboweler? Terrorized the East End of London for several months in the fall of 1888? True identity still unknown? *That* Jack the Ripper?"

Castillo smiles, though he looks uneasy. "The same."

"I have a…friend who's into serial killer lore," I hedge, all too aware of Breitling's presence in this moment. He and I haven't talked about Jake since we started…whatever it is we're doing, and this is not the time to break that streak.

"In that case, I'll spare you the history lesson and cut straight to the matter at hand," Castillo says. "Our compatriots in London have been grappling with a series of murders that bear a striking resemblance to the Ripper crimes, and they've asked for our help. Or to be more specific, *your* help."

His gaze shoves me in the chest. Suddenly, it's hard to breathe. "*My* help? Why?"

"Because of the nature of these attacks. Three, so far. All have been staged in the locations of previous Ripper victims, which are now high-traffic tourist and residential areas in one of the most highly surveilled cities on the planet. Several of them had witnesses, and all of them have been caught on security cameras. We see the victim, the attack, even the moment of expiration. But the killer is nowhere in sight. Therefore, it is possible that the culprit we are dealing with is…well…"

He splays his fingers in my direction.

My throat tightens. I don't want to say it, but I have to. "An Exspiricarius."

Castillo raises his brows in the affirmative. He doesn't look happy, but he doesn't look sorry either. Next to me, Breitling clears his throat. He knows how much I hate what that word represents: a heartless, vengeance-seeking apparition who kills without mercy or forethought. A brutal, unforgiving instrument of death.

A monster.

"What is Scotland Yard's position on the attacks?" Breitling asks in a deft change of subject.

Castillo scoffs and waves a manicured hand. "The NO Police are as useless there as they are here. High caseloads and low budgets mean the easiest solution *will* be the right one, even if it's not the true one. If there's more nuance to it than that, I'm sure Constable McNally will illuminate the situation once you get there."

"When *we*…?"

I glance at Breitling. He seems as surprised as I am. "You're sending us on assignment?" he confirms. "*Both* of us?"

"Indeed, Chief Inquisitor. You leave at ten o'clock tonight, and you're expected at the Tower as soon as you land."

"With all due respect, Prime," Breitling says, "why have *I* been assigned to escort Miss Venture? She's more than capable of handling things on her own."

His words are a gut punch. He doesn't want to go with me? I'd like to ask what the hell, but I can't. Not with Castillo staring right at us. Instead, I pull my shoulders back and continue to appear confused. It's not hard.

"Miss Venture is mere weeks out of her probationary employment period," Castillo says in an officious tone. "It would be inappropriate to send her to an international hold without a senior officer to supervise. There are only two employees familiar enough with Miss Venture's singular Operations to be up for the task, and seeing as Mr. Landry cannot be spared at this time, that leaves you."

"But sir—" Breitling tries to break in.

"*Furthermore*, I am due for a site visit, and as Chief Inquisitor, you have all the clearance you need to carry out that task in my stead. You *will* be her escort, and that's final."

"Yes, Prime," Breitling says, his head bowed as if embarrassed by Castillo's admonishment. But when his eyes slide to me, the look in them is nothing short of victorious. Whatever that was about, it worked out the way he wanted.

"I'll have my assistant forward your tickets to your phones." Castillo stands and clicks the fob. The rattle and whir of the AC floods my ears as the Cone of Silence lifts. "Keep me informed of your progress, and best of luck. To both of you."

He buttons his jacket and leaves the office. Breitling and I, however, remain rooted where we stand.

"Wow," I say. "That's a surprise."

"Yes." Breitling rubs the back of his neck as he stares at the open door after Castillo. "Yes, it is."

He lapses into a thoughtful silence.

"Hey." I place a hand on his forearm. "Are you okay?"

He nods. "I'm fine. Though it seems I have some travel preparations to make."

"Same." The weight of what has happened falls on me, and my head starts spinning. "Holy shit…I'm getting on a plane to London in less than eight hours. I need to pack. I need plane snacks and sudoku books and those tiny little toiletry things and–oh my God, I don't have a passport! How can I–"

Strong hands fall on my shoulders, and his stormy eyes swallow me up. "Don't worry. If the Prime has sanctioned this, all our documents are waiting at the Summit. I will collect them when I go to retrieve my things."

"Okay." I take a breath. "If you're doing that, then I need to go home and figure out if I have anything I can wear on a week-long international work trip."

"Yes. And…try to relax. If what the Prime said is accurate, there are busy days ahead of you."

"Right. Okay." I smile up at him. "Thank you."

"You're welcome." He kneads the tense muscles at the base of my neck. I tip my head back and let myself enjoy the sensation for a moment. He's close enough that I can smell his sandalwood cologne. The scent comforts me like nothing else can.

"Adina, I…I should go," he says hoarsely.

"Mm, yeah," I murmur. "Me too."

He presses his fingers into the back of my head until I look at him. "Need a ride?"

My lips curve into a coy smile. "Desperately."

Three

It's not a long drive between Seychelle and the casita nestled at the foot of the Eastern mountains where I live. You can be there in ten minutes if you take Charleston or Sahara or one of the other major east-west arteries.

Or you can take the scenic route. Go a few miles north and the subdivisions and strip malls peter out into a large tract of nothing. Sand and sagebrush dominate the landscape, broken only by the occasional abandoned gas station and blanketed in smothering silence.

It doesn't stay that way.

"Adina, please," Breitling whimpers as I pull his collar aside and kiss him on the neck. "You're going to make me lose control."

"What's so bad about that?" I purr, trailing my fingers down his stomach. His hands clench around the wheel as, nibbling the skin behind his ear, I take hold of him. With a growl, he whips the car into the parking lot of an old Texaco, fishtails around the back of the decrepit sun-bleached structure, and kills the engine. I begin to dip my head, but he grabs me by the chin and drags me back up. "Get over here."

I'm not about to argue. I sling my leg across his lap as he buries his hands in my hair and pulls me to him. The move makes it impossible to get out of my slacks, but I'm too eager to go back now.

It only takes a few thrusts of my hips to get him hard and pressing into me in exactly the right place. I focus on the spot, moving up and down until I'm humming with delicious heat and he's trembling all over. Before I lose my senses entirely, I unpin the chains fastened to the underside of his lapels. A shudder rips through him as I pull the second skeletal hand away and drop his collar into the cup holder. "Dear fucking God."

"Belt," I mutter against his mouth, pushing his jacket aside. "Both of them."

He unclips his seatbelt first, then handles the one at his waist as I finish unbuttoning his shirt and slide my palms down his flat stomach, the pale skin covered with a scattering of short, golden strands.

"Christ," he sighs as I reach into his pants. "How do you do this to me every time?"

I shrug, working him with one hand as I run the other through his perfect hair. "It's a gift."

"It's magic." His face snaps toward the ceiling. "I swear, Adina, you're fucking magic."

I giggle and rub the tip of him against me, rolling my hips in rhythm with my strokes. "I don't think they covered *fucking* magic in Orientation. Are you sure it's real?"

"Oh…I am now." He takes my face in his hands, thumbs pressing into my jaw as his fingers rest against my temple. I inhale sharply, and he pushes my head back, sending me into the starry blue fog.

The memory is from a couple months ago, right after we started our liaison. He had me pinned up against the wall when a knock came at his office door. I'd expected him to stop or maybe even recoil from me in a panic. Instead, he put a hand over my mouth to stifle my cries and shouted that he was busy and go away. They had protested, and he'd yelled back, his frustration feeding the speed and intensity of his thrusts and making me come so hard I couldn't remember my own name for several minutes afterward. That was the day we'd decided we could no longer use his office for our encounters. But the thrill of the moment shudders me as much now as it did then.

"Oh, Levi." In the car, I grab his shoulders and grind into him, the memory bleeding into reality until I'm about to fall.

His hands slip to the back of my head and pull me down until I'm staring into glowing cobalt irises. "Look at me, Adina."

I do as he asks, pinning my gaze to his until the pleasure overtakes me and I have to squeeze my eyes shut to withstand it. He digs his fingers into the back of my neck and his mouth crashes into mine, silencing my moans as I go limp in his embrace.

It's not perfect, having to be together like this. But with him living at the Summit and my family at home, not to mention both of us running all over town on Order business 24/7, it's the best we can do. Besides, with things being what they are between us, getting caught could mean never seeing each other—or maybe anyone—ever again. With all that on the line, I'm more than happy to take any of him I can get. From the way he's kissing me like he never wants to do anything else, it's safe to say he feels the same.

"Mm." He breaks away, licking his lips and smiling up at me. "You even *taste* like magic."

"You know," I say with a giddy laugh. "I could have been even more 'magical' if I'd known I was going to have this opportunity today. For starters, I would have worn a skirt."

"Soon." He runs his hands over my cheeks and through my hair. "As soon as tomorrow, it seems."

"I hope so," I say. "It sounds like we're going to be working a lot. We may not even be on the same schedule—"

He stops my protests with a soft kiss. "I'll take care of it. I promise. There's no way I'm going to sleep under the same roof as you without having you as many times as I can."

God, I want to believe that. I *almost* can. They'll put us in separate rooms, I'm sure, but they won't be chaperoning us all the time. He's right. We'll get our chance soon. But until then...

I unhook my arms from his neck and slide back into my seat. He winces as if the separation causes him physical pain, but he doesn't stop me. We compose ourselves without speaking, using the silence to ease our mutual frustration. Only after we're back on the dusty highway and heading toward the city do I venture to speak.

"So, this kind of thing–sending Inquisitors and employees to other Order locations–does it happen a lot?"

He shrugs. "The Constables control the five other Order holds around the world, so it's best for the Prime to play nice and share people across borders when necessary. Since you're uniquely qualified for this, I'm not surprised the Tower asked for you."

I pick at the sleeve of my blazer. "You seemed surprised that he was sending you. Even a little upset."

He frowns at my disquieted fingers. "That's what I was going for. The Chief Inquisitor shouldn't appear eager to play escort to an underling. I'm too busy and important for such things."

"But not too busy to fool around with said underling behind an abandoned gas station though, right?" I say with a sly smile.

His mouth twitches. "Anyway, I knew Castillo would expect me to push back, so that's what I did."

"Pretty smart," I concede, folding my hands in my lap.

He's right to be cautious. All Inquisitors Pledge themselves into Order service, forsaking all other fealties as part of that commitment. Sex isn't forbidden, but romantic attachments are. A liaison between the Chief Inquisitor and another employee would be subject to major scrutiny. If we want to keep this up, it's best to meet the expectations that we are colleagues who work well together, and nothing else.

"Speaking of the assignment," I say as I roll down my window and let the desert air blow dry my dark, sweat-dampened strands, "how familiar are *you* with Jack the Ripper? He's your history, after all. Did they teach you about him in high school?"

"Did they teach *you* about Jeffrey Dahmer in high school?"

"If they had, I might have stayed awake in history class."

He shakes his head. "My teachers may have referenced him as a symptom of London poverty and industrial fallout in the 19th century, but I'm sure they omitted the sordid details."

"Then you're not familiar with him?"

He smiles sideways at me. "I never said that."

"I knew it," I say with a smirk. "A centuries-old mystery that no one can solve? Of course you'd be all over that."

"It's a compelling puzzle, and I enjoy the challenge. What's your excuse?"

"I'm American. It's in my DNA to be obsessed with serial killers."

"You might keep that to yourself once we get there."

"Noted," I say. Then, after a pause: "What do you think about the other aspect that Castillo mentioned? That it might be someone like me?"

His shoulders stiffen. "And by 'like you,' you mean…?"

I'm about to utter a smart comeback when the full significance of that question hits me. "You think it could be an Umbralist?"

He taps the wheel in thought. "We don't have enough information to rule it out. Either way, if the murderer is in fact an…ah, what you *used* to be, then I don't need to tell you how dangerous this case could become."

His grim expression makes my skin prickle. For a moment, I'm transported back to the day we met. It still hurts to think of the way he looked at me when he called me that name, with a mix of condescension and revulsion. Now he knows better. But if what's Operating in London can do what I do, but without a moral compass to guide them…

The shiver that runs down my spine shakes me so hard that Breitling reaches over and squeezes my hand.

Yes. If that's what's happening, then this is going to be very dangerous indeed.

Four

Breitling pulls into the dirt patch at the back of the casita, but he doesn't turn off the engine. "Shall I pick you up later?"

"Nah, I can Uber out to the airport," I say as I undo my seatbelt. "It's out of your way, and I've taken advantage of you enough for one day."

"Hardly." The whispered word tickles my ear. I smile as he touches his lips to my cheek, gentle and feathery soft. I want to return it, but if I do, I'll never get out of this car. Instead, I lean in so he can kiss my forehead before he gets out to open my door. Without the tinted windows to protect us, I feel overexposed. One look at the house tells me why. Through the glass patio slider, I see Ruth sitting at my dining room table, her head bent over her laptop. Mama stands across from her, one hand on her hip, staring straight at me.

Shit. My first instinct is to grab Breitling, dive back in the car and head straight for the plane. They've got stores in London, right? My second instinct is to punch my first instinct in the head. She's already seen us. Running now will only be more incriminating. Better to woman up and face the music.

"See you tonight," I mutter as I start for the house.

He wraps his hand around mine and squeezes gently. "Until tonight."

His voice, deep and rough with implications, makes me crave his touch on more than my hand. With extreme effort, I pull away, keep my eyes on the ground, and by some miracle, make it to the porch. I reach for the handle of the slider, but it rockets open before I can grab hold.

"What the–?" I jump back as Mama bursts out of the house.

"Exactly, Adina. 'What the'?" She directs her fiery gaze over my shoulder to where Breitling is, thankfully, driving away. "I thought we talked about this."

"Ma, come on." I push past her into the dining room. Ruth raises her chin in greeting. As Mama storms up behind me, she ducks her head and returns to work. She wants no part of this argument, and I don't blame her. But she's not leaving either.

I race through the kitchen, but Mama is too quick, beating me to the end of the island and blocking my path to the bedroom. "I'm waiting, Adina."

"For what?" I ask innocently.

"Don't be cute, young lady. What on Earth are you thinking?"

"First of all, I'm not a 'young lady' anymore. If you want to scold me effectively, come up with a more appropriate title. Like, maybe, um…"

"Ripe hussy?" Ruth supplies.

"Perfect, thank you," I toss over my shoulder. "Second, to answer your question, what I'm *thinking* is that I can spend time with whoever I want, and I choose to spend time with him because he's a colleague, and a friend, and we have a lot in common."

Ruth snorts a laugh at her computer, but she doesn't look up–or, more importantly, speak.

"And finally, it would be hard to avoid him since our boss keeps pushing us to work together." I think for a second, then turn to Ruth. "Hey, do you know if they have Telemundo in London? I don't want to fall behind on *Los Jovenes del Sol* while I'm gone. Angelique is in a double coma and her husband is having a throuple affair with her hairdresser *and* her twin sister."

Ruth frowns. "What's a double coma?"

"London!?" Mama bursts out. "You're leaving the country? With *him*?"

"For *work*, Ma." I backtrack toward the fridge. "They asked for me."

Finally, Ruth lifts her head. "What's the case?"

I waggle my eyebrows. "A Jack the Ripper copycat."

Her mouth drops. "Oh my God, are you serious? That's, like, the web sleuth Holy Grail! Can I come? The Vigilant has a whole sub-forum dedicated to the Ripper. Tons of theories, and a bunch of documentation on copycats throughout history."

Hm. That does sound useful. "I don't think they'll let me bring a plus-one to London, especially on short notice. But I could probably use you as a remote consultant. How about that?"

"Yes! I'll take it." She pumps her fist.

"I can't believe you two." Mama shakes her head like she's come home to find us covering the walls with glitter and Crazy Glue. "Especially you, Adina. How can you dedicate yourself to these people now that you know what they did?"

I scowl but keep silent, even though I'm dying to throw that question right back at her. She and Russ have been seeing each other on and off since they met at the Stanley Cup Final a couple months ago, and his Order star is most definitely on the rise. But since I want to know as little as possible about their relationship, I don't know if he's told her what he does for a living yet. As much as I want to blow up her spot, I'm less inclined to do the same thing to my direct supervisor.

"Fine," she says with a dramatic sigh. "Can we at least agree that it would be wise to keep a cautious distance?"

I don't know about distance, but the caution part is fair enough. "I will do the best I can, okay?"

Her brows squeeze together, but she nods. "That's all I can ask for, I suppose."

She goes to leave, then doubles back and scoops me into a tight hug. "*Please* be careful, Adi."

"I will." It takes me a minute to pry my arms free and hug her back. "I promise."

"She's not wrong, you know," Ruth says as soon as Mama leaves. "They sent Inquisitors to apprehend the Umbralists before, right? This could be a trap."

I plop down in the chair across from her. "Why would they send us to London when they could just have Breitling drop the hammer on me here? Besides, if that is what's happening—which it *isn't*—he would have told me. He promised as much."

She crosses her arms and stares at me. "And you believe him?"

I shrug. "It was the only thing I asked him to do for me."

"Adina." She regards me with an unwavering stare that says she will accept nothing less than a straight answer.

"Yes," I say resolutely. "I believe him."

"Well…that's something, I guess." She rubs her eyes behind her round lenses. "Still, I'd feel a lot better if I were going with you."

"Sorry, Sis. I can't let you tag along on every magical murder investigation I'm assigned." I reach over and ruffle her hair.

"Hey!" She bats me away. "For the record, the last one was *my* investigation. And it was a disappearance, not a murder. *And* if I hadn't asked for your help, you and Breitling wouldn't be…what was the term you used? Spending time together?"

I glower at her. "What's your point?"

"Nothing, dear sister," she says with a smirk. "Just that the occasional 'thank you' might make me less inclined to bother you—or tell Mom that 'spending time' means 'screwing.'"

"Go right ahead," I fire back. "She could use a little shock and awe. Consider it a fair trade for her…*spending time* with my boss."

Ruth wrinkles her nose and snaps her laptop shut. "On that horrible note, I should probably go. And unless I'm mistaken, *you*'ve got a suitcase to pack."

I glance at the clock on the microwave. Crap–how is it four o'clock already? Cursing under my breath, I dash for my bedroom.

"Have a safe flight!" Ruth calls as she heads out the front door to the pool deck. "Text me when you land."

"I will!" I wrestle my cracked, sticker-covered plastic suitcase out of my closet. As I debate one black t-shirt over another, a corner of my brain continues to mull over my many conundrums.

Despite her insistence on treating me like a child, I do agree with my mother: the Order has a lot to answer for. But while she blames them for my father's disappearance,

I'm less inclined to lay that at their feet. After all, the Order didn't take him. *He* left. That was his *choice*. As far as I'm concerned, he's no different from any other deadbeat who chooses drugs or booze over his family.

I hurl a bundle of black fabric into my suitcase and slam it shut. Besides, even if the Order owes us answers, all this happened almost thirty years ago, before Prime Castillo and a majority of the current Presidium members were in office. A few may not have even been born yet. They're far from perfect, but they are better than *that*.

At least, I think they are.

I grab my birth control off the bathroom sink, then do a quick scan of the medicine cabinet for any indispensable toiletries that may not exist across the pond. My last stop is the living room to search my bookshelves for some in-flight entertainment. The titles blur as my thoughts continue to run.

They know I'm the legacy of one Rafael Venture. It's his name in black and white (or rather, copper and brown) printed on the back of my registration card. But *only* his name. No registered Operations, no listed discipline. A clerical error that wasn't spotted at the time and is too old to correct. Which means they don't know that he's the man who would have been Master—if there were anything left to be Master of.

Unless, of course, this is a matter of keeping your enemies close. Perhaps they *do* know who and what I am and have brought me into the fold to keep an eye on me. Monitor me. Make sure nothing's amiss.

If that *is* the situation, then who's to say I'm not doing the same?

Five

Once I've chosen a few well-worn paperback thrillers to shove into my shoulder bag, I strip off my Seychelle-sanctioned pantsuit in favor of something more comfortable. I'm pulling on a tank top and some sweat shorts when there's a tapping at the window above my bed.

"Shit," I mutter to myself as I slide it open to let Shiva in. I'd been so harried preparing myself to leave that I'd forgotten about my roommate. "Hey, can we talk for a second?"

She cocks her head at me from the narrow shelf above the bed, then hops into her perch in the fake branches sprouting from my nightstand.

"I'm going to be leaving town–and the country–for a little while. Will you be okay here without me?"

Her black eyes snap open and closed.

I shake my head. "I think the TSA will notice if I try to bring a crow in my carry-on."

Ruffling her feathers, she circles on the perch until she's facing the wall.

"Come on, don't be like that," I prod her. "Even if I could get you on the plane, I'll be working the whole time. What are you going to do in London by yourself?"

She drops her legs under her, and her little body lands with an outsized thud.

I throw up my hands. "Okay, fine. If that's the way you want to be about it, go ahead and pout. I'll have Ruth check on you while I'm gone." I sling my bag over my shoulder and haul my suitcase off the bed. "Window open or closed?"

She doesn't answer, so I leave it open. It's too small for a human to get through, the worst of monsoon season isn't for a few weeks, and any trespassing vermin will make great target practice for her. It might even stop her from taking out her anger on my poor throw pillows.

Again.

My phone buzzes as I'm waiting for my Uber outside the casita, my bags gathered around my feet and the August heat sucking the sweat from my pores. It would have been easier to have them pick me up at the main house, but I'll take dizzying dehydration over another lecture from Mama.

I check my texts, expecting to see a message from Mr. Unknown Number with our flight details. But it's not him.

JAKE
Hey u free to talk?

My heart leaps, then nosedives. It's been two months since Jake and I parted ways—or rather, since I ripped his heart out and stomped it into the ground. As much as we both want to stay friends, he's needed time and space to heal, and I've done my best to give it to him. He's texted me a few times though, just to let me know he's still alive. Last week he sent me a link to a website advertising discrete encounters with Lake Meade merwomen and the caption *my next gf? LOL.* It's encouraging progress. But this is the first time he's asked to talk-talk. Good thing? Bad thing?

Only one way to find out. As I type out my answer, a pair of headlights bounce up the hill toward me.

ME

About to get in an Uber. Call me in thirty seconds?

He sends back a thumbs up, and I wave down Romeo in the white Kia Forte. Once I'm settled in the backseat, I have about five seconds to get good and nervous before my phone chimes.

"Hey," I say as complacently as I can manage.

"How's it going, Miss Adventure?" Jake asks with his signature audible grin. The sound fills me with relief. Maybe this is good news after all.

"I'm alright," I say, relaxing into the leather seat. "I'm on my way to the airport."

"Oh." His bouncy tone deflates. *"That's, um…oh."*

The tension returns to my shoulders, and I sit up straighter. "Why? What's wrong?"

"No, it's nothing. There's this band playing at the Backstage Bar tonight, and they gave me and Shanti tickets to come check them out. But she's busy, so I thought maybe you'd want to go. They've got an AC/DC sound with Taylor Swift lyrics. I think you'd be into them."

Hm. This sounds a lot like he's asking me on a date, without making it sound like a date. Combine that with his sweet earnestness…well, it's a good thing I'm leaving, or I might have said yes. Out of friendship, sure, but also out of guilt–or worse, pity. And that wouldn't be good for either of us.

"They sound great," I say. "I'm sorry to miss it."

"Yeah," he says. *"Me too."*

The silence that settles between us is so dense it's almost suffocating. Damn, this is *awkward.* I even catch an uncomfortable glance from Romeo in the rearview. I should have texted him that I was busy, and I'd call later. Stupid hindsight, where are you when I need you?

"So, um, where are you off to?" Jake asks, bringing the painful lapse to an end.

"London."

"Oh yeah?" He perks up a little. *"You gonna visit Whitechapel while you're there? Take the Ripper tour?"*

I smile. Jake may be a late-night radio DJ by trade, but his love of dark music stems from a deeper, more general fascination with the macabre. "Funny you should mention that. There's a Ripper copycat active right now, and I'm going to do some…support work."

"What?" he almost shouts. *"A copycat? Are you serious? Man, that is…well, I mean, it's terrible, but…wow. Is Ruth going with you?"*

I fiddle with my seatbelt. I need to tread carefully here. Jake doesn't know about the Order, or that I work for them, or that I'm an Operator (or that Operators even exist, as far as I know). While we were dating, I let him get the impression that I work in some branch of law enforcement. Ruth's actual position as a Public Information Officer with the LVMPD helped sell the idea, and so far, he's never questioned it. Still, I don't want to put too much pressure on the story. I don't know how close it may be to breaking.

"Uh, no, Ruth isn't coming. But I may be in touch with her if I need help."

"Ah, cool." He draws a breath, and I'm sure his fingers are working their way through his thick black hair. *"You know, I'm no detective, but I've been obsessed with the Ripper case since high school. If she gets stuck or something, maybe I could lend a hand."*

Breitling's quip about Dahmer pops into my head. I smile, only to feel instantly guilty. Focus on the guy you're talking to, I lecture myself. It's the least you can do. "Yeah, that's a good idea. In fact, do you have any good resources off the top of your head? Especially on the first three murders?"

"Which first three?"

If it's possible to do an auditory double-take, I do it. "The...*first* first three? Not sure what you're asking."

"There's some disagreement about which of the early murders were committed by the actual Ripper. There's the Canonical Five, of course, but there's also a fair amount of evidence that suggests—you know what, I'll send you a few links. Should make for some fun plane reading."

"Perfect," I say. Glad he cut himself off before I had to do it. "And...I *am* sorry to miss the concert. Maybe we can do something when I get back?"

The question hangs in the air for way too long. My fingers curl into the leather seat. Too far?

At last, he clears his throat. *"Sure, A. Let's do it."*

Another wash of relief floods me, only this one is strong enough to almost bring tears. "Awesome."

We hang up in the best place we've been since before we started dating.

Six

I leap out of the Uber and into the Departures terminal as quickly as I can. The deep freeze inside the airport turns my sweat into tiny chunks of ice. Rubbing my arms, I check to make sure I'm in the right place, then text Breitling.

ME
At British Airways ticketing. Where are you?

I hit Send, then spot him near the base of the escalators. He's wearing his standard black suit jacket and slacks, but no vest, and the top two buttons of his black shirt are open, revealing a glint of red metal. A leather overnight bag hangs from one shoulder. Between the outfit, the coiffed hair, and the skeptical look he's giving his phone, he's the picture of a sophisticated, jet set business professional.

Grinning, I look down at my baggy tank top, sweat shorts, and flip-flops.

This is going to be fun.

"Howdy, partner!" I yell as I approach him, dragging my beat-up suitcase behind me, its wonky wheel making it yaw in all directions.

He looks up from reading my message. When he sees me, his eyes widen in horror. "What in God's name are you wearing?"

"I could ask you the same thing." I plop my bag down in front of him. "It's a ten-hour flight. How do you expect to sleep in that?"

"I never sleep on planes," he says, tucking his phone into his inside jacket pocket. "Besides, there are more important things to consider. We're going from Heathrow straight to the Tower, and they do things differently there. It's not the come-as-you-are, anything-goes free-for-all the Summit is."

He glowers at me while I try to control my laughter.

"As I was saying, there are protocols to observe, starting with the dress code."

Whoops. "I guess I have some shopping to do."

"Can't you change into something from your suitcase?"

I wrinkle my nose at him. "No, I can't. I *thought* I was going to be buried in the dirt most of the time we were there. Nobody told me I needed to dress for tea with the queen."

"I assumed it went without saying that a professional assignment requires professional attire." He runs a hand over his hair. "It's alright. They know you're new, and it's your first time visiting an international hold. We'll convince them to overlook your misstep."

"And *your* mistaken assumptions." I narrow my eyes before allowing a coy smile to grace my lips. "You do look nice, though."

He evaluates my scrubby outfit again. "Are you expecting me to say the same?"

"Maybe." Standing on my tiptoes, I tug his shoulder down so I can whisper in his ear. "You should see what I'm wearing underneath."

His head jerks toward me, and his cheek brushes against mine. "And what is that, Miss Venture?"

I nuzzle him for a moment before answering. "Absolutely nothing...Levi."

His hands clench as he utters a soft but audible grunt. Emboldened by my victory, I'm tempted to kiss him on the mouth. My sigil dampens that ambition. Not entirely, but enough for me to remember that we're in public. His collar must be responding as well, because he steps away from me with a sigh.

"You are dangerous, my dear," he says, hefting the strap of his bag further up his shoulder. His eyes slide over me one more time before he turns away. "We should go. Security can take a while, and since this is your first time through, we need to account for additional delays."

"Aye aye, sir." I follow him onto the escalator, bringing my gimpy suitcase in line behind me. I intend to struggle with it all the way to the plane. But when we reach the top, he takes it from me without saying a word.

Turns out, Breitling's fears of delay are valid. Something about my passport catches the eye of the TSA, and they pull me aside to sort it out. As Breitling exchanges words with the guard—their superiors have cleared this, I'm a valid citizen, blah blah blah—my phone buzzes.

JAKE
Some lite reading 4u
Have a good flight! {plane emoji} {London guard emoji} {snail
emoji}

My giggle draws a confused look from a nearby security officer. That stupid snail is another baby step back to normal.

A link to a PDF titled *The Enduring Mystery of Jack the Ripper* appears next, followed by a link to a video with the same name. Leave it to a DJ to provide a multimedia presentation.

"Of all the ridiculous things…"

I look up as Breitling approaches, his perfect hair now tousled from his hands raking through it.

"Is everything okay?" I ask.

"Yes, at long last." He casts a final sneer at the guards before taking my suitcase off the scanner belt and heading into the terminal. "Someone mistyped your name on your passport, and the guards took exception to the out-of-date photo. I had to call their supervisor's bloody supervisor to get it straightened out." He slides his fingers through his hair again, trying and failing to comb the blond strands away from his eyes.

"But it's all worked out now," I say. "Next stop, the plane."

"Yes. Yes, you're right." A flush of embarrassment colors his cheeks. "I apologize. I…don't like the thought of something ruining our plans."

"Right," I say. "The Tower is expecting us. We can't let them down."

The smile he gives me is nothing short of lascivious. "That too."

When we arrive at our gate, I sit with the luggage while Breitling goes to the newsstand for snacks and bottles of water. I follow his lead, standing when he stands, approaching the gate when he does, and trailing behind him down the cramped beige jetway to the plane.

The first section is divided into individual pods that look like tiny office cubicles. We sidle down the slim middle aisle into the second section. It's like the first, except that instead of one seat, each pod has two. I plan to keep going toward the aeronautical equivalent of the nosebleeds when Breitling stops in front of the last pod on the left. "This is us."

I take in the spacious seats, wide television screen, and the long counter running below the two windows. "I'm surprised the…um, company would spring for this kind of luxury."

"It's because of me," he says as he hefts my suitcase into the overhead compartment.

I roll my eyes. "Okay, I get it. You're fancy. Enough already."

"Because of my height, I mean." He struggles to contain a smirk. "Regular class seats are murder on my legs and back. A flight this long would take me days to recover. I'm much more useful to everyone if I don't have to waste that kind of time."

"Oh." My cheeks burn. "Well, then, I'm glad I get to reap the benefits of your unfortunate disability."

"If that's your way of saying 'thank you,' then you're welcome." He gestures to the pod, and I take the seat next to the windows. Outside, orange-clad figures load bags and zip around on oversized go-karts. The line of planes parked outside the building stretches well out of my view, reminding me of gigantic white horses at a feeding trough. The roar of engines disturbs the air, and I crane my neck to see behind us as one of those gigantic white horses takes to the sky.

My stomach drops and my hands grow clammy. "Um, Breitling?"

He looks at me over the rim of his reading glasses, the menu in his hand settling on his lap. "Yes?"

"You wouldn't happen to know how many people die in plane crashes every year, would you?"

His brows furrow. "I've heard that one is more likely to die in a car crash than a plane crash, but as far as numbers are concerned, I'm afraid I can't recall. Why do you ask?"

"No reason." I duck my head and stare out the window.

"Adina?" He shifts in his seat, and his hand covers mine. "What is it?"

I swallow the dry lump in my throat. "I just…um…"

His grip tightens. "Tell me."

I turn toward him but can't quite meet his gaze. "I've never flown before."

"Ah." He doesn't say anything else. Instead, he puts the menu away and slips his arm over my shoulders, holding me to his side as the seats fill in around us.

"Welcome to British Airways." The voice of a woman with a posh accent chirps out of the speakers. "Thank you for flying with us."

The plane jerks backward, and my pulse shoots into the stratosphere. I remain rigid as we stutter toward the runway. There's a pause. A long one. I'm starting to think something's wrong when we speed up, going from a standstill to a rocket blast in a matter of seconds. My hand leaps to Breitling's lapel, gripping it like a life preserver.

He rests his chin on the top of my head and strokes my white knuckles. Or they would be white if not for the bruises, so instead they are a pale, muddy mauve.

"It's okay," he whispers. "I've got you."

I dip my head into his chest. The metal creaks and lifts and for a moment I'm weightless, as if the air around me has turned to water. I cling to him tighter as my head swims and my ears fill with pressure. He keeps speaking to me, keeps holding me. After an eternity, the floor levels out and the pressure stabilizes enough that I can tilt my head up to look at him.

"Are you alright?" he asks, his arm still draped over my shoulder.

"I'm…not sure," I say, the grinding of the engines swallowing my words. "Is it going to be like this the whole trip?"

"I'm afraid so. But there are ways to make it bearable." He reaches up for the call button. Within moments, a cheerful blonde flight attendant bounds over to us. "Hello, sir. What can I do for you?"

"Could we please have a bottle of sparkling water and four shots of Jameson?"

"Of course. I'll be right back." She scampers off, as steady on her feet as if she were on land.

Breitling turns back to me. When he sees my wide-eyed stare, he frowns. "What?"

"Since when do you drink?"

"I appreciate a fine spirit every now and then. Besides, this is a special occasion."

The attendant returns with the water, two glasses with a couple of ice cubes, and four tiny green bottles. "Would you like me to pour it for you, sir?"

"That won't be necessary, thank you." He fills our glasses with enough whiskey to cover the ice, then adds the water and hands one to me. "To your first flight."

He clinks his glass to mine and nods at me to take a sip. The bubbles soften the burn of the whiskey, and some of the tension drains from my chest.

"Drink slowly," he says. "And top it off with water every so often. You'll want to stay awake for the next few hours, then get as close to a full night's sleep as you can manage. It will help you adjust to the time change as quickly as possible."

"Got it." I take another, longer drink. "Anything else, O Great and Powerful Inquisitor?"

He narrows his eyes. "As a matter of fact, there is."

He leans over me to set his glass on the counter under the window. But instead of withdrawing, he pulls me into an embrace. I have enough time to notice the absence of red chains beneath his shirt collar before his mouth is on mine, hard and hungry. I hurry to set my own glass down before wrapping my arms around his neck. He scoops his arm under my knees and pulls my legs up onto his lap. I moan as his hand slides up the back of my thigh, hiking my shorts up higher and higher until he pulls away with a startled gasp.

"You were serious?" He sounds borderline scandalized, and yet his palm continues to explore the curve of bare flesh where my underwear should be.

I press my smiling lips over his. "I would never lie to you."

"As I said," he murmurs. "Dangerous."

Seven

I stay awake as long as I can. It's not hard. Between the document Jake sent me, seasons 1-4 of *What We Do in the Shadows*, and Breitling's roaming hands, I have plenty of stimulation, mental and otherwise. Eventually, the warmth of the whiskey and the hum of the engines prove too much, and I recline my seat flat. As promised, Breitling stays upright. I wish he'd lay down with me, but then I'd never fall asleep. Resigning myself to wait until we land for further intimacy, I turn away from him, pull up the Ripper documentary on my phone, and close my eyes.

"In the late 19th century, the city of London was the largest in the world. But in the autumn of 1888, a horrific story emerged from the capital's East End..."

I swear, true crime stories work better than Ambien. The solid, steady voice of the narrator envelopes me, and I snuggle into the velvet darkness of sleep.

Something long and wet slithers across the back of my neck.

"What the hell?" I sit up, disoriented and dizzy, and turn toward Breitling.

But he's not next to me. I'm not even on an airplane anymore. I'm sitting on a craggy stone slab surrounded by gray fog that I wish was too thick to see through. But it isn't, and I can make out serpentine black things squirming on the other side.

"Dammit," I mutter. "How did I get here?"

"I summoned you." The voice emanates out of every wriggling creature clinging to the walls that surround me. I stand up and peer over the top of them. Sure enough, it's Kosmal larvae as far as the eye can see, a roiling ocean of black leeches waiting to burst forth and wreak havoc.

"What are you doing?" I snap at the sky. Its words may come from the Kosmal, but that's an illusion. I know from experience that the being we call Chaos hovers somewhere above me. "Humans call *you*, remember? You can't summon me whenever you want to."

"Of course I can," it says. "The fact that I don't should have you thanking your lucky stars."

I tilt my head. "Wouldn't that be you too?"

"We don't have time for this banter. You're in a bleed-through zone, and I'm not sure how long I have."

I hesitate. If I didn't know better, I'd say it sounded…anxious. "What are you talking about?"

"Where are you off to, Miss Adventure?"

Its refusal to answer my question makes me want to do the same. But that will only drag things out. As much as I hate to admit it, I'm not the one in control here. "London."

"In England?"

"Of course. Why?"

The Kosmal babies shiver around me, emitting tiny, frightened squeaks.

"I don't have influence in the Olde Realm like I do in the New one." It pronounces the first word like "moldy."

That and all the hard consonants make it sound borderline disgusted. "As long as you are over there, I can't reach you."

My heart jumps. "Are you saying you won't be able to get inside my head?"

"I'm saying you will need to be careful. Should you stumble into peril that requires a miraculous rescue— *again*—you can't count on getting one from me."

I frown. While I wouldn't say I *like* my connection to the big, destructive force that lifts people up with as little effort as it cuts them down, I suppose I have, for better or worse, grown accustomed to it. For every horrible thing it's done to me, it has also gotten me out of several jams. Knowing that I won't have that power at my disposal is…confusing, to say the least.

"Miss Adventure? Did you hear what I said?"

"Yes, I heard you. I will be careful."

"I'm afraid there's more. The reason I wield so little influence is not an accident. There is…another. One as powerful as me that claims the Olde Realm as its own. The one they called the Rigour." The Kosmal shiver again. This time, the noise they make is more like a scream. "When you leave my influence, you will be subject to theirs."

I clench my arms and legs to suppress my trembling. Another metaphysical nightmare. Wonderful. "What will it do to me?"

"I am not privy to its machinations. What I do know is that it can manifest its will in many weird ways."

"Weirder than being transported to a leech plane to talk to a disembodied voice?"

It is silent for a moment. "Perhaps 'weird' was the wrong word. 'Unpleasant' may be a better one. Or 'upsetting.' Even…'cruel.'"

My stomach drops. "Cruel how?"

"Again, I cannot presume to know. The Rigour thrives on logic and prediction. It wants things it can track, if not control. It hates rule-breakers and anomalies, and you, my dear, are one of the best. It will try to conform you. If that doesn't take, well…"

Sweat gathers at my temple. "Okay. Best behavior. Got it. How will I know what it wants?"

"It will find ways to tell you. And no matter what happens, remember that I will be here when you return. To…help."

That freezes me solid. Chaos offering to help me recover from whatever is about to happen may be the most unnerving part of this whole exchange. "Okay. Thank you."

It utters a low "hmph," and one of the Kosmal closest to me brushes my cheek, soft and almost tender. "Bon voyage, Miss Adventure, and–" It breaks off as the Kosmal chitter in a chorus of giggles. "I was about to wish you good luck, but…"

"Yeah, better not," I say with a rueful chuckle of my own. "Maybe…stay out of trouble?"

It grunts in disgust. "I suppose that will have to do."

With a whimper, I force my eyes open and examine my hands. They look the same: thin and pale, with brownish-black smudges over the knuckles. But something's different. Somehow, they're both lighter *and* heavier than usual. They move too fast when I lift them, and they're twice as weighty when they sit still.

"Adina?"

I look over at Breitling. He blinks blearily at me. Despite my disquiet, I smile. So much for never sleeping on planes.

"Is everything okay?" he asks hoarsely.

I let my hands float down to my lap. They crash into my thighs like two boulders. "Just a bad dream."

He yawns and stretches, checking his watch as he runs his arm over my shoulders. "Looks like we'll be touching down soon. You'd better prepare yourself—landings can be quite rough."

I nod even though my heart is pounding. His embrace is making my skin itch and burn.

Something's wrong.

His hand slides down my bicep, leaving a trail that feels…slimy. Dirty, and not in a good way. My stomach tightens, drawing me into myself. As I pull away from the seatback, his arm drops and encircles my waist.

"No."

My head wobbles and my knuckles pulse with heat. My sigil does the same.

That's never happened before.

I open my mouth to alert Breitling when a bolt of pain rips from the back of my eyes and down my throat before sinking its teeth into the pit of my stomach. My thoughts scramble, and for a moment, I'm paralyzed.

"Shit!" I shout when the spasm passes. Pressing a hand to my throbbing belly, I scramble as far away from him as my seatbelt will allow.

"What?" He retracts his arm. The pain fizzles instantly. "What's wrong?"

"Nothing," I say as I fumble with my seatbelt. "Sorry. I just, uh…need to use the bathroom."

If he answers me, I don't hear it. The motion and weird atmospheric pressure combine with the panicked surge of adrenaline, making me stumble all the way down the aisle.

What the hell is going on? I shoot the silent question into the ether. If it works for Chaos, maybe it'll work here.

"No."

My head bobs like a buoy in the ocean. Digging my fingers into the seat backs, I crawl up the aisle and launch myself into the miniscule bathroom.

"What do you mean, no?" I pose the question to the mirror. A haggard ghoul stares back at me from sunken sockets, her short black hair sticking out in a ratted halo. "No, I'm not allowed? Or no, you won't answer me?"

"No."

Gritting my teeth around a growl, I slam down on the tap and douse my face with water.

And I thought Chaos was a bitch.

Eight

The landing sucks. Breitling tries to comfort me like he did during takeoff, but between the air pressure, the jostling of the plane, and the monstrous nausea his attempts cause, I wriggle away from him every time he reaches for me. Eventually, he gives up, pinning his hands on his knees and staring in consternation at the floor. I want to tell him what's happening and that it's not his fault, but the velocity of our descent makes talking impossible. Finally, the wheels bounce against solid ground, and my lungs inflate again. Flexing my tense muscles, I attempt to order my thoughts into a reasonable explanation.

I'm still working it out when we reach the gate. The moment the seatbelt light snaps off, Breitling is in the aisle and opening the overhead bin to retrieve my bag. Whether he's mad at me or just ready to get the hell off this plane, I can't tell. We walk in single file down the aisle, off the jetway, and all the way to baggage claim, where we wait at a carousel for his luggage.

"Is everything alright?" he asks me at last. "You don't seem like yourself."

"I'm not sure." Unwilling to say anything too crazy around so many NO ears, I hold up my hand, knuckles facing him, and wiggle my fingers. "My connection is gone."

He frowns. "Are you sure?"

"Oh yeah. Even if it didn't feel so different...it told me. Apparently, Chaos is *entity non-grata* on this side of the pond. We're in 'the realm of the Rigour,' or so it said."

"Dammit." He pinches the bridge of his nose. "It's been so long since I've been back, I'd forgotten about that."

"You're familiar with this concept?"

"I wouldn't say familiar. I read about it once, ages ago. Contrary to popular belief, I don't know everything about the universe and the things that control it."

I arch my brow. "*Who* believes that?"

His mouth twitches, but not enough to overcome the lines of concern creasing his forehead. "From what I recall, the Rigour attempts to shepherd behavior, both of individuals and the populace at large, along acceptable lines."

"And those lines would be?"

"No one knows for sure, but it seems they're rooted in traditional social mores. Propriety, decorum, and so on. All that is subject to interpretation, however, since the Rigour doesn't speak to anyone." He gives me a curious look. "Has it spoken to you?"

"Just one word: No."

"Sounds about right." He struggles not to roll his eyes.

I don't exercise the same restraint. "So, everyone has to walk the line, and if they don't, the Rigour makes them sick. Awesome."

His frown deepens. "And is this the reason for your change in...demeanor toward me?"

My cheeks burn. I don't want to say it, but he deserves to know. "Yeah. I think so."

"Why?" His vehemence draws concerned glances from our fellow passengers. Ducking his head, he lowers his voice. "Why would it do that?"

I shrug. "Your guess is as good as mine."

He fixes a stony gaze on the carousel. It's several moments before he speaks again. "Is there anything I can do?"

He sounds so forlorn, so disappointed. Despite the uncomfortable knot in my stomach, I slip my hand into his. "Maybe there's an adjustment period. You know, like jet lag. Maybe it's hitting me harder because I'm not used to it."

"Perhaps," he says, squeezing my hand. My stomach lurches like I'm on a rollercoaster and I clench my teeth to keep from whimpering. Luckily, his bag comes around the curve, and he lets me go so he can retrieve it. When he looks at me again, his face is an icy mask. "Let's go. Constable McNally is waiting for us."

The evening is cool and humid, with a thick blanket of clouds tinged purple and pink with the sunset. I marvel at the fat raindrops splatting the sidewalk as Breitling orders up a rideshare. It arrives in less than five minutes, and off we go.

The driver talks non-stop as he zigs and swerves through the congestion. Compared to the streets at home, these roads don't seem wide enough for one car, and yet they accommodate two directions of traffic plus bike lanes. As the driver babbles about football, or soccer, or whatever, I wonder to myself why the Rigour is so busy driving wedges into people's love lives when it needs to do something about this miserable gridlock.

"Here is fine," Breitling says after forty-five minutes of vehicular disarray. We're stopped at a light with a park to our left and a cement courtyard to our right.

"Yeah, alright." The driver puts the car in park and jumps out to help us with our bags. He shakes Breitling's hand and nods at me before jumping back into the driver's seat. There's only a single lane of oncoming traffic, and we make it to the sidewalk outside the courtyard unscathed. The whole thing took ten seconds, and we didn't get a single irritated honk.

I don't even want to think about what would happen to us if we tried that maneuver back home.

"He sure was friendly," I say, struggling to get my suitcase to behave on the uneven flagstone.

"Don't get used to it," Breitling says. "Especially not where we're going."

I slow to a crawl. Now that we're done with our crazy commute, I can gauge my surroundings properly. It doesn't take me long to figure out where we are. If the parapets peering out from above the nearby tree line hadn't clued me in, the sign outside the courtyard that reads Tower Hill Terrace would have.

"So…when you said we're going to the Tower, you meant *The* Tower? As in the historical landmark?"

"Yes," he says, continuing his trek down the sidewalk. "As I said, things are different here. The Order and the government–or, rather, the monarchy—have a symbiotic relationship."

My eyes widen, and I hurry to catch up so I don't have to shout my next question. "Are you saying the queen was an Operator?"

He laughs. A real laugh. The kind that lights up his whole face. The kind that, even in my current state, fills me with joy. "That would have been something. But I'm afraid that, with royals, it's NOs all the way down. Perhaps it's karmic revenge for what they did to the druids, and the Celts, and…all the rest."

Good to know that Chaos and the Rigour have a mutual fondness for poetic justice. "The royals are Non-Operational, but they know Ops exist. That's got to be annoying. And terrifying."

"Just so," Breitling confirms. "An Operator with the right skill set and a revolutionary spirit could indeed wrestle power away from them. Bringing the Order under monarchy rule insures them against such affronts."

"And by rule, I assume you mean…" I rub my fingers and thumb together.

He smiles. "What else?"

We reach the entrance to the Tower, where the ticket window stands shuttered for the day. Breitling veers to the right and approaches an iron gate that looks antiquated in every way except for the RFID scanner mounted on the wall next to it. He swipes his Order registration card across it, and the gate pops open. As we walk through it, static licks the back of my neck. An intentions threshold, set on an after-hours high.

We're in the right place.

On the other side of the gate a Beefeater guard awaits us. "State your name and business," he says in a grizzled accent.

"Chief Inquisitor Levi Breitling and Adina Venture," Breitling says. "We're consultants from America here to meet with Constable McNally."

The guard's bushy white brows furrow as he assesses us, with more concern paid to our luggage than our (or rather, my) appearance. "IDs, please."

We hand them over, though Breitling seems ruffled by the extra scrutiny. Figures he wouldn't be used to having his word doubted. That makes me wonder what the hierarchy is here. Does he outrank this guard because he's an Inquisitor? Or is it the opposite because the guard is on his home turf?

After a thorough evaluation of our credentials, the guard steps aside. "You'll find the Constable in his office. Old Hospital Block. Take the path along the wall, turn left at the end and then—"

"Thank you, I know the way," Breitling tosses over his shoulder as he hurries off. I nod my thanks and jog to catch up with his long strides. The light is fading fast, and the evening breeze chills my bare arms and legs. Maybe I should have brought a sweatshirt or coat, but as a born Midwestern girl, there's a part of me that insists I shouldn't need outerwear until at least November. Of course, I haven't been back to the Midwest, or anywhere outside Nevada, in…Christ, over a decade. The wind picks up, and even though it's August, my body erupts in a shiver.

Guess I've got desert blood now.

Unlike the Summit, with its mountain grandeur and modern glass-and-steel facade, the Hospital is a long three-story brick structure that looks like two buildings smushed together, each with a teal green door in the middle. We climb the concrete steps to the patio. Another scanner waits for us on the frame of the nearest door. Breitling huffs impatiently as he digs out his ID yet again.

A soft chorus of caws behind me draws my attention. Six ravens, each the size of a house cat, perch on the crenelated roof of the large square building in the center of the courtyard. When they see me watching, the one in the middle ruffles its feathers and spreads its wings so wide it smacks its compatriots in the face.

"What the hell is that about?" I murmur.

Breitling glances over his shoulder, then gives me a quizzical look. "I assumed you, of all people, would know about the White Tower Ravens."

"Contrary to popular belief, I don't know everything about ravens and the things that control them."

He chuckles. "Legend says that the Ravens are the true protectors of not only the Tower, but the whole of Britain. King Charles II claimed that if the six Ravens were ever to leave the Tower, the kingdom would fall."

"Wow." I shake my head. "That's a lot of pressure for such tiny shoulders."

"Indeed."

As Breitling turns back to the door, I peer up at the bird who flapped its wings. It leans over, as if studying me, then straightens. I've gotten pretty good at reading avian body language over the years, but I've got to admit, the meaning behind this gesture eludes me. Then, as if on some silent signal, all six flutter their wings and rise a few inches into the air. A moment later, they disappear onto the roof of the White Tower.

Breitling scans his card, and the door pops open like it's on a spring. What awaits us on the other side is the polar opposite of what the stately facade suggests, starting with the windows. They're blacked out, and blinking fluorescent overheads cast everything in a sickly yellow light. The room itself is low-ceilinged and wide, but shallow. Only six feet of scuffed linoleum separates us from the dented metal desk stationed in front of the back wall. The lady sitting behind it is in her mid-forties, with mousy brown hair hanging in unintentional waves around her chubby cheeks. She peers at us over wire-rimmed glasses and pushes herself out of her chair. The nametag clipped to her shapeless gray cardigan displays a single word: *Joanne.*

"Hello, Chief Inquisitor." She sounds like she hasn't seen water in days. That would be off-putting on its own, but it's her eyes that make me shiver. They're not just dull; they're lightless. Like two burnt out bulbs. "Right this way."

She trudges over to a narrow steel door carved into the drywall. It opens with a screech the moment she presses the call button.

"First door on the left," she says as we enter a car barely big enough for the two of us. She reaches around the door to stab the button labeled 1N. "He's expecting you."

"Thank you," Breitling says, giving her a small smile. She doesn't return it.

"What's up with her?" I ask when the door has closed.

"Nothing out of the ordinary," he says. "Just the pressure of her position."

"And what position is that?"

"Stuck," he says with a sympathetic sigh. "That's another way things differ between the Tower and the Summit. Once you enter, at any level, you don't move, and with rare exception, you don't leave. I'd bet that she's been sitting at that desk since she was in her twenties, and she'll keep sitting there until, well…" He shoots me a weighty look.

I don't need him to finish that sentence.

Nine

The elevator has two ways out, and the one behind us is the one that opens. We exit into an unassuming hallway with beige walls, brown carpet, and more fluorescent light, all made ten times worse by the baked-in stench of burned coffee. We would have spotted the Constable's office even if Joanne hadn't told us. It's both the first and only door on the left, set in the middle of the floor between two hallways that lead to more offices. Also, it's the only door that's sitting ajar. As a formality, Breitling taps a knuckle against the doorframe before entering.

Inside are two men, one seated behind another dented mass-produced desk, and one in front of it. The one behind is fiftyish, heavy-set, and pasty, with wiry salt-and-pepper hair, watery blue eyes, and a flabby neck. Constable McNally, I presume. He remains seated while the gentleman in front of the desk gets to his feet. He's leaner than the Constable, and older. In his seventies, at least. Who he is, however, is a mystery. I turn to Breitling for an explanation.

He's staring at the older man with a slack jaw. "Uncle Thomas?"

My brows shoot up. I knew Breitling had an uncle, and that he'd played a significant role in Breitling's advancement through the Order's ranks. But I had no idea he'd be *here*. Based on the hand-in-the-cookie-jar look on Breitling's face, he hadn't either.

Thomas approaches us, his thin lips pulling into a warm but reserved smile. Despite being older, he has a sharpness that the Constable lacks. His narrow chin sports a well-trimmed white goatee, his thin white hair is cut close to the scalp, and clear green eyes sparkle behind his round spectacles. While both he and the Constable have nice clothes, Thomas's three-piece suit, made of tan corduroy with leather arm patches, is of far better quality than the Constable's off-the-rack attire.

"Levi." Thomas extends his hand to Breitling. "It's wonderful to see you, though I'm sorry it has to be under such solemn circumstances."

"It's good to see you too, Uncle," Breitling says, sounding more stunned than happy. "But if I may ask, what on Earth are you doing here?"

"He's here upon *my* request," the Constable says with a voice like a battering ram. "This case is a medical mystery, and I need an expert opinion. When I heard *you* were coming, the choice of expert became obvious."

My stomach tightens. He sounds repulsed. Personally, I'm used to that, but Breitling's the Chief Inquisitor. His position alone warrants a modicum of respect, but this guy sounds like Breitling is the *last* person he wants in his office.

"Of course, I was happy to oblige," Thomas says, eclipsing the hostility of McNally's words. He claps Breitling on the arm. "How are you?"

"Well, Uncle. I'm very well." He recovers enough of himself to remember that I'm standing next to him. "Thomas Breitling, meet Adina Venture."

Thomas smiles at me. "A pleasure."

"Likewise." We shake hands, and I duck my head slightly. "Sorry about the outfit."

He looks me over, but his smile only widens. "Think nothing of it. We should be grateful to you both for coming straight off the plane."

"Speaking of which," McNally says with a phlegmy cough. "It's nearly day's end and there's much to cover."

"Of course, Constable." Thomas gestures to the closest of the three chairs in front of the desk. "Miss Venture, if you please?"

I sit first. Thomas moves to the far chair, leaving the middle seat for Breitling. McNally remains standing.

"I assume the Prime has briefed you on this case?" He addresses the question to Breitling.

"In the broadest strokes," Breitling says. "He deferred to you so you could relate what you think is most important in greater detail."

"Is that so?" McNally's voice has taken on a croaky quality as he scowls at Breitling. He sucks a breath through his nose, and I watch in horrified fascination as the folds of his neck inflate until they look ready to pop. "Inquisitor Breitling. Section Three of the Inter-Departmental Communication and Cooperation Memo of 1978 states that all foreign consultants shall be briefed prior to arriving on site. Furthermore, as per Section Thirty of said memo, all breaches of protocol must undergo thorough evaluation to determine commensurate retribution." The bulges in his neck have deflated back to normal during his diatribe. "Have I made myself clear, Inquisitor Breitling?"

Breitling grunts and slumps back. Pink spots warm the apple of his cheeks and beads of sweat cling to his temples. He says nothing, but his rigid posture and furious expression tell me he's using all his willpower to keep himself from lunging across the desk and wrapping his hands around McNally's fleshy throat.

"With all due respect, Constable," Thomas interjects, "I haven't been briefed either. Even if Prime Castillo had told them everything, would we not have to go over it again now?"

McNally considers this, then shrugs. "I suppose that's true." He turns and rummages through his desk drawer without so much as an apologetic glance in Breitling's direction.

What the *hell* was that about? I try to catch Breitling's eye to ask my silent question, but he won't look at me. Despite knowing better, I slide my hand over to brush my pinky against his.

My knuckles warm, and my sigil burns in response. The next thing I know, I'm paralyzed by another bout of brain-stem-to-stomach vertigo.

"No."

I close my eyes and dig my nails into my palms. *I just want to make sure he's okay, and to remind him I'm here—*

"No!"

Okay! I shout silently into the void. *No touching. I get it. Let me go.*

When the tension eases, I remove the sigil from my fingers and slip it into the pocket of my shorts. I can't blame it for not wanting to deal with the Rigour. Doesn't mean I'm going to keep taking punches on its behalf though.

"Now then." From the drawer of his desk, McNally extracts a stack of manila folders and spreads them out like a dealer at the poker table. "About a month ago, we had an odd case come in from the Metro wire. A man was murdered on Gunthorpe Street, about a mile from where we now sit." He points at the folder closest to me. "Forty-one-year-old Tiago Silva, a recent transplant from Lisbon. He was found at eight in the morning outside the door of his first-floor unit at the Fitzgerald Flats."

He flips open the folder to a crime scene photo. The body of a man lies on a slab of concrete, his shirt bunched around his neck, revealing a torso covered with slim, purple bruises.

"Looks like blunt force trauma," Thomas says. "Multiple impacts."

"Thirty-nine, to be precise," McNally confirms. "However, they aren't blunt force trauma. The autopsy report notes internal hemorrhaging, but not from impact wounds. Rather, the tissue beneath the bruising appears to have been perforated."

I study the picture, giving myself time to mentally rifle through Jake's research. But no matter how deep I dig, I find no memory of Gunthorpe Street.

Breitling, who has been skimming the documents in the file, looks up at McNally. "It says you classified it as priority level two. Same one the Summit ascribes to the sale of Operationally loaded dice. A bit low for a deadly attack, wouldn't you say?"

McNally glowers at him. "Strange things happen all the time in *big* cities, Inquisitor. We can't upend our caseloads for every one. In this circumstance, as with every other, we followed standard procedure to the letter."

I lower my head so he doesn't see me roll my eyes. *I bet you love this guy, don't you?*

The Rigour doesn't answer in words. Instead, pinpricks of heat dance over my knuckles, sharp but not painful. It's a response, but whether it's yes, no, or other, who can say?

McNally snaps the first file closed and points to the one in the middle. "Three weeks later, we got another one. Forty-three-year-old Fatima Hassan, attacked on Durward Street. She was visiting from Cairo with some college friends, and they took the wrong exit out of the Tube station on their way to their dinner reservation. Her injuries were similar, only stranger and much worse."

He opens the file to reveal another body lying in a dim, yellow pool of streetlight.

"Oh my God." I press a hand to my mouth. McNally hadn't been exaggerating. A thick black line mars the woman's neck, and her stomach is one big purple stain.

"She appears to have been beaten," Thomas says, though doubt fills his words, "and strangled by a long object pressed into her throat."

"A fair analysis, Doctor. But once again, I'm afraid it's incorrect," McNally says. "Her trachea was severed, as were the fascia and tissue around her small and large intestines."

Breitling shifts in his seat. "She was disemboweled with her throat cut…from the inside."

McNally gives him a severe nod. "With the escalation in injuries, we reprioritized both cases."

"Is this also when you made the Ripper connection?" I'm hazarding another cosmic bitch-slap by speaking out of turn, but I don't have a choice. The second street name didn't ring any bells either, and I'm worried that I slept through more of Jake's documentary than I thought.

McNally's head swivels to me, his gaze heavy with suspicion. "There were some theories at that point, yes.

The locations were near-perfect matches for Martha Tabran and Mary Ann Nichols, even though Tabran is not one of the Ripper's canonical victims. Not only that, but Nichols and Ms. Hassan were also the same age."

My excitement spikes, but immediately plummets at McNally's dismissive wave. "But that's not all that unusual. In many ways, Jack the Ripper never left this city. The strangeness of those murders transcends time. Whenever there's a vicious or unusual attack, especially in the East End, he is bound to surface in the conversation at some point. Nothing ever comes of it."

With a sigh, McNally regards the last file. "The good thing about a Ripper connection is it gives us an idea of the timeline. If this killer followed the pattern, we knew there would be a week between the Durward murder and the one on Hanbury Street."

Finally, a name I recognize.

"I was skeptical about the connection," he continues, "but I thought it prudent to deploy our Reapers to Whitechapel nonetheless. The Metropolitan Police must have thought the same, because there was an increased law enforcement presence during that time as well. Not that it did much good in the end, I'm afraid."

He slides his finger under the corner of the folder, tipping it open as if he doesn't want to have too much contact with it. "Annie Turner. Twenty-five years old from Iowa City. She was about to matriculate at King's College as a graduate student, but she was staying in temporary housing off Hanbury until classes began. Based on her clothes and the early hour of the attack, she was on a morning jog when she was assaulted, dragged into a carpark, and…well…"

I frown at the picture. She's a blonde American and much younger than Fatima Hassan, but their injuries look the same. Those demographics can't be the only reason for McNally's increased aversion, can they?

"Same as the others?" Thomas asks.

"In a way." McNally drops into his chair. "As with the escalation between Mr. Silva and Ms. Hassan, Ms. Turner's injuries are similar, but worse. She suffered a severed trachea and internal trauma, but the big difference is her organs. They aren't damaged. They're missing."

I clench my fists. Annie Turner…and Annie Chapman. Dark Annie, as they called her in the trade. The second canonical Ripper victim. She was the first to have her organs taken. I lean forward to examine the photo more closely. Like Fatima Hassan, Annie the Second's stomach is one big eggplant-colored bruise, but the skin is intact.

"Missing how?" Thomas asks.

"I don't know, Doctor," McNally grumbles. "All I can tell you is that, despite having no external injuries, the medical examiner reported that her intestines and uterus had been cut out of her, as if with a scalpel."

We hold the silence for a long moment as the words sink in.

"What did Scotland Yard make of *that?*" Breitling asks.

McNally snorts a bitter laugh. "Status quo. They believe the world is what they see and what they say it is, regardless of any evidence to the contrary. Left to their own devices, they would find someone to charge as soon as possible. Most likely a person of Common aspect–or a NO, as you Americans say. As such, the Tower will conduct its own investigation, while using all necessary Operational resources to affect a permanent, *accurate* resolution."

"I see," Breitling says with the gravitas of a god surveying his creation. "The Crown must have a lot of faith in your ability to grant you such latitude."

McNally bristles. "An American is dead, Inquisitor. It's only a matter of time before *your* politicians call for someone's head. The Crown knows that. They also know that *we* are the ones who can remedy the problem. The Yard will be brought in when the time is right to handle the public." He cocks his head. "Or have you forgotten how we run things here?"

Breitling leans forward in his chair. "I assure you, Constable, I've forgotten nothing. And might I remind *you* that we didn't ask to come here. The Prime commissioned Miss Venture *per your request*. Correct me if I'm wrong, but *she* will be the one to remedy this problem *for* you–and for the Crown—will she not?"

McNally fumes at Breitling's insinuation, but he doesn't refute it. Satisfied, Breitling sits back in his chair and crosses one ankle over his knee in a rebellious display of casualness. This may be another day at the office for him, but my mind is blown. I'm a low-level Order grunt every other day of the week, but today I'm the Tower's salvation. Or it's destruction.

No pressure.

I clear my throat. "Excuse me, Constable?"

He tears his furious stare away from Breitling and fixes it on me. "Yes?"

"While the Prime didn't tell us much before our arrival, one thing he did explain is why you wanted *me* for this case. You think you may have another Deathwalker on your hands."

He whips his head back toward Breitling so fast the folds of his neck jiggle. "*That's* what you call it over there?"

"Yes," Breitling says. "Miss Venture herself christened it as such. She is the singular expert on this Operation. We take care to follow her lead."

And you should do the same.

He doesn't add that coda, but I hear it in his silence as loud as if he'd shouted it through a megaphone. My face warms with pride. It's the closest he's ever come to paying me a professional compliment in front of witnesses. I wait for the Rigour to chastise me, but it doesn't come. So, platonic admiration gets a pass. Noted and filed.

"Very well," McNally says with a grudging nod in my direction. "All the murders were caught on camera. The murders...but not the killer. When I included this information in our petition for assistance, the Prime mentioned you."

Not gonna lie–hearing that makes me happy. I've never had a supervisor recommend me for anything before.

Okay, so, I've never had a supervisor before, full-stop. Still, it's nice to be noticed.

Sometimes.

I lay my forearm on the desk and lean forward conspiratorially. "So, the cameras didn't see the killer. But they did see *something*, right?"

His brows jump. "Indeed, they did."

He turns to his computer, a (what else?) beige monstrosity from the technological dark ages of the mid-1980s. Clicking a few times with his mouse, he makes the Herculean effort of rotating the monitor in my direction. I'm not sure if it's the capture that's grainy or the ancient screen, but either way, the black and white footage is low on detail. From what I can tell, it's a high-angle view of a brick apartment building on a narrow street. As I watch, one of the first-floor doors opens and a figure emerges.

He takes a few steps toward the camera when he launches himself into the apartment wall and crumples to the ground, mouth twisting and eyes wide until, with a full body spasm, he goes horribly still.

"Bloody hell," Thomas whispers.

"It was the same for the others. Fine one moment, on the ground the next, and dead a few seconds later." Across the desk, McNally regards me again–or, perhaps, for the first time in earnest. The creases in his face have smoothed, and his eyes hold the first glimmer of hope I've seen since walking into this sad little room. Thomas follows his gaze. The spotlight is on me now, and it's already burning. I spent years being sought after by people (or rather, by faceless boxes courtesy of Shiva) who wanted a much bloodier version of my help. Having my skills solicited to *save* lives is still new for me. To have it come from a foreign organization, and one that works not only with law enforcement, but the *government*…

Breitling clears his throat, but I don't turn to him. I need to be able to answer questions without verifying every little thing with him first. "While I can't be positive this is the work of a Deathwalker, it is possible. Maybe even…likely."

McNally studies me for another moment before speaking in a dull monotone. "The Prime has advised us to provide you with anything you need to locate and neutralize this threat. Personnel, weapons–"

"Dirt."

He frowns at me, with Thomas close behind. "Excuse me?"

"I need dirt," I say. "A hole in the ground is best, but any human-sized vessel will work. As long as it's surrounded by lots and lots of dirt."

McNally gapes as if he's worried about my mental stability. Collecting himself, he withdraws a pad of paper from his middle desk drawer. "Right then. Dirt. Is that all?"

"I'll also need an item from someone who lives or works in the Whitechapel District. Walking from here wouldn't be impossible, but it will be faster if I can hitch a ride."

"I'm sure we can accommodate that. Anything else?"

"Yeah. A good night's sleep. I need to kick this jet lag."

Next to me, Breitling sits up a little straighter.

McNally narrows his eyes. "We are on something of a clock, Miss Venture. Time is—"

"I'm afraid I must insist," Breitling says. "Deathwalking can be taxing on Miss Venture's health under normal circumstances. With the added stress of Transatlantic travel, it's best not to tempt fate and risk even longer delays."

"Inquisitor." McNally looks like he may be about to perform his froggy trick again, but Breitling soldiers on before he gets the chance.

"If memory serves, Constable, there were twelve days between the third and fourth Ripper killings, were there not? Miss Venture could take up to a week's rest before anyone is in danger, and yet she's only asked for one night. It's more than reasonable, don't you agree?"

McNally tucks his chin so tight his neck turns into a rippling flesh puddle. "Very well. A night's rest, then back here first thing in the morning."

Breitling nods. "You have my word, Constable."

"And mine," Thomas says.

Both Breitling and I turn to him. "What do you mean, Uncle?"

Thomas smiles at him as if he's simple. "My boy, since we are all working on the same case, it's only logical that you'd stay with me. My townhouse is a few blocks from here, and I've got plenty of rooms for you to choose from. You won't find any hotel closer–or more affordable."

He winks at me. Breitling, on the other hand, looks deflated, with a pained longing in his eyes that makes my heart ache.

"No."

My stomach roils, spitting a geyser of acid at the back of my throat. I swallow it with a whimper. My discomfort must be obvious, because he stiffens, erasing all emotion from his face. By the time Thomas looks at him, Breitling is the picture of a haughty British gentleman.

"That is so generous of you, Uncle. We are most grateful."

I shake my head at him. Since when does he talk like Jane Austen is writing his dialog?

"Excellent." Thomas says. "In that case, let's be off. You could both use a good meal before your rest."

Breitling stands and buttons his jacket. "Constable."

"Inquisitor," McNally grunts in response. He doesn't stand as we file out.

"Before we continue, I'm afraid I must apologize," Thomas says as he presses the elevator call button. "You may not find my house to your liking."

Breitling looks alarmed. "What do you mean?"

"The kitchen, my boy," he says with a grin. "I keep a sparse pantry. However, you'll find that I have an exquisite selection of takeaway menus to choose from."

"I'm sure it's nowhere near as bad as my place." I cock my head in Breitling's direction. "He's always telling me I need to learn how to grocery shop, or at least hire someone to do it for me."

Thomas's smile wobbles. "I see."

My nerves jangle. Was that wrong? Should I not have said that? And if not, why didn't the Rigour warn me I was being inappropriate?

Before I can get any more in my head about this, the elevator arrives. Thomas holds the door for me, his smile firmly in place once again. It's a tight squeeze with three of us, and since I've taken the middle, I have no way of avoiding contact with Breitling. I try to concentrate as Thomas expounds on all the delicious dinner options within the delivery radius of his house, but the hitch of Breitling's chest against the back of my shoulder makes that impossible. His fingers graze mine. I brace myself for the smackdown.

It doesn't come.

My heart leaps. Before I can stop myself, I grab his hand and squeeze. He inhales and squeezes back as a deep throb of desire burns through me.

My head wavers and my vision shutters to nothing.

"Too far."

Goddammit. Gritting my teeth, I let him go. He utters a low growl as his hand falls back to his side. Frustration pours off him in thick, humid waves.

Can't say I don't feel the same.

"And how are you, Levi?" Thomas asks. From the note of worry in his voice, this doesn't sound like an idle question.

"I'm fine, Uncle," Breitling says, his eyes on the floor. "No lingering effects."

"Good. Still, I'd like to run a concussion protocol when we get back to the house, just to be safe."

"Concussion protocol?" I pipe in, hoping to disguise my concern under curiosity. "What for?"

"To make sure there's no lasting damage from the Constable's Operation," Thomas says. "Linguistic stupefaction only works while the subject is speaking, and the disorientation wears off within minutes. But there can be side effects later, especially when it's a skilled Operator performing it."

"It was *nothing*," Breitling insists with even more vehemence.

Thomas frowns, but he doesn't press. I, however, am not about to let him suffer at the hands of his own macho idiocy. The Rigour ties my gut in knots, but I don't stop shooting daggers at the side of Breitling's face until he looks at me. I arch a brow, and he lowers his head in defeat. "But...I suppose you're right, Uncle. It wouldn't hurt to verify."

Thomas nods, but his concerned frown has only deepened. I avert my gaze to the numbers above the door. Can this thing go *any* slower?

At last, we arrive at a cavernous underground parking lot. The moment I step out, a blast of air thick with the smell of damp dirt makes my soul nearly lurch out of my body.

"Shit," I gasp, bracing myself against the wall until I can literally pull myself together.

"Is everything alright, Miss Venture?" Thomas asks. Next to him, Breitling's gone rigid, as if holding himself back from leaping to my aid.

I twitch my head to the side, and his tension eases. "I'm fine. And I think we can tell the Constable that I've found the perfect place to start my Walk."

Ten

We roll our bags through the garage toward Thomas's car, which turns out to be a sleek black sedan that, though smaller, is a lot like Breitling's. I head for the back seat, but Thomas holds the passenger door open for me. "Miss Venture, if you please."

I cast a glance at Breitling, but he's already getting in on the other side. My heart pangs. Even if we don't…can't…touch, I want to be as close to him as I can—

"You're being rude."

My blood ices over. The thick accent and condescending tone remind me of Mary Poppins—if she'd had a second career as a prison guard. Breitling said the Rigour has never spoken to anyone, and now, here I am, getting full sentences. Guess that makes me special. Again. Hoo-fucking-ray.

Thomas's grin wavers. "Is everything alright?"

"Yes. Fine," I say as I get in the front seat. "Thank you."

We're not even on the road five minutes before we pull to a stop in front of a charming two-story brownstone.

"Wow, that *is* close." Suspicion slithers up my spine. "Wouldn't it have been faster to walk?"

He smiles sheepishly. "I hate getting wet. Even something as small as damp trouser cuffs can throw off my whole day."

Then it's a good thing you live in London, I refrain from saying. I also don't tell him I think he's full of it. Either way, his gracious offer of lodging now seems a lot less spur of the moment.

The rain has grown steadier since our arrival at the Tower. Cringing, Thomas grabs the umbrella at my feet and dashes out. I wait for a moment before I remember this is a regular car and I can open my own door. He races up the steps to the covered entrance as Breitling and I silently drag our luggage out of the trunk.

Inside, we're greeted by warm shades of oak and oxblood in the narrow front hall that extends to the back of the house. To our right, a staircase hugs the wall leading upstairs.

Thomas shakes off his umbrella and sets it in the stand next to the door, then claps his hands. "Well then, I suppose you'll both want to settle in a bit, yes?"

"God, yes," I blurt out before I can stop myself.

The Rigour delivers a sharp thwack across my knuckles, and even Breitling arches a brow at me. But Thomas chuckles. "Right this way."

He leads us up the stairs and around the banister. "This one's for you, Miss Venture." He points to a nearby door, then another one a few feet down the hall. "This is the bathroom, and Levi, yours is in the back next to mine.

They aren't big, but I think you'll find them quite comfortable."

"I'm sure we will," I say, feigning happiness despite the sinkhole forming in my chest. We're as far away from each other as it gets while still being in the same house.

Thomas opens the door to my room. "If you'd like to freshen up, I'll get Levi squared away, then order some dinner. Does curry strike your fancy?"

"Sounds great," I say as I hurry into the room and close the door. After taking a moment to savor the silence, I flick the light switch. Buttery light spills from the lamp on the nightstand. The room is as modest as Thomas said it would be, with a squat wooden dresser, rocking chair, and a double bed with a thick knit blanket I want to bury myself in.

I raise my shoulders, and my neck loosens, releasing a tension I hadn't realized had been there. The past day spent locked in small spaces full of people is the longest I've gone without being alone in years. I guess I hadn't realized how much that had been bothering me until now. But here, in this dim, cozy alcove, with rain pattering against the window, I feel like I can breathe for the first time since leaving Las Vegas.

None of us feel up to using the formal dining room, so we eat dinner at the square table in the kitchen, serving ourselves from the paper and plastic takeout containers arranged in the middle like a waxed cardboard centerpiece. It's a silent affair. I'm exhausted to the point of dizziness, and I assume Breitling is too. Not sure what's on Thomas's mind, though at one point I catch him studying his nephew. I duck my head, wipe up a splotch of tikka masala with a piece of garlic naan, and pretend not to notice. As much as I love curry with a side of gossip, all I want right now is to get this food into my stomach and go the hell to sleep.

"So…how are things at the Summit?" Thomas asks, breaking the silence.

Breitling pushes rice around with his fork, his eyes fixed on the table. "The Chaos Intervention Initiative has had a successful test run of an early detection surveillance system. Other than that, status quo."

I frown at the bright orange streaks left on my plate. Just yesterday he was saying what an amazing breakthrough it was and how proud he is of me. Was that empty flattery, or does he simply not feel like talking about it right now? I consider calling him out, but I'm not in the mood for sparring. Besides, what would the Rigour say?

Ugh, did I *really* just think that?

"I trust everything is well with you?" Breitling follows up, his tone polite but blasé.

"Very well indeed." Thomas says. "Though I must admit, I don't think I'm suited for retirement. Not when there's so much need in the world. Last week I consulted on an endocrine ecto-bypass for an eight-year-old with advanced pancreatic cancer."

"Sorry—an endocrine what?" I ask.

"It's…hm." He presses his hands together at his mouth for a moment before answering. "It's an Operation that removes an offending organ without replacing it, and yet the body functions as if it *has* been replaced. That's the simplest explanation for it, mind you. There are a million microscopic connections to make, and it doesn't always work—though it did in this case. The child should be able to go home this time next week, in fact."

"Wow." I knew Thomas was a Biologian pediatrician, but I had no idea he was a real-life hero. "That's amazing. Congratulations."

He beams at me before returning to Breitling. "Speaking of children, I took the liberty of ringing your parents to let them know you were coming to London on business."

The fork stops moving. "And?"

"They're in Brighton at the summer cottage, but they told me to give you their love."

Breitling nods, all but disguising the sudden tightening in his shoulders. "Of course. Please give them my regards as well."

"I will. They considered returning early, but they're paid up through the end of next month. Remind me–how long has it been since you've seen them?"

Breitling remains silent for a moment before answering. "Twenty-two years."

"What?" I gape at him. "That's crazy. Why so long?"

He glares at me but says nothing.

"If I may, Nephew." Thomas dabs at the corner of his lips with his napkin before smoothing it over his lap. "My brother and his wife, while supportive of Levi's career, have never made peace with some of its…special demands."

I'm about to ask what that means when I catch Breitling's pained expression aimed at his plate. A bit of quick math tells me the rest. "You haven't spoken to them since you took the Pledge."

"Just so," Thomas answers for him. "Order above all, Miss Venture. No exceptions, not even for those who bore thee."

I fall back in my chair. Maybe I should have put that together earlier, but I didn't, and it has left me more than a little stunned. "I had no idea—"

"Thank you for dinner, Uncle." Breitling stands, balling his napkin and tossing it on the table. "I hope you'll forgive me, but it has been a long day, and tomorrow will be longer still. I think it best if I retire now."

"Of course." Thomas eyes Breitling's untouched dinner. "Sleep well, Nephew."

I'm about to make my own excuses, but Breitling catches my eye and twitches his head to the side. The corners of my mouth dip down, but I remain seated as he pushes in his chair. "Goodnight, Uncle. Miss Venture."

"Goodnight." I reach for the takeout containers. If I'm going to be here for a while longer, I might as well eat up.

After a few moments of awkward silence, Thomas takes his leave too. He's not even out of the room before my knuckles start to burn.

"What?" I growl into my shoulder in case Thomas is still within earshot.

"You're a guest. Make yourself useful."

It sounds like an eighteenth-century butler chastising a scullery maid. I glower at the dirty plates and half-empty takeout containers. "You can't be serious."

The bone-deep throb in my hands answers that question. With a groan, I clear the table, putting the dirty dishes in the sink and storing the containers in the fridge, all the while listening to the creak of footsteps and the groan of pipes above me. By the time I'm wiping down the table with a damp cloth, the noises have faded along with the pain of the Rigour. Only then do I venture up the stairs. I grab my toiletry kit out of my bag and duck into the bathroom. As I brush my teeth, I examine the deep clawfoot bathtub that looks vintage except for the rainfall showerhead. The idea of a full scrub down is seductive, but the bed is even more so. I locate an empty drawer in the vanity, dump my stuff inside, and head back to my room.

I don't make it.

"Adina."

The gravelly whisper sends shivers down my back, and my fingers freeze on the doorknob. With a shaky sigh, I turn around as Breitling slips out of the shadows. He's put on his gray silk pajama pants, but his shirt is missing.

"Oh…" I slump back against the door. "That is so unfair."

The streetlight filtering in from the nearby window illuminates his mischievous grin. "Think of it as payback for that stunt on the plane."

"That was different," I mutter as he comes to stand in front of me. The throbbing ache has already started in my fingers, pulsing in time with the heat of longing between my legs. "On the plane, we could…and now I can't…"

He presses his hands into the wall over my shoulders and leans forward, his nose brushing against my forehead as he breathes me in. "Can't you?"

"No."

I close my eyes. Even as the pain grows, the proximity of his bare skin makes me tremble with desire. He's *right here*, right in front of me, and it has been so long…

"Oh, fuck it." I grab him by the back of the head and pull his mouth onto mine.

He grunts in surprise before grabbing me by the waist and pressing me back against the door. I spread my legs to make room for him, standing on my tiptoes until I have him right where I want him.

"Oh, yes." His chest heaves as he grinds against me until I feel like I'm going to faint or explode or maybe both.

"No!"

The pain disappears from my hand, only to spring to life behind my eyes, the stabbing intensity making me squeal. He moans back, deepening the kiss as he moves faster, harder, relentless in his mission to bring me to my knees.

The stabbing in my head turns into spinning, and my stomach lurches. If we keep this up for much longer, I'll be sick. I try to break our kiss, try to shift at all. But I can't. He's got me pinned down…God, he's *so strong*…and I can't move without rubbing against him, making him groan with pleasure and making me wonder why the hell I'm trying to get away. I press my hands to his chest, but not that hard, and his arms tighten around me. He still won't let me go, and despite the queasiness, I don't want him to.

"STOP!"

A foul taste hits the back of my throat as bile threatens to flood my mouth–and then his.

With a cry of panic, I shove him away. He stumbles across the hall, grunting as his lower back slams into the balcony railing.

"Dammit!" I shout before I remember we're not alone in the house. "I'm sorry."

"No, *I'm* sorry," he pants, gripping his back with one hand and the railing with the other. "I pushed too far. I should have known better."

"No, you shouldn't." My voice wavers. "I want this. I want *you*. And I don't *understand* why…"

Another wave of vertigo threatens the stability of my dinner. Slouching back against the door, I hold my hands to my burning cheeks until the feeling fades–and so he won't see how close to tears I am. "Why doesn't the Rigour affect you the way it's affecting me?"

He shakes his head. "Perhaps because I'm from here. A subconscious part of my mind must know how to compensate. God, I wish I'd remembered this before we left. If I had…"

"What? You never would have brought me here?" The nausea has faded enough that I can manage a laugh, albeit a humorless one. "Castillo ordered you. Would you really have refused him just because you wouldn't be able to sleep with me?"

He scowls at my feet. He doesn't need to answer that. Frankly, I'd rather he didn't.

"There is another possibility," he says after a moment. "Your connection to Chaos is…singular. Perhaps that is why the Rigour is paying special attention to you."

I narrow my eyes. "So, I'm…what? A Chaos terrorist at the top of the Rigour's watch list?"

"That's a crude way of putting it, but yes. More or less."

"Great." A weight settles in my chest as I follow his thinking to its inevitable end. "And if that *is* the case, I won't feel normal again until…"

"Until we return home." His misery fills the space between us. He'd been looking forward to this. So had I. And to have to deal with yet another roadblock between us is frustrating, to say the least. But seeing him like this…it's worse than frustration or disappointment. And to know that I'm the one causing it, that it's my fault…

No. I can't do that to him. I won't.

"You know," I whisper, my voice trembling with what I'm about to say. "If you want to…to be with me anyway…I wouldn't stop you."

My stomach burns in protest. But the feeling fades just as fast. Breitling's head snaps up and his eyes flash at me. Not with desire or relief, but horror. "No. God, no. Adina, you *know* that pleasing you is what I enjoy most. The idea of you merely enduring it, or that I was hurting you…" He shakes his head as if trying to rid himself of the idea. "I could never. I *would* never."

"But–"

"No, darling." He approaches me, taking my face in his hands. "I will wait. Until you adjust, or until we return to America. Or longer. As long as it takes for you to give yourself to me again."

He runs his thumb over my bottom lip. His words have shifted something inside me, like a stack of bricks falling over. My knuckles tingle as if a cat were nuzzling me with its head. It's so real I look down to make sure no feline has found its way into the hall. Even more significant is that the strokes of his thumb aren't igniting any discomfort. "Levi?"

His hands tremble. "Yes?"

"Kiss me."

His forehead knots, but he does as I ask. The tentative touch of his mouth makes me shiver as we wait for the Rigour's answer.

There isn't one. With a sigh, I allow my hands to rest lightly on his bare chest. "More?"

"God, yes," he moans. "Whatever you want."

His tongue caresses mine so tenderly my knees go weak. Encouraged, he wraps his arms around me, fisting the back of my tee shirt with both hands and pulling me into him once again.

"Enough."

I whip my head to the side, breaking the kiss before the pain can return. "Enough," I pant. "I'm sorry, but…I'm so sorry…"

"It's alright." Despite the strain in his voice, he cracks a small smile. "Remind me–who was it that said, 'if I can't have what I want, then I'll take what I can get'?"

I force a laugh. "I don't think those were my *exact* words."

"Close enough."

Smiling, I press my forehead to his. "I should get some sleep," I say, every part of me shaking at the idea of having to let him go.

His jaw clenches. "Yes. I suppose we both should."

He steps back, giving me room to open my door before taking my hand and squeezing it. "Goodnight, my darling."

I squeeze back, and he raises my hand to his lips. Another thrill runs through me, but it's tainted by the unrest growing in my belly.

"This far. No further."

My smile wavers.

Got it.

"Goodnight," I say, extracting my hand. "I'll see you in the morning."

He nods, his smile only highlighting the longing in his eyes. As much as it breaks my heart to do it, I close the door on him with a resolute click. I want nothing more than to go back out there and throw myself into his arms, let him take me to his room and have me in any way he wants. As those ideas make my body hum with arousal, the nauseating vertigo sweeps them away.

"No."

I slap my hand against the door. "Why the hell not?"

It doesn't answer.

Of course, it doesn't.

I grunt and throw myself onto the bed. "I never thought I'd say this, but I miss Chaos. Its answers may suck, but at least it fucking talks to me."

Still nothing. Apparently, jabs at its ego are one more thing the Rigour doesn't respond to.

I bury my face in my pillow and debate whether it's worth it to change into pajamas when a soft scratching noise makes me shoot upright. Was that my imagination, or is there something at the window?

Another noise confirms my suspicion. My thoughts turn first to Breitling, but I dismiss them. He said he'd give me time, and I believe him. Besides, unless there's a balcony out there, how would he even manage it?

The scratching starts again, and this time it doesn't stop. With a groan, I wheel my legs off the bed. If I wanted to deal with obnoxious noises at the window, I would have brought Shiva.

Oh.

Oh, *no.*

"There's no way," I mutter, stalking toward the window. "There's no freaking *way.*"

I throw open the curtains. Beady black eyes stare back at me.

"You've got to be *kidding* me!" I shout at the rain-splattered glass.

Shiva lets out a brief squawk before resuming her assault.

"Okay! Fine." I pull up the sash. She hops over the sill and onto the floor like she's done hundreds of times at home. Except we're not at home. We're thousands of miles away, on a continent across the ocean, and she's a crow who, as far as I know, does not have a pilot's license.

"How in the hell?" I ask.

She spreads her wings and gives them a sharp flap. Cold droplets of rain smack my bare shins and make me yelp. As I brush off the offending liquid, she hops up onto the bed and settles on the peak of my headboard, staring at me with deep satisfaction.

I roll my eyes. "Well, 'nevermore' to you, too. Show off."

Eleven

Even with the downy pillows and firm mattress, I spend the first half of the night thrashing. My mind spins with scenarios of Breitling and I that are…quite distracting. When I do manage to fall asleep, it's worse. More than once I wake up panting, drenched in sweat, with my stomach twisted into a rotten mess. It gets so bad that at one point, Shiva alights from her perch and stomps across my head to make her irritation known. I even try watching the Ripper documentary again, hoping that the dark procedural will work its usual magic. Instead, the story pulls me in, and by the time it's over, not only am I not asleep, I've created a damn spreadsheet on the inside cover of *The Girl on the Train*:

Name/Age	Location/TOD	Name/Age	Location/TOD
Martha Tabran, 39	George Yard, ~2am	Tiago Silva, 41	Gunthorpe Street, ~8am
Mary Ann Nichols, 43	Bucks Row, ~3am	Fatima Hassan, 43	Durward Street, ~7pm
Annie Chapman, 47	Hanbury Street, ~5:30am	Annie Turner, 25	Hanbury Street, ~5:30am
Elizabeth Stride, 44	Berner Street, ~midnight		
Catherine Eddowes, 46	Mitre Square, ~1am		
Mary Kelly, mid-20s	Miller Court, between 1am-8am		

My throbbing eyes zero in on the six blank cells. If the killer continues as they have been, the location values are a forgone conclusion.

I hope I never have to fill in the rest.

At around three in the morning, I abandon the pursuit of sleep altogether and wander down to the kitchen. My exhausted brain stumbles over itself as I study the counter. Where the hell is the coffeemaker?

I'm still pondering the question when Thomas appears behind me.

"Miss Venture," he says in a subdued voice. "Forgive me for intruding. I didn't expect anyone else to be up at this hour."

I shrug off his apology. After all, it's his house. What concerns me more than his presence is his appearance. He's dressed, groomed, and ready to take on the day. He may have even showered.

"I'm afraid I've always been a bit of a night owl," he explains, as if reading my mind. "I worked the graveyard shift when I was a resident, and the sleep schedule never quite let me go." His brows tighten as he evaluates me. "Is something the matter?"

"I…uh…coffee?" I splutter.

He looks embarrassed. "I don't have any, I'm afraid. Would tea do?"

"As long as it's caffeinated." I sit at the kitchen table as he fusses with the electric kettle. "I couldn't sleep."

"Too excited?"

I rub my eyes. "Something like that."

With the kettle going, Thomas sits down across from me. He clasps his hands and stares at them. My head pounds.

Oh God, what now?

"Miss Venture. May I call you Adina?"

I nod, praying that the water will hurry up and boil.

"Adina, I must confess something. I overheard you and Levi…talking last night."

I maintain a blank stare while my heart and mind take off running. For how important discretion is, Breitling and I have never discussed what we'd do if someone found us out. At the very least, I assumed we'd face the inquisition (no pun intended) together. Worst case, the Prime would have it out with Breitling since he's Pledged and I'm not. I never thought I'd have to handle something like this *alone*. But here I am. So, what's the move? Vehement denial and outrage? Do I throw myself on the mercy of the court and beg him not to say anything? Or–

"Before you panic," Thomas continues (far too late), "I don't intend to expose your secret. My nephew has worked hard to get where he is. He's made sacrifices you can't imagine, and his influence will only continue to grow. He's on track to become a legend. *I* would never jeopardize that."

The stress he places on the word "I" makes my teeth clench. He doesn't even know me, and he's accusing me of sabotage? I want to defend myself, but that's only going to make me seem guilty. Emotion won't help here. I need to play it cool. Folding my arms in front of me on the table, I lean forward and meet his gaze.

"I appreciate your concern," I say in my best business voice. "But I assure you, you have nothing to worry about. I am aware of his position. And my own. We are two consenting adults acting in full compliance with the Order's policy regarding—"

"I beg your pardon, my dear, but I'm afraid you're mistaken," he says, his tone frosty. "What I saw occur in my upstairs hallway last night was not a mere lustful indulgence. I wish it were. Then I could have returned to my room without worry. But the Rigour would not have stopped you if there weren't more to it."

I clamp my mouth shut, hoping to disguise my shock. Judging by his smug smile, I've failed. "Oh yes, I'm quite familiar with the Rigour. It plays an integral part in my Operations."

"I thought you were a Biologian?"

"Indeed. A Biologian who can sense anomalies, no matter how slight, in any organic body. But in order to sense anomalies, one must have something to compare it to. That's where the Rigour's influence enters the picture. Anything that doesn't match its conceit of what is proper and expected is an anomaly, and it must be removed."

He studies me, searching for a crack in my icy shell. When he doesn't find it, he places his hands flat on the table and stands. He's not as tall or as muscular as Breitling, but he's big enough to make me feel small as he looms over me.

"Let me be forthright, because I don't want there to be any confusion. I know what happened wasn't in line with the Rigour's conceit, which means it wasn't in line with Order policy. If there are no further incidents, you can trust me to hold my tongue. However, should you fail to heed this warning, you will leave me no choice but to report your transgressions. Have I made myself clear?"

"Sure have," I bite out. "And will you be giving *your nephew* the same warning?"

He sniffs. "Levi is Chief Inquisitor. He knows his place and his priorities. The only thing he may need to be warned about is how to spot an...inappropriate attachment."

He regards my outfit with contempt. I'm not sure how sweatpants and a coffee-stained t-shirt help his argument. To be honest, I'm not sure what his argument even *is*. Does he think the feelings only flow in one direction? That Breitling can take or leave me, but I'm so over-the-moon infatuated I'll distract him from his "one true purpose," and the Rigour's working overtime to keep me in line? That's ridiculous.

At least, I think it is.

The kettle screams. Thomas lets the shrill cry hang in the air for a moment before stepping away to address it. I take the opportunity to slink into the dark hallway and race up the stairs to get dressed. I'd rather walk the streets of London at three in the morning searching for sustenance than accept anything he has to offer.

Twelve

I arrive at the Tower around six-thirty. No surprise, my ID does not open the door when I scan it, and there's no guard in sight to ask for help. Maybe there's a buzzer or something, but I don't check. I don't feel like facing their scrutiny right now anyway. Instead, I backtrack to the northwest side of the complex, trudging down the bike trail until I find a quiet spot along the guardrail overlooking a grassy expanse that, according to the nearby map display, used to be a moat. Posting up under a tree in case the ominous clouds above me decide to unleash hell, I rip into my butter croissant with the fury of a tiger attacking a juicy cut of meat. Thanks to corporate globalization, I had no trouble locating a Starbucks. A bit ugly American of me, I admit, but give me a break—if ever I needed a taste of home, it's now.

As I crush the butter-stained wax paper into a ball and toss it in a nearby trash bin, my phone buzzes.

RUTH
hows it goin?

I laugh so loud I startle a dog walker, who gives me a wide berth as he passes behind me. Such a simple question, and yet it's riddled with trip hazards. I respond with the most diplomatic reply I can think of.

ME

Ups and downs. How are things at home?

The dots pop up, but it's a full minute before she sends her reply.

RUTH

mom n russ broke up

Ugh, thank God. At least one awkward situation has corrected itself.

ME

Not gonna pretend I'm not thrilled. How is she handling it?

More dots, and another long wait.

RUTH

fine
u got anything for me yet?

Hmm. That's an abrupt subject switch. Either there's more to that story that she doesn't want to talk about, or it's nothing at all, and she's cutting off a boring conversation to jumpstart a more interesting one. Even odds as to which, and I can't undertake a prolonged fact-finding mission at the moment. Whatever is going on with Mama, I'll drag it out of her later.

ME

*Any of your Vigilant friends live in Portugal, Egypt, or Iowa? I
need info on the three victims in this case.*

RUTH

yah i think so!
names plz

I grin as I type the info. Ruth almost never uses
punctuation in her texts. An exclamation point means
she's bouncing off the walls with excitement.

ME

*Tiago Silva, 41, Lisbon. Fatima Hassan, 43, Cairo. Annie
Turner, 25, Iowa City.*

RUTH

cool ill let you know what i find out

ME

Thanks.

I'm glad she didn't ask me why the Order wasn't running
this background. She would have been well within her
rights to do so. It *is* a little strange for me to conduct
another parallel investigation outside the Order *and* the
NO police. But I trust Ruth more than both of them
combined. Besides, a little off-the-books snooping never
hurt anyone, right?

The leaves rustle above my head. I look up as Shiva
struggles to get her balance on a twig that's nowhere near
capable of holding her weight for long. She zeroes in on
me and utters a sharp caw.

They're waiting for you.

"10-4, General." I salute her. The dog walker, now on his way back, fixes me with a wary stare. I smile at him, bugging my eyes a little to see if he'll start running. Sure enough, his pace increases as if he meant to jog anyway. I let out a short but loud guffaw, and he bursts into a full-on sprint that makes me collapse into giggles.

Christ, I'm exhausted.

Wiping away tears, I type one last message to Ruth.

ME
Gotta run. Talk soon?

RUTH
sure thing

And then, after a moment:

b careful sis <3

I smile at the text as the gloomy sky spits out the first drops of rain. Maybe I should have brought her along after all.

Thomas and Breitling stand under a pair of black umbrellas as I approach. Thomas glares at me, annoyed at having to wait. I scowl back at him. It's his own fault, after all. We could have come together if he hadn't treated me like a criminal.

"Good morning," Breitling says, handing me a third umbrella. His tone is complacent, but his narrow eyes reveal his concern.

"Morning," I say with a casual shake of my head. There's nothing he can do about what happened with Thomas, and even if there was, this is not the time.

The guard lets us in without argument. "Constable left a message for you," he says as he hands a cream-colored envelope to Breitling. On the back is a gold wax seal, which he breaks and removes a single piece of paper.

"Seems he got my message," Breitling mutters after scanning the note. "We are to meet him in the parking garage below the Hospital Block."

We cut through a narrow passage into the courtyard. As we pass the White Tower, a chorus of panicked caws pulls my attention to the roof. Four of the resident Ravens bat their wings, their grim oversight disrupted as a fifth bird, black but much smaller, lands in the middle and sends them all scattering.

"Making friends already?" I ask.

Shiva looks at me, cocking her head until it's almost upside down as if she has no idea what I'm talking about.

"Lovely weather we're having," Breitling says as he falls into step next to me. He has lowered his umbrella and drops of rain cling to the golden hair of his sideburns.

I take a quick look around. Thomas has sprinted several yards ahead of us, his umbrella still up and his free hand lifting one trouser leg high enough to reveal the pasty skin above his sock. He's well out of hearing distance and too concerned with the rain to care about much else. Slowing to a stop, I beckon Breitling to do the same. "You want to know something?"

His mouth twitches. "Always."

"Every time it rains back home, I drop whatever I'm doing and go stand outside, like this." I tilt my head up, allowing the warm drops to anoint my eyelids, my lips, and the inside curve of my ears. It feels as strange as it does wonderful. "Rain is so rare in the desert, it's a waste not to enjoy it when it comes along."

"I couldn't agree more."

Breitling's smile looks dreamy and forlorn, and his fist tightens and loosens at his side, as if he's struggling to hold on to something. Or to hold himself back.

Heat rushes through me. With the misty rain and the soft caw of Ravens filling the gothic courtyard, this would be the perfect place for a Hollywood-style kiss, at least in my weird little world. But this isn't Hollywood, or New York, or even Las Vegas, and we are being observed by an audience interested in neither enchantment nor romance. The slightest aberrant move could spell tragedy for both of us. And then, of course, there's—

"Walk." The word comes with a sharp pain in my stomach.

Right on time, the bitch.

"Anyway." I drop my head apologetically. "We should probably go."

His smile fades. "Right. Of course."

He walks ahead of me, raising the umbrella as he goes.

In the garage, we find Constable McNally accompanied by a man of average height and build, with sharp features and close-cropped dark hair. Like the Constable, he's also wearing an off-the-rack suit, and his dark eyes study us suspiciously.

"I see you got my note," McNally says before turning his back on us and stalking toward the rear corner. The nameless man follows, positioning himself behind the Constable.

"Reaper," Breitling murmurs. "Bodyguard."

That guy? I want to ask. I mean, he's no shrimp, but he's no muscle-bound meathead either. Besides, who does McNally think he needs protecting from?

When he reaches the end of the wall, McNally stops and gestures into a narrow, unlit alcove that's all but obscured by a white security van. Large pieces of the concrete floor sit in a pile near the back of the alcove. In their place is a six-foot-long pit of dark, wet dirt. An unhinged door leans up against one cinder block wall, as if ready to slam shut over the pit.

My skin tingles with both anticipation and fear. It's been a while since I've Walked from somewhere other than my shed at home, and I've never Walked on foreign soil. What if it's not the same? Or worse, what if I can't do it at all? I'd never considered that possibility, but given how different everything is here, who knows anymore?

"I apologize for the lack of privacy." Breitling's deep voice settles over my shoulders like a down quilt. "This was the only place they could block off, even halfway. I instructed them to bring enough dirt to provide the proper tactile and olfactory stimulation, as well as for added comfort. With the door closed above you, it will be darker as well. Is it…alright?"

I'm shocked to see lines of worry crease the corners of his eyes. Warmth fills my body and emanates from my smile as I nod. "It's perfect. Thank you."

"You're welcome." He tries to smile back, but he can't quite manage it around his clenched jaw. A pang of nausea hits my stomach, but I ignore it. I won't deny him my approval when it clearly means so much to him–which, in turn, means a lot to me.

Behind us, McNally clears his throat. "Will it do, Miss Venture?"

He phrases the question like a challenge. My delight fades. "Yes, sir."

"Good." He turns to Breitling. "Now that Miss Venture is settled, you can perform your facility inspection as Prime Castillo's proxy."

"I'm staying," Breitling says in a gravelly tone that preempts the digging in of his heels. "The inspection can wait."

Thomas tucks his chin into the upturned collar of his coat and fixes me with an accusatory glare. How is this *my* fault? *Breitling* volunteered to stay. We both heard it. Besides, as my *professional* escort, he has every right to be present while I execute my duties. Not only that, but there's no pain in my fingers, and my stomach remains calm. If this doesn't bother the Rigour, then it shouldn't bother him. Yet he continues to stare at me as if we're at the scene of a raging fire and I'm refusing to call 911. I guess anything that interferes with protocol—*his* idea of it, anyway—will be seen as a manipulation on my part. Or, as he put it, an anomaly to be removed. Better I remove it first, before he has the chance to do so in a messier, more permanent way.

"It's okay, Chief," I say, walking toward McNally and away from Breitling. "You have your duties, and I have mine. We'll reconnoiter at the day's end."

"Are you sure?" Breitling asks. He sounds concerned. More than that, he sounds hurt.

"Yes," I toss over my shoulder. I can't look at him, or I'll change my mind.

"Don't worry, Inquisitor," McNally says. "This is why I asked your uncle to join the investigation. We are all aware of what an asset Miss Venture is to the Order, and the Prime, and, it seems, to you."

Thomas smirks, but I'm the only one who notices. He rearranges his face into a bland mask before stepping into the conversation. "I will take care of everything, Levi. You have my word."

"See?" I force a reassuring smile and face Breitling. "I'll be fine."

"I'll show you to the conference room, Inquisitor. But first." McNally slips his hand into his pocket and extracts a stained blue handkerchief, which he hands to me. "The item you requested, courtesy of one Mr. Gordon Gaye, former Reaper and longtime resident of Whitechapel."

"Former?" The word leaps out of my mouth before I can stop it. I'd thought there was only one way out of the Order's service, at least after a certain level. This is the first I'd heard of anyone making it out *alive.*

"Not by choice," McNally grumbles. "He was one of the best Reapers I've ever seen. Could have been an Inquisitor, under different circumstances. We'd go back and forth for days, sending messages to and fro as we hashed out theories on one matter or another. Gutted me to put him out to pasture, but it was unavoidable. He had a nervous breakdown after his wife died, then crawled into a bottle and never came out. Poor sod was a liability."

He whirls on Breitling. "This is why we should require the Pledge for *all* employees. We'd lose a lot fewer good men that way."

"Mm-hmph." Breitling grunts. I can't imagine that he means it in agreement…but it kinda sounded like it.

"Regardless," McNally says, "you'll find Gordon at The Tied House, downing whiskey and holding court until they send him on his way."

"Great." I wind the handkerchief around my left palm and secure the ends in a loose knot.

"Well, then." His lips purse, and after a moment, he extends his hand to me. "Godspeed, Miss Venture."

"Thank you, Constable," I manage despite my surprise.

He nods, then motions for Breitling to accompany him. The Reaper gives me a suspicious once-over before following at their heels. As they get on the elevator, Breitling angles his head toward me and flashes a little half-smile. My chest loosens.

We're okay.

The moment they're gone, I round on Thomas. "I swear, if you lay so much as a finger on me while I'm out, I will rip it off and feed it to the Ravens."

He tilts his head forward and raises his eyebrows. "I have no interest in laying *anything* on you, if you understand my meaning."

"Oh...*oh*." My aggression dissipates and embarrassment takes over. The tidy appearance, the "confirmed bachelorhood"...man, how did I not put that together on my own? "Does Levi know?"

He shrugs. "I've never told him, but I'm sure he's worked it out. The Constable, however, is another story. I don't know him well enough to know how he'd react, and I'd rather not find out."

I frown. "If it's such sensitive information, why are you telling *me*? Because you like me so much?"

"Because I don't want us to be enemies." He sighs. "I know you won't believe this, Adina, but I said what I said this morning because I care about my nephew a great deal. He is the closest thing I will ever have to a son, and I don't want to see him ruined."

I lift my chin. "Neither do I."

"I believe you." His smile, laced with genuine sympathy, eases my nerves. As angry as I am at him, I don't want us to be enemies either. He's Breitling's family, and I'm…whatever I am. Nothing good will come from being at odds with each other. Besides, there are more pressing matters to attend to.

"Okay." I roll my shoulders and face the alcove. "I guess I should get started."

Thomas bobs his head as a veil of professional detachment falls across his face. "Is there anything you need from me?"

Good question. I step forward to study the pit more closely. It is plenty long, and deep enough that every part of me should fit below ground level. "This looks good, but I need a little privacy. To prepare."

"Of course," he says, rounding to the other side of the van. "Call me when you're ready."

I slip into the alcove, and the shadows swallow me up. My vision wavers as the musty earth smell closes around me. I need to make this quick, or I'm liable to Walk off while I'm still standing and fall on my face. I strip off my clothes until I'm down to my bra, underwear, and socks. My teeth begin chattering immediately. Christ, it's *cold* in here. I swear, I've never longed for the desert more than I do now, standing half-naked in an underground London parking garage, about to lie down in a makeshift grave.

I lower myself to sit. The soft soil hugs my thighs and backside, comforting and even warming me a little. Someone must have added this, because I feel the compressed native dirt not far below it. Gripping the doorknob, I roll back one vertebra at a time, letting myself grow accustomed to the unfamiliar land beneath me. At last, I rest my head on the ground and pull the door closed.

"Okay," I call. "All clear. You can–"

That's as far as I get before the scent of loam and rain spirits me away.

Thirteen

Turns out, Constable McNally found me a perfect artifact. I drop on the sidewalk outside The Tied House at the elbow of a gentleman that I'd thought would be elderly but is closer to my mom's age. His sandy hair has streaks of gray, and his skin is still free of wrinkles except around his eyes, which are sunken and folded as if he hasn't had a good night's sleep in months. His nose and cheeks are stained red, and he misses the door handle a few times before he catches a hold of it.

I peer over his shoulder into the pub's dim interior. The bartender, who can't be over twenty-five, looks disappointed to see him walk in. "Morning, Gord."

"Jimmy," my squire slurs, making no effort to hide his drunkenness as he clambers onto a stool. I stay outside, watching through the glass panel as a reluctant Jimmy pours his drink. Whiskey, neat. At least three fingers of it, and at half-past nine in the morning, according to the Guinness-branded digital clock above the bar. The only reason to get that wrecked this early is when you wish you'd never woken up in the first place.

"Hmm…" I roll my fingertips over my palm, evaluating the phantom silk of the handkerchief wrapped around my hand. How eager is he to be put out of his misery? I could do it. Right now, without missing a step.

But...not really. Of course not. No way I'm going to freelance on the Order's dime, not to mention that having his artifact in my possession might as well be a neon arrow with the words "Here's Your Killer" pointing directly at my face. But I've spent years holding artifacts–and the lives that go with them–in the palm of my hand. Years, using those artifacts to observe and...respond. The two things are linked, like a Pavlovian response. It's not a connection I can turn off overnight.

I leave the unfortunate Gordon Gaye behind and head for the street. For the most part, the Whitechapel Deathplane appears as expected. The buildings are all there, appearing as they do in the living realm. Cars cruise down the street and people crowd the sidewalks, their metal and nylon retractable umbrellas bumping against each other as they hurry toward their various destinations.

But there's more. A lot more. Intertwined with the modern aspects is a shimmering layer of something else. Over and around the cars traversing the pavement, horse-drawn carriages rumble along pitted dirt streets. Women in long skirts and tight bodices amble down the sidewalk or lounge in doorways. Grubby youths with bare feet play in the dirt near the storefronts, prompting the occasional apron-clad proprietor to lean out and shoo them away.

And still, that's not everything. Another layer of grayish wisps, too faded and formless to decipher, fills every inch of space with a semi-translucent miasma. Everything is too close, too crowded, too...rigid.

"Rigour." My shock forces the word from my lips. I don't believe it at first, but the more I think about it, the more sense it makes. These are manifestations of the past, and what are traditions if not expectations founded in history? I am Walking through the Rigour's blueprint.

No wonder it's so goddamned confusing.

"Okay," I say as I reorient myself in this new reality. This is fine. The Deathplane may be different here, but it shouldn't affect my ability to do my job.

I wish I could say the same about my outfit.

"Oh my God, seriously?" I cry as I look down at myself. I don't know if my ethereal stylist can hear me, but I have to try, because this shit is unacceptable. The corset is fastened as tight as it will go, which does wonders for my breasts; as small as they are, they're still about to spill out of my top. The trade-off, however, is that I can't inflate my lungs more than halfway. Good thing I don't *need* to breathe on a Deathwalk, or I'd have fainted by now. The faded mint green dress boasts a full skirt and petticoats, and high-heeled ankle boots pinch my feet. Taken on their own, any one of these features would make movement difficult. Put them together, and it's a full-blown conspiracy.

"Not gonna happen," I grumble as I reach down to unlace my boots. They come off with little hassle. The corset, not so much. Even though the strings are in the front, they appear to have been knotted by a naval officer with a serious hatred for women. It takes a good five minutes of digging with my nails to get them to budge. I shimmy out of the petticoats, then attack my skirt. No surprise, the fabric is cheap, and soon enough I've got a knee-length dress that shows off my stockinged feet. It's hideous, but I can move. Besides, there's no one around to see me.

Or is there? As I ball up the excess fabric and toss it at the base of a nearby garbage can, I spot a figure leaning against a lamppost across the street, his head angled toward me.

Now, people look in my direction when I'm Deathwalking all the time, and while it always freaks me out, it doesn't mean they *see* me. The only exceptions I've come across are Breitling and Neil Green, the Futurist/convicted Chaos invoker. Breitling can do it because he's Deathwalked with me before. Accidentally, of course. But that doesn't change the fact that he has a lingering sensitivity. I'm still not sure how Neil managed it, though I suspect our shared connection to Chaos may play a role.

This time, however, it's more than the attention that bothers me. It's his clothes. He's also dressed like someone out of the Victorian era—or rather, like one very particular someone. His long black outerwear is more like a cloak than a coat, and a black top hat sits upon his dark hair. While I'd like nothing more than to write him off as one of the ghostly echoes floating around me, I can tell that he's as solid as I am. As I study him, his thick brows draw together.

Fuck. He knows I've seen him.

I soften my gaze, as if I had been in the process of searching for someone. Maybe he'll think I'd found the lamppost captivating instead.

With a dramatic swish of his cloak, he darts away, disappearing down a nearby alley.

"Can't believe that didn't work," I mutter as I race across the street. Despite my tailoring, the thick skirt bunches around my knees and slows me down as I try to dodge traffic. I almost make it to the opposite sidewalk when a vaporous carriage appears out of nowhere and barrels right through me.

Without the combustion engine, it doesn't hurt the way a car would. Instead of setting my organs on fire, it's like being impaled with a six-foot-wide timber log. My ribcage compresses, squeezing my lungs into a pulp before springing back into form as the carriage passes.

Stumbling onto the sidewalk, I grab the lamppost that Mr. Dark-and-Sinister had been leaning against. When I've recovered myself, I turn toward the alley—and freeze.

He's there. I mean, *right there*, looming over me. He's a shade under six feet, though the hat makes him seem taller, and the heavy frown makes him extra intimidating. I shrink back.

His eyes widen.

Well. No point in pretending I don't see him. Now what? Fight? Flight? I can't choose, so I opt for diplomacy. Drawing myself upright, I extend my hand. "Uh, hi. I'm–"

His arm shoots out from under his cloak. A long white stiletto protrudes from his sleeve. Before I can react, he plunges it through my bodice and into my stomach.

I gasp, both at the force of the impact and the weird, warm sensation of it. With a frown, I look down at the weapon sticking out of my belly.

But there isn't one. His cuff hangs flush against the ribbing of my corset. No fingers, no hands, no hilt. Almost as if…

My jaw drops. This is no ordinary knife. It isn't a knife at all.

It's him.

"Huh," I exhale. "That's…unexpected."

He blanches in shock. Eyes like two obsidian pools ensnare mine and hold them in place. The wound stings, but not enough to give him the screams he must be waiting for. With a frustrated snarl, he rips his hand away.

I lurch forward a step, clutching my stomach out of instinct more than necessity. When I see what he's pulled out of me, my hold tightens in revulsion. The thing sprouting from his wrist looks like an eight-inch-long bone-white pencil, with a tip that curves into a sharp, narrow fingernail. He studies it, presumably for blood. Finding none, he fixes me with a furious glare.

"What *are* ye?" His voice is gravelly, with a thick accent unlike any I've heard so far. Irish, maybe? In any case, I don't know how to answer his question, so I don't. Instead, I stand up straight, the mild pain of the non-wound already fading, and drop my hand to reveal an unscathed abdomen.

He studies me like a predator who suspects he's underestimated his quarry. I raise my hands in a helpless gesture, back up a step—and hit the lamppost. The cast iron brushes the skin of my neck and immediately starts to burn.

Not good.

Withdrawing his second blade-hand from beneath his cloak, he lunges at me with both weapons.

I screw my eyes shut as the blades slice through the flesh on either side of my belly button. His attack may not kill me, but it's not fun. He grunts with effort, forcing the weapons deeper, until their dual stings punch through my back.

Back. Go back.

This time, he doesn't withdraw. He squeezes, then spreads, making the wounds wider. My teeth clench as pain—real pain—rips through me at last.

"Fuck." The strained curse escapes my gritted teeth. Is this what it was like for the others?

Am I going to die too?

Go back. Now. BACK. NOW.

The dampness of the parking garage douses my skin, and I open my eyes to shadows and woodgrain hovering above me.

"Jesus Christ." I run my stiff, shaking hands over my torso. No wounds. No blood. I'm fine, or at least I'm in one piece. And yet…even as I lay here, unharmed and out of danger, I can still feel those horrible appendages gnawing at my flesh as he tries to saw me in half.

"Adina?" Thomas asks from somewhere beyond the darkness. "Is everything okay?"

I open my mouth to tell him no. What comes out instead is a scream that almost rips my throat in half.

Fourteen

Thomas wastes no time bundling me in his coat and whisking me into the elevator. We ride to the third floor, where he flounders around a beige hallway full of doors until he finds one that doesn't have a nameplate attached to it. On the other side is a small, plain room with a glass coffee table and non-descript gray living room set.

"You can rest here." Thomas deposits me on the couch, then goes to the kitchenette where he fusses with the electric kettle. I sit as still as I can, gazing out the window at the overcast sky and trying my best not to think. About anything.

A few minutes later, Thomas hands me a cup of tea, mutters something I don't catch, and darts out. The drink hasn't even cooled enough to take a sip before the door opens and Breitling rushes to my side.

"Adina," he whispers, placing his hands on my shoulder and my knee. "Are you alright?"

Before I can answer, McNally appears in the doorway. "Who is he?" he demands. "What did he look like? Did you get his name? Can he be stopped?"

He's not hitting me with a Linguistic whammy, but the words come so fast and furious they still make me dizzy.

Shuddering like an overwrought Southern belle, I drop my head and shrink into myself.

Breitling gets the message. "Leave us," he barks over his shoulder.

"Now see here," McNally harrumphs. "The Crown needs answers, and she's the only one that can give them. I'm entitled to a debrief."

"And you'll have it—once I'm sure she's fit to proceed."

"Sound logic." Thomas places a hand on McNally's shoulder. "Come, Constable. We can wait right outside."

McNally grumbles but complies. As soon as the door closes, I unravel from my trauma position and fall back into the cushions. "Thank you. I can only handle so many people in my face right now."

"I understand," Breitling says. "London does love its oversight. It wouldn't surprise me if all these rooms have hidden microphones or even cameras."

"Noted, *Chief*." I glance at his hand, which has slid most of the way up my thigh.

He clears his throat and withdraws. "Right, then. Can you tell me what happened?"

I do as he asks, leaving nothing out. When I recount the assault, he clenches his hands so hard his knuckles turn white.

"Has Thomas examined you?" he asks when I've finished.

I point at the cup on the coffee table. "He got me tea. Isn't that enough?"

His mouth twitches. "Humor me. Please."

The earnestness in his eyes stops my protests. "Fine," I sigh. "For *you*."

He opens the door, speaks a few words, and returns with Thomas, who perches on the coffee table in front of me. "If you would be so kind as to lie back."

It's not a request, but a command, delivered with medical austerity. I comply, letting the coat fall open to reveal my bare legs and stomach. At my waist, two jagged bruises stretch from my sides toward my belly button. As I study the not-even-half-an-inch of space between them, another scream fills my throat. Not one of pain this time, but madness.

What are *ye?*

That's what he asked me. Well, right back at you, Edward Knifeyhands. What in the ever-loving fuck are *you?*

"Jesus," Breitling exhales. "Are you in pain?"

His voice pulls me off the cliff of insanity. I shake my head. Other than the residual stiffness in my muscles that accompanies waking up from a death state, I feel fine.

Thomas prods one mark with his finger. "Does this hurt?"

I shrug. "Maybe it's a little tender? Nothing to write home about."

"Could there be internal injuries?" Breitling asks.

Thomas rubs his chin. "Absence of pain is a good sign, but I would need to do a CT scan to be sure."

"Not necessary," I say at the same time as Breitling says, "Do it."

Thomas shifts his gaze between us. I ignore him and regard Breitling. "You heard the Doctor. No pain, no problem."

"*Not* what I said," Thomas mutters.

"Besides," I continue without acknowledging the correction, "a trip to the hospital will take at least half a day. Now that this…person knows I'm here, we shouldn't waste any time."

"Waste any…?" Breitling's eyes widen. "You don't think I'm going to let you go back, do you?"

I scowl at him. Since when does he "let" me do anything?

Thomas clears his throat and stands. "If there's nothing else pressing, I think the Constable and I will adjourn to his office while you sort this out."

His gaze travels pointedly over my scantily clad figure. With a sneer, I sit up and rewrap myself in his coat. Yeah, I *got* it.

Breitling resumes his seat next to me on the couch. He watches over his shoulder until Thomas exits before speaking. "Do I need to point out that those injuries bear a striking resemblance to our three victims?"

"Do *I* need to point out the one critical difference? I'm not dead."

"Yes, and thank God for that." With a shaky sigh, he takes my hand in both of his. "Did it hurt?

"Not at first. But then…yes." I fidget with the belt of Thomas's coat. "It hurt a lot."

He turns my hand over, one way and then the other. "Why aren't you wearing your sigil?"

Dammit. I should have known I'd have to explain this. "My sigil and the Rigour aren't playing nice. Whenever the Rigour gives me a knock, it goes haywire and I can't move. Taking it off is the only way to stop it."

"I see," he says. "However, I'm afraid you'll have to wear it from now on, regardless of any discomfort it may cause. As you said, this creature knows you exist now. He may come for you."

"And if he finds me while I'm in the middle of a sigil-Rigour power struggle? Paralysis isn't a great defense."

"Then we will have to be extra careful not to…incite such a struggle." With a pained expression, he disentangles his fingers from mine. The loss makes my heart ache, which prompts an immediate slap across my knuckles. I ball my hands into fists and indulge in a quick, nonsensical fantasy of punching the Rigour in its faceless fucking face.

"If I'm at risk of an attack anyway," I say when I've composed myself, "then that's one more reason for me to re-enter the Deathplane. He can't kill me there, and the sigil should lessen the pain of any attack. Not only that, but he won't be able to sneak up on me the way he could while I'm here. It puts us on even ground."

"I'm not sure that's true," Breitling says. "He has abilities we didn't expect. Abilities that *you* lack. And while I didn't like the idea of you going in there by yourself in the first place…" He glances at the door, then leans so close to me his lips brush my ear. "I fucking hate it now."

He sounds so furious, so possessive, I can't help shivering a little. "What do you suggest?"

"That I go with you," he murmurs. "The Lash worked before. No reason to think it wouldn't work again."

The memory of that night—our first escapade together—makes me smile. And of course there's what came after…

I cut off that train of thought before the Rigour has a chance to do it for me.

"As fun as that would be," I say, pulling away from him for good measure. "I don't think it's a good idea. The Deathplane is…different here."

He frowns. "Different how?"

"I can't explain it yet. But it's significant enough that I'm not sure the Lash will function the same as back home. Maybe after another Walk or two I'll know more. But until I do…"

I shrug a shoulder to my ear. He'd brush me off if I told him I feared for his safety, and I can't blame him, considering I did the same thing moments ago.

"If that is your estimation, then we will exercise caution until we know more," he says. "And…until we know more about this creature's motives and abilities, we must extend that caution to your movements on *this* plane as well."

I narrow my eyes. "Meaning?"

He narrows his right back. "Meaning that, until this issue is resolved, you must stay within the bounds of the Tower intentions threshold."

My jaw drops. "You mean I'm stuck here for the rest of the trip? In an *actual* prison?"

He holds up his hands. "This is standard protocol when we suspect one of our employees may be in danger. I would enforce this ruling on anyone, regardless of…personal feelings."

"Well, that's great." I flop back onto the couch. "And I suppose you'll continue to stay with your uncle."

He bristles. "That *is* what's expected of me."

I laugh bitterly. "Of course it is."

"Do you think *I* like this?" he hisses over another furtive glance at the door. "*Any* of this? I'm doing this to protect you, and to help the case. The sooner we sort things out, the sooner we can go home and get back to…to normal."

I frown at my feet. He's not wrong. The intentions threshold stops anyone with bloody motives from passing through it, which makes the Tower the safest place for any Operator in London. Especially one who may now be in the sights of an invisible serial killer.

Huh. I've never been on the receiving end of that relationship before.

I don't think I like it.

"Okay, I'm in. Literally." I fold my arms in resignation. "Let's wrap this up and get the hell out of here."

Fifteen

Breitling insists I eat something before going back to work. I think he may be stalling to see if I show any signs of internal injuries, but I'm hungry enough not to argue. He orders sandwiches from a nearby shop, then calls the Constable to give him his precious update. He also asks him to dispatch an underling to Thomas's house to retrieve my things. It's easy enough for me to instruct them over the phone, since the only items not still in my suitcase are yesterday's clothes and my toiletries. After that, I tune out the rest of Breitling's conversation in favor of picking at my lunch and staring out the window. It doesn't take me more than a minute to spot Shiva, perched on the edge of the Tower's closest parapet, staring at me. From the peak of the structure, a Raven three times her size monitors her with suspicion. She flaps her wings as if she's about to take off, but I mouth "no." We don't know who might be watching.

She settles back down and cocks her head. I lift my shoulder to my ear. I'm about as fine as I can be, given that I've become a captive—though not a slave, thank God. If I wanted to leave, I'm ninety-nine percent sure they wouldn't stop me. But that would mean quitting, and

I have no desire to do that, especially now that I have a target on my back.

Breitling ends his call, and we eat in the silence of two people preoccupied with their own thoughts. As we're finishing, there's a knock at the door.

"It's open!" I call out. The Rigour slaps my hand, but not hard enough to provoke anything more than an eye roll from me. Fine, I won't do that again.

Maybe.

The door opens a crack, and a fresh-faced redhead peeks in. "Miss Venture? Chief Inquisitor? I have the, ah, item you requested?"

"Great," I say, crumpling my sandwich wrapper. "Come on in."

She does, struggling as my trashed and lopsided suitcase gives her all kinds of hell. She's maybe a year or two younger than Ruth, and between the emerald pencil dress, demure pearl necklace, and peaches-and-cream complexion, I wonder if I've fallen into an episode of *Mad Men.*

"Thanks," I say, tightening the belt of Thomas's coat around my waist as I free her of her burdens. "I appreciate you grabbing it for me."

"It's no trouble, Miss Venture." She hands me my shoulder bag, then tucks a strand of hair behind her ear and flashes me a smile as brilliant as her pearls. "Is there anything else I can do for you?"

"No, thank you," I say. With a nod, she leaves, closing the door behind her.

"Well then," I say to Breitling. "I suppose I should let Thomas have his coat back."

"If you think that's best," he says with cool indifference. But I see his jaw tighten, and the sudden rise of his chest. He's…excited. Discontent immediately riles my stomach.

Oh, what? I clench the belt of the coat. *It's not like there's a screen for me to hide behind, and I can't force him to leave. Besides, we're in an unsecured room in the middle of an Order hold, and I have a job to get back to. We're not going to do anything. I swear.*

For a moment, nothing happens. Then my roiling stomach settles.

"Proceed."

I freeze. Did I just argue my point with the Rigour…and *win*? I'm not about to waste time wondering how that's possible. With trembling fingers, I undo the belt and slip out of the coat.

Breitling releases a breath that sounds more like a moan. His gaze slides over my nearly naked form, starting at my knees and meandering upward until our eyes connect. His are dark and stormy, and I'm sure mine are the same.

"Here." I hand the coat to him, stretching my arm as far as it will go while keeping my feet planted. I'm dying to get closer…to touch him…but I don't dare. This moment is a gift, and I'm not about to give the Rigour any reason to take it away.

"Thank you," he says, leaning forward while remaining seated.

I tear myself away and open my suitcase. I can still feel him, enjoying the view of my backside. As much as I don't want to end the moment–and would, in a perfect world, take things much further–I have to be realistic, and not just because of the Rigour. There's a killer at large, and I'm supposed to be out there catching him. Lives don't stop being in danger just because I want to get laid.

I grab the first shirt and pair of shorts I see and yank them on, followed by my flip-flops, before digging my sigil out of the pocket of yesterday's clothes and sliding it over my fingers. "Breitling?"

"Yes, darling?"

I blink, thrown. He never calls me that unless we're...alone. He must have really lost himself for a moment. "Um, can you get Gordon's handkerchief? It's in the coat pocket."

"Oh! Yes. My apologies."

I turn around as he extracts the blue fabric square and hands it to me. "Anything else?"

"Nope. I'm all set."

"Very well." Draping the coat over his arm, he stands up and buttons his jacket.

I frown. "You don't have to go with me. I know the way to—"

"I'm going," he says in a tone like a brick wall. "Thomas may be a brilliant doctor, but he doesn't understand your Operation the way I do. I won't have you injured again."

I arch a brow. "So, if I'm going to get pummeled, better it be on your watch?"

His mouth twitches. "I prefer to think of it as, if I'm going to feel guilty, I'd rather it be for something that's my fault."

I shrug but throw in a smile. "Can't argue with that."

We return to the garage to find it empty. I assume Thomas will be along soon, but I'd rather be gone before then.

Breitling lingers near the alcove entrance as I get myself situated in the ground. It hasn't stopped drizzling all day, and a thin layer of mist hangs in the air above me. The damp smell has grown stronger, infusing with the wooden door and fresh earth. It's how I imagine a forest would smell after a storm. I inhale, smiling in contentment.

"Ready?" Breitling asks.

I open my eyes to see him crouching over me at the foot of the pit. "As ready as I can be."

He frowns at my clothes, and I can see the question forming in his mind. "It's okay," I say before he can ask. "I'll, um, finish once the door is closed."

"Very well." He gives me a strained nod and reaches for the handle. "I'll be here when you return. I promise."

He closes me in. I let out a breath as the tightness in my stomach eases. His desire had been almost painful to witness.

Despite having barely an inch of space between my body and the door, I wriggle and kick my way out of my shorts and shirt. My skin settles into the cool, rich soil as the handkerchief clings to my palm and the surrounding smells thicken until they're almost solid. I take in the aroma with every pore and fiber of my body. By the time I exhale, I'm back in The Tied House, sitting on a stool next to a slumped and semi-conscious Gordon Gaye.

First thing's first—check the outfit.

"Now *this* is more like it." It appears my ethereal stylist took my critique to heart. Instead of an actual Victorian prostitute's dress, I'm wearing something akin to high-end cosplay. The laces crisscrossing the front of my low-cut bodice are decorative, and the stretchy material lets me move with ease. While the skirt still has a petticoat, it's not as full, and the above-the-knee hemline means I won't have to do any ripping. The flat-soled boots aren't the height of fashion, but they're practical. Period aesthetic, modern design. It'll work.

I slip through the glass panel in the door of the pub and return to the street.

No chance of hiding this time. He's waiting for me, in the same place as before. Instead of leaning against the lamppost, he stands with his feet apart, his top hat pulled low over one eye and his cloak draped over his shoulders, concealing his body and making him resemble the Babadook way too much for my taste. His dark eyes lock on me, and his lips curve up in a sadistic smile.

Okay, then. If that's how he wants to play this, then let's play. Stepping in line with the garbage can, I square my shoulders to him as the cars and shimmering carriages flow down the street between us. People past and present surround me, but thanks to my position next to a solid object, no one walks through me. Him they avoid by instinct, as if he's surrounded by invisible razor wire. After a few moments of exchanging death stares, he sweeps an arm to his side and opens his palm.

"Oh no." I make a big show of shaking my head, then cross my arms in defiance. "I went last time."

His extended hand drops. With his other arm he throws back his cloak, revealing a silver-tipped walking stick which he raps once against the sidewalk. Sparks burst from the impact, making me blink in surprise. When I look again, he's disappeared.

"Shit." I scan the length of the road. No sign of him. Wandering down the street a bit, I peer into the alley he'd used to jump me before. As I pass the entrance to the Tied House, an arm shoots out from the vestibule and grabs me around the waist. I scream. Not because I'm scared, but because that's what he's expecting.

Okay, and maybe a little because I'm scared. What can I say? Everything about this is new for me.

He pulls me into the vestibule, letting go of my waist only to take me by the shoulders and hold me still. "What *are* ye?"

Irish. No question.

"I could ask you the same thing," I shoot back.

His eyes blaze with fury at my insolence. "You dare question *me*, creature? I'm the governor and sole denizen of this realm. *You're* the one whose trespassin'."

"Trespassing?" I say with a laugh. "You can't own this place. That's like trying to own the air."

"I *do* own the air, and the Underhalt, and everythin' walkin' or crawlin' on these streets. Including you. You're an innerloper, you are, an' I'll do with ye as I like."

Despite the fear wriggling down my spine, I clench my teeth and force my eyes to roll. "Go ahead."

The cruel smile returns. Grabbing me around the throat, he pulls his other hand back as if preparing to punch me. His fingers join and his palm lengthens to form a single, bonelike blade.

Here we go again.

I brace myself as he stabs me just below the spot where my ribs join.

"There, now." He watches me, his tongue tucked between his teeth, waiting to savor my reaction. "What say ye to that?"

I regard him with an expression as flat as a manhole cover. The sigil has made all the difference—it doesn't hurt in the least. "Ouch."

His jaw drops, and he withdraws his weapon. His gaze flicks from my chest to the blade and back with mounting fury. Instead of cowering or trying to run, I clasp my hands behind my back. "Second time lucky?"

He bares his teeth. "Aye."

I close my eyes as he lays into me, stabbing again and again with both blades. Still, there's no pain. After a while, it actually starts to tickle, and I have to bite the inside of my cheek to stop myself from giggling.

"Goddamn ye!" he roars, raising the blades to my face. I lean back and let him tire himself out. After several minutes of useless slashing, he slumps against the wall across from me in defeat. His shoulders heave and his arms hang limp at his sides, each stiletto splitting into five discrete slivers. I watch the progress until I'm staring at two regular hands with clean, trimmed nails and a scattering of dark hair across the backs.

I run my palms over my face. No blood, no wounds. Such a big tantrum, and I doubt it will even manifest as bruises in the living plane. "Guess I'm not what you were expecting either, huh?"

He glares at me. Now that I'm not being assaulted, I can take a real inventory of him. He's in his mid-forties, with a lean build, narrow face, and full lips pulled into a petulant frown.

"You owe me an answer," he glowers. "What manner o' witch are ye?"

It's an antiquated term, and fraught with connotations both positive and negative. But it's not wrong. "My name is Adina Venture, and I am an Operator, here on behalf of the Order of the Presidium."

"Never hearda it," he snorts. "Why they send you here unbidden and unwelcome?"

"Trouble in my realm," I say, adopting some of his words to speed things along. "Three of our denizens have been killed there within a month. Murdered by a method we can't comprehend. I have been sent to determine if the one responsible is…from here."

I admit, it's not a strong finish. But I don't think it warrants the harsh laughter he responds with. "Your masters think a murderer dwells here, and *this* is what they send as a search party? One willowy whore?"

"Hey!" I stick my hands on my hips. "First of all, thank you. No one has ever called me willowy before, and I kind of like it. Second, the outfit was not my idea. I'd explain, but it's not worth the time. And third, why *not* me? Clearly, I can take anything *you* can dish out."

He grunts. "If there was a murderer skulking around here, I'd surely know about it and put it right. But as I told ye—tis only me."

I squint at him. Does he think I'm an idiot? He's alone in this plane, and he can turn his hands into knives. A plus B equals C. As in, I *C* a killer standing in front of me.

"I would help ye if I could, God's honest," he continues, thumping his palm against his chest. "But I swear on my honor, there's nothin' here."

His demeanor has shifted enough to be, if not friendly, at least genuine. Either he's an accomplished liar, or he's telling the truth. Whatever the case, it's obvious I won't get the answers I need from him.

"How big is this place?" I cast my vision up and down the street as if that will reveal another path forward. "Could someone hide here without your knowledge?"

"No." The word lands as solid and unyielding as a boulder.

"How can you be so sure?"

"You." His eyes sparkle, not with malice this time, but mischief. "I felt ye, the moment ye arrived, ripplin' through my body like a rock splashin' into a pond."

Or a fly landing in a spider web.

I banish the thought, along with my growing sense of unease. Creeping myself out won't solve anything. "Still, perhaps I could look around? At least then I can tell my superiors I gave my best effort."

He appraises me again, his suspicion warring with his curiosity. "I'll be needin' to accompany you. Even if your intentions be honorable, only a fool would trust a witch with the keys to the kingdom. And I'm no fool."

I heave an exaggerated sigh. In truth, I'm more than happy for him to stay where I can see him. "Fine. But if we're going to continue to keep each other company, can you at least tell me your name?"

His expression darkens, and I can almost hear the whir of his shields going up. He thumps his walking stick twice against the ground, turns, and walks away. "Come then, girl. Lemme show ye me realm."

Sixteen

He walks ahead through the rain-spattered streets, pointing out areas of interest with all the swagger and knowledge of the best London tour guide. But I'm barely listening. The longer I spend in this place, the more it clings to me, the air sagging from my limbs like cold, wet laundry. All around me, faces and buildings and vehicles stack and press together into a tableau so dense it makes me dizzy. My feet move faster than my brain, as if being compelled. As we turn a corner, I slip on a curb as some force I can't see tries to drag me into the crosswalk. I yank back a little too hard and lose my balance, stumbling into the wall of the building next to me.

The sound of my shoulder connecting with the brick catches the attention of my guide. "What's wrong with ye?"

"Nothing more than usual," I say, smoothing my skirt.

"If ye say so." His tone sounds benign, but there's a smug expression on his face.

"What?" I demand as we continue down the street. "You know something I don't?"

He chuckles and points his cane at the crosshatch of gold, silver, and gray lines covering the sidewalk. "You know the London Underground, right?"

"The subway?"

"Aye. Movin' cars on unmmovin' tracks. Here's the same. Paths walked so often they're worn into the fabric of time. Easy to fall onto 'em, hard to get off."

That does sound a lot like what I'd felt a moment ago. And yet he moves without any of the same struggles. "But you've found a way around them, haven't you?"

He grins. With a dramatic swish of his cloak, he bounds down the sidewalk on his tiptoes with the precision of a ballet dancer traversing a minefield. When he reaches the end of the walk, he pivots back to me and touches the silver top of his cane to the brim of his hat.

I shake my head, hoping my scoff adequately disguises my smile. This guy may be a psycho, but that was pretty fun to watch.

"Well, girl? What ye think?" he calls.

"Cute," I say, approaching him at a slower and more deliberate pace. "But you haven't been prancing like that this whole time, and the paths still don't affect you. What do you *really* do to avoid them?"

He winks, twirls his cane once, and walks away.

"Ugh, fine. Don't tell me." I trudge behind him, doing my best to avoid walking on any of the threads.

I was right—it doesn't help. There are too many of them, woven tightly together to form an impenetrable rug. Even if avoiding them worked, it would be impossible to do so. With a frustrated sigh, I look up in time to avoid colliding with my guide's back.

"Hey!" I shout as I come around to face him. "I know you're in charge here, but it's still rude to stop dead when you know there's someone following you. I almost—"

His expression silences my rant. The muscles in his face have gone slack, leaving his eyes bugged and his chin resting on his chest. His dark irises and pupils have clouded over, like two orbs filled with overcast skies.

"Uh, hello?" I wave my hand in front of him. Then I snap my fingers. He doesn't even flinch. "What the hell is going on?"

His head jerks up, nostrils flaring as if scenting something in the air. Turning on his heel, he dashes away, his cloak flying out behind him.

"Wait!" I yell with disappointing results. Picking up my skirt, I race after him. It's not easy to keep up. He knows the terrain a lot better than I do, and he's fucking *fast*. After five minutes of all-out sprinting, he stops at the entrance of a narrow lane. On the short brick wall next to me is a sign advertising the location as Henriques Street. It doesn't sound familiar.

I approach him slowly. His head hangs down and his arms dangle at his sides. He's not moving, but he doesn't seem lost either. It's more like he's waiting for something. I peer around his shoulder at his face. The vacant stare remains, and his jaw has dropped so low that his chin and neck are one formless mass.

"What are we–?"

I cut myself off when I hear voices coming from the far end of the street. Two women walk in our direction, both in their early forties, with dark hair and complexions that are too similar not to be related by blood. They're both dressed casually with sensible shoes. One is holding an umbrella, the other has a map. They might as well have "TOURIST" screen printed across their pastel-flowered blouses. If my guide hears or sees them, he doesn't let on. They meander closer, chatting idly, oblivious to the two invisible beings standing in their path. Blood pounds in my ears, giving my anxiety a steady rhythm. Not. Good. Not. Good. Not. Good.

The woman with the umbrella laughs at something her companion says, a lovely, musical sound that ends in a startled scream.

It happens so fast. Literally in the blink of an eye. One second, he's sulking at my side like a broody statue. The next, he's got one of the women by the shoulders, slamming her back against a wrought-iron gate that leads into a parking lot. Her second scream gutters into a groan as her head bangs against the bars. As she goes limp, he grabs her by the throat. His other hand retracts. Reforms.

I know that move. "No! Stop!"

That's all I have time to say before he slashes her throat. A bruise blooms across her skin as blood spurts from her mouth.

"Oh my–Emma!"

Her sister's scream thaws my shock. As he winds up for another strike, I lunge at him, wrap my arms around his elbow, and yank him backward. He's bigger and stronger, but never underestimate the element of surprise. He wobbles for a moment, then loses his balance. I try to untangle my arm from his before he goes down, but I'm not quick enough. His chest collides with mine and we tumble to the cobblestones. He shakes his head, snarling and spitting as he tries to get up.

"Oh, no you don't." The arm I captured is wedged between us, and I clamp down on it with both hands. He wrenches hard enough to nearly free himself, and I wrap my legs around his waist to hold him in place. "You're not going anywhere until you calm the hell down."

He throws his head back and howls, the long nail of his blade scraping and digging at the inside of my leg. As he struggles, I concentrate on the scene playing out around us. Emma splutters, growing weaker every second. Her sister sobs frantically between screams for help. In the distance, footsteps approach. And there, hovering in the air above us…a wheel, big and wooden, like the ones on a covered wagon.

What the hell is *that* doing up there?

"Let me go!"

His scream pulls me back to his milky gaze. "Not. A. Chance."

He bares his teeth, and I pull back just in time to prevent him from ripping into my nose.

"Oh, *hell* no!" Twisting my neck, I chomp down on the top of his ear. He roars, whipping his head back and forth, which only makes me bite harder.

"Snaph owt ah eht!" I mumble around the spongy cartilage.

He stiffens, and I brace for the next assault. Instead, he goes limp, as if someone has yanked his skeleton out of his body. It seems safe enough now that I can let go of his ear, but I don't loosen my grip. His forehead falls into my cheek. Clammy sweat slicks my skin before he pulls back.

"Wha…?" He sounds shaky and weak, like a child who has wandered too far from home and doesn't know how to get back. As he blinks at me, the final traces of fog fade from his eyes. "Wha' happened?"

"You…attacked a woman."

He shakes his head. "Wha' now?"

I jerk my chin toward the wall behind us, unwrapping my legs and loosen my hold on his arm so he can turn. A small crowd has gathered around Emma, who is being attended by someone with a modicum of medical training. Her sister stands to one side, hands pressed to her face as two more people try to offer comfort. To everyone's credit, there's not a cell phone camera in sight.

"Jesus, Mary, and Joseph." The arm I'm holding starts to shake. "You're sayin' *I* did that?"

I frown at the back of his head. "Yes. I saw you."

"I…I dunna remember," he murmurs, eyes pinned on the injured woman. "I dunna remember any of it."

A likely story.

That's what most people in my position would think. Most people, however, have never heard of a man named Darius Canelo, or the strange circumstances in which he died. But I know who he is. Because I was the one who killed him—and until I was accused of his murder, I'd had no idea.

So, as a matter of fact, it *is* a likely story. Because it's happened at least once before.

The wail of sirens at the far end of Henriques Street causes all heads to turn, mine and his included. The ambulance stops in the middle of the road and the medics jump out with a supply kit and gurney. A police car follows close behind. As the professionals take over, my guide drops his head into his hands.

I pull my legs in and cross them in front of me. I'm still holding onto his arm, but for a different reason now. "If you don't remember the attack, can you tell me what you *do* remember?"

He inhales shakily. "I remember you trippin' on the sidewalk. Then…I heard somethin'? Or maybe smelled somethin'? And…now I'm here." He turns so he can see me out of one red-rimmed eye. "With you."

Again, I know from firsthand experience how plausible that is. But I shake my head. "That's not good enough. We already suspected you were the killer. Now we know for sure."

He turns the rest of the way toward me. "I swear, I dinna know what I was doin'. You gotta believe me."

"I *want* to believe you," I say, with the teeniest hint of a smile. "But you need to be about a thousand times more forthcoming than you have been if you're going to convince me. *Or* my bosses."

He looks down to where his hand rests on the gravel near my foot. "I swear to ye, I will be."

"Then let's start with an easy one. Tell me your name."

His shoulders tense. "You ain' gonna like it."

"Try me."

He peers at me from beneath heavy brows. "Heartless."

Seventeen

"Henriques Street!" My corpse-stiff lips crack with the effort of speaking, but I force them to obey. "Wagon wheel. I tried to stop him...police are there...ambulance...need an intentions threshold..."

"We know."

I freeze. Even through the door, I can tell that's not Breitling.

"The Constable has dispatched the Inquisitor and the Doctor to the scene. I am to escort you to the conference room."

"Uh, okay. One second." I scramble for my clothes. Getting dressed in this position is a lot harder than getting undressed, especially with how stiff my limbs are. When I've finished, I roll my neck, then push the lid open.

The mystery voice belongs to McNally's pet Reaper. He nods at me, his face an indifferent mask, before escorting me to the third floor and yet another beige, windowless room. This one contains a glossy wooden table the size of a yacht and a dozen high-backed leather chairs.

He leaves me to my own devices, so I take the opportunity to strip off my shorts and scrape the dirt out of them. Luckily, I've put myself back together by the time the door opens again and McNally appears. Alone.

He said he wouldn't leave. He promised.

I shake my head to dissolve the unbidden thoughts. After all, he didn't *really* leave me. The Constable sent him to secure a crime scene. A crime scene I'd been at, in a way. If anything, he was coming to help me.

And if it had been a different order, to a separate location? You think he wouldn't have left you then?

"Miss Venture?"

I drag myself out of my head and focus on McNally, who has settled himself in the chair at the head of the table. "Did you get the intentions threshold up?" I ask.

He arches his brow. "Reaper Newton is on his way now. He will set a perimeter on the whole of Henriques Street between Fairclough and Commercial."

"Is he the one who brought me up here?"

"Indeed. He's an electrical Materialist, and the best threshold enabler we have. Nothing nefarious will get in or out, I assure you. Now, what can you tell me?"

My eyes flick to the door. "Shouldn't we wait for the others?"

He shifts in his chair. "This attack has come several days earlier than anticipated, which means we can no longer trust the Ripper's original timeline. I need to know what you know. Immediately."

"I understand that, but I don't think the Chief would like–"

"Inquisitor Breitling is not the ranking official here," he snaps. "He answers to *me*, which means *you* answer to me. Now, speak. I won't *ask* you again."

His neck folds jiggle ominously. Crap, I forgot about the whammy. No way I want anything to do with that. I'm about to speak when a spurt of indignant fire rises in my chest to quash it.

I do not care for this one bit. His behavior is unprofessional, boorish, and most unbecoming of a gentleman. As such, he deserves neither your shame nor your cooperation.

I blink. That's not how I talk. It's not how I think. I mean, I agree with it, but still—where the hell did that come from?

McNally clears his throat. His face has turned bright red and beads of sweat cling to his temples. "My apologies, Miss Venture," he says with labored breath. "This situation has me under duress. There are people I must answer to, and they are fearsome indeed. We need to resolve this as quickly as possible, or else…"

He dips into his pocket and extracts a monogrammed handkerchief to mop his forehead.

"That's…okay," I say as I bite back a smile. Guess I'm not the only one who gets bitch-slapped by the Rigour after all.

McNally tucks the handkerchief away and leans forward. Before he can speak, however, there's a soft knock at the door. He pounds his fist against the table. "What now?"

"Sir?" The delicate voice is barely audible. "I have your tea tray, but I'm having a bit of trouble with the door?"

McNally grunts but makes no move to stand. Instead, he stares at me.

So much for being a gentleman. As much as I'd love to lock horns with him, there's someone struggling in the hall. I delay a few seconds to prove I'm not doing this for his benefit, then answer the door. On the other side is the redheaded woman who brought me my suitcase. A large tray laden with a bone china tea service and a plate of powdered cookies teeters in her birdlike arms.

"Oh, thank you, Miss Venture," she says as she enters.

The tray tips, and I leap to help her right it. Together, we set it on the table without catastrophe. "It's no problem…um…"

"Dora." She gives me a small curtsy. "Dora Wood."

McNally clears his throat. She stiffens and rotates toward him like a ballerina in one of those old music boxes. "Yes, sir?"

He sucks air through his nose until his neck bulges. "Dora Wood. Per Section Twelve, Subsection Twenty-Four Paragraph Six of the Pages Handbook, you are not to address yourself to visiting diplomats, outside contractors, or esteemed guests without the express written permission of your supervisor, sub-supervisor, or–"

"Whoa!" I gasp as Dora swoons and falls into me. "Are you okay?"

"She's fine," McNally says, his neck deflating. "And I'll thank you not to interrupt me when I'm speaking to my employees."

Jesus, what an *asshole*. I hold Dora by the shoulders until she can stand on her own. While I can't be certain that this little display violated Order policy, I can say with conviction I am not a fan. I sit back down and cross my arms. "I understand the need for expediency, Constable, and I'll be more than happy to tell you everything I know *once* Chief Inquisitor Breitling returns. Any discussion of strategy will benefit from his opinion and save time in the long run."

McNally's cheeks and neck turn crimson. But I don't flinch. He can pummel me with his bureaucratic jibber jabber until he's blue in the face. I'm not changing my mind.

Frustrated, he turns back to the dazed Dora. "What are you waiting for, Miss Wood? Pour the bloody tea."

An awkward drink and two cookies later, the door slams open and Reaper Newton enters, followed by Breitling. He's three shades paler than normal, and his hair is unkempt and damp. When his eyes land on me, his tense shoulders sag and his face floods with relief. "Oh…good. Good."

My irritation at his broken promise evaporates. All I want now is to wrap him in my arms and hold him until he not only knows, but *feels* I am okay.

"*No.*"

As much as I don't want to, I lower my head so he won't see me grimace. *I wasn't gonna do it. I just–*

"*No!*"

My sigil trembles as the Rigour launches my stomach into my throat. I tear the band off my fingers and toss it onto the conference table before their little spat can turn my limbs to granite.

McNally shoots me a withering glare before acknowledging Breitling. "Inquisitor. What do *you* have to report?"

Breitling watches me for another moment, as if making sure I'm not about to disappear, before turning to McNally. He pulls a small notebook from inside his jacket along with his glasses and reads. "The victim's name is Emma Long, visiting from Cornwall with her sister, Rebecca. They'd already transported both women to Royal London Hospital by the time we arrived on the scene, so I could not assess her injuries firsthand. Thomas is with her now. From what I gathered from the witnesses who had spoken to Rebecca before she left, this appears to align with the previous attacks. Her injuries seemed to bloom from out of nowhere, with no assailant in sight."

"Fine work, Inquisitor." During that speech, McNally's focus never wavered from me. "Your report, Miss Venture. *Now.*"

Breitling arches his brow as he takes one of the several chairs between McNally and me. I smile coyly at him. He, of all people, should know that I'm not so easy to push around. Not by humans, anyway. "*Now,* Constable, I'd be happy to."

I relay my observation of the events: how my guide's demeanor changed, the manner of the attempted murder and my intervention, and how he snapped out of it like a man waking from a dream. For the moment, I keep his name to myself.

"In short," I say when I'm finished, "while he likely executed these attacks, I believe he is being influenced by someone or something else into doing so. He may be a victim as well."

"He attacked you, Adina." Breitling leans forward. "He stabbed you multiple times, and from what you yourself have said, it sounded like he knew what he was doing."

"What he *knew* was that a strange person had invaded his world," I counter. "He did what he thought he had to do to defend it. It was an honest mistake."

"An honest *mistake?*" He groans and rubs his temple like he's trying to ward off a headache.

"Is that all, Miss Venture?" McNally jumps in, seizing Breitling's lapse as the chance to head off an argument.

I drum my fingers. "Yes. That's about it."

"You said you intervened to stop the attack," Breitling says without looking up from the table. "How?"

Crap. I'd kept that part vague on purpose, and of course he'd zeroed right in on it. "I grabbed him by the arm and restrained him until he came around."

"I might have guessed." He huffs out a humorless laugh. I scowl at him, but he's focused on McNally. "Have you decided how you'd like to proceed, sir?"

The Constable heaves a three-ton sigh. "With respect to Miss Venture's opinion, there's no proof to support the theory that this creature is an unwitting accessory. It's more likely he knew you suspected him and, on this one occasion, adopted the guise of madness. It required breaking with the Ripper's timeline, but that's a small price to pay to establish an alibi and hoodwink the investigator. And in that, it does appear he was successful."

That doesn't sound like he respects my opinion. That sounds like he thinks I'm an idiot. "I don't know anyone who can turn their eyes milky white to sell a bit. Do *you*?"

"No," he responds testily. "But if he can form weapons out of the flesh and bone of his hands, a mere recast of eye color is a parlor trick in comparison, wouldn't you say?"

I wrinkle my nose. Good point.

McNally sits back in satisfaction. "No one has encountered a creature like this before. Therefore, it is in the public's best interest to capture him first and ask questions later. Wouldn't you agree, Inquisitor?"

"Absolutely, sir," Breitling says. "Capture and containment would ensure no one else gets hurt." He leans forward. "How do you suggest we do that?"

McNally's forehead wrinkles. "I assumed you would know."

"Not me, sir." He tips his head in my direction. Our eyes meet for a moment. His sparkle with mischief, and I bite back a giggle.

Well played, Inquisitor.

McNally sighs. "Very well, then, Miss Venture. How do *you* suggest we proceed?"

With a magnanimous smile, I get to my feet. "I'll grant you, it's *possible* this creature was pretending to be possessed by an external force. But let's say, for a minute, that he wasn't. If there is a bad actor out there pulling the strings, then taking away his puppet removes our only link to them. The way I see it, there's two courses of action. The first option: we try to remove the creature from the Deathplane. I say *try*, because we don't have a ready method to do that."

"I've been able to pull you out of a Walk before," Breitling says. "Can't we do something similar here?"

"Maybe, if we knew where to find his physical body on *this* plane. But we don't, and as far as I know, there's no way to track it down from the Deathplane side."

"And the second option?" McNally prompts.

"Continued surveillance. I will keep an eye on him in the Deathplane, which will also give me an opportunity to gauge his motives. If he *is* acting alone, he won't be able to hide it forever. If he isn't, that will give you time to investigate how this is happening and who's doing it."

Breitling nods along, but his jaw has tensed. "And if he attempts to attack someone else in the meantime?"

I take a deep breath. He won't like this. "I'll intervene like I did before."

Sure enough, Breitling's face clouds over and his eyes flare.

"I must confess, Miss Venture," McNally cuts in, "there are numerous parts of this plan I find objectionable. The timeline is murky, the odds of success are uncertain, and it puts far too many people at risk, yourself included."

Dammit. I slump in my chair.

"However," he continues, "if there's a chance that this creature has a co-conspirator, we cannot give them recourse to steal away. It is our duty to crown and country to apprehend them as well."

I blink at him. He *agrees* with me? That's a shock and a relief. I'm not even angry that he didn't give me credit for making that same argument ninety seconds ago. Well, not too angry, anyway. "Thank you, Constable."

McNally regards Breitling. "What say you, Inquisitor?"

Breitling glares at him. "It appears we have our way forward."

"Indeed, we do, Inquisitor. Indeed, we do."

His smug triumph makes my heart sink. He doesn't agree with me, and he certainly doesn't care if the plan puts me in danger. He just wanted Breitling to lose.

"Now then—regarding this so-called puppet master…" McNally flaps a hand at Newton, who has been standing sentinel next to the door. "Initiate a database search for all UK-based Aetherists with registered Operations related to telepathy, imbuement, or soul-steering. And, since the deaths resemble historical murders, include all Chronologists with the Manipulative parameter as well."

"A bit broad, isn't it?" Breitling says, and I have to agree. I'm not off-book on official registration documentation, but I know that, after you register as an Operator in one of the six major disciplines, there's at least five additional parameters used to further define the Operation. A search like the one McNally's requesting will return dozens of potential Operators. Good thing the UK is a small country–in the US, it would be thousands.

"We're in uncharted waters here, Inquisitor," McNally counters. "It's only prudent to cast a wide net. We will also need to consider the victimology of this latest attack. Reaper Newton, inform the Scribe in charge of the file that…"

He continues to lob instructions at his underling as I tune out and try to pretend I don't know about the obvious hole in this approach. Because no matter how wide a net McNally casts, there's no way to avoid leaving out an entire Operational discipline.

Mine.

After about five minutes, McNally gets bored with giving orders, and we agree to reconvene at six tomorrow morning to go over the results of the search. As McNally heads to the door, he beckons to Breitling, who rises but doesn't follow.

"I'll meet you in your office. First, I need a few minutes with Miss Venture to debrief."

His choice of words makes me swallow a giggle, but the double entendre doesn't register in his tone. He really does want to talk about the case.

I don't know whether to be disappointed or relieved.

McNally nods severely, communicating that he better make it fast, then stalks out with his minion in tow.

"Are you alright?" Breitling asks the moment the door closes. His eyes travel from my face to my lap, where they freeze in place.

"Of course. Why do you–?" I follow his gaze. There, on the inside of my leg a few inches above my knee, is a long, black bruise. "Oh, that. Like I said, I had to restrain him. He must have grazed me in the struggle. Not a big deal."

"He grazed you…there?" His tone shifts into a growl. "Exactly *how* were you restraining him?"

My blood heats. "He was *murdering* someone, Breitling. I did what I had to do. That's it."

He blinks as if I've thrown a cold drink in his face. "Yes. Of course. I'm sorry, I'm still a bit…shaken." He runs a hand through his damp hair. "When Reaper Newton told us there had been another attack, I didn't know what to think. I checked on you, but…well, it wasn't helpful."

Yeah, I'd imagine not. It's been a while since I've seen my physical body while I've been on a Walk, but I remember thinking that I looked about as dead as I'd ever want to see myself look. Not a great thing when someone's trying to reassure themselves that I'm not dead for real.

"I thought about pulling you out," he says, "but as you said, things are different here. I didn't want to risk it. Then the Constable ordered us to the scene, so I had to go."

"Of course you did," I bite out. He frowns, but I shrug it off, along with my attitude. It's his job, after all, and I know where I stand in relation to it.

My stomach muscles tighten as something sharp pokes into them. Apparently, the Rigour doesn't like that. *You got something to say?*

Silence. Big surprise. As much as I'd like to continue that brick wall conversation, it'll have to wait.

"The point is," I continue, "I'm fine, and we both have our marching orders. You've got to go meet the Constable, and I've got a Walk to resume."

"Right." He stands and extends his hand to me. "*After* you get some rest."

"What? No." I shake my head. "This…being, whatever he is, is confused and traumatized. You should have seen how broken he was after he realized what he'd done. He needs me."

His fingers curl into his palm. "Whether he's Operating alone or on behalf of someone else, they know that their latest attack has failed. They won't risk another before seeing how the chips fall. He's contained for now within an intentions threshold, but he can't stay there forever. Which means that, after we reconvene tomorrow morning, there's no telling when you'll have another chance for respite." He opens his hand again. "Please."

"Fine," I sigh, grabbing my sigil off the table before allowing him to pull me to my feet. "What time is it?"

He checks his watch. "A little past seven in the evening."

"Too early for bed, and anyway, I'm too wired to sleep. Is there somewhere I can go to wind down for a bit? Somewhere that *isn't* that tiny little room?"

A slow smile spreads over his lips. "I know the perfect place."

Eighteen

We head toward the river, heads bowed and shoulders pulled up against the chilly drizzle. If this is summer, I'd hate to know what winter is like. As we pass a half-razed wall near the Tower Green, I glance up. Shiva perches on a craggy outcropping, beak lifted to the sky. On the other end of the wall, the Tower Ravens huddle together, six large birds endeavoring to take up the same amount of space that she does. They stare at her with unmistakable wariness.

Looks like neither of us is particularly good at making friends here.

"I am curious about something," Breitling says as we enter a short tunnel, gaining a brief respite from the weather. "Why do you assume this…puppet master is a person? When you were manipulated, it was Chaos pulling the strings."

"But Chaos isn't here," I say. "And as opaque as the Rigour's logic is, from what I can tell, it doesn't take the same hands-on approach. It nudges, and sometimes that can hurt, but it doesn't seize control. I don't think it would manipulate things this way, not even to further its own agenda."

He nods. "From what I remember reading, that does seem like an accurate conclusion."

On the other side of the tunnel is a cobblestone alley that runs parallel to the river, though the outermost wall of the fortress obscures the view. Beneath a squat overhead bridge on our left, a set of three steps leads down to an unassuming lattice door set in the base of an outer tower. Breitling descends the steps, and I follow. Beyond the lattice, the daylight peters out, giving way to thick, black nothing. An ancient padlock hangs from the bolt, covered in a layer of rust as dark and flaky as overdone pastry. If I didn't know better, I'd say it hasn't been opened in decades.

Taking the padlock in his hand, Breitling slides his finger over the keyhole. A flash of green pricks the center of the tarnished metal. The padlock remains closed, but the door swings open as smooth and silent as any modern fixture.

"Impressive," I say.

He dips his head. "Security has always been a point of pride at the Tower. Especially when they were the seat of power."

He lets me go first so he can close the door behind us. I'm about to keep walking when he grabs my elbow. "Wait."

He opens a small black cupboard mounted on the wall, retrieves a heavy black flashlight, and flicks it on. Now I see why he stopped me—we're standing on a three-foot square that gives way to a steep, narrow staircase.

"Careful," he says as he mounts the top step. "It can get slippery."

He reaches backward with his free hand. I pause, giving the Rigour its chance to intervene, before I grab it.

"Why *did* they switch the seat of power to the Summit?" I ask as we pick our way down the stairs. "No offense to our home field, but when you think of global cities, Las Vegas can't compete with London. And this *place*...I mean, it's basically the Ministry of Magic. Why would they ever give that up?"

"Politics, of course," he says, using the flashlight to swat away a spiderweb. "The Order has existed in Britain much longer than it has in America, that's true. But where there's history, there's baggage. More specifically, there are relationships–ones that may be better off not existing, but for whatever reason cannot be dissolved."

"Like the royal connection."

"Correct. The Tower will never function as an independent entity unless its connection to the Crown is severed."

"And let me guess–the Tower isn't the one holding the scissors."

He chuckles. "More or less. The Crown is too frightened of the Tower to allow them free rein, and the Tower relies on the Crown for financial support."

"But that's not the case in America?"

"No. In fact, the Summit's charter forbids accepting financial support from any outside organization, including and especially the American government, to ensure it will not be subjected to undue influence or pressure. It's funded by the intellectual property created by its employees–Russ's Cone of Silence, for example–and financial contributions from its registered members. The more prestigious the Operator, the bigger the contribution they are expected to make."

"Hmm. So, you're saying that instead of being irritated by how much money Eidolon Haight makes selling

Reverie at his clubs, I should be happy because his profits pay my salary?"

His laugh bounces off the stone walls of the tunnel, warming me thoroughly. "A silver lining if I've ever heard one."

We descend for several more minutes before the ceiling opens up and the flashlight beam hits an arched wooden door with a round iron pull in the center. The entrance is now a dim smudge floating high in the air behind us.

"Take this." He hands me the flashlight and hauls the door open. Orange light flickers from the torches ensconced along the curved wall beyond. There are more stairs, but only a standard number, which deposit us on a sandy stone floor. I take a breath and almost start coughing. We may be deep underground in the wettest city on the planet, but the air down here is as dry as home. Across from the stairs, a waist-high wooden counter spans the length of the room, barring us from what lies beyond. Which is…

"Damn," I whisper. The ceiling of the antechamber in which we stand is normal height, but on the other side of the counter, it disappears, making room for the two dozen bookcases that stretch up and back so far there's no telling where they end. Votive candles fixed to the shelves at random intervals illuminate the aisles, flickering like fireflies in the night sky until the distant darkness swallows them, too. "This is amazing."

"Just wait," Breitling says as we approach the counter where a woman sits reading by the light of an old-fashioned lantern. Her shoulder-length gray hair hangs out from beneath a sack-like hood that's attached to a shapeless dress. Her head bends so low that the hem of the hood brushes the delicate page of the massive tome as she struggles to decipher the tiny red chicken scratch.

"Madame Misty," Breitling says, resting both palms on the counter in front of her.

Opalescent blue eyes squint up at him from behind thick lenses. Her cheeks are plump but saggy, with deep lines that cut from the sides of her pixie nose and frame her thin lips. She stares at him as if in deep thought.

"Shouldn't you–?" I prompt, but he holds up a hand to stop me. Before I can press him further, she speaks.

"Levi Breitling." Her voice is dry, but hearty and melodious. Not at all what I expected to hear coming out of the crone-like persona sitting in front of me. "Is it you?"

"It is indeed."

"My, my!" She clasps her hands together, the crease between her eyebrows easing as her face lights up. "It's been an *age*, dear boy! Come, come, and let me get a proper look at you."

Hand to God, Breitling grins like a schoolboy, then slaps his hands on the counter and vaults over the top of it. My mouth drops open as he lands on the floor in front of her. She claps and giggles with delight.

"Well?" He spreads his arms wide so she can inspect him. "What say you, Madame?"

She looks him up and down, squints, then gives a hearty nod of approval. "Aye, that's my Levi. I could never forget that stature."

He chuckles and, in yet another surprise move, plants a kiss on the top of her head. "You never forget *anything*."

"For better or worse, I'm afraid." She pats the hand he's placed on her shoulder, then regards me. "And who is this stunned young lady?"

"Sorry," I say, returning my jaw to its regular position. "I'm just…uh, hi."

"Hello." She swats Breitling in the stomach. "Where are your manners, boy? Introduce us."

"My apologies." He gestures between us. "Williamina Misty, this is Adina Venture."

"Nice to meet you," I say. She's too far away for a handshake, so I opt for a curtsy-like dip of my knees instead.

"The pleasure is mine, dearie. Welcome to the Catacombs." She fixes me with a warm smile that shows off sporadic teeth before turning back to Breitling. Her eyes roll over him again, slower this time, in an exhaustive evaluation. When they land on his Inquisitor's collar, her smile wavers. "I see you've done your uncle proud."

He stiffens. "Thank you, Madame. I've tried."

"Mm." It's more of a grunt than an acknowledgement. "You wear it well, boy. I should've known you would."

The growing tension crackles over my skin. As much as I'm dying to poke this bear, we came here for a reason, and I'd like to know what it is. I clear my throat to get Breitling back on track.

"I was hoping to show Miss Venture the reading room," he says. "Would that be alright?"

"Of course. If you can remember where it is." Her eyes twinkle.

He grins back. "I suppose we'll find out."

Nineteen

I track him to the edge of the room, where he flips up a section of the counter that has nothing below it, allowing me to pass through without the physical fitness test.

"Who was that?" I whisper as he leads us into the stacks.

"Madame Misty," he says. "Keeper of the Catacombs and one of the most classically skilled Memorists I've ever met. Her recall is beyond photographic, her memories indelible."

Interesting, but not what I want to know. "She seems fond of you."

He nods but doesn't elaborate. My tongue itches to unleash a flurry of questions about their relationship, but the tension in his posture tells me that's not a good idea. Their encounter has him on edge. If I push for answers now, he'll shut me out. Our contact is already minimal, and I don't want to risk diminishing it further.

Breitling leads us to a break in the shelves, turns left, walks past three aisles, and turns in the opposite direction. Despite appearing foggy, the cool air feels as dry as it did in the antechamber. Bad for lungs, but good for books, of which there must be thousands, all snuggled together on the shelves like a vellum fortress.

"Nearly there," he says, taking a right, and then another.

"How can you tell?" I pant, jogging to keep up. He zigs, zags, then stops in front of another break in the shelves. Except it's not a break–it's an archway, bricked with books all around it. On the other side is an area the size of three Olympic swimming pools, furnished with clusters of leather chairs and long wooden tables with banker's lamps placed in front of every seat, their amber glass shades casting circles of warm light in the gloom. More votive candles dot the surrounding shelves and flicker in the fog that hangs above us like a ceiling.

"The reading room," Breitling says, stepping back so I can take it all in. "I spent a lot of time here when I was…when I started working for the Order. Any question I had, any fear plaguing me, this place had the answer. That was a great comfort to me. It still is."

"I'm not surprised." Even though we're alone, I keep my voice reverently low. The sweet, dusty scent of leather and old paper surrounds me, and I breathe it in with pleasure. "It's beautiful. Seriously, if I lived in London, I would never leave."

"I'm glad you like it." His fingertips skim my shoulders as the sandalwood scent of him embraces me. I close my eyes as every mote of jet lag, exertion, and even a bit of death still lingering in my joints begs for the relief that I can only find in his arms.

"I don't suppose you could…stay with me?" I direct the question to him as much as to our invisible chaperone. "Just for a bit?"

"I would love nothing more." His breath warms the side of my neck. "But I must meet with the Constable. I'm already late."

I bite my lip. I want to insist he stay, but duty calls. What's the point in asking if I already know the answer?

His hands stop moving, as if he's waiting for me to say something. But I stay frozen until his touch falls away.

"Well, then...if I may suggest?" He gestures toward the shelves on his right. "There you will find several fiction books written and published by Linguistic Operators. Reading them has been likened to taking a hallucinogenic, or so I've heard."

My jaw drops. "Are you serious?"

"I thought you'd like that," he says. "Don't stay up too late, and I will see you in the morning."

"Wait," I say. "Getting here was a maze. How will I get out?"

He points down the hallway. "Turn right and walk until you hit the counter. Then stop."

"Why didn't we go that way to get here?"

"The way back is always less difficult than the way forward," he says with a mysterious smile.

I arch my brow. "You get that from a fortune cookie?"

He chuckles. "Have fun, and please, don't wander too far away from the reading room. It gets quite twisty back here."

"I promise."

"Good. Then...until tomorrow." He dips his head and disappears down the hall. My aching heart goes with him.

"Well done."

I sneer into the fog. "No one asked you."

Twenty

Ignoring conventional wisdom, I choose the book with the prettiest cover, snuggle into one of the deep leather armchairs, and start to read. The pages seem to move on their own, fast and hypnotic, transporting me into a world of fae and monsters. Adina Venture is gone, and in her place is a demi-goddess with a kingdom to save.

A blink returns me to myself. My eyes burn, my arms beg for movement and everything from my waist down is numb. I set the book on the floor and unfurl in a full-body stretch. The discomfort fades, as do the hallucinatory effects, leaving only a slight giddiness behind.

Breitling hadn't been kidding about the books. In fact, he undersold the experience. If they put those things in NO libraries, all funding problems would disappear overnight.

I stand up, stretch again, and leave the reading room. With the book's afterglow wearing off, sleep feels a lot more possible. I start for the counter when a soft thump over my shoulder stops me. The place was empty when we arrived, and that was hours ago. It's unlikely anyone is working this late at night. Could it be Madame Misty re-shelving something?

"Hello?" I call into the murky aisle. The word irritates my dry throat, and I stifle a cough. Damn, I'm thirsty. "Madame Misty? Is that you?"

Another thump, followed by what sounds like glass bottles bumping against each other. Not something one expects to hear in a library, even one as unusual as this.

I tiptoe toward the sound. Yes, I promised Breitling I wouldn't wander off. But if all I do is take a left instead of a right, that's not wandering so much as taking a wrong turn. As long as I stay in this aisle, I think I'm covered.

The murk gets deeper the farther I go. Then it begins to lift, the color shifting from dark gray to soft bronze. Light. But I don't see the source.

I'm about to give up and turn back when the gloom parts, and I'm standing in the doorway of a small, semi-circular room. The fog lingers above me, hanging much lower than the rest of the library and glowing with that rich, golden light.

How, one might ask, does a room made of bookcases appear circular? Because each case is so narrow, it only fits one book situated cover-out in a marble stand. From the entrance, I can read the title of the one across from me thanks to the dripping candle sconce on the wall next to it.

The Portrait of Dorian Gray.

"No fucking *way.*" I shuffle across the stone floor as fast as my feet will carry me and stand in front of the book. It's not large, but it's beautiful, bound in black velvet and embossed with silver titling. The smell of the pages and the ink circles my head, and I raise my hand to stroke the supple cover.

"I wouldn't."

My heart leaps into my throat and I spin around. Standing in the doorway is a man in a black tailcoat. He's older, though not as old as Madame Misty, with dark eyes and white hair so thin a stiff wind might blow it away. His shoulders are curved with age, but his back is stick-straight. With his hands clasped behind him, he reminds me of an elderly, well-dressed Lurch.

"I'm so sorry," I say, sidling away like a guilty child. "I didn't mean—"

"Not without the gloves." He joins me at the bookcase, moving without urgency or aggression as he opens a narrow drawer below the book. Inside, two stacks of white linen gloves lay pressed and ready for action. He withdraws a pair and hands them to me, then gestures at the room. "We must treat them with respect, you understand."

He gives me a crooked smile. Nodding, I slip the gloves on before withdrawing the book.

"You're a fan of the Gothics?" he asks.

"You could say that," I say, turning the feathery page. "Do you have more?"

He nods and gestures to some of the other alcoves. "Shelley, Stoker, Stevenson, the collected works of Edgar Allen Poe. Gifts all, donated by one estate or another over the years."

I gape at him. "They were *all* Operators?"

His eyes gleam. "Officially, no. Celebrated figures rarely register. These particular volumes, however, have been…illuminated, in a sense. Some by the author, others by an Operational fan of the work. Either way, they belong here."

"I'll say," I mutter, taking extra care not to linger on the words. It's hard to do better than Oscar Wilde, but

I'm not sure I need the firsthand experience of having my soul siphoned into an oil painting. "Thank you, ah…sir."

I set the book back in its stand, slip off the gloves, and try to return them. But his hands remain clasped behind his back. "Are you thirsty, my dear?"

"Uh, yes," I say, setting the gloves on the marble base. "I'm parched."

He shuffles past me, and I follow him to the wall on the right side of the room. Unlike the others, it isn't made of bookshelves, but pigeonholes. Dozens of them, sealed with glass doors and stacked to the cloud ceiling. The cork of a bottle stares out at me from inside each one.

I frown back. Why didn't I notice this when I walked in? I'm not usually that unobservant. I must be more tired than I thought.

"Homer."

"What?" I ask.

He points above the pigeonholes where a quote has been etched into the woodwork: *And wine can of their wits the wise beguile, make the sage frolic, and the serious smile.*

"Well, well." I rub my hands together. "A library with a wine cellar. This place is getting better all the time."

"Is there a type you prefer?"

Anything from the bottom shelf at the Smith's on East Charleston is the honest, yet unhelpful, answer. "Not really. I like reds, but other than that…"

"Not an uncommon state of affairs for the younger generations," he says without a trace of condescension. "No matter. Tell me, do you have a favorite meal?"

I cringe. How do I explain to this man that I don't eat like a normal person? I didn't even keep food in my house until a few months ago, and that wasn't my choice. Breitling did that. And has kept doing it ever since.

"No."

My stomach rolls like I'm on a rollercoaster. I want to collapse into a chair, but this man is still watching me, waiting for an answer, so I grab onto my waist with both hands and study the ceiling. I hope it looks like I'm considering his question, not swallowing bile–and fuming.

What the hell was that for? He's not even here.

"Spaghetti," I say at last. "With tomato sauce. My dad used to make it."

"A good start for a red." From the pocket of his vest, he produces a ring the size of an orange filled with small gold keys. He approaches the wall with reverence, as if he may drop to a knee the way one does before entering a church pew. "Do you know what sort of aromatics he used? What spices?"

I purse my lips. Even though I was only three when he left, I remember sitting across the kitchen counter as my dad made his sauce with the ingredients spread over the big butcher block countertop. Before he added each one, he'd point to it, say the name, and then wait for me to repeat it. But that was almost thirty years ago, and big skips and scratches have warped the memory. Concentrating, I pull out what is still there. "Garlic. Oregano. Pepper. Lots of pepper."

"Mm-hmm, mm-hmm," he mutters, perusing the wall. "What else?"

I contemplate the ceiling and try to think. Dad's words may be gone, but I can still see him, standing on the other side of the counter with a towel over his shoulder, as clear as if it were yesterday. He's tall, with dark hair and a thick beard, and sparkling green eyes. Like mine.

A wave of nostalgia slams into my chest. *That* is not helpful. Stick to what's on the counter.

"Um…a seedlike one?" I say. "Long, pale…I think it's used in sausage a lot?"

"Fennel."

"Yeah, that's it. And a leaf of some kind."

"Bay?"

I shake my head. That doesn't sound familiar.

"Basil."

"No, it was lighter green, like a mint color, and sort of…spongy, I guess."

His head stops roaming between the pigeonholes. "Sage?"

"Yeah, I think that's the one."

"Interesting." He remains still for another moment, then walks over to the door to retrieve a rolling ladder. He scales the rungs with the grace of a sloth, albeit at a much faster clip, and opens a door along the top row. "I believe this will suit."

Descending as deftly with one hand as he had ascended with both, he presents his quarry to me. The crimson label hugs the ink black bottle like silk clinging to steel, with words embossed in rich bronze: *Fratelli Di Erebi Nebbiolo. Gerlatch. 1983.* Beneath the raised print is an inscrutable signature scribbled in blue ink. I bet if I ran my thumb over it, I would feel the imprint the pen had made on the parchment.

"Looks…expensive," I say.

"It is. As expensive as it is rare." He carries the bottle to a white-clothed sideboard that holds wine glasses of every shape and size.

Okay, that *definitely* wasn't there before.

He plucks a corkscrew from the tabletop and plunges it into the bottle. "Care to try it?"

"Oh! I…thank you, but I'm afraid I don't have any money on me."

"It's alright, my dear." He yanks, and the cork releases with a soft pop. "This one's on the house."

He pours a mouthful into a glass, swirls it around, and tosses it back. After a moment's consideration, he swallows. "Of course, a typical Barolo or Baronesco of this age would need at least two hours to decant."

I cough. Two hours? It's gotta be closing in on at least eleven by now. If I don't get to bed soon, Breitling will kill me. Not that he would know. Not until morning, anyway, when I show up to work exhausted and wrecked. Despite whatever else we are to each other, that would still piss the Chief Inquisitor part of him off to no end.

He must sense my agitation, because he chuckles and selects a fresh glass with a narrow mouth and fat base. "This, however, is best savored right away. In fact, were I keeping to tradition, I would dispense with the glassware and invite you to drink straight from the bottle. But as we are in a post-pandemic society, this will have to do."

He hands the glass to me. The surface of the liquid trembles as I accept it with a shaky grip. Being offered an "expensive as it is rare" glass of wine on a whim may be a common occurrence for some women, but I've never scored so much as free cover at a nightclub. And there are barkers on the Strip who literally do nothing but give those away.

Picking through my brain to recall anything I can from the movie *Sideways*, I lift the glass to my nose and sniff. I do smell sage, but only because we've been talking about it. And the fennel, sharp and almost minty. There's something sweet and floral as well. Rose, I think. And…

I reel back so fast the glass goes flying. It hits the floor and explodes in a red and crystal firework. I press a hand to my mouth, hacking against the rotten, humid scent as it slithers down my throat.

"Something wrong, Miss Venture?"

He hasn't moved from his place next to the table, his gloved hands still folded in front of him, unphased by the shattered glass and red wine sinking into the parched stone floor.

"What the hell is that?" I choke out.

"Darkness, my dear," he says. "The one thing all good wine needs. I would expect you of all people to know that."

He takes a step toward me. I stumble away, still clutching my throat as it fills with something foul and sticky. I gasp out a single, critical word. "Umbralist."

His smile stretches wide, and his tongue pokes out from between his long teeth. "Smart girl."

I bump against the bookcase at the far wall. The smell has solidified into a ball in the back of my throat. Gagging, I spit onto the floor. It comes out as a dark glob of goo. I stare, horrified, as it sinks into the ground–and something else emerges. A single fibrous limb, curling out and up, then spreading wide until its tip forms a flat, meaty disc. On the other side of the room, similar growths sprout from the stain my glass left on the floor. Mushrooms, the same shade of magenta as the wine and splattered with dots of deep arterial red.

"It's time, Adina." He takes another step. "Time for you to come home."

I don't wait to find out what that means. As I race for the door, his footsteps rise to meet my pace, then overtake it. I make it out of the room, but not fast enough. Two hands clamp down on my shoulders, and I scream. "No!"

"Miss Venture? Wake up!"

The hands shake me so hard my neck snaps backward and my eyes fly open to see Madame Misty staring at me.

"What...what happened?" I ask.

"You tell me," she says. "I was putting away my books when I heard moaning. I came in here and found you, writhing and whimpering in your sleep." She glances at the book on the table next to me. "I'm not surprised. That one's a bit dire for so late at night, don't you think?"

"I guess so." I run my hands over my face and through my hair. "Sorry."

"It's nothing, dearie," she tuts. "Levi used to fall asleep in here all the time. Imagine having to wake him up from a nightmare."

I cringe. "Not without a full suit of armor on."

"A good idea, though I found a long stick applied to the cranium does the job just as well."

I laugh, and she joins me.

"Now," she says when the giggles fade, "I must insist you leave off your adventures for this evening and get some proper sleep."

As we walk toward the front of the Catacombs, I can't help checking over my shoulder to see if I can spot any of that burnished golden light.

There's nothing there but the gloom.

Twenty-One

I sleep, but I don't rest. The dream returns, though not as potent as before, along with flashes of something else. A place with cool breezes that kiss my cheeks and tangle in my hair…and the cindery smell of autumn…and a sky without a moon or any stars.

And then…I'm awake, with Breitling's gray eyes hovering above me.

"Mm, morning." I push my tangled hair out of my face as he withdraws his hand from my shoulder. "Meeting time?"

"Nearly past it, in fact," he says.

"What?" I grab him by the wrist and check his watch. Five to six. "Why didn't you wake me sooner?"

"I was assisting with the registration queries."

"I thought McNally assigned that to the Reapers?"

"He did," Breitling fumes. "But the Reaper Corp here is…severely lacking, both in number and discipline. There's only twelve of them, half of which are in the field monitoring Henriques Street and the site of the next Ripper murder in Mitre Square, just to be safe. The others, well…except for Reaper Newton, they appear to be allergic to the concept of urgency, let alone the practice.

We're not even halfway finished with the search. Honestly, I don't know what we're going to have to discuss at this meeting. Though I'm sure we'll take an hour doing it."

"Ugh, I'm sorry." As I yawn and stretch, his eyes slide down to my sports bra and bare stomach. After stumbling across the courtyard from the Catacombs and finagling my way into the building, I'd barely gotten my shirt and pants off before collapsing on the couch. I wonder–once he'd gotten a glimpse at what I was (and wasn't) wearing, could that have added to the delayed wake-up call?

"Well, I'm up now." I push myself up on my elbows, giving him enough time to straighten and step back before I sit all the way up. He waits for me to get dressed, making no effort to disguise his interest in my movements. Oddly enough, the Rigour doesn't have much to say about that this time. Not until I catch his eye and flash him a little smile.

"No."

I drop my gaze, wincing as the sandpapery burn scrapes my hand. *Yeah, I got that.*

"I need to use the bathroom," I say once we're in the hallway. "I'll meet you there."

He nods and goes ahead, leaving me to my own devices. As soon as I'm alone, I check my text messages. I've got two waiting, both from Ruth.

RUTH
still working on the profiles
should have somethin by eod PT

Then, a couple hours later:

jake called n said u asked for help w history stuff????

Dammit, I knew I forgot something.

ME

K cool. BTW there's been another attack. Emma Long from Cornwall. If you can add her to your list, that would be great.

There. A fresh body should tide her over until we can talk in person. I tuck my phone back in my pocket, use the facilities, and head into battle.

Reaper Newton opens the door, eying me resentfully from inside the sunken caverns around his eyes. Thomas and Breitling sit on the side of the table near the door, an empty chair between them. At the head, Constable McNally regards me with a displeased glare. If he's expecting an apology for my lateness, he won't get it. Breitling should have woken me sooner, and I'm guessing he's already apologized. That's more than enough groveling for six in the morning.

"How's Emma?" I aim the question at Thomas.

"Stable," he says. "The aid she received at the scene gave the surgeons enough time to repair the damage to her trachea. And the fact that she suffered no further injuries was…critical. She will likely make a full recovery."

"Thank God." I bow my head, partly out of reverence, but also because of the way he's looking at me. His shining eyes and slight smile make it seem like he's in awe, and yet this is the same guy that basically accused me of being a besotted, selfish snake not twenty-four hours ago. It's too weird.

McNally clears his throat. "Would you care to sit, Miss Venture?"

"Actually," I say as I clamp my hands over the back of the empty chair, "I'd rather get back to work. Don't get me wrong, I want to hear the results of your investigation once it's done. But my job is to monitor our culprit–or victim, as the case may be. I can't do that if I'm sitting here listening to a half-finished progress report."

Thomas's brows lift halfway up his head. On my other side, Breitling dips his chin and covers his mouth. His delight makes me grin so fiercely I can barely wipe it off in time to face McNally's disapproving stare.

The Rigour remains uncharacteristically quiet.

"Despite her insubordinate attitude," Breitling says, his haughty, professional mask much more effective than mine, "Miss Venture makes a good point. If we have nothing of consequence to discuss, perhaps we should simply continue our courses until we do. She should rejoin the creature, and we should complete our queries. Of course, the decision is yours, Constable."

With a brief glance at Thomas, who stares resolutely at his hands, McNally hauls himself to his feet. "Inquisitor, you're with me. Miss Venture, proceed as you see fit, but you are to return in no more than six hours to give us a status report. Doctor, you will attend Miss Venture and document any developments of note. Understood?"

"Yes, Constable," we chorus.

"One more thing," I say. "I'll need the intentions threshold lifted. If we're going to draw out the master, it'll help if it's business as usual for his puppet."

McNally nods without stopping to acknowledge me. Breitling holds the door for him and Newton. When he's sure both their backs are turned, he looks at me—and winks.

I gape at him as he leaves. Did that just happen?

"Thank you," Thomas murmurs. "I think you saved us several hours of pointless drudgery—and Levi from having a stroke."

I study him for signs of mockery or malice, but there aren't any. "Don't mention it. McNally already thinks I'm a mannerless monster. Wouldn't want to disappoint him."

He chuckles, then sweeps his arm toward the door. "After you."

Twenty-Two

My formless form drops into a gutter outside a six-story concrete apartment building. Gordon is bent at the waist in front of me, face aimed at the pavement. A wet gurgle lurches from his mouth.

"Ew!" I jump backward out of instinct a moment before he empties his guts into the street. "At seven in the morning? Dude, you've *got* to pull yourself together."

He coughs and spits a few times. I glance around, but the street is deserted. Seems no one in the pub saw fit to make sure he got home safe. God knows how long he's been wandering. "Go home, Gordon. Sleep it off."

"Yeah." He straightens, wiping his lips with the back of his hand as his head lolls to the sky. "Home. Right. Good." Head bobbling, he reels toward the apartment building. As he fumbles with his keys, he slurs out the first part of a children's song:

> *Do your ears hang low?*
> *Do they wobble to and fro?*
> *Can you tie 'em in a knot?*
> *Can you tie 'em in a bow?*

He struggles with both the lock and the lyrics for several minutes. At last, someone exits, and he falls into the vestibule. Christ, I hope he remembers which apartment is his. Or that this is even his building. But right now, I have bigger problems than Gordon Gaye, starting with the fact that my charge is on Henriques Street, and I am not. More than that, I have no idea how to get there.

"This way." The Irish brogue tickles my ear. I whip around, but the street is still empty.

"Follow me voice, girl," he says, only this time the words come from somewhere in front of my forehead. Without a better plan, I do as he says. He keeps repeating the same sentences. "This way. Follow me. This way." Every so often, the direction of the words changes, and I reorient myself to face it. After about twenty minutes, I'm standing on Henriques Street. As I enter, I wait for the static pressure of an intentions threshold, but nothing happens. My request must have made it to the right people.

He's where I left him, slumped against the brick wall with his head in his hands. He's taken off his hat and cloak, revealing a threadbare white shirt and short, greasy black hair. In the burgeoning daylight, his skin glows an ethereal, gunmetal gray. The ghostly wagon wheel still hovers in the air above him. Except it's not hovering. It's attached to a building that is no longer there.

"What's up with that?" I ask as I sit down next to him.

He yanks his hands from his face. "Jesus, girl! Donya know not to sneak up on a man who's wallowin'? You're liable to get your head knocked off."

"Sorry," I mutter, and point up at the wheel. "I was curious about that."

He follows my finger. "This here used to be the socialist club offa Dutfield Yard. Coulda been somethin' to do with that."

"Maybe," I say with a vague nod. Even if I hadn't witnessed the fourth attack firsthand, a name as unique as Dutfield Yard isn't hard to remember. It's one of the Canonical Five murder sites.

"You talk with your people?" he asks.

"Yes. They're investigating how something like this may have happened."

He peers at me from behind dark strands. "Somethin' like what?"

I'd been hoping he wouldn't ask that question. "There are people with powers that can influence someone the way you've been influenced. That's what they're searching for now. If they find the right person, they will question them and hopefully get the answers we need."

"If. Hopefully." He snorts. "So, you're guessin'."

I resist the urge to snort back. If I were in his position, I'd be irritated, too. Pressing my back to the alley wall, I tuck my knees to my chest and change the subject. "Have you been sitting here this whole time?"

"Where else would I go?" The hint of a smile plays upon his lips. "Besides, I knew this is where you'd come lookin' for me. Although, I 'spose I needn't ha' worried. Seems ye ken find me no matter where I am."

"Lucky me," I grunt. If he's trying to charm me, he can forget it. I could not be less in the mood if I tried.

His grin cracks open, revealing pearly white teeth. "Well, I am Irish. Good luck runs in the blood."

I shake my head, chuckling despite myself at the irony of that statement.

"So," he says after a brief silence. "You believe me, do ye? That I had no mind for what I was doin' to that poor woman?"

His hopefulness stokes my sympathy. I'm glad I don't have to lie to him. "Yes. Yes, I do."

Relief smooths the wrinkles lining his face. "And your people?"

"They're…less convinced. But if we can stop whatever is happening to you from happening again, they will have no reason to hurt you."

He nods, but his mouth turns down. "So, then—you're my nursemaid until further notice?"

I shrug. "It's either that or kill you."

"Oh, and you know how to do that, do ye?"

My snide comeback withers on my tongue. Under all that bravado lurks a sobriety that's almost alarming. He's not baiting me. He wants a real answer.

"No," I say earnestly. "I don't."

"Aye, I didn't think so." For a moment, his head drops, only to bounce back up as he leaps to his feet. "Right then. Seein' as we're stuck together, what do ye suggest we do?"

"I don't know," I say, joining him on my feet. "What *does* an invisible man do all day?"

He narrows his eyes, but his smile has returned. Donning his hat, he turns on his heels and walks toward the far end of Henriques Street. "Follow me."

"You know," I say as he swings on his cloak in mid-stride. "If we're going to be spending time together, I need to call you something."

He slows, flapping his collar so it will lie flat over his shoulders. "I told you me handle."

"I'm not calling you that. You need a real name."

"Says you." He tugs at his lapels. "But there again, since you're the one who'll be sayin' it, I suppose your say would count more'n mine. What's your fancy?"

"Um…" Crap. I've got nothing.

He grins sideways at me. "Word of advice, girl: Don't start an argument unless you're prepared to finish it."

I scowl at his long, pale hands. "How about Edward?"

He shrugs. "A bit Imperialist, but if it suits you, then so be it. Now, pick up yer feet. We wanna get there 'fore it gets crowded."

We head north through a series of narrow streets lined with brick buildings in all states of repair, from well-maintained gems to graffiti-coated piles of rubble. With the gray sky of early morning pressing down on us and no idea what our destination is, I feel like a rat in a maze. Not only that, but Edward walks so fast it's like he's trying to escape from something. For a guy with nowhere to go, he's in one hell of a hurry.

"So," I ask, hoping a little conversation will slow him down. "Where did you come from?"

I'm not trying to be funny, and yet he laughs so heartily that the shadows haunting him fade, revealing an exuberance that makes me think I misjudged his age. I'd initially thought him to be older than Breitling; now he looks even younger than me. "How can I answer that? Can *you* answer it?"

"I came from my parents, Elaine and Rafael Venture." My father's name brings a bitter taste to my tongue. "They raised me together until I was three, then my mom raised me alone. See? Easy."

He scowls at the sidewalk. "Tain't so easy for me, girl. All I remember is Whitechapel, and I've always been as you see me now. I dunna change, and I canna leave, no matter what I try. The city, however, that's changin' always."

We spill out onto a major street, dashing through traffic to avoid as many hits as we can. When we reach the other side, he nods at a black Audi cruising through the intersection next to the ghostly figure of a hansom cab. "I remember the first time I saw an automobile in Whitechapel. Spooked every horse it passed. I remember when indoor plumbin' arrived, and how much cleaner the streets were, without shit and all runnin' through them. And I remember..."

The shadows return to his face. "Lightnin'. Great balls of it that fell out of the sky, killin' and destroyin' so many. To this day, I dunno what caused it. Only that the Underhalt damn near collapsed because of it."

"Underhalt?" I ask, ignoring the rest as casually as I can. I don't know enough about World War II to explain the Blitz.

He waves a hand at a building across the street, a stone structure that looks like no one's touched it since the 1800s. From the carbon-copy appearance of its own shimmering ghost, I'm pretty sure I'm right.

"Places disappear and manners change," he says, "but what's gone before never leaves. It's simply halted. Pushed under to make room for what comes next. 'Twas upsettin' at first, but as one year melted into the next and I watched men and missions rise and fall, I realized there's nothing sad or scary about progress. It's the natural way of things. Memories may be static, but time only moves forward, takin' you n' me along for the ride."

"And this?" I gesture at the gold and gray tangles under our feet. I've been able to resist their draw during our jaunt, but it hasn't been easy. "Is this part of the Underhalt?"

"Aye, the most important part of all. The phantom buildings and specters are impressive, no doubt, but they're window dressin'. These, however, still have a part to play."

He squats down on the sidewalk and gestures for me to do the same. "Everyone in the world walks a path. But not everyone walks their *own* path. That's what these are. The brighter the shine, the more people have walked it. The dimmer they are, the more obsolete they've become. Sometimes a path gets so dim, it'll wink out. Any path can be walked, a' course, but the brighter it is, the stronger the call for others to follow it."

"That's how the Rigour works, isn't it?" I stifle a shiver. "It uses these as a map and tries to shove people onto them whenever it can."

He taps the brim of his hat. "Sharp, girl. Very sharp."

"Thanks." I huff out a rueful laugh as I study the thread-choked sidewalk. "Not a lot of space to forge anything new though, huh?"

"You'd be surprised." He straightens and continues walking. "Come. We're almost there."

We pass a few more storefronts, most of them closed at this early hour, before he turns into the one edifice with a healthy amount of foot traffic. I read the blue banner spanning the length of the arched entrance.

Whitechapel Station.

"We're taking the train?" I ask. But he's either too far ahead to hear me or doesn't feel the need to answer. Whatever our destination is, I guess I'll find out when we get there.

"Brace yourself," he says before slipping through the turnstile. "I dun remember much about my first time in a station, but 'twouldn't be understatin' things to say this is going to be a wee bit overwhelmin'."

"Noted." I press through the turnstile after him.

Not an understatement. Not at all. I'm still recovering from the burn of the stainless steel when my feet almost fly out from under me. Commuters would be creatures of habit, I suppose, taking the same route every day from home to office and back. The paths in here tell that story—they're as thick as they are outside, and *blinding*. Even the most faded ones pull at the soles of my boots like magnets. With every step, my feet get heavier. Walking becomes difficult, and then impossible. I try to fight through it, but after a moment or two, I can no longer lift my legs.

"Uh, Edward?" I call out as I start to slide across the linoleum. "A little help?"

He pauses on the platform of the down escalator. When he sees me, sliding faster and faster until I have to pinwheel my arms to keep myself upright, he breaks into a grin.

"Ah, yes. Now I remember." He saunters over way more slowly than I'd like, tucking his cane into a looped leather strap hanging from his hip. "Would you be needin' some help?"

I scowl at him. "If you don't mind."

"My pleasure." He stoops down. Cold lashes the back of my legs and shoulders as he scoops me up.

"Hey!" I shout, tucking my arms into my chest to avoid smacking him in the face. "Jeez, I know you've been alone here for a long time, but you've got to warn a girl before you do something like that."

He doesn't answer me. His fingers flatten and curl against my back and knees, and his arms lift and lower like he's testing my weight. As he evaluates my body with a stunned expression, I get the sense that, until right now, he hadn't believed I was real.

"Everything okay?" I tap his shoulder.

He blinks, shakes his head, and refocuses on me. "Aye, fine. We need to get your walkin' sorted. It's simple once you get the hang of it. But you gotta concentrate."

I frown. Something about that comment feels…familiar.

He sets me back on the ground but keeps hold of my hand. "Physical resistance may work for a bit, but you'll only exhaust yourself. Mental fortitude, that's what ye need. Every step must have intention behind it. You mean to take it, you trust it's right, and you're gonna do it. Understand?"

"It sounds easy enough. But…"

"Aye, I know," he says with a wink. "I'll hold on to ye until you've found your feet, so to speak. Now—you ready?"

I nod and close my eyes. One step forward. One.

"Steady."

I want it. It's right. I'm going to do it.

"Go."

The paths tug at me as I lift my foot. This time, instead of fighting it, I keep my muscles loose and focus on my intention. I want this. This is right. I'm going to do it.

The tug lessens, and the sole of my boot hits the ground exactly where I want it to.

"Good," he says. "Another."

I repeat the process, clinging to his hand for guidance as we move across the floor. People surge around us, through us, their energy making my nerves dance. One last lift of my foot, and my toe strikes the base of the escalator.

"Well done, girl!" He claps me on the shoulder.

"Well done you." I open my eyes and smile at him. "You're a pretty good teacher."

His lips part as his gray face flushes a stunning shade of burgundy. "'Twasn't nothing. Don't even think of it."

Dropping his chin, he mounts the escalator down toward the trains. I follow him with a spring in my step. Now that my feet aren't betraying me, I feel like I can do anything.

Twenty-Three

E dward hustles us onto the platform for the District Line going…somewhere. I didn't think I'd be taking the train much during this trip, so I didn't bother to learn the routes or destinations. It's packed with early birds on their way to work, most of them dressed in chic business attire and almost all of them on their cell phones despite the poor reception.

When the train arrives, I expect him to enter the first or last car as they would be less crowded, but he goes for one in the middle. There's no place left to sit by the time the doors close. We find a bit of standing room in the back where we can avoid being jostled–or, rather, impaled.

"Okay," I say as the train slips into the dark tunnel beyond the station. "*Now* can you tell me where we're going?"

His grin turns wicked. "Who says we're goin' anywhere?"

He falls to one knee and stabs a bladed hand into the floor of the compartment. The wheels seize beneath us with an unholy screech. Everyone gasps. A few people scream, and there are some thumps as those who were not holding on to something pitch forward and fall to the ground.

"What the hell, Ed?" I smack his arm as he stands up. "You want us to get stuck down here?"

He wiggles his reformed fingers. "Perhaps I do."

Before I can ask what he means, the overhead speakers crackle and a put-upon voice informs us that there's been a technical malfunction, they're working on it, and we'll be on our way as soon as possible. The crowd responds exactly how I'd expect them to: with irritated grumbles or broody silence.

"There." Edward leans back against the wall of the car and crosses his arms. "Now we can relax."

"Relax?" I say incredulously. "Stuck underground with a bunch of strangers and no timeline for when we'll start moving? That stresses *me* out, and I'm not even here."

"A'course it does," he says, his expression darkening. "You're like them. Spendin' your days walkin' your ways, followin' your paths without pause, and with no thought given to your next step other than it's the one set before ye, so you're gonna take it."

I cross my arms. "So what? A lot of good people live their lives that way. Happy lives."

He looks at me as if that is the saddest joke he's ever heard. "Then there's no harm in givin' 'em a moment to think on it, is there? Now, hush."

He gestures toward the car. Time passes, and as announcement after useless announcement drones from the speakers, the faces of our fellow passengers morph from irritated to panicked, then furious. Some stay that way, jabbing at their phones and muttering. Some become still and introspective, as if they've put themselves in a trance, or a waking coma, until it's time to move again. The rest adopt either a faraway stare or a sideways squint.

Those are the ones I keep a close eye on. After a while, their expressions crack, and the tears come.

"That's why we're here?" I ask Ed. "To give people a chance to…think?"

He chuckles and shakes his head. "Nah, that's just a bit o' fun. Tell me, girl, how're your feet feelin'?"

"Fine." I pedal my heels to test them. "Light. Loose. Your trick works."

"Aye. And the rest o' ye?"

I'm not sure what he's getting at, but I play along, waving my arms and bouncing on my knees.

He's right. Something's different. I'm buoyant, like every molecule of weight and worry has floated away. Without a doubt, this is the lightest I've felt since starting my Walk—and maybe even since I arrived in England. "How?"

He points at the ground. A wide, solid strip of gold runs the length of the car, so brilliant it's almost white.

"There are lots o' choices on the surface," he says. "You've seen 'em on the sidewalks. The streets are almost as bad. But on the rail, there's only one path, and it's goin' to take you where you mean to go. No choices. No pressure. Respite. Relief." He shakes his head at the fuming, frustrated mob. "Shame they don't realize it."

I frown at the floor. Not sure I'd like to have only one path available to me, even if it did take me where I wanted to go. But obsessing over every little step does sound exhausting.

I lick my lips as a question occurs to me. One I'm not sure I want to ask, especially while I'm trapped in a train car. Then again, it's why I'm here. "If you spend so much time thinking about where your feet are taking you, how can you attack someone without remembering it?"

"I wish I could tell ye," he sighs. "Wish to God I could. But all I know is that it happened. I lost my feet, my mind, my control, and when I came to, someone was hurt. And I as scared as you that it'll happen again."

My stomach clenches. God, I remember how that feels all too well. "You know what happened this time because I was there to wake you up, but you don't remember the others, right?"

He shakes his head but says nothing.

"Were you here during the original Whitechapel murders?"

He takes a long time to answer. "Aye, that I was."

"What do you remember about them?"

"I remember it bein' a terrifyin' time in Whitechapel. But...if I dun 'em like I did these, I don' remember nothin' about it."

I lean back against the wall next to him, and we lapse into a silence that would be uncomfortable were I not so consumed with the puzzle before me. The reason Scotland Yard won't entertain the possibility that the 1888 murders and the present ones are the work of the same person is the same reason Edward's claim of being influenced may be false: the timeline. If the same person did both, they would be at least a hundred and fifty years old. As far as I know, no human has made it past a hundred and thirty, and I doubt they were in any condition to go on a murderous rampage by the end. Edward, however, was here for both. Which leads me right back to the original question—is he lying?

The train lurches forward, then jerks back. I'm not ready for it, and I lose my balance. Flinging out my arms, I prepare to hit the floor. My stomach slams into my spine, and—

I'm on my feet again, my back pressed to the wall.

No. Not the wall.

Edward.

"Steady on," he says. "You a'right?"

"Yeah, I'm fine," I say, waiting for him to uncurl his arm from around me.

That doesn't happen. His nose, and then his mouth, graze the back of my neck. I don't want to shiver, but my body betrays me. He makes a noise that's somewhere between a growl and a whimper and squeezes me tighter.

"Hey!" I grab his fingers and peel them back so hard they snap. He grunts like I've hurt him, but that's impossible. Nothing can hurt you here. He's angling for sympathy. I maintain my hold, keeping one eye on his hand to make sure it stays a hand. "What do you think you're doing?"

"I'm sorry," he pants, raising his free palm in surrender. "I swear, I dinna mean anythin'. I just...I always wondered what it would be like."

I tighten my grip. "What *what* would be like?"

"Touch." His brows tighten. "When I picked you up in the station, that was the first time I ever touched anyone. I...I wanted to feel it one more time."

"You've killed at least three people and assaulted a fourth. Not your fault, maybe, but it was still your hands. What do you call that?"

He whips his head to either side in vehement denial. "That dunna count."

"I think they'd disagree."

"I don' remember doin' those things!" His voice cracks. "I don' remember touchin' 'em, and I know no one has ever touched me. Not until today."

I unleash an exasperated sigh and release him. Mocking a known killer isn't the smartest move in the first place, and especially not when he's spilling his soul on the ground in front of me.

"I'm sorry," he says again as I take my spot next to him on the wall. We must have missed the latest overhead announcement during our tussle but based on the movement and the tension draining from the air, the train is running fine once again. "I dinna mean to be forward with ye."

"It's alright," I say. I have to admit, it felt nice to be touched without the Rigour blasting me for unsavory conduct.

Wait...why *didn't* I get blasted? Because of where we are? Or...or because of who it was?

I cast a sideways glance at Edward. He's staring straight ahead, a thoughtful expression on his dark features.

Match.

One word. That's all it takes to make every muscle in my body tremble with rage. "You bitch."

"I beg yer pardon?"

"Nothing," I grumble. "I'm sick of being treated like a puzzle piece, that's all."

He frowns. "I canna say I know what that means."

"It's a long story, but...there's a chance the Rigour may be trying to push you and I together because it thinks we're a matching set. Apples must be with apples, one and one must make two. Together, we fit its dumb little schematic. "

"Ah." He thinks about this for a long time. "But...inna way, isn' that what we are?"

His thumb curls around my hand and presses into my palm. A second traitorous shiver rolls down my back and I screw my eyes shut. He's a killer, I remind myself. Maybe even a bad one.

More importantly, he's not Breitling.

I shake him off and fold my arms. "How long do you normally stay down here?"

"A few hours," he says, tucking his hand into his pocket. "I can stay on the train from end to end, but no matter where I get off, I always come out at Whitechapel Station."

I check the clock above the door at the other end of the car. It's hours before I need to report back, but damn, I need a break. "If you're going to be here for a while, I'm going to check in with my people. I'll tell them everything you've told me and see if they've gotten any information we can use."

"You're leavin'?"

His alarm makes me pause. "Well, yeah. Either now or later."

"But what if–?" He clears his throat. "What if...*it*, happens again?"

"Well...we could put an intentions threshold around Whitechapel Station. Or some other place where you feel safe, if you have one?"

He thinks for a moment, then nods. "There's a place on the strand near the Tower wall. Rivers flow a lot the same as rails. The lesser number o' paths, the calmer me heart."

"Perfect. We'll get off at the next stop and go straight there. I'll have a threshold put up along the entire bank. That will keep you safe until I return."

"A'right," he says, but he doesn't sound sure.

Despite my better judgment, I tug on his sleeve until he takes his hand out of his pocket so I can hold it. He stiffens, then eases into the contact, his grip molding to mine like he's done it a thousand times. "I won't be long,"

I assure him. "An hour at most, I promise. You'll be okay."

He nods at the ground. He seems so sincere, so earnest...and so scared.

"Hey." I squeeze his hand. He closes his eyes for a moment before he looks at me. "So, what do you think of it? Touch, I mean?"

He smiles, but his brows draw together, as if the question hurts him. "It's wonderful."

Twenty-Four

The spot Edward mentioned is a tiny spit of sand at the base of the motley brick and flagstone wharf between the Tower wall and the Thames, close to the entrance known as Traitor's Gate. I tell him to mark the spot with an X, then stand on that so they know where to put the threshold. When he's done as I've instructed, I pull back from the railing, breathe deep, and return to the land of the living, where I tell Thomas about Edward's location. As I pull on my clothes, he calls McNally and tells him the same.

"Reaper Newton's on his way to the river now," Thomas says after I join him in the parking lot. "And we've been summoned to the conference room. It appears your…ah, display this morning has yielded results. They've finished searching the Operator database and want to go over what they found."

"Great," I say. "In that case, I suppose I'll wait to share what I've learned with the class."

Before the meeting, I stop off in the bathroom and check my messages. All thirty of them. All from Ruth, all with the same general theme: I need to call her *yesterday*. Ignoring the voice in my head that warns of death by international roaming fees, I do as instructed.

"Are you okay?"

Her demand is so loud I reel back from the speaker. "Of course I am. I'm calling you, aren't I?"

"Good." Her relieved sigh distorts the audio. *"We've got news. Kinda."*

We? I do some quick math. The eight-hour time difference means it's after midnight in Vegas. "Is Jake there?"

"Just for another minute or two," she says a bit defensively. *"He came by for dinner—well, my dinner. It was breakfast for him, I guess. We ate and worked on the case, and I guess time got away from us."* She drops her voice to a whisper. *"It's nothing, you know, romantic or whatever, I promise. I guess I've just gotten used to having someone to talk to other than Mama. I mean, she's great, but…well, you know."*

"Oh, I know." I chuckle even as her vulnerability makes my heart throb. She misses me? I have to say, I'm stunned. Our chats revolve around work, soap operas, and boys—or in her case, boys and girls. It's not like I was giving her life-altering guidance or anything. "So, what did you guys find out?"

"Right! Okay, this is so weird. It—what?"

She goes silent as Jake says something in the background.

"What's happening?" I ask.

"Hang on." There's a sequence of sharp rustling sounds before she returns to the line. Her voice has taken on the tinny echo of a speakerphone. *"Okay, we're both on now."*

"Cheerio, Miss A!" Jake shouts in a horrendous Manchester accent. *"How's jolly ol' England treatin' ya?"*

"It's fine," I say. "And you don't have to scream. I can hear you."

"Sorry, love. This accent only comes in one volume, innit?"

"Oh my God," Ruth half-groans, half-giggles. *"Stop being weird and let me tell her what we found."*

"Right-o." Jake clears his throat and returns sans accent. *"Sorry about that."*

"Anyway," Ruth says. *"I posted the names you gave me on the Lisbon, Cairo, and Iowa sections of the Vigilant website, as well as the board for the UK at large."*

"Which is dope, by the way," Jake calls from the near background. *"I'm signing up to get a secret decoder ring of my own the minute I get home."*

"Yeah, so, everyone was a little nervous about investigating something the police are working on, but I kinda…pulled rank, I guess you'd call it?"

"Are you saying you're, like, Vigilant brass?" I ask.

"Yeah, she is!" Jake crows over Ruth's embarrassed pause. *"How does it feel to be related to the Godfather, A? Or…Godmother. Goddess-father?"*

"Ooh, Goddess-father," Ruth murmurs. *"I like it."*

"Goddess-father it is."

"Glad we got that figured out," I cut in. "Now, you were saying?"

"Right, sorry," Ruth continues. *"After I convinced them that this isn't something the police are equipped to handle–without getting into specifics, of course–they ran with it. I've already gotten a ton of intel on the first three victims. Report cards, traffic citations. No medical records yet. Not sure if they can get those, but it wouldn't surprise me."*

"Did they find anything interesting?" I grip the counter to stifle my impatience. I'm glad Ruth is proud of her people. She has every reason to be. But I'm on a clock here.

Silence takes over. Even the scratchy sound of Jake's fidgeting has gone quiet.

"Well…they did, and they didn't," Ruth says at last. *"There's stuff, but it's all different, and it's all pretty minor. Tiago Silva has a couple of outstanding speeding tickets in Lisbon. Fatima Hassan was accused of plagiarizing a paper during college, but it turned out some rival academic made it all up. Annie Turner got a disorderly conduct mark in college for streaking a football game during rush week. And I haven't done much on Emma yet, but so far, she's your average wife and mother who's never even swiped a cookie from one of the many bake sales she's organized. Either they're all secret agents with titanium-coated cover stories, or you've found the four most boring victims in the UK. Maybe the world."*

My shoulders slump. "I can't believe it. There's *nothing* that connects them?"

"There is one thing," Jake says. *"It's super inside baseball, but just the kind of thing a Ripper copycat would know."*

"Go on," I prod.

"Fair warning, you may need to write this down." He takes a breath. *"Tiago Silva and Martha Tabran. Killed at the same location. Fatima Hassan and Mary Ann Nichols. Same location, and both forty-three years old. Annie Turner and Dark Annie Chapman. Same location, same time of attack, and obviously, same first name. And finally: Emma Long and Elizabeth 'Long Liz' Stride. Name, location, age, and time. All match."*

I frown. "Elizabeth Stride was killed at midnight, wasn't she? Emma Long was attacked in the middle of the day."

"Yeah." He pauses for effect. *"Around 12:30 in both cases, correct?"*

Fuck, he's right. "You think they're finding victims that align more closely to the original murders the closer they get to the end of the list."

"I don't know how the hell they're doing it, but yeah. If they keep the pattern, Catherine Eddowes will be next. If I were you, I'd have cops standing guard around Mitre Square, or whatever is there now, and bar access to anyone named Catherine, Kathy, Kate—and maybe Edwina and Edith too, just to be safe."

"I'll pass that along," I say, leaving out the fact that we've already got Reapers all over it. "Nice work. Both of you."

"Aw, thanks, A. We're happy to help."

"Yes. We are." Ruth's pride emanates from the speaker. *"And I'll keep looking for other connections. You never know."*

"Okay. Thank you."

"No problem." There's more fumbling, and Ruth returns to the line, sounding less tinny and borderline scandalized. *"How is everything else going? With…you know…"*

My stomach squirms. The last thing I want to talk about right now is my love life. "It's fine."

"That's it?" Her concern, colored by disappointment, brings a blush of shame to my cheeks. She's expecting tales of sordid dalliances that will curl her stick-straight hair. But I've got nothing.

"It's a long story," I hedge. "I've got to run, but I'll call you later."

"Okay. Take care of yourself."

"Will do. Love you, Sis."

"Yeah. I love you too."

All the usual suspects, except for Newton, are waiting for me when I arrive in the conference room. McNally sits at the head as usual, a stack of manila folders next to him. Thomas is on the far side this time, and Breitling has retaken his seat near the door. He swivels in his chair as I enter, hands pressing on the armrests as if he's about to stand up, but he stops himself. Instead, he gives me a once over, as if making sure I still have all the expected parts, before nodding a greeting. "Miss Venture."

"Chief Inquisitor." I slide into the chair next to him. He turns to the table as well, and as he does, his foot bumps the outside of my leg. I'm not sure if it's intentional or not. Either way, it makes my body break out in goosebumps.

No.

My shoulders tighten, and I duck my head, bracing for the hit. But nothing happens. No pain. Just that one word. *No.*

"Adina?"

I raise my eyes to Breitling. "Yes?"

"The Constable asked you a question."

"Oh?" I turn to McNally. "Sorry, I didn't catch that."

He sucks in a breath. "I was simply inquiring as to whether or not you might be amenable to regaling us with the events of your day thus far, assuming the circumstances of our reconvention are now pleasing to you, of course."

I grip the edge of the table and wait for my head to stop swimming. "*That* wasn't necessary."

Breitling's ears, and in fact his whole body, perk up. "What wasn't–?"

"Nothing," I say as I glower at McNally. His hands lay entwined across his belly as he regards me with a smug smile. It wasn't the full whammy, but it was enough to muddle my brain and piss me off. Maybe it was punishment for embarrassing him earlier. Or, more likely, he enjoys flexing his meager muscles on people who, for whatever reason, can't or won't fight back.

Taking a moment to let my rage bleed out, I relay the events of the morning in faithful detail, even the ones I'd rather forget. When I get to the part about sliding across Whitechapel Station, Breitling tries and fails to stifle a chuckle.

"What?" I ask.

"Oh, nothing," he says around his laughter. "Just that being stuck in an unfamiliar realm with a highly skilled know-it-all who'd rather make jokes than help you…that sounds frustrating."

I narrow my eyes. "It's better than being a rigid authoritarian who refuses to leave the moral high ground long enough to have a good time."

His delighted smirk sparks a litany of emotions I can't do anything about. So, I move on with my story. When I get to the part about Edward picking me up, his delight disappears. "He touched you?"

I shrug. "Only for a minute."

"But he didn't hurt you, right?" Thomas interjects.

I shake my head. "There was a cold shock at first, but it went away. Kind of like static discharge. He said it was the first time he remembers ever touching anyone else, so maybe that's the reason for it."

"Fascinating," Thomas murmurs. Breitling, however, has gone silent. He stares at the table, his jaw clenched and his hands strangling the arms of his chair.

McNally clears his throat. "Anything else, Miss Venture?"

I rush through the rest of the story, but I leave out the part about Ed catching me from falling on the train and everything that resulted from it. No one needs to hear about that.

"Excellent work," McNally says as he taps his phone. "With the intentions threshold now in place on the strand, that should give us enough time to discuss what we've discovered in our registration search. But first, considering the attack on Emma Long, I'd like to start with the updated victimology report."

I sit forward and try to appear eager. I don't want to give away that I already know the answers.

McNally picks up the manila folders, three of which I recognize as belonging to our first victims. They're about fifty percent bigger now. "We have identified a connection between all four victims. Each one has a long history of drug and alcohol abuse. Mr. Silva and Ms. Long also have charges of possession with intent to sell."

"What?" At least I don't have to fake interest anymore. "Are you sure?"

"Quite. We have our best Scribes working this background. I'm sure they've missed nothing." He turns as if trying to hand the files to someone. Recalling that he's unattended, he rises with a groan and passes them around. Breitling and Thomas each take one. I don't. This can't be right. Ruth is nothing if not meticulous. She'd never miss something so big and obvious, and she wouldn't let anyone else get away with that either. Do all four victims actually have cover stories her network can't penetrate? Possible, but that seems unlikely. At the very least, it's something McNally would have mentioned.

Which means someone is lying.

"Very interesting," Breitling mutters in a bland tone. He tosses the folder on the table and clasps his hands. "However, I'm not sure what connection that has with our potential puppet master."

"What did you find out, Chief?" I ask.

For the first time since I finished speaking, he looks at me. His mouth twitches, and while he's still perturbed, he also seems happy I'd asked. "Of the two hundred and six registered Aetherists and Chronologists Operating within fifty miles of Whitechapel, only two have the requisite abilities to either ensnare or influence another person's mental or physical faculties."

He dips into his jacket for his glasses and notebook. Watching his long, pale fingers slide over the pages makes my blood heat. He must sense my gaze, because he lifts his head. Arching a brow, he runs the tip of his finger over his tongue, then lowers it, stroking the paper thoughtfully, sensuously, before turning the page. A soft sigh escapes me. His eyes sparkle devilishly.

"No."

I bite the inside of my cheek. *Why not? I'm settling for this stupid theater, but I want him. I miss him. I–*

My stomach tightens in a warning as the acidic taste of bile climbs up my throat.

Fine. You win. Wrapping my arms around my midsection, I slump back in my chair. "Only two out of two hundred, huh? How did you narrow it down that far?"

His mouth twists in frustration. The feeling is pretty fucking mutual.

"It's not a very common skill set." He skims the page, then addresses McNally. "Do the names Ogden and Noles sound familiar to you, Constable?"

He narrows his eyes. "They're Biologian Aetherists, if I'm not mistaken."

"That's correct."

"And if memory serves, they are *already* in Order custody."

Breitling ducks his head and regards his notebook. "Also correct."

I raise my hand like a kid in school.

"Samantha Ogden and Bertrand Noles are two of the most notorious criminal Operators in UK history," Breitling says without waiting for my question. "Noles owned an apple orchard, and he and Ogden spent the late fall of 1989 selling apples imbued with some very unsavory urges, the most common being cannibalism. Whenever anyone ate one of their apples, the urge overtook them and continued until the material left their system. Luckily, the effect was so frantic and obvious, most of the victims were identified and restrained within minutes. There were no deaths, and as far as we can tell, neither Noles nor Ogden gained materially from their campaign. According to their post-detention remarks, they, quote, 'got off on it,' unquote. When their wares ended up on the dinner table of a member of Parliament, the party ended. They were caught and remanded to the Pit, where I *assume* they remain to this day."

He peers over his glasses at McNally.

"No one who enters the Pit leaves, Inquisitor," McNally says. "They are interred in isolation, given nothing but food rations and adequate water, until they expire of natural causes. Ogden and Noles are alive and in physical conditions commensurate with Order bylaws, but I assure you, neither of them is capable of...well, anything."

Damn. And I thought the Summit had nasty retribution tactics.

"Now then," he continues, "As much as I appreciate your diligence, Inquisitor, it appears your efforts have yielded nothing. We are no closer to finding this supposed master, nor do we have a plan to address the continuing threat that the creature—"

"Edward," I cut in. "Well, technically, Edward Knifeyhands. But I didn't tell him about the last name for obvious reasons."

"You *named* him?"

Breitling's voice is ice cold as it rolls over my shoulders. "I have to call him something. Besides, he said I could."

"In any case," McNally forges ahead. "For all your grand ideas, it doesn't change the fact that this city is still in danger. He needs to be neutralized. *Now*."

Sounds like someone got another strongly worded email from an account with a .crown domain. "That's not necessary, Constable. Ed and I have a rapport now. He trusts me. More importantly, he doesn't want to kill anyone else."

He snorts. "I don't see how that matters. Either he's a liar and your rapport is an illusion, or he's a puppet and it is irrelevant. A mindless killing machine can't stop itself from killing, no matter how much it claims to like you."

"He's not a machine, and he's *not* mindless." I rise to my feet. "Besides, it seems you've lost sight of one small yet crucial fact: I'm still the only one that can reach him. Even if I knew how to go about…*neutralizing* him, I have no intention of doing so anytime soon."

That little trump card should put him in his place. Instead, he smiles at me like I've walked right into his trap. "Are you sure about that?"

"Constable." Breitling sets his notebook on the table. "Would you mind if I spoke with Miss Venture in private for a moment?"

"Yes, I think you'd better." McNally nods like a king deigning to grant a lowly commoner's request.

Suddenly, I feel like I've lost a game I didn't know I was playing.

"What's going on?" I ask Breitling after Thomas and McNally leave.

He pulls off his glasses and tosses them on top of the notebook. "He knows about the Lash. About how I can use it to follow you."

"What?" I gasp. "You–did you–?"

"No," he says, unable to look at me. "Castillo did."

"So you told *him*?"

"It was a relevant Operational discovery that stood to help or harm Order functions. I had to document it in my case report. He never mentioned it, so I assumed it was a non-issue. But after you left this morning, McNally pulled me aside and told me I should prepare for the eventuality of following you to the Deathplane. I am to restrain the suspect and determine how truthful he has been. By any means."

I almost gag on the lump in my throat. "They asked you to perform an inquiry…in the Deathplane?"

"It's not a request, Adina. If you can't—or won't—neutralize him on your own, it's an order."

"But…but we didn't try that when you followed me last time. We have no idea what it could do to Ed. Or—or to you."

He shrugs. "It's an order."

Ugh, that *would* be his answer. But *I'm* under no such orders, and even if I were, I'm not like him, Pledged and compelled to obey. "Fine. If you're all determined to go after him yourselves, I guess I can't stop you. But I wonder–how do you plan to get to him without me?"

His head snaps up. Upon seeing my resolute stare, his eyes fill with alarm. "Before you go off on some ill-advised protest, think about where you are. This is a prison, Adina. An old prison, with old ideas about how to treat inmates."

From anyone else, this would sound like an idle threat. From him, to me, with that specific expression on his face, it's a plea.

Maybe I am being stupid. But I'm also the only one taking Edward's side in all of this. Lingering questions aside, I still believe he's telling the truth. The bizarre victimology discrepancy is further confirmation that something is rotten in the state of London. Until I figure out what's going on, I can't let them tear his brain apart.

Them.

My stomach clenches. Not because I'm staring down a big, bad group of men in suits. That's another Tuesday at this point. What kills me is that this time, Breitling is one of them.

"Sorry." I sit back and cross my arms. "Torture me however you like. I'm not going anywhere."

His brows lower into that appraising look I know so well. "Why do you care about this man so much?"

"Because *someone* needs to. And because he's...like me. We're the same, or close enough."

His body constricts, as if taking a punch. "I see."

That's a big reaction for such an innocuous statement, and I think I know why. I lean toward him, keeping my voice low. "Breitling, are you...*jealous?*"

He glares at me for a moment before busying himself with the manila folder lying open in front of him.

"Fine, don't answer me," I say. "But for the record, I'd be making the same arguments if this were a female ghost-killer. Hell, I think I'd be even angrier."

His cheeks flush. "It's not that. It's...I...I just..."

I'm about to poke more fun at his flusterment when his shoulders slump and he sighs so heavily he seems to shrink by half.

Because he's like me. We're the same.

Oh, God. He is jealous, but not for the reason I thought. At least, not *only* for that reason. Though, in my defense, he's never come out and told me he's the only one like him. His subordinate, Inquisitor Tory, was the one who hit me with that knowledge. And until now, I'd always thought I was the only one like me.

Until now, *he* and I were the same.

My heart throbs. "Oh, Levi…"

He shakes his head at the table. "There will be consequences for this, Adina. For something this serious, this important to the Crown and therefore the Tower, they will deem your refusal to cooperate as a betrayal. They'll detain you, and I…I won't be able to stop them."

His clear desperation makes me want to cave. Digging my fingernails into my arms, I stare at the sharp outline of his profile with cold resolve. "I'm sorry. I am. But I've made my decision."

"I thought as much." He scrubs his hands over his face. His stormy eyes are as resolute as mine. I press my tongue to the roof of my mouth and squint to staunch the impending tears. This isn't how any of this was supposed to go.

But then again, isn't it? He's an Inquisitor, and I'm…me. Was it ever going to go any other way?

He pulls in a breath. "Adina, listen to me–"

But I don't get the chance. The door slams open and Thomas rushes in.

"Levi—" He stops when he sees the composition we're in. "What's happened?"

"Nothing," Breitling says, drawing himself out of his slump. "What is it?"

"You're needed in Whitechapel. Both of you. I don't know how Edward got past the threshold, but there's been another attack. Another death."

Breitling springs to his feet. "We had Reapers stationed at Mitre Square. Why didn't they intervene?"

"Because it's not at Mitre Square. And the victim, it's…" Thomas swallows hard. "Levi, it's one of ours."

Twenty-Five

Breitling drives the service van with Thomas riding shotgun and me in the back, along with a pile of dirt so I can hit the ground running—or rather, Walking—the moment we arrive at the scene. It's not ideal, but I can't use the handkerchief.

I mean, maybe I could. But it's not worth the risk. A ticking clock is not the ideal soundtrack for your first time using the artifact of a dead man.

Steely clouds hang in the sky above the dreary office building, and the wind whistles through the broad entrances that lead from the street into the empty central courtyard. At least, it's empty to those who can't see the golden-gray rat's nest of the Underhalt filling it to the brim. Apparently, this block has been a lot of things over the years: offices and commercial space; a parking structure; public houses with rooms for rent; and, of course, the scene of an infamous, grisly murder.

Actually, make that two.

Three or four cops and a few Reapers cluster in the southeast corner as we approach. They part for us (or rather, for Breitling and Thomas), and I see him: Gordon Gaye, my erstwhile ferryman, sprawled on the concrete. To anyone walking by at a distance, he would look like a passed-out drunk. Up close, it's a different story. Black, purple and red splotches mar his face, and blood soaks the unkempt stubble covering his chin. His ripped shirt exposes the mosaic of bruises covering his broad belly. Though his arms and legs are all present, each one appears crumpled and broken in at least three places. I don't need to see the autopsy report to know that his organs will seem like they've been through a food processor, and his limbs will appear to be disarticulated from the inside. He'll also be missing his intestines, and a bunch of other viscera I don't recognize and have no desire to examine more thoroughly as it lies strewn around the corpse. How Edward managed to pull all of that between the planes, I have no idea. Either way, the fact remains—Gordon Gaye is no longer a man, but a bag of skin filled with too many bones and not enough innards.

The bracing wind rustles Breitling's hair and he shivers. I, of course, don't feel a thing, other than gnawing dread. "Ed, what the hell have you done?"

"Do you see him?" Breitling mutters through almost immobile lips. Given the public setting, and especially in the presence of NO police, it's important that he keeps his comments discreet.

"No," I say. "And to be honest, I doubt I will. Why would he hang around a crime scene when he knows we'll be searching for him?"

He eyeballs my modified Victorian prostitute outfit. "Why do you think?"

"Oh, come on," I scoff. "He wouldn't risk detainment or worse because *I'm* here."

"But I thought you had…*rapport?*"

I grit my teeth and count to ten. He may be able to see and hear me while I'm Walking, but he can't touch me. The opposite, however, isn't the case. I could smack him upside the head right now and he wouldn't be able to do a thing about it. I'm debating if the repercussions I'd face downstream would be worth the immediate satisfaction when I spot a flicker of movement in the shadows to my right.

Ed?

Moving with silent grace so as not to alert Breitling, I slip away. Edward has balled himself up in the corner, his chin resting on his knees, hat missing and dark hair hanging over his face. His walking stick lies on the ground next to him. The sight of it fills me with guilt. It had given him the ability to teleport through the Deathplane once before. That must be how he escaped the threshold. Goddammit, *why* didn't I think of that? Unwilling to make the same mistake twice, I fling the walking stick into the courtyard and out of reach before kneeling in front of him.

"Ed," I whisper. "It's me."

He stiffens. "Dun do that."

"Do what?"

"Be kind to me." He buries a hand in his hair. "I killed 'em, din' I? I don' remember it, but I musta done. What other explanation is there?"

As much as I wish I had another to give him, he's right. There isn't one. "What *do* you remember?"

Setting his head against his knees, he rocks back and forth, preparing to recount the story. I glance over my shoulder. Breitling has moved closer to the middle of the courtyard. He stands with his hands on his hips and his head down as McNally rails at him about something. Off to the side, Thomas has one arm wrapped around his torso while the other covers his mouth. Whatever they're discussing, it's upsetting to all three of them.

"I was at the river's edge, right where ye left me." Edward's soft, shaky voice pulls me back. "Just sittin' there by the water like I like, when a feelin' come upon me like someone had grabbed hold a' me head with both hands and was yankin' and pullin' like they meant to rip it off. I tried ignorin' it at first, thinkin' I could wait it out and maybe it would stop. But it kept comin', gettin' stronger an' stronger. And then…"

He rolls his forehead, his fingers picking at the beds of his nails. "Next thing ye know, I'm standin' over that poor bastard, and he's lookin' up at me–right fuckin' at me– askin' *why*. Beggin' me to spare his life. I saw people walkin' by on the street outside, and I shouted for help, but they kept goin'. They didn't see the blood. Just a crazy old man screamin' at nothin'. 'Twasn't 'til some barback comin' off his shift walked through and spotted 'em that he was seen to, but by then he was…he…"

Edward curls into himself, shaking with stifled sobs.

It sounds like what I'd seen on Henriques Street, and though I don't know for sure, I'm guessing the corner where Gaye expired more or less matches where they found Mary Kelly, the Ripper's fifth and final canonical victim.

But the pattern…the pattern is wrong. Tiago Silva and Martha Tabran shared a location. Mary Ann Nichols and Fatima Hassan shared location and age. Annies Turner and Chapman–location, name, and time of death. And Emma Long–Location. Name. Age. TOD, albeit in reverse. With every death, another point of similarity.

Until now.

I hug my knees. While I don't know much about Gordon Gaye, I know he was decades older than 25, which was how old Mary Kelly was when the Ripper got her. Their names obviously don't match, and while I can't remember her exact time of death, I think it was between six and ten in the morning. It's a little past four in the afternoon now, which makes that strike three. Even the location isn't quite right. We should be at Mitre Square, the site of the fourth murder, where half the Tower's Reaper Corp has been standing sentinel, waiting to sound the alarm. Instead, we're here. The pattern, such as it was, had been moving toward alignment. Now, it's all the way back to one. Maybe even zero.

What the hell happened?

Edward hiccups, then turns his tear-stained face to me. "What're they gonna do with me now?"

My chest pangs. Suddenly I'm back on my couch in the pool casita, covered in a blanket and holding a crushed sleeve of Saltines, asking Breitling the same question. Now, I'm the one who has to answer.

"I hate this." I don't mean to say that out loud, but it's true. I'm a killer of *bad* people. I never wanted to have someone innocent hand me their life with the feeble hope that I don't crush it in my fist. I hate it, and I don't want it…and that's too fucking bad. I'm here now, and he's waiting for my answer, and I have to tell him something.

"I think—"

A sharp pain pierces the back of my neck and spreads down my limbs. My body goes rigid and a high-pitched screech rips from my throat.

"Mother o' God!" Edward yells as he scrambles backward. "What's hap'nin'?"

I don't know, is my instinctual response. Only that's not true. This pain may be sudden, but it's not unfamiliar. And thank God, it's temporary. A moment later it's gone, and I fall forward over my knees.

"I'm…going…to *kill* you," I growl.

Edward's eyes widen in terror. "What?"

"No. Not you." I round on the gigantic, blond, soon-to-be-dead man looming behind me. "Him."

I swear, my ethereal stylist has one hell of a sense of humor; Breitling is dressed exactly like a Victorian-era cop. Silver buttons run down the front of his long navy jacket, which is cinched at the waist by a black belt with a silver buckle. He's even got the domed hat with the stupid little chinstrap. I want nothing more than to laugh at him. The fact that I'm too angry to do that only fuels my rage.

Edward gasps, but I don't hear him move. The shock of this intimidating and unfamiliar presence must have paralyzed him.

Breitling seizes the opportunity. Sidestepping me with ease, he lunges for Edward.

"Don't!" I shout. He doesn't listen, so I dive for him. Edward may be frozen, but I'm not.

I catch Breitling around the leg, upsetting his balance and bringing him to one knee. He grunts, but he doesn't lose focus. With his long reach, he grabs Edward's head with both hands and drags him close.

My heart rate spikes. Abandoning his leg, I throw myself on his back and grab hold of his biceps. It won't stop him, but it's all I've got. "Please. We don't know how—"

"It's this or I kill him."

My heart drops. This sounds nothing like the man I know, the man I…care about. Right now, he sounds every bit the cold, unfeeling Inquisitor I once thought him to be. "He can't be killed."

"Are you sure?"

"Dammit, Levi!" I dig my nails into his arm. "Please don't do this."

"I have to. He's a murderer."

"He didn't know what he was doing!"

"And an inquiry will prove that!"

I rock onto my heels. It's been a long time since he's shouted at me like that. I want to shout back, but my logical mind asserts itself before I have the chance. As hurt as I am about what he's done, it *is* done, and...dammit, he *is* right. His inquiry technique is infallible, and his word is gospel. If Chief Inquisitor Levi Breitling swears Edward wasn't responsible for his actions, everyone will believe it.

With a deep breath, I let him go. "Fine. But you and I are not finished. Not at all."

He bobs his head, then addresses Edward. "This will be easier for you if you don't resist me."

Edward blinks, his panicked gaze fixing on me.

"It's okay," I whisper over Breitling's shoulder. "He'll see the truth. And when he speaks, people listen. Important people."

"Will it hurt?"

Fuck. I'd been hoping he wouldn't ask me that. But I'm not about to lie to him. "Yes, it will hurt. But if you cooperate, it won't last long."

His brows crush together. I can feel Breitling's agitation rising with every silent moment. How long do I wait before pointing out to Edward that this is happening with or without his say so?

At last, the frantic look fades, and his eyes settle on Breitling. "Go on then."

Breitling doesn't hesitate, slamming Edward's head back until he's gaping at the sky in a silent scream.

"Show me," Breitling murmurs, irises glowing their brilliant cerulean blue.

Wait, how can I see that? I'm sitting behind him. I mean, I've seen his eyes during an inquiry, so I can conjure the image of them in my head. But this isn't a memory. They're right in front of me. So is Edward, but he's filmy and blurred, like he's wrapped in crinkled plastic.

"Show me," Breitling repeats, and the blue eyes in front of me disappear. "Yes…I see it."

"I know." The translucent waves of the Thames stream across my vision. "I see it too."

The waves stutter. "What?"

"Don't worry about it." I grope around until I find his shoulder. "Just concentrate."

His muscles shift with his nod, and the picture stabilizes, growing more solid with every moment. Weak sunlight illuminates the water that stretches out in front of me. I sit with my knees drawn to my chest and the toes of my shoes digging into the soft sand. It's even colder than usual, and the stench of old trash and rotting fish almost smothers me. But at least it's quiet, the noise and bustle of the crowds a mere whisper beneath the rush of the river. I gulp in the rank air, feeling unaccountably at ease.

It doesn't last.

The pain is as Edward said it would be, like something has trapped my head in a vice and wants to rip it off.

"Good God," Breitling groans. "What *is* that?"

"I don't know," I say, my fingers kneading his shoulder. "He told me this is how it happened, but I—"

We both gasp as the pain intensifies. Black splotches stain the waves as my spine stretches beyond what I'd thought possible. My fingers dig into the sand, trying in vain to hold myself to the spot.

"Please, no. Please, please, no."

While I agree with that sentiment, those aren't my thoughts. They aren't thoughts at all. It's Edward, suffering on the shore and in the courtyard, tears streaming down both sets of cheeks.

Breitling curls forward, his body wracked with chills. He must be getting the full hit of whatever this is, and it's edging toward too much. I grip him tighter, grind my teeth, and pray that it ends soon.

"On your feet, Heartless."

That's not Ed. Or me. Or Breitling. It's high-pitched and nasal, with a gritty, mean quality lurking underneath a posh accent.

"Adina?"

"I heard it," I say as the pain, the images, everything disappears behind a curtain of black. "Wait. Is that...?"

The curtain falls away. Gordon Gaye lies sprawled on the concrete. He's battered, dying, but not dead. His mouth forms words I can't hear as he reaches for me. I look around the empty courtyard, then down at my hands.

My bloody, knife-shaped hands.

"Enough," I hiss. "Enough of this."

The images fade and Edward appears in front of me. "Did ye see it?" He reaches around Breitling and grabs my face in both his hands. "Did ye see?"

"Yes," I say as Breitling slides out from between us. "We know."

"Oh, thank God." He slumps forward into my arms, convulsing with sobs.

"It's okay," I say. "You're going to be okay."

"I'm sorry." He wraps his arms around me and buries his face in my shoulder. "I'm so fuckin' sorry."

I rock back and forth, one hand stroking his matted hair. "You have nothing to be sorry about."

I hold him until he stops trembling and his breathing returns to normal. When he speaks again, the first thing he manages is a soft, "Thank ye, girl. Thank ye."

Tears of my own threatening to fall, I say nothing and squeeze him tighter, enjoying the feeling of his smile against my shoulder. With a cleansing sigh, he presses his tear-soaked eyes against my neck. "What now?"

I crane my head toward the crime scene. Breitling stands outside the circle of activity, watching as the police load Gaye into a body bag. The organs, of course, will remain—most likely forever.

"Good question," I say loud enough for him to hear. "What now?"

Breitling turns away from the scene and returns to stand over us. His words are as stiff as his posture, and he delivers his speech to the wall. "With this new information, it's clear there's another player involved. We'll need to confer with the Constable about next steps, though I imagine he will be much less obstinate about using Tower resources to find this puppet master."

"What about me?" Edward asks, withdrawing from my arms but keeping hold of my waist.

"You will return to the strand, where I will incapacitate you. Painlessly. We will put another threshold in place and install a Reaper guard. That is where you will remain until the matter is resolved."

"Can you stay with me?"

Somehow, Breitling's face grows even colder. I turn around; Edward's staring at me with wide, desperate eyes.

"You'll be safe with the Reapers," I say, taking his hands from my waist and holding them in mine. "They can't hurt you, and they will make sure you don't leave without someone knowing about it."

He nods, but his shoulders slump. "I just...I don' wanna be alone anymore."

"It won't be for long," I say. "I promise."

"Well then...if it's *yer* promise I'm gettin', then I agree. Only yers." He raises one of my hands and his lips graze the bruised skin of my knuckles.

"Time to go." Breitling's frigid anger makes Edward tremble, but I'm not at all inclined to quake with fear. My anger sees to that.

"You don't make the calls here, *Inquisitor*," I say as I stand up. "This is *my* world. Mine, and his."

Extending my hand, I pull Edward up and head for the street.

"What are you doing?" Breitling calls after us. "You need to take me back. We must brief the Constable on all this."

Fresh rage surges through me. Of all the entitled fucking bullshit. "Wait here," I say to Edward, then whip around and charge at Breitling. He doesn't even flinch, the bastard. "Right now, I don't give a shit what you want. You Lashed me even though you knew I didn't want you to."

"It worked, didn't it?" he counters. "Now we know he's telling the truth. We even heard the puppet master's speak, for God's sake. Don't you think that's more important than—"

"Than what?" I cut him off. "My consent?"

His mouth moves, but no words come out. My heart slams against my ribcage as I wait. For an explanation, for an apology, for anything.

He drops his head and remains silent.

Well. That's an answer, all right. Tears burning in my eyes, I turn my back on him and dash out of the alley. "Come with now or come along later. I don't care. But I'm not leaving this plane until *I'm* ready."

Twenty-Six

Our walk to the river is one of the most painful ten-minute stretches of my life. Edward and I don't talk or touch, choosing instead to fill the time with sad, thoughtful silence. Breitling keeps pace with us but hangs back, maintaining a distance of about twenty feet.

He always was a smart one.

When we arrive at the Tower Wharf, Breitling lifts his hand over Edward's forehead, then grabs him around the waist before he can hit the ground. He won't wake up again without an Order-regulated antidote. Between that, the threshold, and the Reaper guard, he shouldn't be able to hurt anyone else.

I hope.

Breitling hefts the unconscious Edward over the railing and gently lowers him onto the X still carved in the sand. He's taken off that ridiculous hat, which means I can face him without laughing. But my anger—that's still there.

"Right. Now that that's done…" Wiping his hands, Breitling nods toward the Tower entrance.

Shaking my head, I stalk off in the opposite direction, weaving through the dense afternoon crowd of tourists. The van is probably back in the garage by now, our bodies inside it, with Thomas and McNally not far away, waiting for us to wake up. Well, they can fucking wait.

"Where are you going?"

And so can he.

I quicken my pace as Breitling's turn-of-the-century shoes tap on the stone path behind me. "Adina, the Constable needs this information so it can be acted upon immediately."

I don't answer him. I don't even turn around. Maybe it's unprofessional, but I need a fucking minute.

"I know you're angry," he continues. "And you have a right to be. But if I can explain—"

"Yeah, yeah," I toss over my shoulder. "McNally gave you an order. You had a job to do. What more is there to say?"

"There *is* more to say. A lot more. Just—Adina, stop!"

His footfalls cease. I take a few more steps before I pause as well. I'm being childish and stupid, and I know it. We're Lashed, and we work together, and…all the other things. I can't outrun him forever. But that doesn't mean I have to admit defeat. Raising my chin, I face him. "Fine. If you have more to say, then go ahead. Say it."

He narrows his eyes as if sensing a trap. "Despite what you may think, I understand why you're adamant about this…about Edward. And you were right—he *is* a victim. But while your instincts may have been enough proof for…certain people, we were always going to need something more concrete to guarantee his protection. An inquiry may well have been the only way to get it, and the only way I could perform one was by joining you here.

You *know* all of this. Frankly, Adina, I don't understand why you were so opposed to it."

"Because–" I hesitate, unsure if what I have to say is something I want to say out loud. "Because I was…scared, okay?"

"Ah," he says to the ground. "That's understandable. But as you can see, Edward came through it fine."

I tip my head back and laugh. "God, you're an idiot."

"I beg your pardon?"

"Forget it." I shake my head. "Anyway, you have the information you need, and I have 'at least no one's disfigured or worse.' It's all good, except for one thing."

"Which is?"

"You. And me. I know I have no right to expect loyalty from you when it's me versus the Order, but I never thought you'd *actively* betray me."

His face pinches, and he takes a tentative step forward. "Adina, I didn't–"

"I know," I cut him off. "You didn't have a choice. But it still sucks."

He halts his advance a few feet away from me. The crow's feet around his eyes deepen and his teeth clench as his head moves to either side. I've seen him do this before. That's his strategizing face. He's trying to figure out what words he should use to get the results he wants.

My stomach drops. After everything else, he's going to try to manipulate me too? *Fuck* that.

I turn and run.

"Adina!"

"No!" I shout. Childish and stupid? Most definitely. But I don't care. I need to get away from him, even if it's only for the next minute or two. He's not going to see how much he's hurt me. He's not going to see me cry.

He's lost that privilege.

I maintain my lead for a long time. With no need for oxygen and without the burden of lactic acid, plus how much more experienced I am with Deathplane calisthenics than he is, I could have raced him across the city. But then two things happen. One, his longer stride overcomes my experience; and two, I emerge from under the London Bridge overpass and instead of continuing straight along the river, I turn right into an alcove between the bridge and a stone building. I'd planned to make a clever detour and lose him in the twisty London alleys, but I'm foiled by a wrought-iron dead end. Pivoting on my toes, I reorient myself toward the river. That's as far as I get before he grabs me by the waist and spins me to face him, crushing me against the rough blue serge covering his chest.

"Let me go." I squirm as he wraps me in a bear hug that pins my arms at my sides.

"I'm done playing games," he says, my resistance not troubling him in the least. "Take us back to the land of the living."

"No."

"Why the hell not?"

"Because I don't want to. You can't barge in here and start telling me what to do. You and the Order make the rules everywhere else, but when you're in here, I'm in charge."

"Is that so?" he asks. "Because from where I'm standing, you're not in charge of anything, my dear."

"You'd like to think that, wouldn't you?" But we both know I'm posturing. I'm no match for him when I've got both arms free. Now, the only thing I can do is glare at him. So, I do it, with every furious fiber of my being.

Blinking rapidly, he averts his gaze, focusing on something above and behind me instead. "Stop it."

"Stop what? I can't do anything, remember?"

"Stop looking at me like that."

"Why? Because I'm angry?"

"Because...you're beautiful." His eyes fall to my lips, and his hold on me tightens.

No. I shake my head, determined to maintain my steely expression. "Don't you dare."

"I'd love to know how you plan to stop me."

His amusement reignites my fury. I lift my chin higher in defiance. "Fine then. Go ahead. You've made it clear you're going to do whatever you want. Why not go all the way with it?"

That slaps the smile off his face. "Do *not* insult me like that, Adina. You have no idea how hard this has been."

"Don't I?" I shoot back. "I'm the one who can't even think about you without getting smacked with an invisible ruler."

"You think that's made it easier for me?" His sharp tone cuts my last word in half. "You think it's easy to bear this constant ache like I'm missing a part of myself? Is it easy when every time I'm near you I want to touch you so badly I can't breathe? And then Edward. Seeing him with his hands on you, knowing that he can hold you like that whenever he wants...it's driving me mad."

His body heaves with air he doesn't need. To be honest, I'm breathing a little heavy myself. He's never gone off on a rant like that before. He's been protective, even possessive, but *never* like this. No matter how angry I am, seeing the pain clouding those beautiful, stormy irises hurts me too.

"He *can't* touch me whenever he wants, because *I* won't let him." I don't want to yell, but in my current state I can't pull off empathetic, so I settle for gentle scolding. "I don't want him, Levi. I want you. But you've made a commitment that I can never compete with. Compared to your Pledge, I'm nothing."

His jaw drops. "Is *that* what you think?"

I shrug as best I can in his death hug. "It's what I agreed to, isn't it?"

His forehead creases, but he doesn't seem angry. If anything, he seems horrified.

"Levi?" I ask after several moments of silence. "Are you okay?"

He blinks, and the look disappears. "Take us back, Adina."

The resolution has returned to his eyes, but not his grip. My lips curl into a triumphant smile. "No."

I throw myself backward. His hold breaks, and I race out of the shadowed alcove toward the river.

But he's so *fast*. I don't make it past the side of the building before his hand closes around my wrist and his other arm slams into my chest. He yanks, capturing me again, this time with my back to him.

"Take us back," he demands. "Now."

"No!"

He growls in frustration. "Then at least forgive me."

"Why should I?"

"Because I'm sorry. And because I asked you to."

"Not good enough." I roll my head away from him, but he grabs my chin and holds me in place. His strength and the heat of his breath on my neck threaten my resolve.

"Forgive me," he murmurs.

I clench my teeth and wait for the Rigour to kick in with its objection. It's bound to happen any minute now.

Any…minute…

He tugs my face in his direction. "Are you—?"

"Shut up." I shake off his grip and look down. The patchwork of paths is as dense here as it is everywhere else, but I don't feel their pull. Not at my feet, not at my stomach, not anywhere. I haven't since I started this Walk. Is my sigil doing this? Is it the Lash? Whatever the reason, one thing is for sure: at this moment, in this place, we're free.

"Adina?"

"Shut up." I turn to face him. "Just…shut up."

Standing on my toes, I press my mouth tentatively to his.

"Oh…" He moans as I run my tongue over his lower lip, but he doesn't return the kiss. I pull back and see a mix of emotions in his eyes. Fear. Desire. Hope. He swallows what sentiment he can before speaking. "Will you?"

Good question. I'm still mad at him. And I want to stay mad at him, at least for a little while.

But I want this more.

"Yes. I will."

That's all it takes. I knew it would be. The arm around me tightens while his other hand slides up the front of my skirt and pushes my undergarment aside. His first touch makes me shudder. My head falls back against his shoulder. "Mm, Levi…"

"Oh God, yes." He grabs my breast, pinning me against him. I gasp as he slides his fingers inside me, curling them in time with the relentless strokes of his thumb until my knees give out. I sag backward, heaving and arching against his chest as I fall to him.

"Good girl," he whispers when my cries have faded. "Now–forgive me."

He wants it. Maybe even needs it. But he hasn't earned it. Panting, I shake my head.

"Very well then."

He starts moving again, rubbing and stroking so fast, so fucking perfect, my head swims. Once wasn't enough—he's absolutely set on destroying me. He drags his teeth across my neck, and I whimper. That only makes him go faster, work harder, building me into a frenzy. God, I never knew it was possible to feel this much good all at once. How *is* it possible? We're in the Deathplane. A realm of the soul. This shouldn't be happening here. And yet…

"Oh, *fuck*." I grit my teeth, my head snapping back as I succumb for a second time.

"Goddammit, Adina," he groans. "*Forgive* me."

He doesn't wait for my denial before giving me a soft shove into the stone wall of the building. I start to press away when he falls into me with all his weight, bending down until his lips tickle my ear. A moment later, I hear the whisper of a zipper.

"Oh, my God." I want this more than anything, but I'm already weak from his manipulations and so sensitive down there the slightest brush makes my muscles jump. "I don't know if I can take it…"

"You can." He splays his fingers over mine, sealing my palm against the brick. "I'll show you."

His harsh murmur brooks no argument, and I don't plan to give him one. I spread my legs, angling my hips until I feel him slide between my thighs. His first thrust, hard and full, takes my breath away.

"Yes," I exhale, my body going slack as I give myself over to him. "Fuck, Levi, *yes*."

His growl ripples against the back of my neck. I claw at the stones as he grinds into me so deep, I can't hold back my scream. It doesn't stop him, though. He withdraws only to enter me again, and again, until I'm seeing stars. He's not being gentle, and I don't want him to be. I want him to have whatever he wants. I want, at last, to be his.

"Son of a bitch."

That's not an excited utterance. It's desperate. Panicked. "What's wrong?"

"I don't know," he says, his voice tight. "I'm right there, but I can't...I can't seem to..."

He slows his efforts. Concerned, I glance over my shoulder. The narrow look he gives me makes me a little nervous. "What?" I ask. "What is it?"

His eyes narrow further. Then, wiping a hand over his sweat-slick face, he falls to his knees and tugs on my wrist. "Come here."

Under different circumstances, I might refuse. Hell, I might have refused ten minutes ago. Now, punch drunk and ears ringing, I'm not going to refuse him anything. I drop a knee on either side of him, my inner calves pressing against the rough fabric of his patrolman's uniform as I drape my arms over his shoulders. He sighs, every one of his tense muscles easing as I settle into him.

"Thank you," he whispers before placing his hands on either side of my head, thumbs at my temples, fingers below my jaw. It's a familiar configuration. Only this time, it's backwards.

"What are you doing?"

"Trying something," he says. "I don't know if it will work, and I know it's a lot to ask, but...please. Trust me, Adina. Just one more time."

My heart stumbles. What does *that* mean?

He doesn't explain. Instead, he pulls my head down so he can kiss me on one temple and then the other. A promise to be gentle. "Do I have your permission?"

My heart pangs, but I smile anyway. "Yes."

He bows my head. There's no pain this time, no explosions of light. Only the star clusters, winking one by one into existence. But they're different. Unlike the blue constellations I've seen before, these are a brilliant mercurial silver, each one edged with delicate white fractals. Like frost.

Oh my God. Is this…?

The stars dim as a long, silver wand appears in front of me. Despite not having hands, I pick it up. One cluster twinkles, and I tap on the first star.

I'm in a school room papered with finger paintings and Popsicle stick art and packed with kids in plaid uniforms. They're all four or five years old, and tiny. All except one–a blond boy, sitting at a table hunched over a slim leather-bound reader. Based on the size of his head and shoulders, he'd be at least a foot taller than the next tallest kid in the class if he were standing up. But he just sits there, reading in silence.

And yet, I hear him anyway.

You can't play with them. Every time you do, someone gets hurt. You can't control your abilities, so you must stay here. Let them have fun. Ignore it. Do your work and ignore it.

"It is," I whisper in awe. "It's you."

Twenty-Seven

I tap the wand against another star. I'm in a different classroom now. This one is darker, with an interior that's more like a Gothic church than a public school. The Order Academy, I presume.

There are only eight students in this room. Instead of one age group, it ranges from a woman in her mid-twenties to…that same little boy. He's sitting in the front corner, far away from the rest of the group, like he's trying to separate himself from everyone else.

A wadded-up ball of wet paper sails through the air and hits him in the back of the head. He tenses, his face contorting with discomfort, but he doesn't move, not even to swat the disgusting blob away. Across the room, three teenaged boys snicker and slap hands.

They're intimidated. That's what Mum says. That's why they tease me. That's why they gave me that nickname. If you ignore it, they'll stop.

My stomach clenches. What nickname?

The image freezes as a chorus of shouts fills my head, a cacophony that spirals down into a single word.

Mindfucker.

It's followed by the unmistakable crack of a fist connecting with bone.

"Oh God," I moan, my heart sick for the little boy in the classroom, all alone, with a wad of paper stuck to his neck.

I flick the wand between the stars in this cluster and find more snapshots of his early life. His return to public school when he was ten. Sunday dinners with the family. Movies on the weekend with his friends. Quiet evenings in his room, doing homework. And a dark-haired girl with freckles and big, green eyes. First love, perhaps? Either way, I don't delve any deeper. Even here, some things should remain private. All these memories glow with a peach-colored light that reminds me of summer vacation, and youth, and hope.

He was happy.

I move on to the next cluster. He's in America now, working at the Summit. Excelling, in fact. Apprentice, and then a Reaper, all before his eighteenth birthday. There are more romantic dalliances, but none of them last longer than a blink. Every memory oozes a smug, cool lavender. All except one, which is soaked in deep, royal purple.

He's wearing Inquisitor black, kneeling in front of the altar in the cathedral at the back of the Depths. The Prime–not Castillo, so it must be his predecessor–pins the boney silver hands to his lapel. His pale skin is as smooth as porcelain and his gray eyes sparkle with swirls of cobalt. He's young. Twenty, he's told me before. Still practically a kid.

When the Prime steps back, Breitling stands. The Prime retrieves a book from the lectern behind him and holds it out.

You've worked so hard for this.
You may never see your parents again.

Uncle Thomas has done so much for you.
You'll never have a family of your own.
Everyone is counting on you.
You'll be an Inquisitor forever.
You'll be an Inquisitor...forever.
Stop this. You're here now. That's all that matters. Say the
words. Ignore the rest and say them.

Placing one hand on the cover and the other hand on his chains, he opens his mouth to speak.

I fling the wand as hard as I can. At *anything* else.

There are more commendations, more accolades. About fifteen years' worth. I shake my head in awe as his office, a much smaller one than he has now, fills with newspaper clippings and certificates. He really is the Order's golden boy, isn't he? I'm sure it didn't surprise anyone when he became Chief Inquisitor, in a ceremony much like the first one. It's all very impressive, and yet as time goes on, the shading of the memories dulls. What began as passionate purple fades to silver, then a wizened brown. I almost expect them to curl at the edges.

I tap another star. Color explodes around me, not purple or peach this time, but neon pink. It's a shock, but not the biggest one. That honor goes to this memory's location.

My house.

He's sitting in the armchair across from the dining room table. Moses Mendelsohn stands in front of him, silhouetted by the brilliant morning light from the patio, staring at my bedroom door with crossed arms and the expression of an exasperated schoolteacher. Breitling nods as if agreeing with something, but his thoughts are a different matter.

Moses is being ridiculous. It's not like we're dragging a poor old
woman out of bed by her hair. We're being civil, waiting for her to

awaken in her own time. Besides, even if one could barge in on a ghost, what's wrong with that? Especially this ghost? If there's an element of surprise to be had, we'd be fools not to take it. As it is, we may wake up tomorrow with throats slit, the both of us.

Damn. He really thought I was a monster.

He turns to my bedroom door as I emerge, dirt-streaked, disheveled, and blinking in the harsh light.

Ah, good, she's...oh. My God, she's so young. And...naked?

I smirk. And here I thought he hadn't noticed.

I cycle through the other stars in the cluster. The images from our first case together rush past me in a blur that I all but ignore. I lived through it. I don't need to see it again.

But I do listen.

I can't believe she's going to put me through this farce of an investigation. If she'd confess now, it would be so much easier. For everyone.

I'll give her this—she's a good liar. Exceptional, even. It's almost as if she believes she didn't kill Canelo.

There. I knew it. She's guilty, and she admits it. And...that's that, I suppose.

She wants me to look? Look at what?
    In her head?
    Oh. She's submitting. To an inquiry. To...me.
    Why would she do that? She's heard the stories. She knows what Inquisitors do...what I do to people during an inquiry.
    It's a trick. It has to be. Unless...
    Could she have killed Canelo and still, somehow...be innocent?

What you're feeling isn't real. Ignore it and it will pass.

Russ wouldn't exaggerate about Chaos. If it's marked her...
No. It won't hurt her again. I won't let it.

What you're feeling isn't real.

She's amazing.
Ignore it.

She's gorgeous.
Ignore it.

She's...touching me.
Ignore it and—
No. I can't ignore this. I care about her. I want her.
And I'm going to have her.

"Holy shit." My mouth falls open, and so does my hand. The wand disappears, and everything fades into the silver fog. I shake my head to dispel it, but it doesn't work. "Levi?"

"Stay with me, darling." On the other side of the clouds, he raises my chin. But he doesn't let me go.

My body temperature spikes. Sweat slicks my skin and my heart jumps into warp speed. "What...?"

My words disappear along with all the thoughts in my head. I moan to the sky, and hear it echoed in his throat. Everything is in stereo, doubled, and then quadrupled, like a piece of paper folding over and over on itself.

His hands slide down. One settles on my low back while the other splays over my heart. My fingers tingle with the supple warmth of my own skin. He's sharing himself with me, in real time. And I feel it all. The heat, the longing, the love.

My God, the love. It's bigger than anything I've ever felt, an ocean of light and warmth that holds me and consumes me and drowns me and fills me. It steals my breath. And then it breathes for me.

"Oh my…" I drop my forehead against his shoulder in a delicious daze.

"Adina?"

"Hmm?"

"Forgive me."

I should have guessed. With a disoriented moan, I roll my head to either side. "Not yet."

Grunting with discontent, he grabs my ass and pulls me into him. "Then fuck me until you do."

I laugh in surprise as his words burn through me. Dragging myself up, I lock eyes with him. "Finally, a reasonable request."

His mouth twitches. I sling my arms around the back of his neck as he puts himself where he needs to be. My lips hover over his as I rock up and down, making him quiver inside me.

"Oh, God," he moans, his face taut with ecstatic desperation. "More. Please. More."

"Yes," I pant against his mouth, moving as fast as I can without losing him. "Everything, Levi. Everything."

The hand on my chest drops. He pushes my skirt up to my waist, and once again, it's my turn to curse. My breath catches as I tighten around him, drawing him into me, my body begging for more of his.

"Yes! Oh fuck, *yes*." I cling to him as a third orgasm rips through me. "Oh God, Levi. I love you."

He stops moving. Stops breathing. I pull away. He stares up at me in disbelief. "What?"

Maybe I shouldn't repeat it. He doesn't look in any condition to hear it again. But my brain is a muddled mess of hormones and emotions, both mine and his, and I can't stop myself. "I love you."

His eyes roll closed, and he presses his face into my breast. "Adina, I...I'm sorry."

"I forgive you." I run my hands through his hair and kiss the back of his head, still delirious and not sure what he's talking about anymore. "I love you."

He tightens his hold on me, his body shaking like he's going to break apart. "I'm sorry, my darling. I'm so, so sorry."

I come to in the darkness, our words still echoing in my head.

I love you.

I'm sorry.

I forgive you. I love you.

I'm sorry.

"What have you done?"

My throat itches, and I flutter my eyelids open. This isn't the van. It's my pit, back in the parking garage. I press on the wooden lid, but there's something wrong. My limbs ache so badly I can barely lift them, let alone anything else.

I love you.

I'm sorry.

"Get..." I wheeze through dry lips. "Get me *out* of here."

Dim light washes over me as the door pulls away. I don't stop to see who released me before scrambling out of the hole, hugging the wall as I stumble on rubbery legs toward the elevator. Someone calls after me, but I don't listen. I need to go. I need to get away from here. From him. From everything. I need–

My organs pancake and I go down hard, writhing and gasping at the ceiling. The Lash. That's what they'd been yelling about. That miserable fucking thing that has ruined my life in so many ways.

"Adina, calm down."

Not Breitling. If it were him, the pain would be retreating, and it…is…*not.*

Thomas appears in my vision. I close my eyes so he won't see my tears.

"Lost. All lost. Why did you do this?"

Why do you care? I snap back at the Rigour a split-second before I realize what's happening. What has been happening this whole time.

I'd assumed the Rigour didn't affect him, but it did— only in the opposite way. It hasn't been trying to stop my feelings. It's been trying to protect me from them, at least until it could work him into enough of a frenzy to…what? Declare his love like some fucking Regency romance? Whatever path it tried to shove us onto, it's safe to say it has failed. On *all* counts.

"Son of a bitch." With no air in my lungs, my curse comes out as a formless grunt. *You're a real asshole, you know that. Chivalrous, maybe, but an asshole, nonetheless.*

"Levi, she needs you," Thomas calls out.

"No…" I moan even though I know it won't make a difference. He's the only one that can remove this Lash.

Rapid footfalls crunch toward me. I roll over until my face scrapes asphalt. A large hand clamps onto the back of my neck, and warmth rushes in as the Lash disappears, the pain morphing into the throb of returning blood flow.

"Breathe," he says, his voice shaky and low enough for no one else to hear. "Just breathe."

"Poor thing. Poor, poor thing."

I love you.

I'm sorry.

I inhale once, twice—then turn and throw up all over the craggy concrete wall.

Twenty-Eight

Thomas helps me to my feet and half-carries me to a service hallway that contains a closet-sized bathroom. When I'm certain there's nothing else coming up, I rinse out my mouth and splash my face with cold water. It tastes and smells like minerals and old pipes. Most people don't like that, but I find it soothing.

I love you.

I'm sorry.

"Goddammit." I brace against the rust-stained porcelain sink as panic and despair well inside me. That was it, wasn't it? That was what "things going too far" looks like. Which means this was the last time…the very last time…

My stomach lurches again. Instead of vomit spewing out of me, it's a full-body sob. I fall to my knees, the sound of my misery bouncing off the tile walls, filling the space and boxing me in.

Dammit. Stop crying. Thomas is right outside. Stop it. Now.

But the shaking only gets worse, my wails growing louder and rougher, like the keening moans of a dying walrus.

"Ugh, stop it!" I bite into the fleshiest part of my palm until I taste blood. Edward is still out there, lying on the shore like a landmine. If his master pushes the button again, someone else could die. I may be a wreck, but I'm a wreck with a job to do.

I suck air through the tight gaps in my fingers. Once. Twice. By the third one, my chest has stopped hitching like an overwrought toddler. Four. I stand up and drop my hand from my mouth.

Five. I splash more water on my face and check myself in the mirror. I don't like the red eyes or the crimson splotches on my pale cheeks. They make me look weak.

Six. Seven. Eight. I close my eyes and breathe deep, unhindered.

I love you.

"No." I jerk my head to the side, picturing the words as a venomous snake and my refusal as a silver sword slicing through its neck.

Nine, and…ten.

When I open my eyes, they look less red, and the bright splotches on my face have faded to a dull pink. The monsters will be back, but later. Which is fine. Later, I can fall apart all I want. Edward needs me now.

Nodding at my reflection, I stride toward the door and yank it open. Thomas spins around, withdrawing his hand from the back of his head.

"Is everything okay?" he asks with what sounds like genuine concern. "I heard…well, it sounded bad."

"It's fine. That can happen sometimes upon exit—especially when there's another person with me. Against my will."

There's nothing veiled about my accusation. At least he has the decency to look ashamed. "Would you permit me to conduct a brief physical evaluation? We should make sure there's no—"

I stalk past him out of the hallway. I'm not interested in sympathy or concern. Not his, and not anyone else's. I want to finish this case, go home, dive under my covers and never come out.

The van's rear doors are open, and Breitling sits on the floor of it with his head bowed, his fingers clamped around the bumper. McNally stands in front of him, belly pushed out and hands clasped behind his back like a condescending penguin. When he hears the service door open, he turns his arrogance on me. I want to ream him for ordering the Lash—it was irresponsible, and it violated my trust, and so many other fucked-up things. But what would be the point? It's done, and no amount of screaming is going to change it. I doubt it would even make me feel better.

He glances down and takes in my state of undress. His cheeks flush crimson and for one glorious moment, I think he might keel over from a heart attack. Instead, he averts his eyes and waits for me to handle the situation.

I *guess* that's for the best.

"Are you alright?" Breitling asks as I enter the van to retrieve my clothes, my shoulder pressed to the wall opposite him. As much as I don't want to, his words make me flinch. He sounds exhausted, with a brittle edge that suggests he's been crying. Or trying hard not to.

"Yeah," I say through gritted teeth. My clothes sit in a folded stack at the back of the van. My sigil rests on top of it.

"I took it off," he murmurs in my direction. "I didn't want...I wasn't sure how it would affect the Lash, so I thought it best to remove it."

My nerves flame. Slipping the sigil on, I wait for it to do its thing before responding with a bland, "Okay." I feel him watching me as I dress and comb my fingers through my hair, but I don't dare look.

Work now. Fall apart later.

I make myself decent, then escape the van as quickly as I can. The three men watch me as I find a bit of wall to slump against. McNally clears his throat, and they turn into each other once more. "You were saying, Inquisitor?"

"The voice of the master didn't sound familiar," Breitling says, "and the gender was indistinct."

McNally scoffs. "No way a woman would murder five people this way. It makes no sense."

"Oh, but a man doing it makes *perfect* sense," I mutter.

Breitling snorts, the corner of his mouth twitching though his eyes look sad. "From what I observed, Edward was compelled to act by the owner of the voice. Not only that, but he does indeed have no memory of committing the attack. Whoever is compelling him must take control of his thoughts and senses as well. He is another victim of his master's crimes."

I bite my tongue before the words "I told you so" have the chance to jump out. They could have saved so much time if they'd trusted me from the start. "Now that we're all on the same page, how do we catch the master?"

McNally gapes at me like I've announced I'm running for Parliament. "The creature has been subdued by Inquisitor Breitling and detained inside an intentions threshold. What would be the point in dedicating more man hours to eliminating what is already a neutralized threat?"

My heart drops. "You're suggesting we leave him like that?"

He shrugs. "Why not?"

"Because it's inhuman!" I shout. "He may be paralyzed, but he's still conscious, and from everything I've seen, this is an immortal being we're talking about. You'll condemn him to an eternity of suffering."

"He's a killer," McNally sniffs. "You'll forgive me if I don't shed a tear."

"You forget, *sir*," I shoot back, "the master isn't finished. There's one more murder left in the Canonical Five."

"She's right," Breitling says, taking to his feet. "We're missing Mitre Square."

"We're not *missing* it," McNally counters. "The Mitre Square incident should have taken place on the same occasion as the attack on Emma Long. But we disabled him before he had the chance—"

"Oh, *we* did that, did we?" I can't help sniping.

"—and he moved on to the last incident at Miller Court. Perhaps that was why he included the George Yard attack in the first place, as a contingency. If something went wrong, he'd still get his five."

"You can't be serious," I splutter, my tongue going numb with fury. "We have to figure out who's behind all this. We owe it to the victims. To *Ed*."

McNally whips around and advances toward me. "That *thing* has done nothing but terrify and aggrieve this country from the moment he slithered into existence. He can rot on the strand until kingdom come. If you don't like it, you are free to join him."

The last of my patience evaporates. My hands curl into fists, and I slide my foot back until I'm in a fighting stance. I'm no brawler, but if this bastard comes any closer, I'm gonna punch him in his flabby neck.

"Sir." Breitling steps up to McNally and places a hand on his shoulder. He doesn't pull him back, but his hold is tight enough that McNally stops coming at me. "It has been a trying day, and Miss Venture's nerves must be frayed. Might I suggest a brief recess so that she may recover herself?"

My jaw drops. "Excuse me?"

McNally assesses Breitling, trying to determine what his game is. He must decide there isn't one, because he waves us out. "Go. She's your subordinate, after all. But be warned, I don't want to see or hear a word from her until she's ready to listen to reason."

"Thank you, Constable." Breitling shoulders past him, grabs my arm, and leads me away. I'm about to shake him off when I realize I don't have to. His grip is loose, and the way he pulls me looks harder than it is. As soon as we're on the elevator, he lets me go.

"What now?" I ask, crossing my arms. "You gonna bleed me with leeches to relieve my feminine hysteria?"

He shakes his head. "We are *going* to go back to your quarters before the Constable orders us off the property and the case."

"He wouldn't do that."

Breitling's silence insists otherwise. I drop my arms to my sides in defeat and spend the ride up to the third floor sulking. When the door opens, my anger dissolves under a crushing wave of anxiety. My room. The two of us. Alone. And I haven't heard a peep from the Rigour since I splattered stomach acid all over the parking garage wall.

I love you.

I snap my teeth together. No. Not yet. Not when there's still work to do.

He lingers across the hall from my door to let me go in first. Chivalrous though his intention may be, it also burdens me with having to choose where to sit. The couch seems like an immediate no, but if I don't take it, he'll have to sit there instead, which would be even worse. So, I do the only thing I can–I make for the window and stare outside. Shiva perches in the same place she'd been earlier. This time, one of the large Ravens cuddles up next to her.

At least this trip has worked out for one of us.

Twenty-Nine

The door closes behind me with a soft click. It's silent, and for a moment I wonder if maybe he's left me to "recover myself." The creak of a nearby floorboard dashes that hope.

"I know you won't want to hear this—"

"Always your worst opener," I mutter without turning around.

"--but the Constable isn't entertaining this decision simply to infuriate you. He expanded the search for the master to the Continent, but the parameters are at once too specialized *and* too broad. It's untenable."

I twirl my finger. "English, please."

He sighs. "There are dozens of Operational combinations that could allow someone to manipulate a being like Edward *in theory*. But no such registered Operator exists in *reality*. Not in the free world, anyway."

"Why didn't he just tell me *that?*" I grumble at the window. Now it makes sense why McNally would be eager to close the matter. It's tough to justify spending so much time and energy searching for someone when it seems more and more likely you're chasing a ghost. Or a dream.

On the other hand, someone *did* do this. They're out there. And if we don't find them, who knows what they'll do next now that they've lost their puppet?

With a bracing inhale, I turn around. Breitling stands next to the armchair, his hands on his hips with his eyes pinned to the coffee table.

"Fine," I say. "If the registered Operator database is a dead end, then it must be an unregistered Operator doing it."

"Or we're misunderstanding the Operation," he says. "Neither solution will be easy, but...perhaps if we review our combined knowledge, it will reveal something we've missed."

My heart leaps as my mouth dries. He wants to keep working together? Is that wise? But then, what is the alternative? McNally won't let me investigate alone, and Breitling doesn't have enough background to handle it without me.

"Adina?"

As much as I want to keep avoiding him, I can't help it. He's raised his chin enough to look at me. His forehead is etched with worry and his eyes burn into me with concern and regret and...

No. Goddammit, I don't want to see that. But I do see it, and it makes me want to...well, thank God there's a table between us. Though I wish it was a wall. Or maybe a building.

He must sense my discomfort, because he turns away, running both hands over his face and through his hair.

"I can do this," he says loud enough for me to know he's not talking to himself. "Regardless of what happened. Of what I did, and...what was said. I can set that aside for now and finish this." His head twitches in my direction. "Can you do the same?"

His ominous tone chills my blood. Knowing what awaits us at the end of this case is bad. But either we work together or say goodbye now.

God help me, I'm not ready for that.

"Yes," I say at last. "I can do that."

"Good." He turns back around. I almost smile at his placid expression. I don't know how he does it; even with my sigil working overtime, I can still feel the horrid emptiness overtaking my chest.

He sits down in the armchair and takes his notebook and glasses out of his jacket. "Let's start with today and work backward. You observed my inquiry. What were your impressions?"

I lean back on the windowsill and recount everything I can, grateful to have something other than my emotions to focus on. He nods along, his head bowed to the paper, recording my words in tight, precise handwriting.

"Did I leave anything out?" I ask when I'm done.

"I don't think so. It matches what I remember as well. Sitting on the riverbank, the pain, the voice…" He frowns. "Did *you* hear what it said?"

"'On your feet, Heartless.'" The words send a chill down my spine. "I don't think I'll ever forget it."

"It's an interesting phrase, isn't it?"

I run my hands over my arms. "That's one way to put it."

"The 'on your feet' bit makes sense," he muses. "Edward was resisting, and his master was trying to goad him into compliance. But Heartless? Why call him that?"

"I don't know. He's irritating and he did stab me. Twice. But he's also wracked with guilt over what he's done. Whoever controls him hasn't met him, because anyone who has wouldn't call him heartless."

"Oh." Breitling raises his head. "Now *that's* something."

"What is?"

"By his own admission, Edward has lived in his current state since at least the Autumn of Terror, 1888. Though he has no memory of it, we suspect he's responsible for those deaths as well. But with over a hundred years between then and now, and no currently registered Operator who fits the bill…"

His meaning dawns. "*He* hasn't changed, but his master has. It *is* what we've always said it was—a copycat. Sort of."

"Which means that the method being used to control him is transferable." Breitling takes this down, his precise writing abandoned in favor of excited scrawls.

"Operations can be transferred?" This is news to me. "How?"

"Rarely, and with great difficulty." He eyes me over his glasses. "You remember Ogden and Noles with their apples? Or Eidolon Haight and Reverie? It's like that, only instead of transferring the effect of the Operation, you transfer the Operation itself. However, there's an exponential loss of efficacy. The more transfers there are, the more the Operation degrades, and the more it degrades, the less effective the results."

"That explains the change in severity too," I say as another piece falls into place. "It's the same method, except that the transferred Operation isn't as strong as the original. Instead of blood and guts, you get bruises and internal injuries."

"We've been going at this backward." He snaps his notebook closed and stands. "The current registry may be unwieldy, but the one from 1888 will be significantly smaller. If we figure out who created the original

Operation, and how, perhaps we can figure out who it was transferred to." Smiling at me, he opens the door. "It appears another visit to the Catacombs is in order."

🖋

Madame Misty's grin illuminates her face as we approach the counter. I expect her to focus on Breitling, but she's looking at me. "Welcome back, dearie. How are you today?"

The question stings. There's no good way to answer it and still be honest. "Fine, thank you."

Her smile wavers and her eyes grow suspicious. "Is something wrong?" she asks Breitling.

"We need to see the active registration records from the year 1888," he says.

"Oh." She blinks, his stern tone catching her by surprise. The fine lines in her forehead deepen. "For records that old, I will have to see your identification, Miss Venture."

I present my card. As usual, it receives extra scrutiny.

"Can't say I recognize *that* name," she says, tapping the back of it. "Who is Rafael Venture?"

I hope the flickering firelight disguises my cringe. "He's my dad."

"And his Operation?"

"Uh, well…"

"We're not sure," Breitling steps in. "The paperwork is incomplete—clerical error—and unfortunately, he has…disappeared."

"I see." She studies me for a long moment as if she's struggling with a question she may or may not want to ask. In the end, she returns my ID without another word.

Lifting her lantern by its top ring, she shuffles into one of the shrouded, narrow aisles. "This way."

Breitling lets me go first, and we follow her between the book-laden shelves. She moves fast for an old lady. The murk dances around the edges of her figure, swallowing her when she gets too far away. I fix my gaze on the bobbing light of the lantern, its diffuse glow making the gilt-stamped words on the bindings around us gleam.

We walk for what must be a mile before Madame Misty comes to a stop. "Here we are then. 1888." She taps the spine of a thick, leather-bound volume. "Popular year, that. Someone else came in asking for it not too long ago."

"What?" Her comment must stun Breitling, because he walks right into me. I lurch forward and almost crash into Madame Misty when he grabs my wrist and pulls me back.

"Sorry," he mutters. "Who asked to see 1888 besides us?"

She opens her mouth, then closes it again, her brow furrowing. "I…I can't remember."

I wince as his grip tightens. "How is that possible?"

"Don't insult her," I whisper, shaking him off me. "People forget things. Especially people of…you know, advanced age."

"Not her," he says. "She doesn't forget anything. Ever."

"What a peculiar thing." Madame Misty sucks in her lower lip, the gesture making her appear much younger. "I remember what they asked for. The words. But everything else about them…I don't…I can't…"

"It's alright," Breitling soothes. "Don't worry about their appearance. What did they *say*?"

She squeezes her eyes shut, concentrating. "It was July 16th. A Tuesday. I was annotating the latest edition of *Organic Materialism in the Modern Age* when...." She drops her right ear to her right shoulder. "I would like to see the names of all registered Operators from 1886 to 1890."

Her head tilts the other way. "Access to any document created prior to 1992 is restricted to Reaper rank and above."

Right shoulder. "How about just 1888?"

Left shoulder. "Not without the proper clearance."

Right shoulder. "Oh, but I do have clearance. See?"

Left shoulder. "I don't–"

Her head snaps up and her eyes fly open. "That's all. Does it help?"

I glance behind me. Breitling nods, doing his best to keep her from seeing the disappointment clouding his eyes. "It might. Thank you, Madame."

"Of course, boy." She hands me the lantern. "Take all the time you need."

We press our backs to the shelves as she shuffles past us and starts the long walk back to the distant light of the reception desk.

"Curious," I say.

"Indeed." He nods at the book. "Let's see if we can find what they were searching for."

His arm bumps my shoulder as he passes by, and I catch the smell of his sandalwood cologne. I want to retreat. Both from him and from the shivers his touch arouses. But I'm backed up against the leather spines, and there's nowhere else to go.

"My apologies." He clears his throat, grabs the book off the shelf, and nods down the hall. "This way."

We take the zigzag path to the reading room. A scattering of what appear to be off-duty Order grunts sit in the overstuffed chairs and hunch at the tables, engaged in silent study. Breitling leads us to the closest table, and we sit down next to each other. I set the lantern between us as he dons his glasses, opens the book, and bends toward the first page. I follow suit, keeping as much distance between us as I can.

The print isn't as tiny as the book Madame Misty had been slaving over on our last visit, the blue ink less faded. It's like a spreadsheet, albeit an old one. Rows and columns contain numbers and words that might be English, but they're arranged in a way that makes no sense. As I struggle to decipher them, the characters slither around the page and reform. I try to focus, but every time I think I've got it, the writing changes again.

"What's it doing?" I ask, shaking my head as if that might help. "Or is it me?"

"Right. Sorry." Breitling lays his thumb over a black square in the upper left corner of the first page. He nods at the matching square on the right. "Put your finger there."

The spot sticks like oil to my skin, and the writing on the page snaps into solid, immutable text.

"It's a Linguistic encryption," he says before I can ask. "A final layer of security. Anyone without the proper clearance needs to be sponsored."

"So, even if whoever it was got past Madame Misty, they wouldn't be able to read it, anyway."

"Not without help," he mutters, already absorbed by the book's contents. I try to follow his lead, but it doesn't work. The column headings make sense: name, date of birth, Efflorescent age (how long they've been an

Operator), registered discipline, and so on. The entries in each row, however, appear in cursive so fluid and abstract they're more like art than words. After about ten minutes of laboring in vain, I sit back in my chair and rub my eyes.

"Giving up already?" he asks.

"You've always been better with paperwork than I have."

Even in the lamplight, I can see his mouth twitch. "That reminds me, I still need your notes on the latest draft of the Sang Treaty. We've only got a few months before the assembly."

"Only you would take my avoidance of work as an opportunity to talk about other, more boring work."

He chuckles, then coughs as if he has something caught in his throat.

"What's wrong?"

"Well, with their Western outfit in disarray, the Sang will no doubt request we hold the meeting at their New Orleans headquarters, and to avoid hosting them day and night at the Summit, the Presidium will most likely agree. Which means...we will be traveling together again. Soon."

The regret and–dare I say it?–dread in his tone carries so much weight it knocks the wind out of me. What might that trip have been if this one hadn't been fucked from the beginning? And how...oh God, how are we going to deal with it now? This isn't like breaking up with Jake or anyone else. There's still work to be done. Work that only we can do. Together.

Suddenly, this cavernous room feels about as big as a shoebox. Sweat gathers at the base of my neck and I jump up so fast I almost knock over my chair.

"Are you...uh, where are you going?" He lifts his head, but his eyes remain on the book.

I silently congratulate him for pivoting away from his first question. With everything that's happened, it should be pretty damn obvious I'm not alright. "I'm going to go look around. Not that it isn't fun sitting here watching you read, but…you know, it isn't."

He grunts an affirmation and flips the page. "Don't wander too far."

"I'll leave a trail of breadcrumbs," I say as I exit into the hall. My head jerks to the left, and I examine the distant darkness for any spectral light or spooky figures before turning in the opposite direction. My fingers wander over the cracked spines as I head toward the soft, warm light in the front. When I reach the end of the last bookcase, I peer around the corner. Madame Misty sits in her usual chair in the middle of the long counter, nose hovering inches above her book.

"I may be old, but I'm not deaf," she says without looking up.

I gasp and pull myself halfway back into the aisle. Instead of rounding on me in accusation, she leans forward and blows on the ink of her most recent writing until it dries. "Now, now, don't make me shout at you. Come out of there and keep me company."

"Sorry," I say as I approach. "I don't mean to interrupt you, but he's in the zone and I don't want to get in the way."

"I don't blame you one bit." She turns the page with a snap and scans over the next one, her pen fluttering with hummingbird quickness as she makes notes not in the book, but on a bright yellow legal pad. "All this old handwriting makes everyone's eyes cross. Why do you think Levi has to wear those reading glasses now?"

I hop up onto the counter next to her. "He's read a lot of these books?"

"Almost as many as I have. He always was insatiable."

I clamp my teeth together to stop my brain—and my tongue—from riffing on the obvious (and I hope unintended) euphemism. "He must have spent a lot of time here when he worked at the Tower then."

She studies me over the rims of her glasses. The gesture reminds me so much of Breitling I almost expect the corner of her mouth to twitch as well. "He didn't tell you?"

"Tell me what?"

She sits back in her chair so she can face me fully. "I met Levi when he was ten years old. His parents had just sent him back to his NO school, much to his uncle's dismay. Thomas practically drove his brother to madness, haranguing him to keep Levi at the Order academy. In the end, they compromised by securing him an internship at the Tower–here, in the Catacombs–after school. It wasn't practical work, but he got a fine education."

My mind wanders back to those peach-colored memories I'd witnessed. "And he was okay with that?"

She glances over her shoulder toward the stacks, as if she's worried he'll overhear. "He loved it. It was only supposed to be two days a week, but it wasn't long before he was here every afternoon, buried in the stacks, devouring books and learning everything he could about any subject he had permission to access. I thought maybe he'd take my job someday when, one morning when he was about fifteen, his uncle swept down the stairs and announced that Levi would go to the States to start an apprenticeship at the Summit. I've never seen anyone look so devastated."

That's not the word I expected to hear. "I thought being an Inquisitor was his dream. I mean, it's a big change, and leaving his life and his family couldn't have been easy. But...devastated?"

She nods. "Levi always knew the expectations for him were high. But between you and me, I think that, deep down, he'd hoped it wouldn't work out. I'll never forget the way his face fell when he got the news, then turned cold and rigid. That was the moment I realized Thomas was right. He would make an excellent Inquisitor one day. It was like watching him turn to stone before my eyes." Her head drops to her chin. "If ever there was a memory I'd like to forget, it would be that one."

I want to say something sympathetic, but the words won't come. A weight has settled in the middle of my chest and it's hard to breathe around it, let alone speak. If I didn't know better, I'd say my heart had turned to stone as well.

With a sigh, she pulls herself up as much as her old bones can manage, then settles back to her work. "I'll say this much for Thomas, though—he saw Levi's potential from the beginning, and gave him every opportunity to make the most of it. Knowing Levi, I'm sure he's done just that."

"Yes," I whisper. "He's a talented Inquisitor, and a good Chief. Everyone respects him very much."

"Mm-hmm," she grunts. "And how is he as a man?"

My heart breaks into a gallop. "What do you mean?"

"You know. Is he happy?"

"Oh. Uh..." Once again, I'm at a loss. She shouldn't be asking me that, and I definitely shouldn't answer. "I...I'm afraid I couldn't say. We just work together."

"Of course, dearie." She pats my hand with a dry, feathery palm. "Of course."

I take my leave of Madame Misty and wander back into the shadows of the stacks. Between her insinuations and sad recollections, and the awkwardness awaiting me, I don't hurry. And, as it turns out, I didn't need to— Breitling hasn't moved since I left.

"You're still at it?" I ask as I sit.

"I've only got one pair of eyes." He leans back. "Did I hear you and Madame Misty talking?"

"It's not polite to eavesdrop." I roll my head over the back of my chair, staring up at the ceiling fog as if I'm bored and not at all terrified to hear his commentary.

"I said I heard you talking, not what you were saying. The desk is too far away for that." Adjusting his glasses, he resumes his study. "What did you discuss?"

"Nothing much." He won't buy that answer, but I'm not giving him a chance to press me. "You said her Operation is total recall. So, it would take an even more highly skilled Memorist to wipe themselves out of her memory, right?"

"If it *was* a Memorist that tried to access the book. There are other possibilities. A Biologian could have disabled or overstimulated certain hormones that could tamper with her recall. An Aetherist could have shrouded themselves to prevent a memory from forming. And the TechnOps have many gadgets that will confuse and disorient a subject."

I groan. "So, it could have been anyone."

"Yes. As long as they are currently employed at the Tower in a position with lower clearance than a Reaper, it could be anyone at all."

I roll my eyes. "You think you're so smart, don't you?"

He shrugs, but it doesn't hide his smirk. "The only levels below Reaper are Page and Scribe."

"I thought Page was a NO position?"

He tilts his hand back and forth. "It's a bit more complicated than that. Pages don't have Operations the way we do. They are measured by their OAL—Operational Affinity Level—on a one to five scale. The higher the number, the greater the chance they may Effloresce into a full Operator someday. Of course, OALs are kept confidential, especially the high ones. We don't want to give anyone false hope. Instead, we offer them a job, both to monitor them and so they don't feel alone. That way, if things do progress, we know where they are, and they know where to turn."

His words, along with the gentleness in his voice, bring a smile to my lips. "You told me once you're not good with the young ones."

"So?"

"So, I wouldn't expect someone who thinks that of themselves to sound so…paternal."

His face turns bright red, and he flips the page with more force than necessary. "I believe I was referring to the young Inquisitors when I said that. It's different with NOs. The ones with high OALs are outsiders. Fragile. Looking for their place. They need someone to guide them."

My heart fills almost to bursting. That may be one of the sweetest things I've ever heard him say—and if I don't change the subject right now, I'm going to do something very, very embarrassing. Like swoon. "Anyway…the question stands: Could a Page have done this?"

He scrubs his jaw, then shakes his head. "I don't think so. They would have to have an abnormally high OAL—and I mean, off-the-charts high—to assume another's Operation. Someone like that would undoubtedly stand out. And even if they did manage to go unnoticed, there's no way a person with mere affinity, no matter how strong, could affect Madame Misty like that. It's far more likely we're looking for a Scribe."

"Okay. A highly Operational Scribe with a desire to kill people because…" I frown. "Because why?"

"I keep running into that problem as well. Why kill? Why now?"

"And why *them*? Why these five?"

"We know the answer to that. The substance abuse."

Crap. I'd almost forgotten about that gigantic discrepancy. "Yeah, about that—"

"Wait." He spins the book toward me and points to a line on the page. "I think this is it."

Squinting, I force myself to parse the flowing script.

Name: Declan O'Dowd
Born: May 2, 1834
Died: December 2nd, 1888
Date of Efflorescence: September 3rd, 1853
Registered: Organic Materialist (Biologian),
Aetherist

"Those Operations sound like a fit, and he died within a few months of the last murder. He's even Irish," I muse. "Coincidence?"

"Perhaps." Breitling's sly expression says he's not finished. "Did you see his occupation?"

I examine the second-to-last column. Goosebumps prickle my flesh as phantom words echo in my head.

On your feet, Heartless.

"You see it?" Breitling prods.

I nod, waiting for my pulse to stop racing before I speak. "Declan O'Dowd was a heart surgeon."

"Not just a heart surgeon." He taps the far-right column, which is so packed with microscopic print I don't even bother trying to read it. "An ecto-bypass specialist."

"Like Thomas?"

"Indeed. Only Uncle Thomas is not an Aetherist. With that additional Operation, it's possible, even likely, that Declan could transfer his own power and essence into an organic item."

"Like Ogden and Noles," I say. "Except instead of a craving for human flesh, it was a full-on Operator-slash-serial-killer. And instead of apples…"

"A human heart." Breitling runs a hand through his hair. "And when it's something as complicated as one's own avatar, he couldn't use just anyone's heart. It would have to be…his own."

"Holy shit." I flop back in my chair as I picture a man–Ed, but not Ed–lifting a scalpel to his iodine-slathered chest. I shake the image away before it goes any further than that. "He must have been crazy."

"Very possible," Breitling says, drumming a finger over the Date of Death entry. "If we assume the first of the Ripper murders occurred right after the procedure took place, in late summer of 1888, he only survived a few months before his death in December."

"You say that like it's a failure. Most people die within moments of having their hearts cut out. I bet the ones who do it themselves don't even make it that long."

He shakes his head. "Either the Operation was flawed, or he never intended it to last longer than that. Whatever the case, his demise left his avatar stranded in the Deathplane until someone else took up Declan's mission."

My stomach lurches. "Oh God. Please tell me that doesn't mean what I think it means."

"I'm afraid it does," he says. "Somehow, someone found Declan's heart, used its imbued Operation to perform a cardio ecto-bypass on themselves, and then replaced Declan's heart, wherever he'd been hiding it, with their own. They've been able to control his avatar— Edward—ever since."

Thirty

We return the book to its proper place. As we hurry out from behind the counter, Madame Misty stands up.

"Boy!" she shouts, her voice echoing off the stone walls.

Breitling skids to a halt so he can double back. She hands him a folded piece of yellow legal paper, which he slips into his pocket. Leaning over the counter, he kisses her on the top of the head. "Thank you."

"Good luck." She pats his cheek, and with a nod in my direction, retakes her seat.

"What did she give you?" I ask as we trot up the stairs as fast as the narrow steps will allow.

"Notes on an unrelated matter," he says curtly. I'd like to push him for more, but it's taking all my energy and concentration to get to the surface without tripping.

After the staleness of the Catacombs, the fresh, dewy air tastes wonderful. We're halfway back to the Hospital Block when my phone bleats with a call. Jake's name appears on the screen, and my heart, already pounding from the upstairs dash, slams even harder into my ribs.

"Why is *he* calling?" Breitling asks from over my shoulder.

I want to tell him it's none of his business, or at least remind him that we agreed to keep our personal feelings locked away until the case is over. Instead, I let my sigil help me craft a more professional response.

"He and Ruth have been doing some background for me. Victimology and...Ripperology, I suppose you could call it. He's practically an expert, and no one else is working that angle."

He arches a brow. "And why the victimology?"

"You'll see." It's a coward's move, but I'm going to hand this particular grenade off to Ruth. She can explain what she did and didn't find and he can draw his conclusions directly from her. Also, he's a lot less likely to accuse *her* of intentionally undermining Order authority.

I press the green button and turn on the speaker. "Hey, Jake. What are you still doing up?"

"Come on, A. You know I don't sleep. Besides, Ruth's been cracking the whip on the Vigilant site all night. I've been her entertainment while we waited for updates."

I smile. "Well, it is what you do best."

"Aw, go on," he says as Ruth shouts a greeting from the background.

"Hey!" I call back. "So, let me take a wild guess: Emma Long was another dead end."

"Yeah," Ruth says sulkily. *"I even have a guy in Cornwall who went to high school with her. He dug into her background the same way he would with anyone else, but everything he found matched his own perceptions."*

"Which were angelic, I assume?"

"In every possible sense of the word. Strict family, superior academics, no police record or any evidence of run-ins with the law. Also, my guy says her parents were super protective of her

extracurricular activities. Like, no-drugs, no-dating, no-fun-until-you-graduate kind of protective."

"Yeah, but high school kids find ways around that sort of thing all the time, right?"

Breitling makes a noise that sounds suspiciously like a laugh. Sure enough, he's got a big smile plastered across his face. "What?"

He shrugs. "Nothing. But...well, you would know, wouldn't you?"

I chuckle. Of course he remembers the rebellious teenager who snuck out from under the oppressive gaze of her cop stepdad to go smoke pot in her friend's basement. When the rebellion ends in an unintentional Deathwalk and subsequent blacklisting by all your friends, it's not exactly an easy thing to forget. Believe me, I've tried.

Static bursts on the line, followed by an irritated *"Hey!"* from Ruth.

"What was that?" I ask.

"Nothing," she bites out. *"Jake was asking who's there with you."*

Shit. I wince in embarrassment, and Breitling wipes a hand over his face. At least I'm not the only one who feels stupid right now.

"Anyway," Ruth says pointedly. *"While you make a good point, I'm sure you also remember how stupid teenagers can be. If Emma was the type to sneak out from under her parents' rule, she would have done it compulsively until she got caught. But there's no indication that it even happened once."*

I hate to admit it, but that all tracks. "So, that's it. She's as normal as the rest of them?"

Ruth laughs. *"She's the Vanilla Queen. She graduated college, got married, had kids, started doing charity work, and lived the domestic dream. She's barely even left Cornwall, except for the requisite yearly vacation with her husband and kids. This one, a girl's trip with her sister, was the first of its kind."*

"It's a damn shame," Jake pipes in. *"She didn't even get the chance to make one bad decision before that psycho got a hold of her."*

I shake my head at the phone. The first four victims were average people. Not perfect, but not terrible. All NOs, and as Jake pointed out on our last call, each one was a better match to their corresponding Autumn of Terror victim than the last.

And then…Gordon Gaye. A former Reaper, and as far as walking trainwrecks go, he was in line to claim the top prize. Not only that, but he appears to have absolutely nothing in common with his 1888 counterpart. How does *he* fit into this?

"Hey, Jake?"

"Yah?"

"What can you tell me about the fifth Ripper victim?"

"Ooo, so glad you asked. Mary Kelly, the last of the Canonical Five. She was a lot younger than the others, she was found inside a locked apartment, and the scene was Brutal with a capital B."

"Kelly was a departure from the Ripper's MO?"

"I'd say so. In fact, some people think she was the actual target all along. She'd been living with a guy until he decided he couldn't stand her profession anymore and moved out. The theory is that he killed the other women to try to scare her out of 'the life.' When that didn't work, he murdered her in highly Ripperesque style and banked on the cops conflating her with the rest."

"Do you believe that?"

He chuckles. *"To be honest with you, A, I don't know what to believe. There are so many stories out there, people can't even agree on a single profile, let alone the most likely killer. All I can tell you is that almost everyone agrees the Ripper had a relatively thorough understanding of human anatomy."*

My ears perk up. "The way a surgeon would?"

"Like I said, there are a lot of theories. But it's not not possible."

"Got it. Thanks, Jake."

"Anytime."

"Is there anything else you need?" Ruth asks.

I confer silently with Breitling. He shakes his head, and I agree. The only person left for them to investigate would be Gordon Gaye, and setting a bunch of web sleuths on the trail of a Reaper is asking for trouble. "Not at the moment. But I'll let you know if anything else comes up. Thank you, though. This has been a huge help."

"No problem. This has been…kind of a blast," Ruth says. *"Be careful and come home safe."*

I nod at my feet. "I will. I promise."

"Good luck, A!" Jake adds. *"And hey, when you catch the bastard, make sure you give him an extra kick in the nuts from us."*

"Will do." I chuckle as I disconnect. They may be far away, but it's nice to know someone out there is cheering for me. Two someones, even.

"I'm surprised Ruth's people couldn't find more on our victims," Breitling says after he's sure the call has ended. "Public intoxication and DUIs are public record in nearly every country, and everything else inevitably finds its way to social media."

I heave a sigh. "The Vigilant may not be cops or Inquisitors, but they aren't idiots. And even if some of them were slacking, Ruth wasn't. If they didn't find anything, it means there was nothing to find."

Breitling narrows his eyes. "Are you suggesting that someone in the Order falsified the reports?"

I'm about to tell him that's exactly what I think when Jake's words jump into my head. "Conflation."

"I beg your pardon?"

"One murder with one real motive, and four others to cover it up. Is it possible...?" I pause, giving myself a chance to develop the theory before speaking it out loud. "It could be that someone wants us to connect all five victims through substance abuse so they could cover up their one intended victim. The only one that *actually* fits this non-existent pattern."

"Gordon Gaye." Breitling completes my thought. "Then you *are* suggesting someone falsified the reports."

I shrug apologetically. "All I know is that Ruth is good at what she does. Can you say the same about everyone who works here?"

"Not after what I've seen this week," he scoffs. "Still, why go through all that trouble? Wouldn't... I can't believe I have to say this, but wouldn't it have been easier to simply murder actual substance abusers?"

"That I can't tell you." I quicken my pace toward the Hospital Block. "But since we're looking for a Scribe anyway, I say we start with the ones who compiled those victim profiles. Whoever they are, they're our new prime suspects."

Thirty-One

I'd pictured the Scribery as a richly paneled hall with floor-to-ceiling bookshelves and vaulted windows. Imagine my horror when the elevator slides open on the second floor and I'm greeted by a drop-ceilinged cube farm with fritzing fluorescent lights. The ever-present stench of burned coffee is thick enough to coat the back of my throat, almost like some psychopath made it into a plug-in air freshener.

Breitling points to the line of offices on our right. We edge that way, clinging to the wall as if the tessellated mass in the middle of the room may reach out and swallow us at any moment. He stops in front of a door with a brown plastic nameplate that reads *C. Margaine, Director,* and raps with his knuckles before pushing in without waiting for permission.

"Oh!" The man behind the file-covered desk jumps up. He's tall and lanky, with floppy chestnut hair and horn-rimmed glasses. "Inquisitor–Chief! What a...how...what can I do for you?"

"Sorry to barge in like this, Colin," Breitling says. "I'm putting together a dossier on this Ripper copycat for the Prime, and I need to make sure I've got everything buttoned up. No loose threads, no missing pieces. You understand."

"The Prime? Oh, yes. Of course. Absolutely." Colin pets his tie like it's going to run away if he doesn't keep it happy. "Anything you need."

"Excellent." Breitling pulls out his notebook and glasses. I examine my shoes to hide my smirk. And he mocks *my* theatrics. "Let me see…yes, here it is. The names of the Scribes who compiled the reports on our victims have escaped us. If you would be so kind as to produce them, we have some follow-up questions."

"Of course." Colin clicks his mouse, still too amped to sit down. "Bear with me a moment. I need to check the assignment roster. We put our best on it, of course, but let me…huh. That's odd."

Breitling and I exchange a look. I've never liked that combination of words, and I'm guessing he feels the same. "What's odd?"

"Well, I know I assigned it out to the senior pool, and it has been marked as completed, but the assignment names are blank."

I clench my teeth. *Of course* it wouldn't be that easy.

"Who has edit access to those records?" Breitling asks, all pretense of paper-pushing camaraderie evaporating into patented, barely restrained Inquisitor fury.

"I do, of course, and the work zone leaders."

The corporate nightmare continues. "What the hell is a work zone leader?" I ask against my better judgment.

"It's like a coach," Colin says. "They're in charge of a subset of Scribes with similar Operational abilities and skill levels. They have the final say in triaging assignments. This one would have gone to Alpha Zone, which means you'll need to talk to Teagan."

"Well, then." Breitling juts his chin at the phone, and Colin dives on it like a life preserver. His fingers shake as he stabs the plastic buttons. It's an over-the-top reaction, but I suppose these people aren't used to seeing the Chief Inquisitor walking around the Tower every day. Back home, he literally lives at the Summit, and…well, it's easy to forget how other people perceive him when he and I spend so much time together.

But that's going to change soon, isn't it? With our personal relationship ending, professional engagements will be fraught to say the least. I doubt we'll add any new ones beyond our current assignments. Then again, Prime Castillo has pointed out on more than one occasion how well we work together. Why wouldn't he want that to continue? Or even…become permanent?

I take a deep breath and wait for the sigil to take away the anxious pain burning in my chest. What a fucking mess.

"She'll be here in a second," Colin says as he hangs up. I didn't catch any part of his conversation, but it must have been terrifying because there's a knock at the door almost instantly.

"Come–"

He's halfway through his invitation when a short, stocky woman bursts into the room. Her curly strawberry blonde hair is trapped in two pigtails, and she's wearing blue overalls, green Chuck Taylors, and a bright yellow t-shirt that says, "There's Always Money in the Banana Stand."

"I didn't change a thing!" she cries. Not sure if her voice is high-pitched and squeaky because she's upset, or if it's always that way. "I assigned it out the moment it came in. I would have taken it myself, but I'm already six pips over my quota for the week. If I slotted any more,

I'd have to sell a share to Beta, and I need that for my trip to Edinburgh next month–"

"Oh my God, make it stop," I murmur toward Breitling's shoulder. I have nothing but respect for nine-to-fivers and the world they live in, but there's only so much of this I can take.

Breitling holds up his hands in a defensive gesture. "That's alright, Miss Teagan. We only need you to tell us to whom you assigned the case, if you can recall."

"Of course I can," she says, sounding somewhat indignant. "A project like that stands out. You don't forget who…ah, who you…huh. That's odd."

That refrain has officially worn out its welcome. "Let me guess," I say. "You don't remember."

She rubs the back of her neck. "I swear, I had it a second ago, but as I was reaching for it…" She screws up her face until her eyes almost disappear. With a loud exhale, they pop back to normal. "It's there. But it's fuzzy. I…I'm sorry, but I can't recall."

Colin makes a choking sound, which I think is his attempt at sounding stern. "Can someone please tell me what's going on?"

"That's need-to-know." Breitling gestures toward the open door, and I walk ahead of him. "We'll be in touch if we think you can be of any more help. Colin, Miss Teagan." He bobs his head at them and follows me out, leaving the two bewildered worker bees behind.

"Now what?" I ask as we walk toward the elevator.

Breitling holds up a finger, using his height to peer over the tops of the cubicles. "Not here."

He quickens his pace. We don't speak until we're behind the closed elevator door.

"Someone in the Scribery is not only doctoring reports, but changing internal records and altering employee memories, both of which are major violations of Order protocol."

"Plus, you know, aiding and abetting five murders," I remind him. It's not the first time an Order higher-up has viewed violating protocol as worse than taking lives, and I'm sure it won't be the last. But I'll keep reminding them that, for normal folk, *murder* is almost always the worst.

"We need to tell the Constable." He stabs the button for the first floor.

"Are you sure that's a good idea, seeing how he told us not to come back until we could see reason?"

"No offense, but…he told *you* not to come back." Breitling's shoulders rise as if preparing for a physical blow. Wise man–my hand itches to smack him in the arm. "I, however, must finish my duties as the Prime's proxy. Which naturally has led me to question what the *Prime* would do were he to ponder the lingering questions in this case. I have continued down a legitimate path of investigation with the much-needed help of a knowledgeable colleague, much as the Prime would have done."

I arch a brow. "That wouldn't be justification after the fact, would it?"

He grins. "No comment."

Thirty-Two

The door to the Constable's office whips open the moment Breitling sets his knuckle to the veneer. On the other side, Reaper Newton looks ashen and shaky.

"What the hell do you think you're doing, Inquisitor?" McNally bellows from behind his desk.

Newton's shoulders tighten as he steps aside. The overwrought appearance now makes sense. If I'd been cooped up in a room with this asshole for who knows how long, I'd be halfway to a nervous breakdown too.

"I received a call from Mr. Margaine." McNally stands with hands on hips and his stomach thrust out. "What business do you have harassing my Scribes when I specifically told you—"

"Pardon me," Breitling interrupts. "As Chief Inquisitor and the Prime's proxy, I am perfectly within my right to examine *any* investigation more closely, including this one."

McNally harrumphs. His soggy blue eyes slither over to me. "And *her?*"

Breitling scowls. "As you may recall, Constable, Miss Venture is still in residence here at the Tower. With

Edward in custody, she is now mine to command. I will use her as I see fit until I'm thoroughly satisfied."

I bite my lip as that string of jargony nonsense sends a hot shiver through my body. Dammit, I need to get the hell out of England.

"Now then." Breitling stands behind the middle of the three chairs in front of the desk but makes no move to sit. "Would you like to know what our search has uncovered?"

His cool demeanor does nothing to ingratiate him to McNally, whose grinding teeth I can hear from across the room. "Quickly."

"We located an Operator from the 1800s who fits the profile of the puppet master. Declan O'Dowd, a heart surgeon, registered Aetherist and Biologian, whose date of death roughly coincides with the end of the Autumn of Terror. You can verify it with Madame Misty if you wish."

"What does it matter?" McNally demands. He's long dead."

"No, he isn't," Breitling says. "Not all of him, anyway."

"What do you mean?"

I expect Breitling to continue. Instead, he turns to me. "Miss Venture, would you care to explain?"

Gulping, I face McNally. Time to sell it. "We believe that Declan O'Dowd used his combined surgical and Operational skills to remove his own heart via an ecto-bypass, like the ones Thomas performs. O'Dowd, however, was also an Aetherist, which allowed him to imbue the discarded organ with a mirror of himself and his Operations. He hid the organ somewhere in Whitechapel. When he died, his mirror was doomed to walk the Deathplane forever, never allowed to travel more than a certain distance from the heart. Now, someone has found that heart and used it to perform their own ecto-bypass. They then discarded it and replaced it with their own, thus gaining control of O'Dowd's mirror. Of Edward."

As I've been talking, McNally's face has cycled through a rainbow of hues. When I'm done, it's the color of a Red Delicious apple. "Who?" he demands. "Who do you think recovered this supposed heart?"

"That is the question," Breitling says. "Whoever it is, they're able to access computerized records, falsify reports, and alter memories–including Madame Misty's. The only thing she can remember are the words of someone without clearance trying to access records from 1888."

Breitling hesitates. I nod at him to go ahead. McNally needs to know, and there's no sense dragging it out. "Constable, we believe the culprit is a Scribe working here in the Tower. More than likely, it is whoever was tasked with researching and assembling the background on our victims. They tried to create a false pattern of drug use where there wasn't one, when in truth, they only cared about a single target: Gordon Gaye."

McNally goes still. His frown deepens, sinking into his folded neck until he looks like a frog about to explode.

And then–well, he explodes.

"Of all the ridiculous, preposterous, idiotic rubbish! Gordon Gaye was a saint among men. What's become of him wasn't his fault, and everyone knows it. He hadn't an enemy in the world. Besides, we vet everyone to the bone before they set foot on the property, and I review each candidate's dossier *personally* before we hire them. A killer of this caliber wouldn't make it within ten blocks of the Scribery without me knowing about it."

I barely stop my eyes from rolling. I've heard this speech so many times, from so many men like him. We could stand here all day trying to reason with him, and it wouldn't make a difference. He'll never admit he made a mistake, no matter who it might kill.

"We're not saying you didn't do your job," I say after I've tamped down my irritation. "But the puppet master is still out there—or rather, in here. If they decide to activate Ed again, who knows what will happen? Maybe all the safeguards will work, and we have nothing to worry about. But if the call is coming from inside the house…they might not."

He wrinkles his nose at his desk blotter. I can't play to his sympathy for the potential loss of life, since I'm pretty sure he doesn't have any. But try as I might, I can't bring myself to utter the words, "And the Crown won't like that, will they?"

"Sir," Breitling says, picking up where I left off, "if the master *is* in this building, they may believe they've gotten away with their crimes. We need to exercise our advantage now while their guard is down. If we wait too long, they may flee, and really *will* get away with it. Like Declan did."

McNally's jaw clenches so tight I'm afraid he'll need a crowbar to open it. "What do you need from me?"

Breitling leans forward, gripping the back of the chair with both hands. "How many Scribes do you have working here?"

"About a hundred and fifty."

"A hundred and *fifty*?" I gasp. I've never even seen *one* Scribe working at the Summit, let alone a gross of them. "Why so many? Especially since you've only got a dozen Reapers and, as far as I can tell, no Inquisitors?"

"The Tower has been around for centuries, Miss Venture," McNally says with a put-upon sigh. "Our era of gallivanting about the land with flags flying and swords drawn ended long ago. Accurate record-keeping and procedural documentation are our primary functions now. Over the years that has translated into more Scribes and less of every other role. We simply don't have the same need for Reapers and Inquisitors the way…the way we used to."

I narrow my eyes. "You mean the way we do in America."

He scowls, then turns back to Breitling. "Anything else?"

"Do you know the name of the Scribe that compiled the background on the latest Ripper victims?"

He shakes his head. "I don't know. Dora never mentioned their name."

"Why would she know who they are?" I ask.

"She's my go-between for all correspondence and paperwork. I assume she spoke to them when she retrieved the reports."

"Can't you do that sort of thing through email?"

He sneers at me with such vehemence I may as well have accused him of treason. "I like the personal touch of face-to-face interactions, and I don't always have time to handle them myself. Does that offend you, Miss Venture?"

It depends, I want to say. Do you handle *any* of the interactions yourself, or do you sit behind a desk while your servant girl does the legwork?

"May we speak with Dora?" Breitling interjects. "Perhaps she will remember something."

"She's gone home for the day," McNally says. "She's been run off her feet these last few weeks. A case like this generates a lot of back and forth between departments, and she asked for the afternoon to recuperate. I told her that was fine, so long as she makes up the time tomorrow."

Man, am I glad he's not *my* boss. One of us would end up dead, and it would *not* be me.

"With your permission, Constable," Breitling says, "may we call on her at home? Time may not be on our side."

McNally shrugs. "If it gets you out of my office and off Tower grounds for a few hours, I don't care what you do."

Thirty-Three

Breitling conducts our Tube ride to Dora's house. We emerge from the Gloucester Road station and walk a few blocks until we're standing in front of a three-story brick building nestled in the middle of a quiet street. I start up the wide stairs to the front door, but he stops me.

"Not there." He nods to the left, where a low gate guards another set of stairs that lead down. "There."

Under the stoop is a white door with a cross-window covered in frilly curtains. I ring the bell while Breitling waits on the bottom step—he's too tall to fit in the entryway without hunching. The curtains ripple, and a few seconds later, the door opens.

"Miss Venture?" Dora asks, peering timidly out at us. When she spots Breitling, her eyes widen. "And Chief Inquisitor! Oh, my…what are you doing here?"

I groan inwardly, annoyed with myself. *He's* the celebrity, and therefore the more obvious way in. I step back, and sure enough, she descends on Breitling like a fangirl meeting Elvis.

"It's an honor, sir." She grabs his hand in both of hers and pulls him toward the door. "Please come in. I'm afraid it's a bit of a mess. I so rarely have guests. But I can offer you tea. Or coffee, since that's what you're probably used to in America, right? Oh, and I have these excellent vanilla ginger biscuits! You must try them. You too, Miss Venture."

She rushes past me with Breitling in tow. He shoots me a pleading look as she drags him inside. "Help me," he whispers.

Biting my cheek to hold in my smile, I follow them in.

"Here, please sit." She hurries him into an emerald-green chair. "I'll get the tea."

"That's not—" He tries to stand, but he's no match for the saggy cushion. By the time he pulls himself to the edge of the seat, she's already gone.

"I think we just met the president of your fan club," I mumble.

"So it would seem," he says with a wry smile. "Thank you for all the help keeping her off me, by the way."

"Anytime." I wink and smile back. He doesn't look away, and like an idiot, neither do I. My face, and then the rest of me, start to tingle as I examine the hard line of his nose, the tension in his cut jaw, the curve of his lower lip…

No. Not the time. Work now.

I turn away and examine the framed pictures on the mantle. They're all moody black-and-white shots of inanimate objects or animals. If they weren't so blurry and poorly composed, they could be the stock images sold with the frame. The rest of the house is equally strange. Dried flowers sit in vases, not in a decorative way, but as if someone let them shrivel and then forgot to throw them out. The stems and leaves are withered, and flaky petals lay scattered around the crusty bases. The tall windows filling the back wall are smudged and covered with vines, making the room feel smaller and the light seem dirty. The smell of overcooked carrots hangs in the humid air.

"Kettle's on!" Dora sweeps back into the room holding a plastic serving tray lined with paper napkins and filled with crumbly, anemic cookies. She sets it on the coffee table and sits down on the end of the couch nearest Breitling, cozying up so close to the arm that her knee bumps his. "Now then. What brings you to my home, Chief?"

He clears his throat and shifts position, putting a modicum of distance between them without being rude. "We have a few questions for you. About your work on the Ripper case."

"Oh." Her brows tighten. "Okay, then."

I turn back to the mantle and fade into the background. If she can believe it's just the two of them, the more forthcoming she'll be.

"Constable McNally told us you handle all his correspondence. Is that correct?"

"Yes, sir," she says. "Every bit of professional conversation he has goes through me."

"Then you must have shepherded the victimology reports between the Constable and the Scribery."

"Indeed, I did, sir. I handed the Constable's initial request to Director Margaine himself, and retrieved the reports the moment they were ready."

"Retrieved them from whom?"

"Zone Leader Teagan, sir."

"Did you ever have contact with the Scribes who created the report?"

A soft shushing noise disrupts the silence, as if she's running her hands over her legs. She's nervous. I pretend to study a photograph of a dog on a beach. I don't want her to suspect I'm listening for a lie.

"As the Constable's Page, I interact with first- and second-tier department leaders only. I don't mean for that to sound arrogant. It's just…more efficient that way. I'm sorry."

I let out a disappointed breath. No deception. Just worried about looking bad in front of a superior.

"That's alright, Ms. Wood." Though I'm sure Breitling is as irritated as I am about this dead end, he hides it under a thick layer of placation. "I can appreciate the need for efficiency, considering the volume of tasks you must face."

"Yes, sir." She heaves a relieved sigh. "It takes it out of you, you know, running to and fro all day. You learn to take shortcuts wherever you can."

I shake my head at a lopsided snapshot of a poodle. I haven't heard the phrase "to and fro" since preschool, and now I've heard it twice on this trip.

No…three times.

"But it's not so bad," Dora continues, her words adopting an almost sultry edge. "I get to meet a lot of…*interesting* people."

Breitling shifts in his chair again, this time with enough force to make the old wooden legs creak and scrape across the floor. I should rescue him from this awkward exchange, but I can't. My mind has frozen, and my body along with it, as a scrap of innocuous conversation forces its way into the forefront of my memory, recited to the tune of a bizarre nursery rhyme.

Do your ears hang low? Do they wobble to and fro?

We'd go back and forth for days. Sending messages to and fro.

McNally. Gordon Gaye. And Dora, the girl who ferried those messages to and fro…to and fro…

"That's how you met Gordon."

It shouldn't be loud enough for her to hear me, but she does.

"Excuse me?"

My shoulders hitch. Her tone hasn't lost its breezy sweetness, but there's an edge to it now.

"You delivered the Constable's messages to Reaper Gaye. At first, you dropped them off, like you did with everyone else. But they corresponded so often that you figured it was faster, more *efficient*, to wait in Gordon's office while he wrote out his responses." I turn away from the mantle. "Or did he invite you to stay the very first time?"

She doesn't answer me, but the flash of shock in her eyes tells me I'm on the right track. In the corner of my vision, Breitling's lips part in surprise. I suppress a smile–now is not the time to gloat. Still, I'm proud that I've put it together before him.

"No one spends that much time in the company of someone else without developing rapport," I continue. "At first, it was friendship. And then it turned into more."

"His wife was sick," Dora says, her tone imploring even as her hands tighten into fists. "He was lonely. And…so was I."

"Did he tell you he loved you?"

"He *did* love me," she insists. "But she was dying. He couldn't leave her."

"And then…she died."

She nods. "Even though he knew it was coming, it devastated him. He started drinking. Lost his job. I would have helped him through it, but I couldn't."

"You didn't want to?" I draw a breath and strike. "Or he didn't let you?"

Her doe eyes narrow. "What?"

"You loved him. He said he loved you, but he couldn't do so openly. So, you held on, waiting for the day he would be free. That day came, and he fell apart. But you didn't leave because of that. After all, you were in love. You would have walked into hell itself to help lift him out of it. No–after all your patience and sacrifice, he spurned you." Another breath, another strike. The big one. "And you decided to make him pay."

I expect denial, defensiveness, rage. Instead, she hangs her head so low her red hair falls over her face.

"It was you?" Breitling has recovered from his surprise enough to join the party. "Reaper Gaye, Miss Long…you killed them all?"

She doesn't move. I arch a brow at Breitling, indicating he should rouse her. He shakes his head tightly, his mouth firm, condemning my impatience.

"I've had Operational affinity my whole life." Dora's gentle voice breaks the silence before we can continue our argument. "My parents had me tested, and while the administrators didn't give me my exact OAL, I could tell they were impressed. They knew it was just a matter of time before I Effloresced. So, I enrolled as a Page right away. I wanted to be ready when it happened.

"I got older. And older. And still nothing. But I was patient. It would happen. They'd practically said as much. It would happen, and then I could move up. Be a Reaper someday. Or maybe more." She stares longingly at Breitling's collar for a moment before returning her gaze to the floor. "But that's not how things work here, is it? Even if I had Effloresced, no one was ever going to let me be more than I am now."

"So, you *made* yourself more. That's where O'Dowd came in." As I say the name, something else occurs to me.

"Dora Wood. Declan O'Dowd. I assume the similarity isn't a coincidence."

She shrugs. "His wife changed their name after he died. She didn't like the suspicious looks she got when Londoners found out she was Irish."

"*That's* why you snuck into the Catacombs," I say as another puzzle piece clicks into place. "You come from a long line of Operators, and you wanted to know more about your origins. Declan O'Dowd is, what? Your great, great…great grandfather?"

Her head dips lower.

"Did you know he was Jack the Ripper before you searched the records?" Breitling asks.

Her shoulders tremble. "My older relatives gossiped about it, but there was nothing concrete. Suspicion, that's all. A few bizarre notes scratched in old journals. I didn't expect it to be true."

"You believed it enough to start with the 1888 records though," he continues. "Can I presume that, when you saw what he was and how he died, those 'bizarre notes' in his journals made a bit more sense?"

She shakes her head, but in a circle, like she isn't sure what the answer is. "He'd lost his senses near the end of his life. Everything was all about the plague of sin that had infected the city, and how a heartless angel of the air would come to cleanse the people and cut out the rot. Everyone assumed it was his Catholic faith and surgical background mixing with his growing madness."

"Hm." I grunt, hoping to disguise my discomfort. *A heartless angel. Cleanse the people. Cut out the rot.* It sure sounds crazy–unless, of course, you already know what it means.

The skin over my knuckles tightens.

"Match."

My mouth drops open. "*Blood* match. Is that it?"

Breitling frowns at me with confusion, but I forge ahead. "With the familial connection between you and Declan, you knew his heart would give you the ability to perform an ecto-bypass on yourself, like he had. The journals must have told you where to find it. That's how you gained control of...of the heartless angel. It was everything you wanted–including a tool for your revenge."

"That's impossible." Breitling stands, looming over Dora in that intimidating way he's so good at. "Even with genetics to help you, you're a Page. There's no way—"

"That's what everyone thinks, isn't it?" The words, low and tense, emanate from beneath her fiery strands. "A Page can't be good for anything besides running errands and ferrying memos. Talentless drones, that's what we are, or toys to be used for one's pleasure and discarded when we're not shiny and new anymore."

Something like a giggle, only much meaner, escapes her throat. "But I don't need to tell *you* about that, do I, Miss Venture?"

Her words slap me so hard they leave me stunned. From the way the color drains from Breitling's face, the statement has hit him equally hard.

"You and I are *not* the same," I say as I advance on her, my shock giving way to rage. She stiffens, and even Breitling backs away a little. "I never killed innocent people out of spite."

"They *weren't* innocent," she snaps, her eyes flashing up at me. "You saw the reports. Junkies and alcoholics, every one of them. They were throwing their lives away anyhow. I just sped things along."

"Stop it!" I bring my foot down with enough force to make her jump. "We know that's not true, and even if it were, it's not *your* place to decide when someone's life isn't worth living anymore."

Breitling arches a brow at me, but I shrug him off. There's no time for irony when you're in the middle of unmasking a killer. "You fixed the reports and records to create the appearance of a pattern that fit with Gaye's addiction. But this had nothing to do with drugs or alcohol. That was all a smokescreen for your vengeance. What I can't figure out, though, is why? Aside from being criminally average, they'd done nothing to you, or to anyone. Why choose them?"

"I didn't. Heartless did."

"That's not true either. I was with him during the attack on Emma Long, and we inquired about Gordon Gaye. He had no idea—"

"She doesn't mean Edward," Breitling says gently, cooling my rage. "She means the Operation. It must have selected victims based on proximity to the original locations. They were, in a way, random."

Fresh chills roll down my back. "Not random. The Rigour. That's why it kept getting more specific. The Operation used the Rigour to find the right people on the right path at the right time, growing more efficient and precise with each one."

My mind reels and I fall back a step. Even Breitling looks a little stunned.

Dora, on the other hand, is disaffected. "Whatever you want to call it. It didn't matter to me. Once I completed the ecto-bypass, the Operation ran itself."

"Not completely," Breitling says. "There was still the matter of Gordon Gaye. He didn't share any commonalities with Mary Kelly. How did you get to him?"

She scoffs but remains silent.

"I bet it was easy," I volunteer. "The Operation may have been on autopilot, but it was still hers. She could have controlled it all along but chose not to until the very end. We heard what she said to Ed before she attacked Gordon. Remember?"

He glares down at her. "On your feet, Heartless."

She shudders and curls in on herself, her hand pressed against her chest.

"Right. With us on the case, she had to speed up the timeline or risk being stopped before she got to her real target. She had to initiate that attack directly. All she had to do was make sure Gaye was in the right place when she did it. What did you do, Dora? Ask him to meet you for lunch somewhere close by, for old time's sake?"

She grinds her teeth. "I'm done talking."

"Oh, but we have more questions," Breitling says. "It's easy enough for the Constable's PA to change victim reports. But how did you manipulate so many people? Declan's heart may have transferred the ability to perform an ecto-bypass, but it held no Memorist Operations. How did you hoodwink Madame Misty into forgetting your face, or Colin and Teagan into forgetting to whom they assigned the victim research? And, perhaps most importantly–" He leans forward until she has no place else to look but straight at him "--where is *your* heart now?"

Despite his subzero tone, she manages a smug smile. "You already know the answer to that one."

"Oh, do I?" he snaps, her attitude clearly wearing on him. "Hear me, Miss Wood: If I don't know yet, I will soon enough. One way…or another."

Her posture remains rigid, but the quiver in her lower lip gives her away. She's terrified.

She should be.

He straightens and buttons his jacket. "Dora Wood, I am detaining you on the charges of performing an unregistered Operation, false imprisonment of a sovereign entity, assault, and murder. Stand up and face me."

The hand pressed to her chest clenches, but she remains seated. "You're going to regret this. I promise you that."

"On your feet," he growls. "Now."

After another tense, motionless moment, she complies. Tilting her chin up, she meets Breitling's gaze. Her cold, blank expression makes my skin crawl. "Whatever you say, Chief."

His throat bobs, and he flicks his fingers at her forehead. Those unnerving eyes shutter, and she collapses, unconscious, onto the couch.

"Jesus," I whisper as Breitling runs a hand through his hair. "She's…something else."

"Indeed," he says as he pulls his cell phone from his pocket. "I'll apprise the Constable and request he send someone with a vehicle to retrieve us. We can't bring her on the Tube in this state."

I nod and start for the door–no point in waiting for the cavalry in this stuffy, weird little apartment–when Breitling grabs me by the arm.

"Adina," he says softly over the ringing of the phone pressed to his shoulder. "What she implied about you…"

I shake my head. "It's idle gossip, I'm sure. A way for low-level employees to feel important. She doesn't know anything real."

He lowers his chin. That's not what he meant, and we both know it.

With a shaky smile, I squeeze his hand before removing it from my arm. Of course her inference was wrong. He's not using me, and I'm not his toy.

After all, that's kind of our whole problem.

Thirty-Four

Half an hour later, Reaper Newton arrives in the service van. He examines Dora, then checks his watch.

"It'll be dark soon," he says, his tone as bland as his expression. "We'll wait until then to move her. Walk her out like a drunk. It's more discrete than taking her by the wrists and ankles."

We do as he suggests. When it comes time for the lift, I tap in for Breitling, being closer in height to Newton than he is. We drag her up the stairs and across the sidewalk with her arms slung over our shoulders, all the while muttering things like, "You're okay," and "Let's get you home," before loading her into the back of the van. I don't know about Newton, but I use a bit more force than necessary.

"There's space for one of you in front," he says when she's squared away.

"I'll ride in back," I say. "I don't mind."

"Nope. No belts back here. Can't allow it." He slams the doors shut for emphasis.

I want to point out that I've already ridden in the back once today, but I don't feel like arguing about whether being alive versus in a corpse-like state makes it more or less safe. I turn to Breitling, but I can't quite look at him. "Maybe we can take the Tube back and–"

"It's alright," he cuts me off. "I need to do a sweep of Ms. Wood's flat. We still don't know how she occluded so many people's memories, or where her heart is—or Declan's, for that matter. It may not control Edward anymore, but it still contains a powerful Operational transfer. The answers will be in his journals, and they are most likely here somewhere. You go. I'll stay."

That's what I was afraid of. With a furtive glance at Newton, I slide a step closer to Breitling, raising my eyes as far as his collar. "I…don't want to."

He inhales and his hand rises almost all the way to my chin. But he catches himself at the last moment, and his arm falls back to his side.

"I will see you soon," he whispers. "I promise."

I nod and turn away. I don't want him to see my doubt. "Guess it's you and me," I say to Newton.

"Fab," he mutters.

Well, this is going to be a fun drive.

Breitling escorts me to the passenger's side. He reaches for the handle, but I grab it first. Newton may be aggressively indifferent, but he's not stupid. I can't stop Breitling from closing the door after me, however, or looking at me through the window like he's trying to memorize my face. Or standing in the street, hands in his pockets, watching us drive away. Thank God he didn't say goodbye. I've already broken my rule about crying in front of an Inquisitor several times over. I don't need to do it in front of a Reaper too.

We zip through town, the semi-late hour and the lack of rain making traffic almost bearable. As we approach the Tower's underground parking garage, my brain conjures what the next few hours will bring. I'll convene with Thomas and McNally while Newton dispatches Dora to the Pit, which I assume is somewhere on the Tower grounds. I have no desire to learn anything more specific than that. Breitling will return, we'll go through the facts of the case as we understand them, and McNally will take it from there. Applause and laurels all around. McNally will probably be knighted, which is irritating to think about. Maybe Breitling will too. Picturing him kneeling in front of the monarch as he struggles not to roll his eyes almost makes me smile. Then we'll get on a plane and go home.

And that will be that.

I take a breath and let it go. The release relieves some of the tightness in my chest. I've known all along that my heart would be smashed to pieces eventually, but it's always been at some nebulous future date. The fact that I know when it's coming and the events that will lead up to it should make me sad. Instead, it's oddly comforting, the way it stretches out in front of me, step by step, creating a clear and inevitable path. All I have to do is walk it.

Except...we're still driving.

I look out the window at the buildings towering high above us. None of them are familiar. As we turn down a narrow one-way and glide to a stop, I check the white sign affixed to the corner.

Mitre Street.

Oh. Fuck.

"We're here." Newton's cold, dead voice sends a surge of adrenaline shooting through my limbs. I scramble for the door handle and almost get it open when five strong, thick fingers wrap around my neck.

"You don't want to do that," he hisses in my ear. Electricity sparks from his palm, sizzling down my spine and impaling my lower back. It's not a full-on spasm, but it hurts enough to let me know he's capable of disabling me with very little effort on his part. My sigil sparks as it tries to compensate for the assault, but it only dulls the pain. The rigidity, and the danger, remain.

"Okay." I hold my hands up in surrender. "I'm not resisting. I'll do whatever you say."

He grunts and lets me go. I watch him exit the car, keys in hand, his eyes fixed on me through the windshield as he comes around to open my door.

"Put your hands down," he says when I'm standing on the sidewalk. I comply. Grabbing my wrist, he leads me leisurely across the street. If anyone happens to see us, we'll look like a couple out for a nighttime stroll, and if I start to make a fuss, he's in an ideal position to bring the pain. Pretty clever, goddamn him.

Heart pounding and head spinning, I try to take stock of my surroundings as covertly as I can. We're on an out-of-the-way street in what might be a business district. No one's around. On the next block, light filters out from a few of the ground-floor windows. Restaurants, I think. Maybe I could make a break for it. Run into one of them and start screaming my head off. If this were the Deathplane, that would be a no-brainer. But in the land of the living, I'm a middling athlete at best, and Reaper Newton is pretty fit. If he caught me before I got to safety, I'd be even more fucked than I already am.

Halfway down the block, Newton veers to the left and cuts through a small city park. My stomach knots as I spot a placard on one of the central flowerbeds. We're too far away to read the text, but I have no trouble seeing the drawing of a woman's portrait.

That's it. The murder site of Catherine Eddowes, second to last of the Ripper's Canonical Five and the only one Dora Woods has failed to replicate.

Until now.

"Son of a bitch," I whisper, dragging my feet a little more heavily across the flagstone. "Did you even put up an intentions threshold around Ed before Gordon Gaye was killed? Or did you just wave your hands until the air crackled enough to fool everyone?"

"Shut up," he grumbles.

Suspicions confirmed. Which means I can assume there isn't one in place now either. But as far as I know, Ed's still incapacitated, and they can't undo Breitling's Operation without a regulated antidote.

Again—as far as I know.

"I bet you got her into the Catacombs too," I continue. "You cleared her to read whatever books she asked for, and afterward you zapped Madame Misty to scramble her memory, and Colin, and Teagan, and whoever else she pointed her pretty little finger at."

"I *said* shut up." He yanks on my wrist, lighting up the nerves in my forearm.

I jerk back despite the pain. "And what about me, huh? I couldn't have been part of the plan the whole time. Is this improv? Or…or payback? After all, someone should have died here yesterday, right after Emma Long, if I hadn't gotten in the way. When Dora found out I'd stopped her third attack and prevented the fourth from ever starting…is that when she decided to swap me in? Told you to keep an eye out for opportunities, and strike when the time was right?"

He meets my questions with condescending silence. That infuriates me more than anything he could have said.

On the other side of the square is an L-shaped brick structure that surrounds a fenced-in playground. He stops in front of a sliding glass door and places a hand on the motorized mechanism. It clanks in protest, but the door opens. The scent of Elmer's glue and sharpened pencils floods my nose. No doubt this used to be a school–and a low-rent tenement a hundred years before that. But the bare walls and boarded windows say it hasn't been anything for a long time.

"In there." He wheels to the left and tosses me into what was once an office. I stumble over the puckered, dingy carpet and smash into the far wall.

"What is the matter with you?" I regain my balance and storm back across the room, coming to stand in front of him. "You're a *Reaper*, and the Constable's personal bodyguard, and you're taking orders from a *Page*? You've got to be kidding me."

"You're kidding *yourself*." For the first time since I met him, his eyes hold an emotion: pure, all-consuming hatred. "Reaper. Page. It's all shit. We're dogs told to heel and fetch and lie down and obey. That's all we'll ever be."

I scoff. "*She* told you that?"

"She didn't have to," he sneers. "At the Summit, or any other hold, I'd be an Inquisitor by now. Instead, I'm an errand boy for Constable Shitface. I've tried for years to get out. Tried *everything*. And what do I get for my trouble? Denials, and delays, and sorry-but-you-forgot-form-12-fucking-C-better-luck-next-time. All of it amounts to the same thing: I'm not going anywhere. And if I'm not going anywhere, then why *not* let it burn?"

I gape at him, fists clenched in the face of such stunning selfishness. "I can't believe I'm saying this—me, of all people—but you're a fucking disgrace."

He slaps me. Stars explode in my vision, and I stumble but stay upright. Despite the fury of his action, the calm expression remains plastered on his face.

Fuck this guy.

I lunge for him, my clawed hands aimed at his throat.

An invisible arm slams into my stomach and throws me across the room. My shoulder smashes into the wall, and I sink to the floor.

He's already here.

"Goodbye, Miss Venture." With an expression as dull as mud, Newton steps out of the room and slams the door.

Thirty-Five

"Ed?" Clutching my bruised shoulder, I huddle against the wall. The room is a ten-by-ten square and empty. Three small windows sit high in the wall over my head, their frosted panes the only meager source of light. Even if I had a way to break them, the iron crossbars make escape impossible. Besides, I'm sure Newton is standing outside the door. He'd be on me the moment he heard the glass break. Screaming for help–same problem. All that's going to do is get me another slap in the face. But that, of course, pales compared to what's coming.

My throat tightens as I recall, very much against my will, the details of the Mitre Square victim. Catherine Eddowes didn't get it as bad as Mary Kelly, but it was close. Slashed throat and belly, as per usual. Intestines shredded. Face mutilated. Womb and left kidney removed. Unlike Kelly, however, Eddowes came out of it with all her limbs still attached. So…that's something, I guess.

A soft scrape against the carpet draws my attention to a spot six feet in front of me. Still holding my arm, I slide my back up the wall until I'm on my feet. "Ed, please. Don't let it end like this. At least…let me see you."

For a moment, there's nothing. And then he's there. Not six feet away, but right in front of me. The weak streetlight from the window illuminates his milky eyes and gaping mouth. I shrink back as far as the wall will let me, but only for a second. I've seen him in Dora's thrall before, so his appearance doesn't surprise me. It's the contradiction of him. How can someone seem so passionless and so bloodthirsty at the same time?

"You can fight this," I whisper. "Just because a path is set doesn't mean it has to be walked. You told me as much."

He grunts as if I've shoved him in the chest. That's a good sign, right? I glance down at his hands. Ten fingers, all present and accounted for. Definitely a good sign.

"You may not be a person, but you're still human," I continue. "You're one of the most human beings I've ever met, in fact. You can resist her. You're doing it already."

With trembling hands, I reach for him.

My fingers slip through his like they're not even there. Which, technically, they aren't. Christ, I'm such an idiot. I know how this works better than anyone. It doesn't change just because I'm on the other side of it now.

With a wolfish growl, he withdraws a step and raises his arms. My heart drops as the fingers of both hands melt into each other.

Well, that failed. I have about two seconds to come up with Plan B. My brain is screaming at me to run, to duck and cover, to do *something*. But my feet won't move. Neither will my arms. All my muscles have checked out, already steeling themselves against the impending assault. The only thing still capable of movement are my eyes, following his human fingers as they transform into twin stilettos.

Is it me, or are those bigger than before?

He lowers his freshly weaponized arms to his sides. I expect him to lunge, but he just keeps staring at me. Something shifts behind the white film. My heart leaps. Is it working? Can he throw off her power?

His shoulders lift, then settle in a heavy sigh.

Not resistance. Resignation.

He inches closer.

Finally, my feet get the frantic messages my brain has been sending, and I dart to the left before he can fall on me. His head turns, tracking the move, but he doesn't pursue. Flexing my fists, I take one last look around. Door guarded. Windows barred. The drop ceiling may provide an exit, but there's nothing to climb on to get up there. No desk, no chairs, not even a broken table leg to use as a weapon. Not that it would work against him anyway.

Now his languid demeanor makes sense. He's not chasing me because he doesn't need to. There's nowhere for me to run. Even as my heart sinks through the floor, I've got to hand it to Dora and Newton. I couldn't have picked a better death chamber myself.

He takes a step in my direction. I slide further to the left. He follows, in no hurry. Good; neither am I. We circle each other, distant at first, but growing closer with each step in our dance of death. It's a decent delaying tactic…except I'm not sure what I'm delaying *for*. No one knows where I am, and no one is coming for me. I am alone, the way I've always been. The way everyone is, in the end.

He takes another step toward me. When I don't move, he takes another. Still, I stay where I am. His brows shoot up with a question.

I tip a shoulder to my ear. "Let's get this over with."

He lunges at me with uncanny speed. Behind the white film, his pupils constrict in frustration. Raising a hand, he drags one stiletto down my cheek. The nail scratches, but not hard enough to draw blood.

"Prepare yourself, girl," he says. The words have no empathy. No life.

I close my eyes. With no other path to take, I do as he suggests.

He draws the blade from my jaw to my throat. I dig my nails into my palms as tears slide down my face. "I'm sorry. I failed you. I'm so sorry, Ed."

"Wha'?"

That's not the same zombie monotone he had a moment ago. With hope I have no right to feel, I crack an eyelid. Dark irises stare back at me, disoriented and confused. "Adina?"

"Ed?" I venture, still unsure that what I'm seeing is real. "Ed, can you hear me?"

"Aye." He steps back, and his hand falls from my throat, the blade already shrinking and splitting. "Wha' was that?"

"Dora...your master...called you to kill me," I say, my body trembling with adrenaline.

He rubs the back of his neck. "'Twas like somethin' crawled up inside me and donned me arms and legs like a soddin' jumper. Never happened like that before."

"Because she never Operated like that before," I say. "I was forced onto Catherine Eddowes's path. Seems she had to force you onto yours too, by Operating at full power."

"Power o'er my body, aye. 'Twasn't the only thing different this time though. I...I *knew* what I was doin'. I couldn't control it. Couldn't stop it. But...I knew."

His head drops.

"It's okay." I go to place a hand on his shoulder before remembering it doesn't work that way. "You stopped yourself before you went through with it. You resisted her."

"Nah." He shakes his head. "I didn't resist her. She disappeared. If she hadn't, I woulda slit your throat like it was nothin'. *Hungry* for that, she was. Didn't stop thinkin' about it the whole time she had a hold o' me."

My stomach clenches. "What do you mean, she disappeared? She had me. I was dead. Why would she just…give up?"

He shrugs and wipes his nose with the back of his hand. Giving him a chance to recover himself, I tiptoe over to the door and press my ear to it. Silence. If Newton can hear what's transpired, he isn't trying to intervene.

"We need to check on Dora," I whisper. "She's incapacitated in a van one street over. But if she released her hold on you, it's possible she's…escaped, or something?"

I can barely finish that sentence, it's so illogical. Even if Newton had gotten his hands on the antidote to pull her out of Breitling's fugue, he hadn't done it. I would have seen him.

So, what happened to her?

"We need to get out of here. Can you…handle Newton?"

His forehead puckers. Dammit, I shouldn't have asked him to do that. He's been through a traumatic event. It's insensitive to make him—

"He the one locked you in here?" he growls.

I nod. "Yes. He is."

Beneath his heavy brows, his eyes gleam with unbridled delight. "In that case, 'twould be my absolute pleasure."

He's through the door before I can say another word. As Newton's grunts of surprise devolve into shrieks of pain, my lips part in a delighted smile of my own.

When silence reigns once again, Edward starts to hack at the lock on the office door. It takes a while, thanks to the interdimensional barrier, but eventually he does enough damage that a hard slam with my good shoulder is enough to force it open.

Newton sprawls on the scuffed linoleum tile near the administration desk. Thin, black bruises mar his face, and both his arms are as limp as wet noodles. His ribs expand and retract in a shallow, irregular motion that only adds to my joy. "Nice work."

Edward dips in a slight bow, then steps aside to let me lead the way out of the building and through the square to the street.

When I spot the van, my jaw drops. Breitling stands with his back pressed to the rear door, his hair and suit disheveled and his head tilted to the sky like he's trying to catch his breath.

"How–?" I exhale before breaking into a sprint. "Levi!"

He snaps upright. "Adina?"

He barely has time to open his arms before I throw myself into them, burying my face in his chest and wrapping him in a hug so tight he grunts in surprise. A second later, his arms are around me too, crushing me to him as if his life depends on it. If the Rigour has anything to say about our behavior, I don't feel it. And I don't give a shit.

"It was Newton," I say, my frantic words swallowed by the soft fabric of his vest. "She and him were in it together. Her call must have been enough to overpower your Operation because she brought Ed here. And Newton brought me. And he—he was gonna…"

"Shh," he murmurs, holding me tighter. "It's alright. It's over now."

Nodding, I squeeze him a little tighter before pulling away and looking up at him. "How did you find me?"

He tilts his head toward the roof of the van. I follow his gaze to the pair of beady black eyes peering down at us.

"You're kidding?" I say around a giggle.

"Not a bit. Apart from having to convince an Uber driver to 'follow that crow,' she's better than GPS." He pushes my hair back so he can hold my face in his hands. "Of course, by the time she arrived at Dora's house, I already knew you needed me."

My heart swells. That's right. He can feel when I'm in trouble. I'd almost forgotten.

Swallowing the emotions rising in my throat, I give Shiva a small salute. "Thanks, buddy."

She ruffles her feathers, caws twice, and takes off. Far be it for my near-death experience to ruin her vacation.

"What about Dora?" I ask when Shiva has disappeared into the night. "Is she still incapacitated?"

"No." His eyes fall to the ground. "She's dead."

The statement almost knocks me over. "What? How?"

He releases his hold on me and opens the back door. Dora appears the same as she did when we put her in the van. Then I look closer, and my stomach roils. Her eyes are not only open, but bulging, until I can see all the whites and the deep, wet red of her sockets. Her jaw sags past her collarbone as if dislodged from her skull. The only thing keeping it attached to her face is her pale, distended skin. Her hands form white-knuckled fists, and her nostrils are frozen in a permanent flare. She must have died in terrible pain.

Or bone-deep terror.

"My God," I gasp. "What happened to her?"

"She was like this when I found her," Breitling says. "When she clutched her chest during our interrogation, it wasn't out of emotion. She was calling Edward to execute this…final task. Without the Rigour shouldering some of the burden, plus the effort of overcoming Edward's incapacitation, *and* Operating while physically incapacitated herself…it was too much for her to bear."

I stare at Dora, her corpse a nightmare I can't look away from, as questions surface in my brain. Edward did say it had felt different this time. Still, something doesn't add up. "The heart failed at the exact time Ed attacked me? That's one hell of a coincidence, don't you think?"

He shrugs. "Declan survived just four months after he began his crusade. With the decline in veracity, the ecto-bypass Dora performed on herself would have been even less stable. Considering that she isn't even a true Operator, it's a wonder she lasted as long as she did."

"But–"

"Adina." He glares at me, his eyes flashing with a hint of spectral blue. "She was dead when I found her. Understand?"

I shut my mouth. Can't get much clearer than that.

"Good." He closes the door. "Where's Newton?"

"In the school, unconscious with what I hope are many internal injuries." I glance over my shoulder. Edward lingers on the sidewalk near the square, his attention angled away from us. "Ed knocked him around enough to put him down for the count."

"Good man." Breitling nods in his direction.

I blink in surprise. "You can see him?"

"As clearly as I can see you when you're in the Deathplane."

"Interesting," I murmur. But my anxiety outweighs my curiosity. "So, what happens now?"

He inhales and draws himself upright. "I will inform Constable McNally of the situation, who will send a unit to apprehend Reaper Newton. Then we will return to the Tower. All of us. Thomas will attend to Dora, and you and I will debrief. As for Edward…" He sighs. "Right now, all I can say for certain is that there is much to discuss."

That's about the best I can hope for, I suppose. That, and the opportunity to fight on Edward's behalf. Without a master, he's no longer a threat to anyone. I'm sure of it. He could continue living as he always has. Assuming we find Dora's heart, that is.

And once we do…what do we do with it? Could the Tower hide it? They must have a vault or something where they keep dangerous artifacts a la *Raiders of the Lost Ark*. Or maybe Madame Misty could find a place in the Catacombs, some cobweb-covered nook where no one would ever look for it. There's got to be a solution. After all, this is the Order we're talking about. They didn't get to where they are by being bad at keeping secrets.

Thirty-Six

B reitling gets us back to the Tower in record time. I don't know if it's the high emotion or the thrill of being on the right side of the car, but he drives like a maniac, whipping around hairpin turns and running yellows mere moments before they turn red. In Vegas he's so reserved and defensive, but get him behind the wheel in London and it's demolition derby time? I want to ask what the hell, but I'm afraid if I distract him, he'll hit something, so I grip the windowsill, grit my teeth, and wait for it to be over.

I had offered to let Edward sit in the front, but he'd refused, climbing into the back before I could argue. It's understandable–if I could sit in the company of my creator, dead or otherwise, I'd jump at the chance too.

Against all odds, we pull into the underground parking garage unscathed. McNally is waiting for us outside the elevator with not one, but two Reapers at his side.

"Miss Venture," he says as I join him at the back of the van, his expression a bizarre combination of nervous and sullen. "Where is…ah…?"

I gesture to the vehicle as Edward jumps through the doors, startling Breitling, who had been about to open them.

"Sorry, brother," Edward says, straightening the shoulders of his cloak. "I'd forgotten you had the sight o' me now."

"It's alright," Breitling mutters, tugging at the lapels of his own jacket. "I suppose I should have expected that."

I smile at the two of them. Even with the differences in complexion, they carry themselves in much the same way. I wonder if Breitling sees the similarity too. Could that be part of the reason he's been so frosty about Edward and me? The more I think about it, the more sense it makes. Edward and I having things in common is one thing. But if Edward shares characteristics with Breitling too…

Match.

I swallow hard. To be fair to the Rigour, I can't find much fault with that assessment. Edward and I *are* a match in a lot of ways. There's just one problem.

I'm not in love with Edward.

"Inquisitor Breitling, can you please direct us to our guest?" McNally prompts as the Reapers approach the van. They look ready to pounce as soon as someone tells them where to go.

"Stop right there." Breitling moves casually but strategically, placing himself between Edward and the Reapers. "He came of his own free will, and he is no longer under the control of a master. He does not present a threat, and therefore should not be treated like a prisoner."

"Aye!" Edward claps Breitling on (and a bit through) the shoulder. "Well said, lad."

I stifle a laugh, both at the sight of Breitling trying not to react to Ed's touch and the way his face contorts at being called "lad" by someone who appears to be ten years his junior.

"I see," McNally grumbles. "In that case, Inquisitor, I suggest you join us in my office, where we can discuss the night's events and how to proceed."

I scowl at him. "Gee, I didn't hear *my* name in that sentence."

"Rude."

The knuckle-slap is swift, but there's no fire behind it. Am I finally getting used to it?

Or is *it* getting used to me?

Whatever the Rigour's opinion may be, McNally has had enough. He rounds on me, his neck swelling bigger than ever.

Shit. Here comes the whammy.

"Miss Venture. Section Seventeen of the–"

"Stop!" Breitling's bellow shakes the walls and steals the words right out of McNally's mouth—or shoves them down his throat. McNally's eyes bug as his distended neck bobbles but doesn't deflate. He hacks and splutters, his face scrunching like he's tasting something rotten.

"Insubordination," he wheezes, the air trapped in his neck closing around his throat. "Level one. You'll be censured for this, Inquisitor."

"So be it," Breitling sneers. "And it's *Chief* Inquisitor, Constable."

With that, he turns his back on McNally and faces me. "They can't hear him without having me there as a relay," he says in a soothing whisper, "and I will bring him back to the conference room when we're done. I promise."

He's been saying that a lot, with mixed results. But this time, I have no trouble believing him. "Okay."

"Good." His hand jerks forward, as if to grasp mine, but he stops himself. "Then let us proceed, Constable."

McNally mops his forehead with his handkerchief. His neck has returned to normal, but when he addresses the Reaper on his left, his voice is raspy and subdued. "The Doctor is waiting in the morgue. Make sure he gets...everything he needs."

The Reaper approaches the van as McNally extends his hand toward my cohorts. "If you would come with me...Chief."

Breitling bobs his head and turns to Edward, who casts a concerned glance at me. "You gonna be alright, girl?"

"Me?" I chuckle despite the tension in my chest. "You're the one going into the lion's den."

"Aye, but with a lion at my side." He slaps Breitling's arm again.

"Indeed," Breitling says stiffly. "Are you ready?"

Edward winks at me, then nods at Breitling. "Go on, then."

They get on the elevator, along with McNally and one of his guard dogs. I don't join them.

"Did you want to ride up?" Breitling asks.

"No thanks," I say as I head for the stairwell. After everything that's happened, I could use a little alone time. Besides, "a Reaper, an Inquisitor, and a murder-ghost walk into an elevator" is an awkward enough setup. I have no desire to be there for the punchline.

I go back to my room to splash some water on my face and change clothes. The ones I'm wearing–nay, the ones I was almost murdered in–go straight in the trash. I yank on my last pair of clean yoga pants, a black t-shirt, and my hoodie. As I slide into my flip-flops, I peer out the window into the dark courtyard. A row of avian silhouettes sits on the battlements of the White Tower across from my window. Six big, one small, with little space between them.

Seems about right.

I make my way to the conference room, passing nothing but closed doors, with only the incessant drone of the HVAC fans to keep me company. Where does everyone go at night? Do they have barracks somewhere like at the Summit? Maybe, but I doubt it. Like everything in London, space appears to be at a premium. Smart money says they sleep in their offices on cots or something. As if confirming my suspicion, I swear I hear the creak of springs and a single, soft snore.

With everyone else occupied, I'm not surprised to find I'm the first to arrive. I settle into a chair across the table from the door and load up Angry Birds, preparing to defend my streak. I'm in the middle of debating whether I need to use Hal's boomerang ability on a tricky stack of pigs when Thomas enters. He's flushed, and the fluorescent light reflects a sheen of sweat on his face.

"Rough night?" I ask as he takes the chair across from me.

"To put it mildly." He reaches for the pitcher of no-doubt lukewarm water in the middle of the table and fills a glass. I pretend to focus on the birds bouncing around my screen as he takes a long swig. "In fifty-odd years practicing medicine, I don't think I've ever had anyone demand a post-mortem to be that fast *or* that thorough. Word of advice, Miss Venture: when the Constable asks for a rush job on anything, *run*."

I can only come up with a thin smile. Right now, I don't care about the process. Only his findings. Before I can say anything, however, the door opens. McNally enters first, followed by Edward and then Breitling, with the two Reapers bringing up the rear.

"Oh good, you're both here," McNally says in monotone as he bustles to his regular chair, a Reaper at his side. The other Reaper hovers relatively near Ed, who drops into the seat on the other end of the table. Breitling takes the spot to my immediate right. I catch Edward's attention and mouth at him: *Are you okay?*

He flashes me a crooked half-smile. I'm about to relax when I notice his eyes have lost their vigor. When he catches me watching, he drops his gaze to his hands folded in his lap.

I turn to Breitling. "What's going on?"

McNally raps his knuckles on the table. "Well, Doctor. Have you anything to tell us about Miss…ah, that is…the body?"

His stumble sparks an unexpected pang of sympathy. Sure, he's a dick, but he was the only one that had a personal relationship with Dora. Having to deal with her betrayal *and* her death, all while appearing calm and in control…that can't be easy.

Thomas lays his forearms on the table. "The standard post-mortem examination revealed extensive damage to the ribs and chest cavity indicative of an unskilled heart removal. I noted the presence of a foreign biological specimen as well, however as it was not surgically attached in a way that would support Non-Operational functionality, I cannot in good conscience call it a heart transplant."

My stomach lurches. Declan's heart has been inside her this whole time? *Why?* Did she need it to keep the

Operation going, or as a Page, did she just not know any better? Either way, Breitling was right—it's a miracle she survived as long as she did with a two-hundred-year-old heart flopping around inside her.

"Furthermore," Thomas continues, "a 60-second perimortem ocular projection depicted green and blue phosphenes that suggest her eyes were closed, followed by a brief flash of whitish light at the moment of demise. There will be more tests to conduct, but I can say with confidence that her death was the result of a massive cardiac event."

"Unfortunate," McNally says after a brief silence. "Though not unexpected. Thank you, Doctor."

Thomas sits back in his chair. Tucking his chin, he peers over the rims of his spectacles, looking at me first, and then Breitling. An all-too-familiar twitch lifts the corner of his mouth.

McNally turns to my side of the table. "As to the other matter—"

"Before you say anything," I say, resisting the urge to stand up, "I'm aware this is a unique circumstance. Ed is unlike anything else in this world, and I know that's scary. But it's also why we need to protect him. He's special, and kind, and no harm to anyone as long as the heart that contains him doesn't fall into the wrong hands. Which it won't. We'll find it, and we'll secure it. We'll have to be vigilant, and it's possible it may go wrong, but I believe this is the only viable, humane, and moral solution."

McNally regards me with a raised brow. "Practiced that speech, did you?"

My cheeks warm. "You did leave me in here alone for quite a while, you know."

He grunts, but his mouth turns up. If I didn't know better, I'd say I just made the Constable laugh.

"I will admit, the thought of Mr. Edward's continued presence in Whitechapel does concern me." He raises his hand when he sees me gearing up for Round Two. "However, after a lengthy discussion with Mr. Edward himself as well as the Chief Inquisitor, I must agree. The risk of future harm doesn't justify destroying a sentient life form. God help us all if it did."

I'm not about to tell him how wrong he is when I'm so close to winning this argument. "So, you agree? He can stay?"

He and Breitling exchange heavy looks. "I have invited Mr. Edward to continue residing in Whitechapel, or indeed anywhere else he prefers, as long as he agrees to abide by the same social contract under which we all live. But I'm sorry to say, he has refused."

His words send my stomach plummeting through the floor. I whip toward Edward. "You *refused*? Why?"

His jaw tightens. "Because things canna go on like this. Not after all that's happened. It's gotta change. For good."

That doesn't make sense. He doesn't change. He can't change. Not unless…

Everything snaps into place with a clarity so brilliant my head throbs. "Dora's heart?"

"Aye," he says. "I believe I know where it is. I'll take you to it and you'll be doin' what you want with it. I canna stop that. But know this—as long as it lives, so too does Jack the Ripper. Ain't nowhere in the world you can hide it that'll keep it safe forever. It needs to be destroyed."

Chills race down my arms. "And…that will kill you."

He closes his eyes. "Aye. I reckon that's about the size of it."

A fog descends over my mind. After everything that's happened, *this* is where it ends?

"No." I shake my head. "No. I don't accept this."

"Adina," Breitling whispers, his hand sliding under the table to reach for mine.

The clouds in my head turn to flames. I rocket to my feet so fast my chair rolls into the wall behind me. "What happened?" I shout at Edward, slapping my hands on the table. "What did they say to you to get you to go along with this?"

Edward wipes a hand over his face and casts a desperate look...past me.

At Breitling.

I round on him. "Did you convince him to do this?"

He shakes his head, then stands and addresses the others. "Gentlemen, I believe a recess is in order. Shall we?"

They waste no time getting to their feet. Breitling holds the door open as McNally exits first, followed by the Reapers, and then Thomas.

"Take all the time you need," Breitling says as he steps out.

"Obviously," I snap at the closed door. With a steadying breath, I focus on Edward. "What the hell is going on?"

"I'm sorry, girl," he says, his voice thick with pain. "I dunna want you thinkin' I'm not grateful for what you've done. The time I had with you was a gift, no doubt, and one I'd treasure for the rest of me days. But that's the thing. The rest o' me days...there's so many of 'em, with nothing and no one to fill 'em."

"You have *me*," I choke out. "I can come back and visit. Or maybe we can figure out a way to move you, and you could come back to America with us."

He shakes his head. "You're young. You got your own life to lead. I canna put meself on ye that way."

"You can't stop me. Not if…not if I replace Dora's heart with mine."

His dark eyes flash at me. "No."

"Yes," I shoot back bobbing as the answer forms in front of me. "We even have a premiere ecto-bypass surgeon to do it. You tell us where the heart is, and Thomas could perform the Operation *tonight*. I know there are risks, but you and I are so similar. That…oh my God, that's what the Rigour's been trying to tell me this whole time. We're a *match*. Not for each other, but for *this*."

He gapes at me, horrified. "You canna do that. It'd be mad."

"No, it wouldn't. You've had two masters already. A third would be no problem. I bet I would take to it better too. The Rigour has said as much. It's perfect, isn't it?" Tears of joy fill my eyes. "Like it's meant to be."

"Dammit, girl, listen to me." He springs from his chair and grabs me by the shoulders as best as his incorporeal form will allow. "Whatever the Rigour may be thinkin', it don' matter. Not to me. I…I'm tired, Adina. I've been shufflin' along this mortal coil for nigh on two centuries, and what time I haven't spent under the thumb of a killer, I've spent alone, watchin' other people live in ways I can't.

"And then…here you come along. You gave me minutes and hours I never thought I'd have. It's more than I coulda e'er ask for, and it's more than enough. Besides." He smiles ruefully as his eyes slide to the door. "Unless I'm very much mistaken, I think your heart is already spoken for."

I laugh bitterly. "Yet another reason to remove it."

"Hey now," he says, growing uncharacteristically sober. "Take an old man's word on this. You an' I may witness more'n most, but even we only have one pair o' eyes. There's *always* more to see than what lies in fron o' ye."

All his joy and mischief has faded, replaced by a conviction so cold and sharp it pins me to the spot. "I dun know where we go from here. No more'n anyone else does. But I'm ready to find out."

My blood rages in my veins, urging me to keep pushing. There's got to be a way to change his mind. But my mouth stays closed. I could rant until I'm hoarse and faint, and it wouldn't make a difference.

He's chosen his path.

I take a breath and let myself go numb. It's the only way I'm going to make it through this. "Okay. If this is what you want...okay."

His eyes flutter closed, as if my permission comes as a huge relief. "If I may...there is one last inconvenience I'd hazard to impose."

My heart quickens, but I nod at him to continue.

"Stay with me, Adina." He peers at me from beneath his dark lashes with all the fear and vulnerability of a child. "I want you, and you alone, to be with me at the end."

My lungs deflate. I try to pull in air, but they won't cooperate beyond sharp, shallow gasps. I utter a strangled "yes," then drop my face into my hands and let the pain shatter me.

Thirty-Seven

After I pull myself together as best I can, we summon Breitling, Thomas, and McNally back into the room. Edward retakes his seat and the four of them settle in to discuss his "departure." I, however, have had enough. Breitling can relay Edward's opinions to the others, and they are more than capable of handling the logistics of ending a life. I am a cog in their machine, and I'm sure they will call for me when I'm needed. Until then, I need to get the fuck out of here.

I lean back against the brick facade of the Hospital Block and let the night breeze cool my flushed face. Security lights flood the courtyard beneath the starless black sky, turning the verdant grass of the Tower Green a morbid shade of vermilion. Shiva roosts on the far side of the lawn, looking content and morose amid the brilliance. A single Raven stands beside her. Close. So close, in fact, that when she turns in his direction, the side of her face brushes the feathers of his chest. I search the grounds for the other five and spot them on the crenellated wall of the

White Tower, gazing down on the pair, their hunched silhouettes looking less like Ravens and more like vultures.

"Adina."

I jump as the door opens, and Thomas appears next to me. "Finished already?"

"Almost," he says. "I've been sent to inform you that your presence will be required at dawn."

"Great." I swallow the lump in my throat. "Anything else?"

"Only that they—we—are sorry for your...for what you're going through." He slides his hand inside his jacket and extracts a pack of cigarettes. The warning label, which takes up almost the entire front panel of the box, reads SMOKERS DIE YOUNGER in blocky black letters.

"Seriously, *Doctor*?" I ask as he puts one in his mouth and lights it.

He exhales a languid blue cloud. "I'm seventy-three years old. Dying young is no longer a concern. Besides, I don't need to tell you what a stressful week this has been. Everyone is entitled to their release valve, even if it's not the healthiest thing for them."

I snort. "That's ironic coming from the man who's done everything he can to shame me about my...*release*."

He takes a long drag before responding. "I was only trying to prevent two talented Operators from making a mistake that would ruin *both* of their futures."

"You shouldn't have bothered," I say. "Those two Operators are perfectly capable of *not* making mistakes on their own."

His brows draw together. "I'm afraid you lost me."

I let out a frustrated sigh and flop back against the wall. "It's over. Me and him. We're done."

His jaw drops and he nearly loses his cigarette. "You are?"

"Don't sound so surprised. You were right. It's not worth it. There's too much emotion, too much conflict. And that damned stunt with the Lash…" I rub my temple, dispelling the memory—*all* the memories—associated with that event.

"Hm." He replaces the cigarette between his lips, his forehead creased with dozens of tiny lines.

"What?" I ask warily. "Something I should know?"

"Well…" He glances at the front door of the building before he continues. "I can't speak to everything you said, of course. But what I can tell you is that the Lash was the Constable's decision, and his alone. Even I advised him against it."

I snort. "Oh, really?"

"Yes, really," he says, parroting my snarky tone. "New Operational applications must undergo rigorous testing in controlled environments before they are cleared for field use. Lashing you while you were already on your Walk was not only untested, it bore a cursory resemblance to the original circumstances at best. It was my duty, both as a physician and an Order consultant, to warn the Constable of the risks. Plus…I didn't want anyone to get hurt. *Anyone.*"

I scoff despite the surge of gratitude. It's nice to know *someone* had my back. "Maybe McNally would have changed his mind if Lev–if *he* had tried to reason with him too."

The wrinkles in his forehead deepen. "Adina, he *did* try."

His words break over me like ice water, and I stiffen against the chill. "He did?"

"Vehemently. Honest to God, he was almost begging McNally not to make him do it by the end. But the Constable's rule over the Tower is absolute and second only to the Prime. Levi may outrank everyone else here, but he cannot disobey the Constable."

Of course he could, I want to insist. We're human beings with free will, and these are some stupid, arbitrary rules that a bunch of control freaks made into law.

But every law, no matter how arbitrary, comes with consequences. If Breitling had refused an order from a superior, it would have brought unwanted scrutiny on him.

And…on me.

My chest deflates. Oh God…please tell me that's not what happened. That this wasn't yet another hurt-me-to-protect-me chivalrous asshole thing.

"Sorry."

Ugh. Not the time, the Rigour. Not. The. Time.

I flex my fingers, trying to soothe my frayed nerves. "Why didn't he tell me?"

"Levi cannot always choose his actions, but he'll take responsibility for them. Blaming someone else would be a show of cowardice. He may be Pledged, but he's not a coward. In fact, until quite recently, I would have bet hearth and home that he wasn't afraid of anything."

I swallow hard. "And now?"

He smiles at me, curls of smoke framing his face. "Don't be coy. You and I both know what Chief Inquisitor Levi Breitling fears the most."

Heat sizzles through me, and I look away so he won't see me blush. Across the green, Shiva gets to her feet, her beak coming within a hair's breadth of the Raven's. She spreads her wings, flapping to dispel the moisture, before pitching forward and taking to the air. The Raven's head lifts as it watches her disappear into the night.

"They don't fly, you know."

"Hm?" I murmur, tilting my head toward Thomas.

"The Tower Ravens," he says, nodding at the bird still sitting on the grass. "They don't fly."

I frown at the five feathered sentinels perched on the roof of the White Tower. "Then how...?"

"Oh, they *can* fly," he amends. "But the Tower's Ravenmaster keeps their flight feathers trimmed to discourage too much of it. Plus, they are so well-fed and comfortable here...well, I think it would take something very, very special to get them to leave."

He drops the stub of his cigarette into the smoker's outpost next to the door. "I must get back inside. Miss Wood's family will be here in the morning, and I need to finish preparing her body."

"Thomas?"

He pauses, his hand on the knob. "Yes?"

I fix him with a knowing gaze. "Just between us—how did she die? Really?"

He lifts his chin and regards me carefully. I hold his stare. After a long moment, he nods, the corner of his mouth rising ever so slightly. "Godspeed, Miss Venture."

He turns and disappears inside.

Thirty-Eight

The next thing I know, someone is shaking me by the shoulder. "Adina?"

I pry my eyes open and peer up at Breitling. I don't remember going back to my room after my little chat with Thomas, but here I am.

"Adina," he says again, still holding my arm. "It's time. Are you...up for this?"

I try to laugh, but the anxiety and lack of sleep make my stomach cramp, and it sounds like more of a groan. "No. But I'm doing it anyway."

He keeps a hold on me as I stand. In different circumstances, I might find that patronizing. But right now, in the wee hours of the morning, on my way to commit a ritual murder, my pride is nowhere to be found, and I allow him to help me get on my feet.

"Thanks." It's a bad idea to look at him. But my willpower seems to have run away along with my pride, and I can't stop myself.

The foggy pools of his irises suck me in and invite me to drown in them.

"I'm so sorry, darling." His words are so quiet I almost don't hear them as he clutches me by the shoulders. "I wish you'd never had to come here, that there had been another way…"

My head throbs. I'm dehydrated from how much crying I've done, and somehow tears still threaten. I should say something like "it's okay" or "me too," but the words won't come out. Instead, I disentangle myself from him and stumble toward the doorway.

"Where is he?" I address my question straight ahead.

"The strand," he says. "He said he'd wait as long as it takes for you to…prepare."

"No time like the present." I grope at the doorknob.

"Adina, slow down. There's no need to–"

But I'm already out of the room, plodding on rubbery legs toward the elevator. He's worried about me, but he shouldn't be. I'm fine. As fine as someone who's lost everything can be, anyway. That Edward still exists, or that Breitling still…cares, is an illusion. It's all over but the shouting.

Might as well get that over with too.

The sky lightens from pitch black to inky indigo as we trudge along the Tower Wharf. I keep as far away from the water as I can. Despite heading in the opposite direction of my ultimate destination, I don't want to risk seeing Ed–or him seeing me–until I'm ready.

When we reach the edge of the Tower Bridge, Breitling gestures toward a concrete platform under the overpass. "There's a network of ladders that lead from here down to the water. Shall I go with you?"

I clamp down on my desire to accept that offer. I don't want to be doing this at all, and I really don't want to be doing it alone. But Edward asked that I be there. Just me.

"No," I say at last. "Thank you. But I'll be okay."

"Very well." He folds his arms and leans on the railing overlooking the water. "I will be right here when you're done."

"I know." Without thinking, I reach out and squeeze his forearm. He stiffens, staring down at my hand like it's an alien appendage. Before he can say anything, I withdraw and dart into the shadows below the bridge. It's easy enough to locate the ladders he mentioned. After about twenty feet of climbing, the sole of one flip-flop hits rocky sand. Good thing it's the dry season—at least, as dry as it gets here—or all this would probably be underwater.

Edward is right where I expect him, a dark figure standing on the shore. He watches me approach but doesn't make a move to greet me. Despite the brightening sky, I can't see his face, still shrouded as it is in the shadow of his hat brim.

"Morning." My voice sounds too loud and hollow in this dim, deserted version of a place that's always filled to bursting with noise and people and life.

"And to you." He touches his hat. "'Twill be a lovely day, I think."

"Sure," I half-gasp, half-giggle. My nerves have chilled me to the point where my feet are numb and my arms won't stop trembling, and yet he's standing on the shore as if he does this sort of thing every day. Why am I the one who's having a hard time here? It's not like anything is happening to me.

Then again, isn't it? He's going, sure, but once he's gone, that's it. The hard part will be over—for *him*. That's why funerals are a $20 billion a year industry. Because it's not about the dead people. It's about us, the poor bastards that have to cope with being left behind.

"Hope ye don' mind," he says, pulling me out of my cheerful thoughts. From beneath his cloak, he extracts a lump of soiled coffee-colored fabric. "I dinna think you'd like to go diggin' for such a gruesome treasure. Wadn't sure it would work, with these no-hands o' mine, and it did take a fair bit o' time indeed, but here she is."

At our feet, the X mark he made has been disturbed, as if that spot, and that spot alone, was hit by the world's tiniest earthquake.

"I should have known," I say as I take the parcel from him. The warmth emanating from beneath the fabric thaws my fingers, and a steady rhythm pulses from the center, each beat accompanied by a soft, wet squeak. It should repulse me, and yet I find myself cradling it like a newborn.

"Dammit," I mutter. "I'll never forgive it."

"Never forgive what?" he asks.

"The Rigour." I wipe the shoulder of my hoodie against my cheek. I'm not crying—yet—but it's a comfort, nonetheless. "The only reason Dora could use you like she did was because the Rigour shuttled those poor people into the Ripper victims' paths. Without that, none of this would have happened."

"Now, now," he scolds like a benevolent teacher. "Aren't you being a wee bit unfair? Declan O'Dowd wasn't followin' anyone's path when he created me, was he?"

"Who knows? History is full of evil people. Maybe he got shoved into doing what he did, too. Chaos may be unpredictable, but the Rigour is a monster."

"Nah, you got it wrong. I canna speak to what the Chaos is like on your side of the world, but this much I can say: The Rigour is not an enemy, nor is it a friend. It's a fool function, trying to organize all the bits an' bobs flyin' about. But all that sortin' makes it a slow learner. That's why it takes so long to change."

I scoff. "I didn't think it could change."

He unleashes a delighted laugh. "Good God, woman, *everything* changes. The Rigour pushes humanity, but humanity pushes back just as good. The Rigour shoves ye onto one path. You cut away and find a new one, and then ye make yer own. With enough effort and time, change is not only possible, it's damn near inevitable."

"That's the problem," I say. "Time. We only get so much."

"And yet I seen people work miracles and tragedies in a wee handful o' years. An' a lifetime? That's more'n enough to remake the world as fine as you like. Twice."

He winks at me. I smile back, though it's half-hearted. Pained.

With a sigh, his expression turns serious. Placing his hands lightly on my shoulders so they don't sink into me too far, he traps my gaze in his. "Are ye ready?"

I glance at the dingy bundle in my arms. "Are you?"

He tilts his head up to the sky. His eyes shutter as the first rays of sun kiss his skin and scatter sparkles over his beard stubble. The smile that spreads across his face contains neither sadness nor conflict. He's more serene than I've ever seen him.

Or maybe anyone.

"Okay then," I whisper as loud as the lump in my throat will let me. "Then I guess I will–"

"Just one more thing," he says, retraining his dark eyes on mine. "Would you permit me to…kiss you goodbye?"

I press my lips together. Maybe Breitling's stare burns into the back of my head. Maybe it's my imagination. It doesn't matter either way. "Yes, I would."

He steps closer, leaning down slightly to cover my mouth with his. There's no wild passion, no desperate pawing. His hands don't move an inch down my shoulders. But the way he lingers, his grip sinking into my skin as his chest rises and falls rapidly…I don't know how to explain it. It's not the kiss of a friend *or* a lover. If anything, it reminds me of when you're a teenager and you finally kiss a person you really, *really* like for the very first time. It's giddy and thrilling, and awkward, and a little sad, because once it's over, that's it. You only get one first kiss.

Which, I suppose, is pretty much what this is.

He moans, pulling me closer to him before breaking away.

"Thank ye," he whispers, cupping my face in his hands. "For all o' this. For everything."

I nod. It's all I can do without crying. He holds me for a moment in silence before he speaks again.

"I love ye, Adina." His words are inches from cracking. "You know that, right?"

"I know," I say, my own voice dangerously fragile. "I love you too, Ed."

His body shakes as he exhales. "My one saving grace. And thanks be to whatever God there is for it." He kisses me one more time on the forehead before stepping back, his arms falling to his sides. "Right then. I'm ready."

The water bites my ankles with teeth still frosty from the night air. I wait for my body to adjust before wading out a few more feet, wincing as the lubricious currents lick my thighs and thick mud squelches between my toes. What the hell could survive in this muck?

I shove the thought away. *This* is why I don't swim. Not in lakes or rivers, anyway.

When the water reaches my waist, I stop. Lights flicker on in the windows of the tall buildings on the opposite riverbank, a sign of the city waking up to a new day.

I look down at the sand-covered, squishy lump in my arms. Its warm pulse thumps against me as I pick at the delicate edge of the muslin swaddling. The fabric gets darker and slimier the more I unwrap, until it's so soggy it practically dissolves in my fingers. When the last of the bandages fall into the water, I'm left with a perfect, pink heart the size of my fist. It glistens in the morning light like a rose-colored diamond as it pumps its steady rhythm.

I release the wrapping into the water. It catches the current and floats off as I take the heart in both my hands and hold it away from me.

I've never put much stock in prayer. When the only gods you've met are an insane dice-player and a taciturn control freak, begging for help seems pointless at best. But right now, I'm tired and sad enough to close my eyes, bow my head, and say "fuck it."

"I don't know if you can hear me," I say to the water lapping at my waist. "I don't even know if there's anyone out there that cares enough to listen. But if there is…please, go easy on him. He's been through enough."

I'm not sure what I expect in terms of a response. A whisper, maybe, or a warm breeze. But there's nothing like that. Nothing except the rush of the river and the rising sounds of traffic as the world around me comes to life.

I shrug in the heart's direction. "I tried."

Maybe it's my imagination, but I swear its pulse speeds up.

Christ, I *hope* it's my imagination.

"Okay. Here we go." I roll my shoulders up to my ears and drop them back down. Guess the only thing left to do is…what needs doing. Giving the heart one last comforting squeeze, I lower it into the water.

It jerks in my grip, as if shocked by the cold of its new surroundings. The thumping increases, and for a moment I expect it to struggle, the way an animal might if it were being held under.

A dull thud comes from behind me, followed by a strangled gasp. Pain burns through me. I want to turn around, but I don't dare. If I see what's happening, I won't be able to finish this.

The organ buzzes in my hands. Between that and the cold water, my palms go numb. It's frightened. Panicked. Dying. I tighten my grip, screw my eyes shut, and wait.

The frenetic energy lessens, then stops. In real life, it only takes a minute or two. But for me, it's years. And yet even when I'm sure it's over, I don't move. I stand there in the cold water and let the tears flow until I'm numb inside and out. Only then do I turn around.

An empty shoreline is all that greets me.

Breitling is right where he said he would be, with his arms folded on the railing and his head bent toward the river. He straightens as I approach.

"Here," I say as I hand him my wet, balled-up hoodie. Though the Wharf is still deserted, I'm not about to go parading around with a human heart for all to see. "It's harmless now, I think. But it didn't seem right to toss it in the water."

"I'll take care of it." He tucks it into the crook of one arm. With effort, he brings his gaze to me. "Are you alright?"

The light of the sunrise shimmers in his eyes, burning off the fog and turning them a dazzling aquamarine that I can only describe as "dreamy."

My breath hitches. I want to ask him to forget this trip ever happened. I want to fall to my knees and beg him to let us go back to the way things were. I'll abandon my feelings–hell, I'll kill them dead if it means I don't have to let him go. There's got to be someone somewhere within the Order's tentacular reach that could do that for me, right? And yet, even as my mind conjures up a multitude of workarounds, I know it's hopeless.

I love him. I know he loves me.

And that's the fucking end of it.

At last, I tear myself away from those beautiful eyes and stare at the ground. "I want to go home."

Thirty-Nine

I stand on the bottom step of the Hospital Block, staring up at the brick edifice. With the job now done, I refuse to spend one more second in that place, so I've opted to wait here while Breitling wraps things up with the Constable. As for why I'm staring at the building, well…maybe it's silly, but I can't bear to look at the courtyard right now. Or its inhabitants.

After about twenty minutes, Breitling returns, my shoulder bag and gimpy suitcase in tow. I reach for them, and he turns them over to me without question.

"We're booked on a flight this afternoon out of Gatwick. It's further away than Heathrow, but it's the only way we could get a same-day departure. I will also need to stop at Thomas's flat for my things."

I flinch at the recitation. His words are starched and impersonal, like a secretary reporting their activities to their boss. I try not to think about the lead-up to our last flight together, and how different it was. It hurts too much.

The rideshare meets us out front of the Tower, not far from where we arrived, and shuttles us to Thomas's.

Once again, I wait outside. The driver tries to make small talk, but a few clipped grunts shuts that down real quick, and we both go back to staring out the window. The vibrant colors and clear blue sky spark rage in my belly. It should be cloudy. Rainy. The worst thunderstorm in a hundred years. If ever there was a day for dark and dreary, it's today. But no. The people of Whitechapel are out in force, walking their dogs, making their deliveries, running their routes. Business as usual.

What will they make of this when it all comes out, I wonder? The Constable said that Scotland Yard would be the one to come up with a credible cover story. Will they find a scapegoat? Some criminal whose prior bad acts mean they've forfeited their chance at a decent life?

God, I hope not. And I doubt it. Between uncovering a murderous conspiracy inside the Tower and the shame of calling in the Americans to clean up the mess, the best thing that could happen would be for the whole sordid business to fade away. Another scandal will pop up soon, I'm sure, and public interest will shift. That's the thing about modern times. There's always a new tragedy to focus on. Except for the families, of course. But they're pretty easy to sweep into the shadows once everyone has lost interest. I would know–that's when they used to come to me.

And maybe, now that my life is well and truly fucked, they will come to me again.

We've crossed the river and are heading south when Breitling's phone rings.

"Levi Breitling," he answers.

I frown at the passing scenery. If he knew the person calling, he would have addressed them by their name. Which means it wasn't a known number. Which means...

"No, you're mistaken," he says testily. "We cleared that up before our departure. Everything is—"

Whoever is on the line cuts him off. I hazard a glance over my shoulder. His teeth grind and he's scowling at the back of the driver's headrest like it owes him money. His fist sits on his left knee and he's kneading his fingers into his palm. "I see." Pause. "I see." Pause. "Fine, then." He drops the phone to his lap and wipes his face. "Goddammit."

"What's wrong?" I ask.

"It seems the passport troubles we had in the States have made their way here. They've suspended your ability to re-enter America until they can verify that you're a citizen."

"What?" My jaw drops. "Are you saying I'm stuck here?"

"Not just you," he grumbles. "Since I'm listed as your traveling companion, they've suspended my re-entry privileges as well."

"Oh, that's great." I flop back against the seat. "What do we do now? Call Thomas? Go back to the Tower?"

"That won't be necessary." Breitling leans forward and addresses the driver. "There's been a change of plans."

The driver pulls over and they sweat out the technological and financial steps of our reroute. Meanwhile, I fix my gaze on the pristine park out my window and take some calming breaths. It'll be okay. The Summit has all the resources they need to take care of this in no time. I may be a grunt, but there's no way they'll let their Chief Inquisitor languish overseas any longer than necessary.

We get moving again, circling the far end of the park before heading back toward the river in silence. Breitling's phone has consumed his attention, and I don't want to bother him. Not that I have anything to bother him with.

Another twenty minutes of winding through city streets puts us back in front of the Tower–and then past it. The driver turns onto a quiet dead-end road surrounded by glass-fronted buildings and stops. "Here alright?"

"Yes, thank you," Breitling says as he exits.

"Care to enlighten me?" I ask as we retrieve our bags from the trunk.

"Castillo and Russ are working on our travel arrangements," he says, guiding us toward the far end of the street. "But it's tricky. Any other system they'd muscle in, get it done, and beg forgiveness later. In this case, with Homeland Security involved, it requires more finesse. Which means more time."

"How much more time?"

"Twenty-four hours. At least."

I groan loud enough to startle a pack of seagulls ripping into someone's abandoned soft pretzel.

"Indeed." Breitling pauses in front of the entrance to the last concrete-and-glass building on the street. Above the sliding doors, the words IDYLL HOUSE - THREE QUAYS hang on the wall in blocky iron lettering. Inside are pristine marble floors and meticulous flower arrangements that can only belong to a very expensive hotel.

My throat tightens. "Are you sure this is necessary?"

"It's this or go to the airport and hope for the best."

I almost laugh. To say I'm thin on hope at the moment is miserably inadequate. Sighing, I gesture to the door. "After you."

The lobby is everything I hate about modern design. Weird geometric shapes, blank walls, and cold, impersonal lighting. I stand as close to the front window as possible while Breitling confers with the front desk. From the volume of his voice, it's going about as well as it did with the airline.

"More problems?" I say when he returns. Even to my own ears, I sound way more tired than curious.

His discontented grunt confirms my suspicion. I follow him to the elevator, which we take to the fifth floor. He leads us a few doors down where he stops and pulls out a keycard.

Just one.

My heart crumbles. "Don't tell me…"

He slams the door open so hard I'm pretty sure he cracks the drywall. On the other side is an expansive room that's as sleek and modern as the lobby. Windows fill the far wall with a view of the river. A maple wood desk sits under a painting of purple and red squares, and a flat screen TV perches on a low dresser opposite the bed. The single, king-sized bed.

Because *of course* it is.

"Unbelievable." I throw my suitcase against the wall almost as hard as Breitling opened the door.

"I agree," he says, both hands buried in his hair. "How they gave away one of our rooms in the ten minutes since I made this booking is a stunning display of incompetence."

"Make sure you include that in the Yelp review. Verbatim." I stomp to the window and press my forehead against it, hoping the cool glass will soothe my anger.

How can this be happening? The Rigour has spent days keeping us apart and dismantling our relationship, and *now* it drops us in the middle of a romantic comedy screw-up? That's not only stupid, it's cruel.

It's also confusing. The Rigour nudges and prods. It doesn't take direct action. Only Chaos–

My brain stutters. The problems followed us from America. That's what he'd said. Could it be…is it possible…?

"I'm sorry, Adina," Breitling says. "This wasn't…I want you to know that I didn't plan this."

"Oh, I know," I murmur as I gaze down at the river. The sunlight catches the small waves, silting the muddy expanse with flecks of gold. "You didn't have to book us somewhere this nice, you know. A Best Western, or Eastern, or whatever you call them over here, would have been fine."

"Don't worry about it. I had credit."

"Credit? What for?"

His only answer is a heavy sigh.

"Oh." The word blooms in a light fog over the glass. "This is where we were supposed to stay. Before Thomas. Before…everything."

He doesn't answer. He doesn't have to.

I turn around. He's standing with his hands in his pockets, as still as I've ever seen him except for his eyes, which roam all over me with a hunger so desperate and hopeless I can feel it throbbing in my own belly. "Levi…"

"Don't," he exhales. "Don't do that. It's hard enough being here with you…like this."

Like what? I want to ask. Like colleagues? Like friends? Like people who feel nothing for each other than wild sexual attraction? Or like what we *really* are?

And what, I wonder, would be so wrong with that? The job is done, but we haven't returned to business as usual yet. There's no one here to judge us, no one to tell us we can't. It's just...us.

Heart hammering, I take a tentative step forward. His head quirks and his eyes narrow, not with suspicion, but curiosity. Is that a good sign?

I'm about to find out.

I take another step, and another, until I'm standing in front of him. Hands still in his pockets, he watches me with the ghost of a smile. It's wistful and full of regret. But it's still a smile.

"Levi," I whisper, pressing my hands to his chest.

His eyelids flutter. He makes no move to stop me as I press my mouth to the underside of his jaw. A shudder ripples through him and into me as I undo the first pin holding his collar in place. Only then do his hands emerge from his pockets and take me by the elbows. His touch is firm but delicate, as if he can't decide whether to push me away or pull me closer. Trailing kisses down his neck, I unclasp the second pin, and his collar falls to the floor.

"Adina..." He tries to fold me in his arms, but I'm not finished. I push his jacket off his shoulders, then unbutton his shirt and vest and remove those, too. He moans as I nibble at his collarbone, and tries to ensnare me once again, this time with his mouth and arms both. I let him, but only for a moment, allowing the thrill to build before I break away. His look of confusion and desire follows me as I sink to my knees, stopping to anoint his stomach with licks and gentle nibbles until my lips graze the smooth metal of his belt buckle.

"Adina, stop."

I do. Not just because he told me to, but because there's something extra in his voice that makes me.

Something urgent, almost panicked. I peer up at him and see the same emotions darkening his features. "What's wrong?"

"Nothing, just..." He swallows hard. "I've never had anyone give me, um..."

The color rising in his cheeks finishes the thought for him. My eyes widen. I can't help it–I'm surprised. "Never?"

He shakes his head. "It's not that I didn't–or don't–want to. But I've never been with someone that seemed...that I could..."

He falters, and his hands clench at his sides, his words failing him.

"It's okay," I say, resting my hands on his thighs. "Nothing you say is going to scare me away. You know that."

"Yes, I know it." He looks me over, his lower lip pinned between his teeth. "I... I want this, Adina. I want *you* to do this for me."

My heart swells with tenderness as well as despair. Clinging to the former, I adopt a sultry pout and try my best to push the latter away. "Are you sure?" I ask, dragging my fingers across his thighs to stroke the bulge growing between them.

He grunts an affirmation through sealed lips, as if he's already struggling to hold on. "I trust you, my darling. Completely."

A lump forms in my throat. I don't know if my heart can take much more of this. Instead of letting him see how affected I am, I throw myself into the next steps. His buttons and zipper undone, I slide his slacks and boxer briefs to the ground so he can step out of them.

Dear. God. He's gorgeous. Every single inch of him. After weeks of carrying on like we have been, it's strange that this only occurs to me now. Then again, this is the first time he's stood in front of me like this, naked and exposed. Vulnerable.

I've never loved him more.

"Do you, um…" I hesitate, feeling the flutter of a couple butterflies myself. "Do you want to sit down?"

He glances from me to the bed and back. "No." Reaching down, he pushes the hair back from my face. "I want to see you. All of you."

I arch my brow. "Well, if that's what you want…"

He watches in appreciative silence as I pull my t-shirt over my head and toss it aside. Despite his nerves, he cracks a smile. "Do you think you'll ever wear underwear on a plane?"

"Not sure." I wink at him and slip out of my leggings. "But it doesn't look good."

His brow lifts as he evaluates my bare breasts. "I…may have to disagree."

"Do you?" I run my hands through my hair and arch backward.

"Mm, yes," he moans, his eyes molten. "Disagree. Thoroughly."

With a nervous giggle, I take him in my hand and start to stroke.

"Adina," he says, his voice rough. "If I do anything wrong, anything you don't like…"

"I know," I say. "I trust you too."

And to prove it, I take him in my mouth.

"Holy fu—" His head falls backward, his words fading into a deep moan.

I pull away, startled. I didn't expect such a big reaction that soon. "Too much?"

"Perhaps a little," he says shakily. "You'll have to go easy on me, I'm afraid. I'm a bit…overwrought."

No kidding. This has been such a frustrating week, and he's been so patient. "I'll keep that in mind."

I take him again, shallow this time, teasing him with slow, gentle licks. When his grunts of exertion ease, I slide my lips down his shaft, taking more of him. And more. As much as he'll let me, until he hits the back of my throat. It seizes, and I pause. Breathe. The smoky sweet scent of his skin helps ease the spasm, making room for the rest of him.

"Oh, *God*..." His hand lifts, but hesitates over my head, as if he's afraid to touch me.

I withdraw, my hand gliding up and down as I circle the tip with my tongue, slow at first, then speeding up, until he's panting and trembling all over. I take him deep again, and again, stealing a glance up at him as I move.

His smoldering eyes capture mine, sending a bolt of electricity shooting through my core and settling in a deep, low ache. Whimpering, I avert my gaze.

"No." The hand that has been so reticent to touch me grabs a fistful of my hair. "Look at me."

I do as he says. Another bolt rips through me, and this time I can't help myself–I slip my free hand between my legs, desperate to ease the throbbing need pooling there.

"God, I love you like this," he says, loosening his grip on me, moving as I move. "At my feet, on your knees, writhing...ecstatic...*mine*..." His abs tense and he sucks air through his teeth. "Adina, I'm...fuck, I'm going to come."

He yanks his hand away, as if he's expecting me to pull back. I do no such thing. Cradling him with my tongue and encouraging him with my hand, I suck hard and fast until, shoulders heaving and muscles shaking, his release floods my mouth as my name spills from his. As his tremors recede, I take him in from shaft to tip one more time, licking him all the way clean.

"Jesus Christ, Adina." He regards me with something akin to shock. "Where the hell did you learn to do that?"

I run a finger over my lower lip. "A lady never tells."

"Fair enough." He rakes a hand through his sweat-dampened hair. "God, I feel like a fool. I should have asked you for that a long time ago."

The weight of those words stabs my chest. Will this first …also be the last?

No. I won't think about that. Not while we still have time.

I start to get up. One of my feet hits the floor, then I'm down again as he falls to his knees, wraps me in his arms, and pulls me on top of him. I yelp in surprise, my legs wrapping instinctively around his waist.

"Where do you think you're going?" he growls into my neck before setting me on the floor in front of him. With a kiss so tender it makes me weak, he guides my hand back between my legs. "Finish."

Oh, God. Talk about firsts. I've never done *this* in front of anyone before. None of my youthful encounters were what you might call long-term prospects, and while things were better with Jake, he and I didn't even round all the bases, let alone go into extra innings, if that's not stretching the metaphor too far. This is so…intimate. Private, beyond even what happens between two people behind closed doors. I don't know if I can…

"I don't know if I can." The words are out before I realize I was planning to say them. But once they're said, I'm glad.

His lips compress, not in anger but consideration. Ever the problem solver. Lifting his hand, he drops his fingers over my eyelids and eases them closed. "It's alright, darling. Nothing you do will scare me away either."

I smile. Yes. I know. "Okay," I say, letting my hand settle. "I'll try."

My fingers flutter with practiced enthusiasm—I am an adult woman, after all—as I use the embers he kindled to build a fire. Physically, he's nowhere. I hear him breathing, feel the occasional puff of air against my neck, but that's all. In every other way, it is like he's not here.

Except in my head. In my head, he's everywhere. Every time and place. The first time, in my kitchen. The second time, in his office. Every time in his car. Even the silly fooling around on the plane. Every touch, every kiss, every restrained look of desire. It's all there, each one an indelible scar on my brain.

"Levi," I sigh, moving faster, growing hotter and wetter even as the tears gather in my eyes. Is that why he asked for this? So he can see what my so-called love life will be like once he's gone? Because…this is it. After we get home, this is all that will be left of us.

My arousal shrivels like a dead leaf, and I'm left with nothing but a dull, empty void.

"Shit," I whimper, pressing my palms to my face to disguise my shame.

"It's alright." He takes one of my hands in his and kisses the back of it. "I'm still here."

I know that already, and yet hearing him say it fills me with relief. Dropping my other hand from my face, I open my eyes. I'm so used to seeing his irises shining bright blue in these moments, an overflow of his power brought on by the heightened emotion. Staring into the pearly fog of his normal eye color is surprising. And concerning.

"Are you alright?" I ask.

He winces. Then, after a moment, he shakes his head. "No. I'm not. Not at all."

"Join the club," I say, using the back of my hand to wipe a tear off my cheek.

He smiles ruefully and runs his thumb over the same spot. "Adina, I need to tell you something. After we return to Vegas…"

My stomach clenches so hard it almost pulls me upright. Oh God, we're doing this now? While we're both naked and…in the middle of things? I mean, I *can* think of worse times, but not many. The idea of never being with him like this ever again…it hurts so much, I can't comprehend the depths of the pain.

But…

But I'll deal with it. I will. I'll suffer through all that and more if it means I can keep the rest of him. The man and the friend. And if I'm lucky, he's about to tell me the same thing.

He drags in a fortifying breath. I do as well, then nod for him to go ahead. God, I hope he knows what he's doing.

"Darling, when we return to Vegas, I am going to tell the Prime that I am revoking my Pledge."

I shoot up so fast he has to fall back on his heels so I don't smack him in the head. I must have gone temporarily insane, because there's no way I heard that right. "You…can you do that?"

"I don't know," he says. "I asked Madame Misty to check the records, and as far as she can tell, it's never been done before. But 'never been done' and 'not allowed' are two different things. I was going to wait to tell you until I had a real answer, but…well…"

With a gentle smile, he wipes another of my tears away.

I shake my head, still in shock. "What do you think the chances are of Castillo accepting it?"

"I don't know that either. But I have to try."

"But...if you revoke your Pledge, you won't be able to keep your position in the Order, will you?"

"No." His palms slide up my thighs. "No, I don't imagine I will."

I scoot backward out of easy reach. We need to finish this conversation. "You would no longer be an Inquisitor. You'd be giving up everything you've worked for, everything you've spent your life trying to achieve, just for—"

He springs forward and locks his hands around my waist. I don't even have the chance to think about resisting before he scoops me up in his arms.

"Hey!" I squeal. But his serious expression doesn't waver as he lays me on the bed, then lowers himself onto me. I let my knees fall open to accommodate him—and gasp. He's hard. At least as hard as when I first took him in my mouth.

Maybe I *am* fucking magic after all.

I stifle a moan as he moves against me, slow but sure, rebuilding the pressure and heat that I'm so desperate to yield to.

"Let me be very clear," he says, his voice even lower than usual. "There's no 'just' about this. You are everything to me, Adina. Everything. Even if I could let you go, or if...if you decided you didn't want me, I couldn't go back to the way things were. The way *I* was. It's too different now." His mouth grazes mine, gentle at first, then harder, hungrier, as if he knows he'll never get enough but will die trying. "You've made me want to be different."

Whatever will I had to continue the conversation evaporates. Holding his face in both my hands, I spread my legs wider. I'm aching wet, and when he enters me, it's almost enough to push me over the edge. But I grit my teeth and hold on in every way I can. I claw at his hair and squeeze his hips between my thighs, bucking in his tight embrace until his familiar full-body spasm rises against me. Then I push him onto his back and ride him into the ground.

"Goddammit, Levi," I cry out, cresting one orgasm, only to fall directly into another.

"Yes," he growls, his neck muscles corded and straining. "Scream for me, Adina. Tell me you're mine."

I want to. God, I want to. But I shake my head. "You first."

His brow arches, as if he's never heard anything so ridiculous. Or so delightful. Then, with a smile bright enough to light up the room: "I'm yours, Adina. I'm all yours. I think I have been since the day we met."

His words leave me breathless. My request was a challenge that I didn't expect him to meet. But he did. And now that he has, I realize how much I've wanted to hear him say that, and for how long, and for it to be the truth.

He runs his hands up my stomach to my breasts, then my face, and pulls me to him. "Your turn, darling."

His kiss makes me shudder. It always does, but it's different this time. Because now I know it's mine.

"I'm yours," I whisper. "Oh God, Levi. I'm so fucking yours."

He shivers and tries to pull me into another kiss. But I break away, raking my fingers through my hair and trying to gather my shattered wits even as I continue to fuck him stupid. His fingers dig into me, not to slow me down, but to keep me close. I open my legs as far as I can, reveling in his desperate groans as I take him all the way into me.

"That's it." I swirl my hips as I brace my hands against his stomach. His muscles are so tense, I'm afraid they may snap. "Come for me, Levi. Just for me."

"Yes, darling. My God, yes." His head falls back as he lets go with a roar like I've never heard. I ride his final jerking thrusts until he collapses back onto the mattress, his eyes screwed shut. Cerulean light seeps from beneath his eyelids like neon tears.

I lean down and kiss them away. They burst on contact, soft and ticklish like static electricity. Before I can withdraw, he grabs me by the back of the head and kisses me hard.

"Holy shit," he murmurs without breaking our connection. "I love you, Adina Venture. I love you so goddamn much."

"I love you too, Levi Breitling," I say, my lips still buzzing with his strange, beautiful magic. "No matter what happens, I always will."

Somewhere in the recesses of my consciousness, I swear I hear two faceless, smart-ass demigods give each other a high five.

Forty

I sleep the sleep of a thousand corpses. When I wake up, the sun has started to set. I haven't slept through the day since my early twenties, and I don't feel the least bit bad about it. Not until I rouse myself enough to realize where I am: lying on my stomach, arms and legs splayed, with a six-foot-six blond Brit pinned beneath me.

"Oh," I say as I tip my chin toward him. "Hi."

"Hello." Levi smiles at me, his glasses slipping to the end of his nose. In his free hand, the one that's not tracing the length of my spine, his phone murmurs with the comforting sounds of the evening news. "I'm sorry, love. Did I wake you?"

Love. I bask in the glow of my new moniker, before I answer. "No, you didn't wake me. Besides, I'd much rather you watch TV than watch me sleep."

"To be fair, I *did* just lie here staring at you until about an hour ago. Then I got bored."

"Yeah, right." I giggle and press my forehead into his chest. "Why didn't you shove me over?"

"I wouldn't dare. You're so majestic when you sleep. Like a…drunken octopus."

I snap my head up, mouth agape. "Oh, *now* you're going to give me shit?"

"Maybe." He kisses the top of my head. "If you take it half as well as you give it, I think you'll be fine."

I sigh, forfeiting further banter in favor of draping myself over him again so he can keep rubbing my back. We've never done this before. Lain in bed together, like regular people. Like...a couple. It's strange. And nice.

Really, *really* nice.

"*—most violent summer London has seen since the 1800s may be over. Hamish Newton, 32, has been arrested after confessing to what police believe is the latest in a string of attacks recreating the infamous Jack the Ripper murders.*"

"What?" I spin up and grab his wrist so I can see his screen. "Reaper Newton's in NO custody?"

"It would appear so." He increases the volume of his phone.

"*Newton, himself a resident of Whitechapel, has admitted to kidnapping a young woman and detaining her in a van near Mitre Square, a location that coincides with one of the historical Ripper attacks. During the commission of this crime, the woman appeared to suffer a fatal heart attack. Prints and DNA evidence found at the scene coincide with Newton's account. A representative of Scotland Yard refused to comment on whether Newton will be charged with the five previous crimes but did confirm that the investigation is ongoing.*"

"Well then," Levi says. "Even if they don't bring official charges against Newton for all the attacks, the people have their villain. Case closed."

"I guess." I lay back and pull the duvet up to my collarbone.

"Something on your mind?" he asks.

"Just...I know why Newton would choose confession and a NO prison over the Pit. But I'm surprised McNally would allow a traitor—a Reaper he trusted with his *life*—to get off that easy."

"I'm sure he didn't want to. But the Yard and the Crown need a perpetrator, and Newton *is* the most logical choice. We should be grateful that, at least in this case, the person they're charging is guilty of something."

I scrub my hands over my face. "Jesus, this country is a mess."

He smiles mischievously. "Not to complicate things further for you, but I should point out: Until the murder of Gordon Gaye, all the victims were Non-Operational. Without the Crown there to put pressure on the Tower, Order protocol by its letter would not have required the Constable to act at all."

My stomach tightens. "So, if this had happened in America, the Summit would have let four bodies drop and done nothing?"

"It's possible, yes. Good thing *you* were running your previous Operations in America though. If you'd been Operating in England, I'm not sure you'd be here right now."

"Wow." I chuckle. "Not only is the system fucked, it doesn't even have the decency to be fucked the same way across the board."

"Indeed. Now then." Tossing his phone and glasses onto the nightstand, he rolls on top of me and pins my wrists above my head. "Say 'fuck' one more time."

I raise my chin in defiance. "Make me."

His mischievous smile widens. "With pleasure."

He kisses me, his touch delicate but with something big and heavy behind it, a raw power he can barely contain. He only stays for a moment, long enough to make my body temperature rise, before pulling the duvet off me so he can run his tongue over my breasts and down my stomach to the inside of my thighs. My fingers curl into the bed as he explores me, licking and teasing with studied precision until I'm convulsing.

"Fuck, Levi," I gasp.

He growls in triumph as my eyes roll up to the ceiling. The sun is all but gone, and shadows stretch from the window over the smooth, white plaster, longer…and longer…

And longer.

In my growing delirium, I watch the darkness slide down the wall to the floor. Across the floor.

And back toward the bed.

"Oh my God…"

I draw a sharp breath that has nothing to do with Levi's tongue. He must sense my anxiety because he lifts his head. "Adina? Is everything–?"

I point to where the dark finger has crawled up onto the mattress. My jaw drops, but no sound comes out as fibrous magenta tendrils burst from the ceiling and split the wallpaper.

"Jesus!" Levi grabs me and drags me to the other side of the bed. He faces the invader, pinning me against the headboard with his back to my chest. "What the hell is that?"

I can't answer. I'm too busy punching myself in the brain for not telling him about what happened in the Catacombs. Dammit, I'd really thought it was a dream. Or maybe that's just what I'd wanted to believe. Now, as I watch this putrid thing coming toward us, seeding blood-spattered purple mushrooms over the pristine white linen, there's no avoiding the truth.

"Umbralists," I say at last. "I don't know how, but they've come to take what's theirs."

He turns his head toward me. His gaze touches mine for only a moment before refocusing on the shadow, but the look he gives me is nothing short of savage. "Over my dead body."

I swallow hard. He means it. And that scares me more than anything. I won't lose him. I *refuse*.

Closing my eyes, I wrap my arms around his shoulders.

The thing surges toward him, eager to sink its corrupting rot into his flesh. I clench my arms, and with all my strength, I roll him over me. Despite his size, it's easier than I thought it would be. Element of surprise and all that. With almost no resistance, he lands on the floor with a thud.

"Sorry," I pant as something wet and cold slithers up my back. "It's my turn to be the chivalrous asshole."

"No!" He scrambles for the bed. "Adina, please. You can fight."

But it's too late. The shadow has wrapped itself around my waist, its damp chill freezing me to the bone. From the way his face falls, I know he's seen it too.

"I will find you, my love." His fingers tangle with mine. Though his voice has broken and his cheeks are wet, his eyes burn with bloodthirsty rage. "I will find you, and I will make them *pay*."

I don't doubt it, I want to say. But I only have time to half-smile. Then I'm flying backward and his fingers, his hand, his eyes…everything disappears as the darkness swallows me.

They will pay…

DEATH IN THE SHADOWS

The Fourth Miss Adventure Misadventure

August 2025

Visit <u>www.sgtasz.com</u> for release updates, social media links, newsletter signup and more.

Afterword

In the fall of 2006, I had the extremely good fortune to be able to spend the first trimester of my senior year at Lawrence University's London Centre. At twenty-one, I'd never been overseas before, and now I'd be spending ten weeks in a city with which I only knew from books and movies.

It was intimidating. So much so that, for several days after I arrived, I found every reason I could not to leave the Centre. Then, during an Intro to London class (yep, that was a real thing), I received this piece of advice: "The best way to get to know this city is to go get lost."

Looking back, it's not exactly the most responsible directive, especially in a time before the ubiquity of smartphones. All I had was the London A to Z—which, if you're not familiar, is a small but thick book that contains heavily detailed maps of every section of the city. But fancying myself as an A student (okay, maybe a B+), I decided to give it a try. Armed with my maps, my iPod Nano, and nothing else, I set out to get lost.

Stepping from the stoop onto the sidewalk was probably one of the scariest steps I've ever taken. Surely there was at least one moment where I considered rushing back inside. But in the end, I steeled my nerves and dropped my foot. One, then the other, and repeat. I practically ran the first block, out of nerves and to put some distance between me and the ability to return to safety. I walked without thought or care, and after about twenty minutes, I had done it—I was lost.

I'd like to tell you that my return home was an epic journey filled with crazy characters and valuable lessons. The truth is, I don't remember much about it. I walked, I listened to music, and eventually I found my way back to the Centre, safe and sound. The point of this exercise wasn't to get into trouble. It was simply to get myself off the stoop and onto the sidewalk. It didn't matter where I went after that—the point was the steps themselves.

When I first conceived the *Miss Adventure* series, I knew right away that I wanted to write a Jack the Ripper mystery. At the time I'd hoped I'd be able to get back to London before the book went to print, but unfortunately, things didn't work out that way. I conducted all the research for this book remotely—something that was much easier than I'd thought it would be, thanks to Google Maps, the Tower of London website, and Jack the Ripper Virtual Tours. However, without my experience at the London Centre to shape and color my research, this book would be a mere shadow of what it is. I had no idea at the time, but that step onto the sidewalk all those years ago put me on a path that led, through countless twists and turns, to *Death in Whitechapel*.

Since my time there, the Lawrence London Centre has relocated from the brownstone building on Brechin Street I knew to a location just down the road from the British Museum. Still, the Centre of my memories is as real to me as if I were there yesterday.

And even though I never entered the basement-level apartment of the Centre in real life, I have seen a version of it in my imagination—and now, after reading this book, so have you.

As always, big thanks to my beta readers Melissa, JE and PB; to Marcin, who's still suffering through those first drafts; and to everyone at Sin City Writers Group and Coffee House Tours for their continuous support at every stage of the writing process.

A special thanks goes out to all my advanced readers. You all had to take that cliffhanger without knowing when the next book would be out. Apologies again, but I promise, it'll be worth the wait. I'd also like to give a special shoutout to Emma, *Miss Adventure's* longest and most dedicated ARC reader. The fact that I chose your name for one of the victims in this book is purely a coincidence, I swear.

Finally, I must give credit to the documentary *The Enduring Mystery of the Jack the Ripper* for providing much of the historical facts in this book. And yes, it *is* what Jake sent to Adina for research. It's just that good.

Until next time, my friends.

-S

About the Author

S.G. Tasz is an urban fantasy author from Las Vegas, Nevada. Her work includes the YA paranormal comedy series *Dead Mall* and the urban fantasy-romance *Death by Miss Adventure* which was named Best Urban Fantasy 2023 by Indies Today. When she's not writing, she's thinking about writing. When she's not doing that, she enjoys watching football (Go Pack!), hockey (Go Knights!), and anything on Dropout.tv (especially Dimension 20). Other hobbies include reading, crafting, role-playing, and axe-throwing.

For the latest updates, subscribe to my newsletter by scanning this code:

Also by S.G. Tasz

The Dead Mall Series	The Death by Miss Adventure Series
An Original Sin	
Welcome to Halcyon	*Death by Miss Adventure*
Veiled Threats	*Death in the Desert*
The Long Moon	*Death in Whitechapel*
The Mourning Sun	
A Midwinter Nightmare	Other Works
The Lost Weekend	
Everything Must Go	*Mr. Lucky: A Holiday Novelette*